BELLA FIGURA

BELLA FIGURA

JOJO CAPECE

NEVILLE PUBLISHING LTD.

LONDON

Neville Publishing Ltd.
35 Piccadilly
London W1J ODW England

First Edition May 2013

Cover: Variation of Sandro Botticelli's
"The Birth of Venus" 1486
Uffizzi Gallery, Florence

Back Cover Photograph:
View from Hotel Caesar Augustus, Capri

Map of Capri, circa 1810
Current Map of Capri courtesy Axel Munthe Foundation
Sketches by Jojo Capece
Author's photograph courtesy of LONDON EVENING STANDARD

ISBN: 9781482076615
Library of Congress Control Number: 2013901708
Printed in the United States of America

Writer's Guild of America Registered 1105704

Outside historical personages, the characters in this story are the imagination of the author including the personality of the narrator. They bear no resemblance to persons living or dead. Only the cities are real.

To the most unprejudiced of men

my husband

Edgar dePue Osgood

forever young at heart

Also by Jojo Capece

ALL ROADS LEAD TO ROME

Screenplay

FOR BETTER OR WORSE

BELLA FIGURA

Part Four

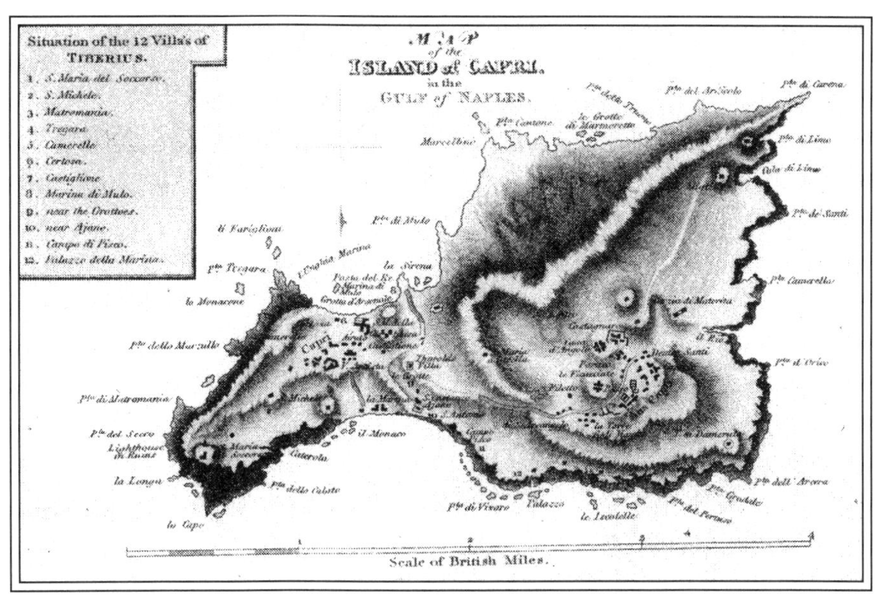

MAP
of the
ISLAND of CAPRI,
in the
GULF of NAPLES.
Situation of the 12 Villa's of
TIBERIUS.
1. S. Maria del Soccorso.
2. S. Michele.
3. Matromania.
4. Tregara.
5. Camerelle.
6. Certosa.
7. Castiglione.
8. Marina di Mulo.
9. near the Grottoes.
10. near Ajane.
11. Campo di Pisco.
12. Palazzo della Marina.
Marcellino
Pta di Mulo
la Sirena
Pta Tregara
lo Monacone
Pta dello Marzullo
Pta di Matromania
Pta del Secco
Lighthouse
la Longa
lo Capo
Pta dello Cabito
il Monaco
Pta di Vivaro
Palazzo
le Isolelle
Pta dell' Arcera
Pta Camarella
Pta de Santi
Pta di Carena
Pta di Limo
Scale of British Miles.

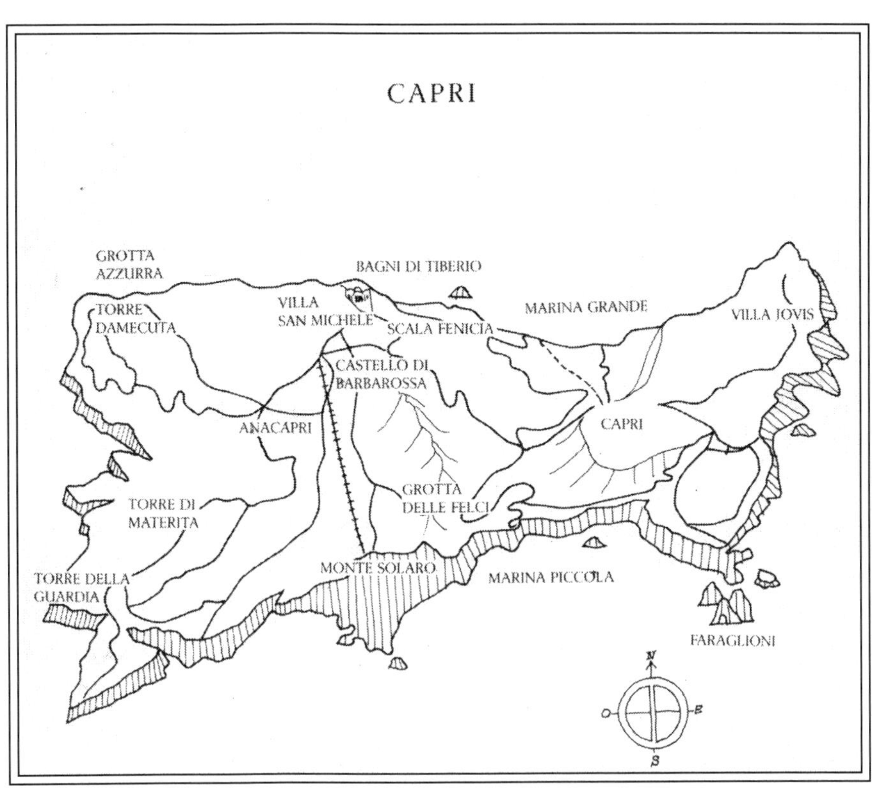
CAPRI
GROTTA AZZURRA
BAGNI DI TIBERIO
TORRE DAMECUTA
VILLA SAN MICHELE
SCALA FENICIA
MARINA GRANDE
VILLA JOVIS
CASTELLO DI BARBAROSSA
ANACAPRI
CAPRI
TORRE DI MATERITA
GROTTA DELLE FELCI
TORRE DELLA GUARDIA
MONTE SOLARO
MARINA PICCOLA
FARAGLIONI
N
O
E
S

Judge not, and you shall not be judged:

condemn not, and you shall not be condemned:

forgive, and you shall be forgiven.

Luke 6:37

BELLA FIGURA

For too many years I have postponed telling this story knowing that the ugliness of prejudice is best kept suppressed with political correctness.

No one is without prejudice – whether it be age, race, religion, class, gender or nationality.

What I write is not an invention. In time you will discover who I am, my motives and why I have no intention to remain a mystery.

Suspend judgment until you read my narrative.

Every word is true.

Esmeralda Pembrooke, a legend in her time, astonished everyone whose life was entwined with hers.

Our journey begins in Capri…

PROLOGUE

Capri

The enchanted island of Capri begins at the southern tip of the Bay of Naples. Poets, writers and painters have recorded its unique beauty forever. Legends have spun about its mythical heroes, gods of the universe and sirens of the sea that came to call with ancient mysteries. Storytellers Homer, Dickens, Dumas, Wilde, Fitzgerald and scores more expressed awe over centuries with dramatic tales of Capri.

History tells us the Emperor Augustus was intoxicated by the island's mystique discovering fossilized remains of *homo sapiens,* split in two so the marrow became a feast, eaten by the first inhabitants, cannibals called Laestrigonians, the ancient people of Capri.

It was here Ulysses tried the herb from the god Hermes as the antidote to the spell of Circe, and here Virgil spoke of the twenty wives left behind because a nymph bore Telon a son. In the upper part of Capri, Anacapri, Greeks claimed their place enjoying a species of plants first supplied to Semite Phoenicians. Wild boar and quail roamed the rocky island's terrain and, in time, magnificent Capri became a possession of the Caesars. Latin was spoken, intellectuals congregated and its Greek name kept for centuries.

Historian Suetonius' accounts of the Augustan age on the Imperial isle recall Emperor Augustus so taken by the superior geography, climate and beauty of Capri, he exchanged his private domain, Ischia, the larger, neighboring island, with the Republic of Naples for Capri because he sensed the paradise he was searching for was exclusively here. The venerable leader desired peace in his late years. Spectacular gardens and serene glades made him believe he'd found *the* precious jewel of the Imperial crown. Sumptuous villas and temples were built, including what remains today, *Villa Jovis,* destined to become home to Emperor Tiberius, his successor and adopted stepson. Tiberius, an anti-Semite, prejudiced against women, aristocrat and general, was a complex individual who gave Capri the importance to be the second Palatine of Imperial Rome.

He ruled the Roman Empire twenty-three years, was distinguished as a statesman and a man of exemplary virtue (issuing an edit against promiscuous kissing at New Year) and passed his last ten years on Capri. The Capresi still say Tiberius' ghost haunts the isle from that day to this. His public life was one of devotion and service to his country, ruling at the height of its splendor that encompassed the world. His move from Rome to Capri with his entourage made the Neapolitan philosopher Giovanni Bovio write, *"The law of the world is conceived at Capri, sold in Rome and imposed on the whole earth."*

The house of the Caesars brought literary assemblies and individuals of remarkable quality to congregate and pay tribute to Tiberius. The Bay of Naples was splendid. Vesuvius had yet to erupt and in this setting Tacitus, eighty years after the death of Tiberius, wrote of the Emperor Tiberius' evil deeds, catamites, secrets and sordid sensuality arousing moral distaste for the leader that included malevolent crimes marking his chapters with Tiberius' symptoms of *dementia senilis*, coloring him as an embittered old man living in intense solitude, after the death of his only child.

One must consider was Tacitus' pen history or gossip to satisfy the public's lust for reports of the scandalous orgies of Capri? Beginning with these tales, whether fabricated or true, stories began the island's fortune in fantasy. Later, Voltaire recorded Tiberius selected this remote isle as the scene for debauchery.

Whatever one believes, whatever course astrology prophesized for Tiberius and those that came before and after him, and whatever truth was spirited away in the effort to enflame the public's leisure time with excitement, old age had come to call Emperor Tiberius.

His *bella figura* was that of a man with exceptional power, attaining the astonishing age of seventy-seven, still demonstrating he could rule and enjoy life - attending javelin tournaments on the mainland robustly stalking wild boar. Nevertheless, circumstances changed the course of history.

Tiberius caught chill while hunting precisely when he received concurrent messages of vital importance. Firstly, news from Pontius Pilate that a certain Jesus Christ (who claimed he was King of the Jews), had been crucified in Jerusalem and secondly, on Capri, a one and only earthquake brought evil to call with an omen so severe it precipitated the collapse of the Roman Empire.

Feverish and shivering, Tiberius was taken to the sumptuous villa of Lucullus on the north-western end of the Bay of Naples, Cape Misenum, where the situation became grave and his life ebbed.

This gave nimble handed Caligula, his grandnephew and adopted grandson, (a guest at the villa the same time), power to hasten destiny by smothering Emperor Tiberius's face with pillows facilitating death.

Tiberius never thought Caligula would betray him evidenced by the fact that months earlier he'd bequeathed to Caligula and his biological, teenage grand-son Tiberius Germellus, joint power upon his death to rule the vast Roman Empire in his Last Will and Testament. On becoming Princeps, Caligula's first act after murdering Tiberius, was to void Tiberius' Will and have Gemellus executed.

These harrowing events brought Tiberius and Capri's glory days to end. The story of Imperial Capri was lost in obscurity until the tenth century when the Dukes of Amalfi built a fortress to protect the island and its inhabitants...that was until Barbarossa, the Ottoman pirate, captured the isle, securing dominance over the Mediterranean in 1535. This victory permitted Barbarossa to take the short sail to the richest city in Christendom, the Kingdom of Naples - and loot it. This act of barbarism terrified the isle's population. They fled to the citadel as refuge, 1,352 feet above sea level, on Mount Solaro.

The ruthless Barbarossa led his attack to conquer, kidnapping and robbing all, destroying the castle in 1544. Today, this breathtaking archaeological ruin derives its name from its pirate destroyer.

With the passage of time, all became peaceful once more....best described by Goethe's poem two hundred years later, detailing where we are about to go ~ Capri ~

You know that land where lemon orchards bloom,

Its golden oranges aglow in gloom,

That land of soft wind blowing from blue sky,

Where myrtle hushes and the laurel's high?

You know that land? That way! That way

I'd go with you, my love, and go today.

You know that house, its roof on colonnades,

The halls agleam, the rooms of gems and jades?

The marble statues eying all I do:

"Oh wretched child, what have they done to you?"

You know that house?

That way! That way

I'd go with you, my guardian, today.

...and now, with a scenario that echoes history, hundreds of years later, our story begins in Capri in the year 2004 A.D.

PART ONE

I

Esmeralda and Nigel Pembrooke

Villa Pina, Capri, September 2004

"Grazie, Esmeralda.....*grazie...*" Nigel caressed her long strawberry-blonde hair gazing at her, satiated. Her full lips parted with a gentle smile, feline style she rolled over exhausted as he left her bedroom gloating.

The sybaritic joy to linger in bed and deliberate the future ignited Esmeralda's imagination. Stretching her body, she studied the fresco of nymphs and satyrs on the ceiling. The expressions of erotica the artist depicted amused her calling to memory her past and present. Her mind raced with countless thoughts...what had been...what was - and what was to come.

"From Baroness to Countess in a dozen years and now marriage to Nigel ...seems incredible..."

A beam of sun glistened through *persianni* shutters. Esmeralda threw off her covers and exited to the balcony viewing the calm cerulean sea without a definitive mark. The only break in the scene appeared as an apparition from the distant Bay of Naples. The wake of a ship was spotted in the midst as fog began to evaporate, unfolding a spectacular view. Soon the vessel would move parallel to the shore taking a leisurely turn towards Marina Grande.

"This week will change things. I feel it instinctively, like an omen. Extraordinary change....is going to happen." A swarm of butterflies lit upon a mimosa tree nearby. Memories consumed her. "I've lived incognito as a woman of power in many places ...an expatriate wanting to lose myself in the intoxication of all things foreign...." The fickle butterflies flew to the jasmine plant. "Others may judge me, they have and they will. Life isn't a popularity contest, it's about self-discovery and survival. To survive is the test of a person's character." The butterflies flew away, as a chill went through her, believing in her omen.

No matter how Esmeralda tried to dismiss forces that brought a life many craved, Esmeralda returned to the web of herself questioning how she could continue and if she'd have courage to face her tomorrows.

She was a woman without fear – except the fear of disclosure. Esmeralda Pembrooke could do anything because she had done everything to be in the position she achieved.

Her view from Villa Pina was remote and extraordinarily beautiful, set at a cliff that plunged into the sea six hundred feet from the peak where Capri met Anacapri. Towering cypress framed the setting reaching an unending expanse of sky. Esmeralda was bequeathed the villa by her beloved late husband, Count Giovanni Zianni and now she resided a few months every year at this residence with her present husband, Nigel Pembrooke, younger brother to the Earl of Norfolk. Known as the finest villa on the island, built in 1370 by the monks of Certosa di San Giacomo, Doric columns, ancient ruins, and unparalleled panorama complimented floriculture of peach and lemon trees that colored the terraced gardens. Beyond were white washed villas sprinkling the terrain, closer to the sea, punctuating the landscape as if a painter had placed them there with his imagination.

Stefano will be here. The only one who comes near my past, she thought and suddenly *déjà vu* swept over her. Serena, her second husband's sister, illuminated. The instant was a sinister collision with her past and her future. Startled, she moved inside to steady her nerves as a flood of memories descended, stirring her emotions.

While at the same time…

Nigel Pembrooke whistling *Funiculi, Funicula* was in his dressing room preparing for the day, studying his face in the mirror, just as a woman of a certain age would do. Ignoring the sparse cranium that put his age beyond fifty, he brushed grey tendrils of his remaining chestnut hair with matching silver brushes, considering himself splendid.

It had been an exceptional orgasm, fine way to begin the morning, he thought, letting him forget his long wait for a title and inheritance. Damn his brother, who'd live forever with no issue and was surely not interested in women. Prince Charles is in the same fix, waiting...endless waiting... for a relative, in his case, the Queen, to die and take control. "Wretched situation to be in," Nigel proclaimed, speaking to himself as was his habit.

Taking back stairs from their dual bedrooms, Nigel crossed the library below and opened French doors leading to the veranda viewing the spectacular panorama of Capri counting himself lucky with this marriage to Esmeralda. Capri encapsulated the best of Italy, the best of life. Everything he beheld was a masterpiece, as one views a Monet landscape. The *Coast Amalfitana* retained a hazy shadow from the precipice at Villa Pina yet he could tell immediately, another brilliant September day was guaranteed.

"Ah…*la vita!*" Nigel inhaled deeply.

A patch of vibrant blue broke through the clouds illuminating the promontory and rocky crest of the mountain.

"Bel..la….fig…u…rrra."

"I beg your pardon Sir?" A manservant appeared with his linen blazer.

Nigel nodded thanks, stretching his arms to accommodate the assistance smiling as he appraised his tall form in the garden window, proudly running his long fingers down his muscular chest giving scant attention to the pouch beginning to form.

*"Bel..la....fig...u...rrra...*practicing my Italian, Sanjeev."

"Yes, Sir."

"Confounded language! You think you know what it means, then you learn it's an idiomatic expression...."

"Yes, Sir."

"Bella figur..rr..a." Nigel Pembrooke relaxed leafing through his dictionary talking to himself. "Funny that...One would think it means beautiful figure – Ha! Wrong!...Here it is! ...*Bella figura:* how people act to gain respect and recognition. Sounds like my Esmeralda. *Bella figur...rrra*. That's better. I'm rolling the r like an Italian."

"Yes, Sir."

Nigel's be-speckled eyes remained fixed on the slow pace of the three-mast schooner coming into port. A cool breeze met his cheek, and for the moment he fell under the hypnotic spell of nature, lost in thought. It didn't bother him that he was unable to speak Italian, everyone of any importance on the island spoke English, like himself and why involve himself with Capresi whether rich or poor? Esmeralda kept her distance relishing privacy too, they had that in common here. Import guests was the answer. What Brits do every weekend at their country houses to have élan.

Tourists, far below in Capri, were not part of this life. Languishing on the terrace suited him - well, to a point. How he wished he could be in control of his family's estate in Norfolk using the sale one of the houses Esmeralda owned to pay delinquent estate taxes. Damned UK taxes... threaten an existence that's been the Pembrooke's forever! Something! Anything! would do instead of this film Esmeralda wants! He dismissed the notion of taxes with a heavy sigh.

"May I serve your breakfast, Signor?" the Sri Lankan manservant, inquired holding a tray. Sanjeev was a fixture to this scene thirty years.

"Yes please and let me see the guest list for the weekend." For the life of him, Nigel couldn't understand why months ago Esmeralda invested in Hollywood glitz when he would have preferred a board seat at Covent Garden, a bonus to his allowance and that miniature painting of Lucien Freud's for his library. Now he'd be forced to endure a long week of people from tinsel town who wanted an Oscar acting like circus performers.

Sanjeev appeared with the list. Nigel scanned the names noting his wife's remarks, fingering his crest ring on his pinkie finger. "Let me get this straight before Act One begins…" He jested uttering what he believed was the truth, (his opinion)….

Monty Daniels, journalist – PR for the film - "I owe him..."

Rupert Davidson – arriving with Naomi – "I don't see why she invited him"

Dame Naomi Griffin, Poet Laureate – "same with her"

Ambassador Stefano de Gesu – "A favorite of Esmeralda's – he'll add smaltz"

Stella Gregotti, screenwriter – "Feminist bitch"

Whitney and Lynne Jameson – backers – "Serious money, the lucky bastard."

Sir Brian Korthorpe - backer? – " Brains but backer? Esmeralda must be joking…"

Véronique Joulin, astrologer - "Hocus-pocus...with flair..."

Mark Levy, producer + current girlfriend – "Glitz, pure glitz! God help me get through the week with them!"

Elizabeth Mackenzie, Naomi's daughter – (courtesy) weekend guest only

Dr. Samir and Jacqueline Redat –backers – "Must ask him about my heart"

Marco Ricci, actor – STAR of the film – "good, entertaining fun"

Olympia Sanford - solo without fiancé –"Man eater"

Princess Shabadiba – window dressing –"Old times …old money…"

Niccolo Viscounti- 'family' – "Not 'family but Esmeralda thinks so…"

Zofra Zofany – friend of journalist Daniels – "God knows what the cat's dragged in!"

"Old friends, strangers, VIPs, nobodies…" Nigel evaluated the mix considering Véronique's astute astrological predictions surmising they would be needed with the assortment of characters and performance everyone would give. Véronique creates uneasiness – physic shit - with that astrology, thought Nigel, nevertheless, I can trust her, the others? Of no importance except Daniels. Nigel's muttering returned, "...covered my tracks hushing one story or another. He'll poke around for a scoop about Esmeralda."

Nigel turned his attention back to the incomparable view considering how money separates people, "the great socio-economic divide," he heard himself mutter observing birds and butterflies atwitter, lizards peeking from bougainvillea, dogs and servants energized. The place was magical. Even the vine pickers in the grape arbor sang a sweet song. The scent of jasmine permeated the air. Surveying the grandeur of the landscape, lemon and orange groves in bloom, he reconsidered Esmeralda's idea about this week's agenda concentrating how the unexpected was certain to happen. Confidence came to him until his mobile phone vibrated in his pocket breaking his concentration. Pembrooke checked to identify the caller. *Restricted number.* Robotically, he accepted the call, wondering who was "Restricted."

"Pronto…"

A brief one-way conversation ensued.

"I'll consider it." Responded Nigel. What he heard put him off guard, his hands became clammy.

Obsequiously Sanjeev continued with the daily ritual. It was eleven o'clock. Nigel Pembrooke enjoyed Sanjeev tending his every need. "This is what I was born to," he told himself, *"la bella vita."* Figs from the garden were peeled. His 3 1/2 minute soft-boiled eggs were cracked open with tops removed, Espresso *corretto,* poured with an exact measure of Anisette placed in his cup. Sanjeev noticed until that phone call everything was perfect. An unnatural silence was obvious, Pembrooke was tense. It changed everything that was serene moments before. Mercurial behavior, considered the butler, continuing his tasks silently.

"Island mentality," Nigel muttered *sotto voce* trying to dismiss stress. "This island's taught me lessons, much like my island, England." Sanjeev understood Nigel's mumblings were no invitation to engage in conversation. He observed him, stone still staring at the vessel. "Capri's changed me." He remarked aloud. "Me, of all people! There's no reason to strive anymore. No need to pretend. I have everything here, like Augustus and Tiberius. How marvelous to relinquish the idea to be one of the bloody crowd and be myself."

Nevertheless, with his English restraint contained, that telephone call gave him the jitters. He drummed his fingers on the table and his right leg shook with impatience. He sipped café, reached for *The London Times*, scanning the headlines, 10th of September 2004.

As part of his daily ritual, Nigel turned to the stock quotation of ZIP, Zianni International Pharmaceuticals, checking how many points rose since yesterday. This gave him self-assurance validating why he let Esmeralda rule his life.

"The most arduous journey always gives the best reward," Nigel reflected. "Hell to those Chinese who say, *"Tis better to travel with hope than to arrive,"* they don't know Capri and my plans!"

Dazzled by the view and impatient, he glanced at the sea again forgetting the call redirecting thoughts to Esmeralda and the guests on the yacht.

Capri!...Isle of history and mysticism…aristocrats, bourgeois people, clowns, lovers, artists and millionaires arrive everyday from every corner of the planet to experience a sense of legendary magic from this rock in the middle of the Mediterranean. Capri never disappoints them.

Our guests know how to arrive. They'll have no problem with timetables or connections. The privileged lucky bastards to visit us for a week! Not like the masses that shove and sweat next to each other arriving hourly on the *aloscafii,* weather beaten and tired, too Italian and crude – except for a few.

The color of the sea and pure air made Nigel feel years younger. There was freedom here but it was not true freedom. Are we ever free? The cynical Nigel knew humanity was not to be trusted. Like the wind in Capri when it gusts and one is unable to linger on a cliff looking to the ocean, unable to stay afloat on a boat between the mainland and this island, the elements steer you to a different trajectory and in that detour one never senses the danger gazing at a Capri sea or witnessing its *merenda*• of intense blue streaked with red.

The idyllic setting fascinated him yet Nigel was no fool to circumstances. Capri's beguiling paradise had an evil twin. He'd auctioned himself with this marriage three years ago and boredom set in. The coming week's activities with the business of Esmeralda backing a major motion picture would bring change ...inevitable change....just like the weather.

"Change," he declared to Sanjeev, "is the only thing certain in this world. Watching the tempests of Capri turn to glorious days, I've learned about change preparing myself for the tempests to arrive again. Like people, each with our own tempest…"

"Yes, Sir..."

I don't want things to change. Nigel thought. If everything could stay exactly as it is right now, even with that phone call, I'd be in paradise.

———

• sunset

How many of us have wished the same thing? Within an hour, a plethora of guest would descend on Villa Pina and pandemonium commence.

———

Nigel relished his last moments of solitude spying a Liberian flag on the mast of Whitney's yacht.

"Millionaire defrauding America."

"I beg your pardon, Sir?"

"Oh Sanjeev, I was remarking about phenomena, private thoughts."

"Yes Sir, anything else you require?"

"No. I'm quite content." He watched Sanjeev walk off.

"Content! Phenomena! Ha! I'm about as content as a rat in a cage!"

How could he be content when everything he was waiting for was on hold? After love making this morning, when he was in ecstasy, the last words from Esmeralda echoed in his brain: "Who are you, Nigel Darling, to question my investment of twenty million? A film like this comes along every five years." Then with that angelic smile of hers, impossible to read, she turned over.

"Who am I?" he wanted to howl - instead all he could think of was "Let her control me!" Nigel paused, pompous fashion, expanding his chest. "Fucking impossible to dominate Esmeralda. Not with her money and God damned mystery."

Reaching for *Corriere della Sera* he spoke loudly, "I hope to hell it isn't boring." Struggling to read the front page, frustration mounted. "Bloody Italian! Three years and I still haven't mastered it!" His eyes rolled and realigned themselves to the view and the vessel closer. "That flag! Some phenomena! What's new about avoiding taxes?" His brooding temperament went in circles as he paced the mosaic-tiled terrace and his Labrador watched.

Nigel pulled a *stogie* from its case, inserted it into a tortoise filter and ignited the tip with his gold lighter. The flame called to mind his arousing morning with Esmeralda. For once he had his way. His aristocratic mouth smiled with the victory of control, even for a brief hour. He drew a long inhale from the *cigarillo* and Pembrooke sighed a sigh that would have brought him an Oscar if this were a film.

"...But wasn't it a film?" He deliberated. "Don't we all make our own movies? Take in our own dramas? Live in the cutting room? Don't we edit people and scenes in life for a better spectacle? Wasn't it Marco who said the same thing? And, soon he'd arrive from Positano, with his *amante*, that ball buster, the famous screenwriter, Stella."

Nigel's mind wandered back to his peace of solitude and his intolerance of liberal ideas. Suddenly, it was shattered by the sound of Esmeralda at the piano.

"God Damn it! I wish that cunt would learn to play!"

He took no notice of the devoted houseman clearing the table. His hand reached for the buff colored Labrador at his feet and kicked it off his espadrille. "The time is NOW – view the clowns and be one myself."

He extinguished his smoke, stretched broadly, pausing to look at the sea.

"Bella figura has begun...!"

"Sir?"

Nigel Pembrooke shoved the dog at his side and abruptly exited the terrace.

"Countess, I thought you should know the yacht's been spotted in the harbor."

"Thank you, Sanjeev." Esmeralda rose from the piano and hid her music in an adjacent cabinet. Her ability wasn't up to par but she could lose herself in music with intense concentration. It was the one time she forgot her yesterdays.

"Now begins another chapter," she ascended the sweeping staircase to her bedroom to prepare for the visitors who'd invade her world. Suddenly she sensed the omen again and tried to divert her mind from this and the sting of loneliness.

———

What Esmeralda needed in life was the greatest of all luxuries: a true friend to understand and accept her and the bizarre actions of her past. How well she remembered her first time in Capri, brought to the glorious isle by her husband, Count Gianni Zianni.

Love promised everything. Now, gazing at this magnificence in the middle of the Mediterranean something different enveloped her. Her guests would bring distraction, spice, activity and begin to set a course for a new beginning. Nigel didn't understand that. He was too selfish to have a larger scope of life; he wanted things to remain the same, suffocated by lineage, venerating his aristocratic life and pleasures.

On the landing she adjusted the Modigliani painting of his mistress, a gift from her second husband reminiscing...with Gianni here in Capri how we lived! Every kiss brought inspiration...How we loved! The rhapsody of our bodies, the joy of his words! There was laughter too... laughter is the secret to life. We must laugh even at ourselves, even in the sex act when it is very good and we've discovered something together.... but in this marriage, there is no laughter......no rhapsody...This marriage, so different from that marriage....it isn't working... hasn't from the beginning.

Starting to dress, she considered the charade one plays in marriage. To control Nigel financially bored her. Money wasn't her *modus operandi*, unlike him, a taker. "Maybe I'm too hard on myself and Nigel but self knowledge doesn't deceive you."

"*Truco*,"• she uttered glossing her lips using the Italian word for cosmetics, knowing it the perfect way to express how women bewitch their audience with make-believe. She glanced in the gilt mirror of her *Belle Epoque* bedroom calling to mind how people viewed her while admitting to herself. "Everyone has secrets but I'm caught in this trap thirty-seven years with too many lies, too many lives. Pretense surrounds me."

All expected Esmeralda Pembrooke to be perfect vision of loveliness, endowed with everything because of her wealth and beauty. Wealth was relative. Wealth could vanish, like beauty. She was wise to both having seen life from other perspectives. She dabbed Shalimar on her thighs and through her long strawberry-blonde tresses.

"To control one's mind and emotions is the key to life..." she made this her mantra, repeating it three times, closing her eyes haunted by a voice within ...alone in this marriage, alone with all the glitter...those who loved me are dead just as a part of me is dead....I must go on...I must control my mind and emotions....

She slipped on her lingerie dwelling on the forces of destiny that brought her to this life envied by all. Let the troubadours sing with praises. They want me to enrich their lives with gold dust. Everything was performance. No one walked in her shoes.

What did she do that redirected the course of her life? Who could understand what she had at stake and that her only fear was exposure? Esmeralda could deceive everyone but she didn't deceive herself.

• trick

She looked at the wedding picture on her dressing table. "Nigel and I mirror each other." She whispered hearing her husband's footsteps in the adjoining bedroom knowing they were opportunists stung by Fate and opulence, living a sham of a marriage. *mariage de convenance,* the French called it...nonetheless, Nigel's past is nothing like mine.

She reached for her hidden photograph with Gianni, stashed behind her mirror and kissed his face. The hairs on her back bristled thinking of the rest. At that precise moment, Nigel entered from his room.

"Esmeralda…"

"Yes Nigel," she said breaking reverie, hiding the photograph while at the same time understanding he'd seen what she'd done and chose to say nothing about it.

"Seems first to arrive will be old chums. God knows how the others will react."

"Let's try to enjoy it, Nigel and not bicker." She gave him a smile full of hope. "They'll be gone in a week and who knows? This may be a remarkable time." She held her wrist towards him to fasten a gold bracelet, not divulging her omen, smelling the scent of putrid cigars on his breath, not like the aroma of her first husband, Baron Martin Beck's meerschaum pipe.

"Yes," he said coolly, returning her smile. "Who knows?"

His topaz eyes fixed on her in a lacy satin brassiere and panties, desiring his wife, feeling the stir of an erection, stealing a kiss on her breasts while taking his advantage running his hand along her firm buttocks. God! she was beautiful!

Gently Esmeralda pushed him aside. Her denial was always like this, stimulating his want - with only his eyes to feast on that want.

Esmeralda put him off balance and although he stirred sexual need in her, it was desire, no more, without a fire of love, tenderness or passion she'd known in the past. The fact that she was a woman of mystery enticed Nigel and kept him enticed. Nevertheless Esmeralda realized from the beginning a man of his dimension would never understand the chasm of her sexual personae. He would always leave her wanting. She knew the difference. His ego and veiled barbs didn't escape her. The crucial decision how they viewed their marriage hadn't changed from the bargain they cut when wed three years ago.

Now Nigel would wait for her to finish dressing eyeing her with lust, not knowing what was going through her head. The routine would be as before. She'd have last minute details to tend to and then, together, they'd exit downstairs looking elegant and greet their first guests smiling.

Bella figura.

The Pembrookes excelled in giving a great impression.

Before visitors arrive at Villa Pina, events from the past make me speak of the happiness Esmeralda knew with Gianni Zianni, her second husband.

From the moment Gianni Zianni glimpsed at Esmeralda he wanted her to be his wife. Love produced a force that required no explanation. He decided what was to be and pursued Esmeralda with an intensity known only to those who've experienced a magnificent sensation of this magnitude.

The power of love is a time when doubt knows no place.

Fear is a stranger.

It is the rare time we trust ourselves entirely.

Words mean nothing, instincts command…and before the fleeting arrow Eros targeted vanishes, opportunity is seized.

Love is the time miracles happen.

II

The Arrival

"BASTA!"......... "STOP"

"Do not proceed. This is an order!" A siren blasted, a megaphone screeched, rupturing silence.

A speedboat marked POLICE drew alongside the three-mast schooner, circling Whitney Jameson's vessel. His skipper furled sails immediately. A uniformed officer, megaphone in hand, watched the crew working intently. The two boats idled at sea, engines humming.

All eyes fixed on the officer with gold epilates, creating drama Italian style. *"Passoporti! Passoporti per favore."*

"Si Capitano," the skipper bowed his head respectfully giving a sharp cry, "*Signor* Whitney! *Signor* Whitney!"

Whitney Jameson appeared from the stern with natural composure. *"Buon Giorno Signor* Police! May I help you?"

"Passoporti per tutti!"

"You want *Passoporti?* Here..." he began to unzip a small attaché case his Italian skipper handed him to deliver for examination, engaging him in conversation. "Pardon me, My Italian is not good. *Otto ospiti, nove impiegati* ...Eight guests, nine crew. I'm Whitney Jameson. This is my boat. Come aboard, have a café.... study the documents."

The police captain liked this man. He had a genuine quality of nonchalance, completely unaffected for a man who could have a yacht like this. The officer. smiled agreeing, *"Si."* Whitney extended his hand helping the officer aboard.

In accented English, the *Capitano* said, "Funny name, your vessel. *The Other Woman!"* They laughed although the coast-guard police with medals gleaming in his blue uniform was dazed at the disparity of the two boats rocking to and fro, side by side, juggling the tide."My boat no other woman." Whitney patted him on the shoulder, motioning guests assembled to come forward. "This is my wife, friends," he passed along the passports to review.

"You stay at Contessa Zianni's villa. You, the American – *Si?"*

"Yes. My wife and I are American. We have two British guests, Sir Brian here and ….two women holding French passports, the Italian Ambassador de Gesu on board…"

"Ambassador de Gesu?"

"Yes."

"*Pardondami, Signor* Whitney," he exclaimed bowing, "I leave you to enjoy arriving in Capri."

His exit was as unexpected as his entry. Nonplussed, the crew, Lynne, Véronique and Brian watched as he ignored his café and disembarked. Within seconds, the POLICE speed boat raced off, siren screeching, towards another boat.

"It's always like this," Whitney laughed turning to his crew and Brian Korthorpe close by, "guarding Capri, an island without crime, one mention of Stefano's name and I knew we'd sail through."

"Capree?....an island without crime? You say… except Mafiosi on vacation," Brian jested.

"Brian, the correct way to say Capri, if ya'll don't mind me sayin' so is with the emphasis on the first syllable. You say it terribly." said Lynne.

"I say it like the song...*'Twas on the Isle of Capreee that I met her..."* "

"Wrong!...Brian, ya'll listen to me..your ways a cock-up. I'm just wild about Italy and I know what's right."

"You jest about pronunciation and that Capri has no crime" answered Véronique... but what about superstitions?"

"Anyone who has ever lived in Italy believes in superstition and knows never trust the police or crime statistics," advised Whitney.

Véronique moved along the deck and Brian followed her. "The Capresi say when the eclipse of the sun arrived with its dual bolt of lightening..."

"Véronique!" Is your conception of life always through the stars, the sun and the moon?" her lifelong friend Sir Brian Korthorpe wanted to tease her, moving his glance from the magnificence of Capri to the slender, elegant woman he'd studied for decades.

"With due respect, Brian, one day all your scientific principles, will make you come down from your academic pedestal and admit the first science was astrology."

"Because our stars are aligned on some hemisphere and this is our Fate?" He was in good humor returning to Villa Pina after several years.

"Stop demeaning MY life's work when I laud yours, naughty boy!"

"Naughty boy! I wish." It pleased him to have the comfort of Véronique's company wondering what dramatics would present themselves this week.

At seventy-five only his hands and neck gave his age away. Other than that, women thought him ten years younger which pleased the sprightly septuagenarian with his abundant lionesque white hair. Vanity was not a dominant part of his character, nonetheless, as age increased and his scientific fame became second nature, a certain macho ego reared its head. There was no need to advertise his advanced years, a fact he detested that the press continually inserted into an article whenever he gave a news conference. As his blue eyes caught sight of Villa Pina towering above them, he was silent ...how strange Fate had disrupted plans he thought would succeed.

"Sorry, Véronique, I was lost in thought seeing this overwhelming spectacle...I'm not myself."

"Nervous returning to Villa Pina, seeing two women from your past?"

She threw her head back engaging him with her remark. A breeze came from he sea and churned through her glistening auburn mane. Véronique was alluring. Her oval face spotlighted lively black eyes, the most dramatic he'd ever witnessed. Studying her (as he had for years), he thought it remarkable they'd never had an affair. She kept a certain dignity, sex was never on offer and she, his junior, kept a reserve between them.

Nonetheless, those exceptional eyes brought an observation that seized him studying people. Eyes portray the soul and mind. Véronique's brain was richer than most, some called it a 'Rolls Royce brain,' cultivated by birth, travels, her amatory history and the depth in which she examined the human condition through astrology. When one discussed the soul, Véronique's, he was certain, was on some celestial stratosphere unknown to science, in a class all her own.

A dozen years ago when the Queen bestowed knighthood upon him for his scientific discoveries to retard the rapid development of Alzheimer's, Brian Korthorpe chose Véronique to stand alongside him with the one woman he ever loved, acclaimed poet, Naomi Griffin, Lord Dartworth's daughter. He had mixed feelings meeting Naomi again. That beast ego was involved in his neurosis. The space of too many silent years between them made him leery.

How will I approach her when we meet today? He questioned himself. Ridiculous, he thought answering his question, the one person I could unveil my soul to and now with the idea I'll be in her company, I'm speechless! Emotions, smothered for what seemed a century, percolated testing him to experience life again.

The invitation to Villa Pina he accepted, learning later Naomi would be a guest at the same time. He hadn't set eyes on her for a dozen years.

He wanted to turn his mind to something else, "Véronique the beginning of this conversation you mentioned something about the Capresi..."

"What I started to reveal was to this day, the Capresi say when the eclipse of the sun arrived with its dual bolt of lightening that year on the third of October..."

"Yes, yes, I know. What about the Capresi?"

"The Villa's main wing was destroyed at the same time Gianni met Esmeralda."

"Two years later on the exact date..." she hesitated...

"Gianni lost his life at Windsor thrown by his horse, trampled to death." Brian's words came from the pit of his heart .

".....the family fortune changed hands."

Véronique and Brian's eyes met in a long take as the last sails were furled securely and the yacht readied for anchor.

"What are we doing here, Véronique? "

"You'll see." She linked her arm in his and squeezed it to her body.

"Loyal friends coming back to view the wreckage."

"It is going to be more than that. There's a reason we're invited and a blessing we can see this through together."

While at the Villa...

"Sanjeev. I need to speak to the chef. Send him to me please."

"Certainly Contessa." The devoted Sanjeev walked off and Esmeralda was delighted how things were progressing.

Fascinating mix of people this week, she thought including Brian Korthorpe. The Zianni Foundation at Cambridge is due to his scientific discoveries enriching the family but I won't keep endowing his coffers...not unless..."

Diverted by the buzzing of a bee whose irritating noise distracted the peace of her study, she questioned the insect: "Are you trying to tell me Brian Korthorpe has the brains and ambition to make history?" The bee flew off.

"Contessa you asked to speak to me?"

Methodically Esmeralda drew her clip-board from her desk and began discussing details about menus for the next several days. Politely he listened knowing he would inflate the bills from the butcher and *vinaio*• and pocket the rest.

• wine merchant

Her chef, Mario, held her in esteem. This gorgeous female is a marvel, he contemplated...studied culinary arts in France and Italy and drives me *pazza* with likes and dislikes. Too much of a perfectionist. None of these guests understand her exacting standards.

• crazy

He looked over her body and Esmeralda realized this uncomfortably. She raised her chin without meeting his eye as only the aristocrat in her could do. Instantly, she became more distant with the man who created her delectable feasts.

This was a practiced exercise. Most men who admired her found her reserve appealing. Infidelity with the likes of a chef amused Esmeralda and when she was alone in England and read how the press lauded chefs as 'society,' she was more amused. If she ever let Mario have his way, she'd be taking that vulgar streak all women have for the thrill of the forbidden. There were boundaries and hers on the subject of class were impenetrable.

Mario shifted the weight of his nervous body considering his boss, I bet she's a great lay. She treats me fairly... God bless her, with this cold husband...

"Si Contessa. Everything will be as you wish."

The ship dropped anchor, the *portobaggagi* scrambled to assist the crew with the baggage. From below deck, Samir and Jacqueline Redat appeared, looking as they'd engaged in a sexual adventure minutes before while from the portside, skeletal, overdressed Lynne Jameson spoke at high pitch to Whitney who followed her to the main deck like a dog.

"Now this is the way I like to come to a place, Whitney honey, ya'll hear?" Lynne scampered beside him clutching her Bible. "Next time we evva go to a place that can be reached by watta, make sure ya'll organize somethin' like this again, honey..."

The withered, once beautiful South Carolina *belle* adjusted her Burberry jacket that matched her Burberry shoes and purse. Armani spectacles that turned darker according to the light of day, hid her lined eyes. Stiff, overly bleached, cropped hair fixed permanently to her head, resembled her rigid opinions on every subject.

For an instant, Whitney's shadow blocked the sun from his wife's face revealing the vestiges of misery in her fixed expression that was no stranger to a surgeon's knife. Theirs was a toxic, thirty-year marriage of means, his means.

"I'll say one thing," Lynne began pointing her finger at the guests, "ya'll know Jesus's lookin' after ya'll when you can have friends sailin' like this from Portofino."

Véronique and Brian smiled courteously, as did the Redats while Whitney, distinctly different from his spouse, motioned to Samir. Lynne thrust herself in a deck chair to re-read the 23rd Psalm – at least, thought Whitney, it's better than hearing her carp morning, noon and night.

They distanced themselves from the party in what seemed a guise to avoid their wives as they went to chat alone on the starboard. Samir, an Egyptian, living between London and Cairo, was the perfectly attired Asian gentleman with dapper moustache, navy blazer, white ducks and Gucci loafers while billionaire Jameson was in sailing kit that had seen several storms and five America Cup races. They made an odd pair yet respected each other's intelligence enormously.

"What's the current feeling in Egypt today, Samir with the Muslim world at odds with Western sentiment?"

"The poor are desperate. The current regime in Egypt doesn't take kindly to fanaticism. They treat them in an inhuman way, arresting and torturing people. Religion in Egypt is used as a cover for social unrest, a way to empower those people who are not empowered."

"I sense huge disruption when Mubarak ends his career."

"Yes, Whitney you're right. In Egypt we have Islam for the rich and Islam for the poor. They are separate with their own mosques, own sheikhs, own ideas. The rich use religion to ensure the status quo for they don't want change, but the poor, the poor everywhere, want change. They want it because they're desperate and have been deprived all their lives and the lives of their parents for fundamental rights. They don't want that for their children."

Samir, similar to Jameson in age was broad shouldered close to sixty and like his friend from Cambridge years, had his own insecurities not inherent in his professional life. Samir became withdrawn in any ambiance of social significance. Boston Brahmin, Jameson, conversely, was completely at ease in society yet insecure himself. Their wives reflected their insecurity.

When the chef left her study, Esmeralda again experienced *déjà vu.* This recurring sensation made her wonder if she was imagining things or could someone possibly be a villain to disrupt her plans? Gianni's friends were linked with Nigel and had never caused anything of an acrimonious nature.

Her mind began to churn. Jacqueline and Samir Redat loved each other and exhibited kindness to all. Princess Shabadiba likewise and certainly she didn't contain a morsel of jealousy. Not like prune-mouthed Lynne Jameson, fixed in her ways. But Lynne knows her place. The gentlemen are gallant – Whitney with his money, Samir with his brains like Brian Korthorpe, Stefano with his charm and Rupert, totally meek. Madness to be edgy, she thought and turned her mind how they'd all attended her wedding to Gianni six years ago...and then she busied herself with preparations for the party.

What a mixture of individuals...

Samir's wife, Jacqueline, was an intoxicating woman twenty years his junior who liked to believe she dominated her famous surgeon husband, nevertheless knew he would always have the last word. Jameson's wife, Lynne, his contemporary, dominated and fed upon Whitney's insecurities. She was the A-typical, American wife, in continual therapy, and Whitney was a hen-pecked spouse. Her dominance in the past had been in the bedroom. Now when passions cooled to arctic levels, all that was left were joint investments made for tax reasons because Lynne had presented him with two miserable children who didn't speak to him anymore.

The President bypassed him for political appointments he salivated, which, he was sure, was because of Lynne. No matter how philanthropic he was to lobbyists and political coffers, Jameson was excluded from the Chief's inner circle. How he had wished to be Ambassador to London, Paris or Rome! He told himself Lynne didn't contain the polish one would need to be an Ambassador's wife, questioning continually why his one wish, a presidential posting, was never met. It had to be her not him, of course…but was it?

All his god damned money thrown away to hoodlums who'd invade the Senate, all his party giving for miserable phonies, too superficial for his liking with Lynne gushing all over everyone and nothing came to fruition. Nothing!

To return to Villa Pina, his former haunt where he could relax would be good, nevertheless tragic not to be there with Gianni. At least the movie launch was exciting, the old crowd would be together and Nigel wasn't all bad.

Jameson was comfortable with Samir, kinky haired Samir, who would always be on the outside looking in, yet a part of the legacy of Gianni. Screw the Social Register, people like Samir who came from the slums of Cairo to his position of importance today, would never be listed. Who gave a damn anyway? Lynne, that's who.

I prefer a man of accomplishment like Samir, who knows his place, a man of genius, humble. I favor him. We don't have to try to impress each other; he's above those double-talking creeps in Washington who'd sell their grandmother for a vote.

Back at the Villa, Nigel caught sight of Sanjeev going to the wine cellar.

"Which wine did Mrs. Pembrooke say we'll serve at lunch Sanjeev?"

"She noted the Brunello di Montalcino vintage from '89, Sir."

"And dinner tonight?"

"Tonight's dinner is in the *piazzetta*, informal, with a stroll through Capri."

"Oh, I forgot," he said quickly once again reminded of his mind's inefficiency to retain details as before.

"Will that be all Sir?"

"Doctor Samir doesn't drink. Have you that fruit juice he likes?"

"Yes, Sir."

"Anything else Sir?"

"Not for now. Always good to have a heart surgeon as a guest." He laughed at his joke and became anxious he'd forgotten the dinner in town.

Nigel Pembrooke compared himself to his peers.

Samir, with professional alliances to de Bakey and Yacoub, was one of today's extraordinary heart surgeons making history worldwide saving lives. Whereas Jameson, unfulfilled professionally, struggled writing books published through vanity press for recognition telling everyone Proust did the same thing. Years paled to be an Ambassador. This upset Nigel and Samir respecting Jameson who retained his fair haired handsomeness, cutting an attractive figure nevertheless to view their chum succumb to browbeaten remarks from his wife, Lynne, appalled the Egyptian and Nigel who viewed women differently.

"Whitney failed politically because the hard crust one needs for that game Whitney Jameson doesn't possess." Samir told his wife, Jacqueline. Yet how could he ever explain that to the golden spoon boy? He'd mentioned this to Nigel and his input was, "Or that everyone who spends five minutes with Lynne, loathes her social climbing behavior."

———

Samir, no stranger to extra marital relations, loved his present wife and their two children. Without Gianni how would this week's holiday develop? He let nostalgia envelope him. His old culture made him consider things carefully. The reasons he was asked to return to Villa Pina after many years and were not clear. It has to be more than to back a film.

"Zee sea es as I like it," Jacqueline Redat 's French accent and hourglass figure drew the dockhand's attention as she buttoned the last fastening on her skin-tight Pucci blouse. "Are ve all here?" She leaned down to adjust her gold and diamond ankle bracelet, smiling at her husband.

"We'll be twenty," Véronique replied. "Others are coming by different means and I think we're missing the Princess…has anyone seen her….?" A yelp from Groucho, Shabadiba's Maltese was heard. All looked around.

Appearing instantly with pup in arm, she made her entrance elegant as royalty, jaw thrust upward, engrossed with herself, as one would expect from Garbo. Shabadiba always dominated the scene. Her sophisticated voice was two tones lower than most women. Her smile was dangerous. "*Buon Giorno tutti!*"

One sensed mystery in her smile, the only part of her anatomy visible from the over-sized cobalt sunhat that shielded her face and matched every part of her costume except for quail-sized South Sea pearls decorating her neck, ears and wrist.

Following was Stefano de Gesu speaking Arabic, *"Efendim! Tamum! …Maşallah!,"* finishing a sentence to Shabadiba. He bowed diplomatically demonstrating, as always, formal manners, *'a born Ambassador'* people said, *'a true friend'* said others.

"Forgive me everyone, I was at the climax of a story with the Princess about how certain countries get rich, falsifying passports and selling visas, as was the case in the Dominican Republic with Porfirio Ruberosa, my old polo mate."

He smiled dispersing kisses, a man accomplished at charming and deceiving women. "How lovely you look this morning Lynne... Véronique... Jacqueline…" The purrs of the women pleased him between the shouts of the dockhands to the crew.

"Take the rope!"

"Handle the dog!"

"Give me your hand, to the right, watch your step…"

Within minutes, *paparazzi* in profusion snapped photographs as the illustrious guests disembarked the gangplank. Chauffeurs in peeked caps met the VIP entourage driving fringed-topped convertible limousines up the breathtaking climb to Villa Pina where their extraordinary adventure would commence.

Esmeralda checked her vintage Cartier watch from 1928, it was, like her, always precise. The moment she had dreamed of was close at hand.

Olympia Sanford

"At this point Tong I am on the *aloscalfi,* I had to come this way because it was all last minute." Olympia Sanford twisted her abundant sable hair into a chignon speaking on her cell phone to Tong Wan Park, her fiancé, the Korean entrepreneur.

"We're eight hours apart for your information. Jameson's coming with a group from Rome, something about backing a movie. Frankly, I was asked on his yacht but thought it too much with that wife of his!" Fumbling with the array of satchels in front of her, taking up three seats across much to the disagreement of the Italian passengers, the hydrofoil's engine commenced and she continued…

"This telephone connection is not the best, we're pulling away from the dock in Naples, but to be in this circle means that show I want at the Tate"

"I said the TATE or the MOMA might materialize since you won't spring for it…Gianni's friends might….Call me later Sweetheart."

She rang off without a hint of emotion, readjusted her things, pulled her sketchpad from a case and consumed herself making *croquis* of people aboard.

Olympia's style was horsy English chic, an eccentric socialite and member of the London set who rubbed shoulders with people who made the town buzz. She was not beautiful but contained a certain energy when she entered a room that made her outshine all other women by her dazzling presence. Her height was medium, frame slim, and although approaching forty, no one guessed this to be her age. Tilted gazelle eyes, the exact hue of her hair, dominated a macaw-like nose that defined her Hebraic persuasion. A wide sensuous mouth painted in fiery tangerine brought thoughts of sensuality when viewing the self-assured artist.

———

Simultaneously…

Esmeralda glanced at the guest list again thinking of the mix of people...

Olympia's amusing. Not a hint of snobbism is a part of her character. She commands respect without uttering a word. But when she speaks! Good God!...not giving mind to political correctness. I hope with all her effervescence, she'll consider others."

———

Although married twice, Olympia's independent soul preferred being single. On this journey to Villa Pina, she had time to reconsider her solitude. In the past, she'd formed unions only to regret them.

Marriage destroyed something within that paralyzed her artistic spirit. Older men were her desire, exotic ones - similar to Tong. Nevertheless, with all Olympia's therapy, a recurrent father complex loomed, difficult to shed.

Whatever age, men suffocated the artist with all their wants. She reckoned it was all ingrained dependency. She made a note to speak to her therapist about this because she knew changes had to come – she couldn't take the pressure any longer. Love affairs caused distraction from her true love: art. And love affairs were tedious once the chase was assured. Who could she ever marry who would let her side step from a union to immerse herself in art? No one. Not one single soul. Men always put their needs first.

———

Nigel thought of the guests. Olympia's been part of the polo set, equestrian life's her subject. The racing set includes investors interested in art that appeals to Olympia's nature. A portrait of Esmeralda on her favorite horse caught his eye. Esmeralda's bought a few paintings, but Olympia's frustrated, she needs a good screw... and acclaim from critics. She'd kill to get into Gagosian's Gallery...but unless she changes her fetish of one man after another and focuses, she'll never accomplish her dream to be famous. What in hell all those men fancy in her, baffles me, she's talented, I suppose for creating…he snickered…on canvas and in bed. He laughed a naughty laugh, poured himself a drink and spoke aloud, "Lucien Freud would love that remark."

———

Olympia had taken Esmerala into her confidence years before when she bought a triptych for Beaumont Manor. "Esmeralda I want to be at the TATE or the MOMA, lauded by all! That's my ambition." Her candor impressed Esmeralda who was no stranger to ambition.

"If Olympia plays her cards right, something will spring from this week. Maybe Mark Levy will commission something for the LACMA."

———

Olympia meanwhile was daydreaming recalling her fate....She told Tong, "I will never accomplish my dream, to be famous and have a show at a top museum." She could have been speaking Greek. She told him in

Korean. It went unnoticed. She told him in English. "You are mine now." was his answer. "This is now a finished conversation."

How could she live with a man like that even if he gave her a diamond as big as a search light from Harry Winston's? She remembered she didn't answer him and thought instead of the tabloids that followed her behavior in this month's news. Her lips played with that memory as a sly smile came to her face remembering how TATLER quoted her: *"Art is everything for me, people a shallow second. I spent half of my life in bed - not ever sleeping but without the fulfillment I find in art."*

So what if that remark didn't endear her to Tong or other men in her life? Free spirited Olympia didn't go with the herd. Being saucy suited her. All tolerated her candor and some her trysts, which never went unnoticed.

Suddenly, she saw the rocky crest of Capri from the hydrofoil's speedy entry through windows wet with foam.

So much better to be independent, she thought and concealed her remembrances of the passengers in her sketchbook as one would conceal cocaine. In less than an hour she'd have to mingle with people she couldn't stand, people who could change her future.

People! People! People! The thought of all those people will shatter my nerves! At least I had the foresight to say I can't stay the full week because I have to go to Korea and see Tong. Better a lie than endure superficiality.

The time was nearing one. Esmeralda's trained eye looked plans for room designations while Nigel stirred his swizzle stick in his gin and tonic.

"God! I hope this is going to work."

"Nigel, relax.

"Olympia's amusing..."

"And Stella?"

"Stella, Nigel? She's written a great screenplay, and your attitude will contribute to how much enjoyment you have. Remember, you can always go back to your club in London or be with Lynne Jameson and read the Bible."

"Whitney's a saint. And a fool. All men are."

"A saint? Like you, I suppose?"

"Touché and to you, my beautiful wife!" Nigel lifted his glass and walked to the garden.

Stella Gregotti, Screenwriter - Marco Ricci, Star

"Marco, God Damn It! Get your hide in gear and MOVE! Otherwise we're going to miss the ferry and the next one will be too late to show *bella figura!*" She thrust her Armani blazer on, pushing up the sleeves. Marco didn't answer. It infuriated her! "You're always late…lunch is at two promptly…." Stella called out stuffing more material into her attaché case.

Casually entering the front hall came Marco. "Me? Late? I've been ready for an hour! it's you wanking off with calls to L.A. and God knows where. Let me remind you, Stella, these people we're visiting love me! Yes, Me, Marco Ricci not because I'm an actor but because I know how to talk to them, I'm full of ZEN, I know how to tell it like it…"

"Shut up. Shut up and don't say another word about ZEN, ying/yang or anything! If you didn't have me with my money I wonder where your career…" she ran her long fingers through her short streaked hair and smeared sunblock on her face.

"Stella……S T E L L A….Darling…I'm your karma…the reason why you are. The luckiest day in your life arrived when I entered your banal landscape…you fortunate, fuckingly beautiful Goddess…" Marco moved his Sicilian body close to hers. Actor that he was, he exuded sex appeal. He whiffed Stella's scent, the scent that drove him to ecstasy. He, a man who loved women, appreciated women, understood women had the woman he desired. He pressed his hips close to hers.

"Don't you dare come near me until later...*Andiamo!*"

They crammed themselves into their vintage Masserati *"Rapido"* Stella ordered the chauffeur bolting down the crest of Sant'Agata sui Due Golfi towards Positano at top speed to meet the ferry.

This was another hasty farewell from the precipice overlooking the Galli Islands that Browning called *'those isles of the siren,'* and the Salerian Gulf, to go to the precipice of Capri all in the name of glitz, Hollywood, the world of cinema and they loved it, loved each other, loved life and took it all in stride with common purpose unless, of course, they wanted to smite each other. Then they would fight like alley cats but the making up was so sweet.

Marco liked that best of all because that's when Stella was *his* woman - without the sham of money, fame and bossing him around like the God damned feminist she'd become. Then he brought her to orgasm like no one else - she was dominated as she truly wanted to be and he, Marco Ricci who had been from the pits to the heights knew that everything that ever mattered was his and how gorgeous life had become...it reached perfection.

The thought of going to entertain Nigel and Esmeralda was work, singing for his supper...but supper had been good to Marco...a staring role in a fine film, written by his beloved General wife Stella, well not his wife but after so many years who's counting? Wife or mistress or what? They'd been through hell together and would remain together because of their energy, because no one else would put up with them and because it was Fate, yes, Fate. He'd speak to Véronique about this, brilliant Véronique who can out talk him about all the stars, not the mundane stars of Hollywood! Holy Christ not those! The stars in God's Fantastic Universe!

Véronique's real, real like most people are not, like no woman he knew could ever be except Stella when exhausted from lovemaking and then she would purr...but her purrs lately seemed to be erratic. Sometimes they were hard to come by - other times, the glory times - WOW! She could whine like a tigress in heat.

"Esmeralda, Monty's just texted. He's bringing his new partner, a guy named Jarvis Engleton." Nigel called to his wife from the library and could hear Esmeralda huff from across the hall in the dining room. As she walked across to him, Sanjeev followed.

"Sanjeev make the double room with the view to the tennis court for Monty Daniels please, shift the single to that Hungarian woman he's acquired. Frankly, Nigel he's got some cheek to bring two people along."

"Think of the press we'll get, Esmeralda…for you and your film…"

"Yes, for the film I suppose you're right but I don't want him to write anything personal about me! I can't bear these people who always upset plans just before take off!"

"What do you expect?" Nigel drained his drink. "Manners?" He walked to the garden realizing his wife would continue to bitch at him if he lingered.

Monty Daniels, Journalist - Zofra Zofany, his guest Jarvis Engleton, uninvited beau of Daniels

"At the end of the day Zofra, you've been a darling. I bet you score at this shindig," Monty Daniels good-looking face was intent on steering his motor launch towards Capri. Lean Jarvis Engleton's hand rested on Monty's naked thigh, pleasing him as it approached his jewels. "We're all in it for something. Let's be straight."

"Straight, coming from you, Darling?" The black haired Hungarian cougar eyes alighted taking in the two aging swans sitting across from her. Daniels was a good friend to arrange for Zofra to be in this posh company. What did she care if he and Engleton had been screwing each other for the last two days everywhere they went? Everyone had a story and she knew Daniels' to a degree.

In his mid-forties with looks that made him an instant success in his first career, a gigolo, his work today as a gossip columnist was a far cry from his past, promenading rakish-style from via Veneto to Mayfair, L.A. to Park Avenue.

Those years, he'd find some millionaire who'd trade his D'Andrea smoking jacket for rough affection. Monty would be impressed with his conquests' wealth but never their neediness and lack of brains.

Thick tousled curls on his statuesque head matched a steroid-physic, *'the image of Michelangelo's David,'* said admirers. Confident with this assurance, Daniels' gait sauntered in key cities, prowling and searching, wanting the high life. Ambling along for years, parading his talent, he scored with one of his conquests: A New York heiress on vacation sitting in Piazza Navona, fresh out of rehab, forty-two years old, passed over by suitors of her class. Married at a price to shake the stock market, nine months later, he fathered a child. A rapid divorce followed, producing a settlement in his favor and he launched his second career: *Journaliste par excellence!*

"Smart Son of a Bitch." His ex-wife howled, "*Bella figura* the Italians call it," was his reply.

Monty Daniel's bi-sexual life meant nothing to anyone because his true passion was reporting gossip. Today, at the peak of his career, people treated Daniels prudently, spoiling him endlessly with gifts, trips and favors.

"Imagine me, able to strut into Villa Pina carting whomever I please," his pride bubbled over with thoughts. Everyone wants to be in my column hoping to read their name in twenty-seven god damned syndicated countries. What the shit do I care if some call me guttersnipe press?…sig their libel lawyers on me when I pen a piece? More power to me! There's gargantuan pleasure when I succeed, ravenous for a scoop and report antics of the high falutin' jet set.

He revved the boat's engine. Engleton, his present partner, high strung and incapable of relaxing, was close to fifty who thrived on the perverse (mostly in conversation). He could be found continually fingering his monocle that hung from his neck like a thin black noose.

He didn't matter to Zofra, anymore than the way the two of them adopted the Italian vulgar gesture of continually touching their *coglioni,* whether to assure themselves all was there or languish in the momentary pleasure of petting their cock. What mattered to Zofra was that she was climbing the ladder she wanted to climb, social entry into the right circles would put her exactly where she wanted to be: married to some gullible guy, preferably younger by ten years, who would never sniff anything except her perfume and consider himself blessed the day he met her.

Zofra's looks had taken her as far as she could manage and forever she would consider Fate smiled on her the day she received an E-mail from a man Dates.com recommended who wanted an escort for a VIP party in New York. It was Jarvis Engleton, in his quest to pass as a heterosexual. That was important to Engleton, *bella figura*, appearing to be what he was not, poor sap Jarvis, a bore really but he interested the muscular Daniels and Daniels knows everyone.

Zofra began to daydream....I've watched them and photographed them and who else would do that? It would take a wrecked soul like mine but I've come from hell...not one of these people know where I've been, and none of them have to know. Let Daniels tell everyone I'm a public relations rep.

Fine, I can handle that. It sure beats being a hooker, my pussy continuously on a bidet, working my bum off in the lap clubs with all those dribbling, elderly, drunken men, and those women!

Whatever becomes of me will be better to what I am now. Something good will happen in Capri with all those polo millionaires' monotony plaguing them. I can turn myself in a knot to achieve the end I want.... Amazing when you speak with a little accent, wear the right clothes, have slender legs and roll your eyes men fall at your feet. Stupid men. Women are much more interesting. I wouldn't link emotionally with any man but women are so much more able to understand....women don't need men anymore...disgusting what we do for men, I hate it. I prefer to be with these two pathetic gays. They're miserable but they leave me alone and pretend. We all pretend in this farce of life! A trumped up farce, that's life - and I'm a Toulouse Lautrec character.

"Are you listening Zofra? I told Jarvis although he's not been formally invited have no fear...he will be ...no one's kinder than Nigel Pembrooke. Well, kind might not be the right adjective."

Daniels cleared his throat and spit in the sea, "Frankly he owes me big time for keeping his name in and out of the tabloids. Now what I intend to do is have a good visit at the Villa with you two....Zofra... Zofra..."

"Darling...I've heard every word...I was just thinking..."

"You don't have to think. Look gorgeous. That's all you have to do."

Daniels pushed the toddle to maximum, raising his affected voice to be heard. "Jarvis, impress everyone with your knowledge of antiques and music. That's a turn on for the wives in the crowd. I need to dig around for a dynamite story for HELLO...this is...between us, understand?"

"I feel ill at ease Monty with the lack of a formal invita..."

"Cut the bullshit Jarvis. I know who's who and Esmeralda does what I say and Nigel tells her. This is a fab opportunity for me to get a scoop on the bbackers of the film, Marco Ricci, the star, and more importantly a low down on the whole saga of Gianni Zianni. If I play my cards right, it makes for a whopping best seller, a segment on 60 MINUTES and first chapter rights to VANITY FAIR..."

"Is this a working holiday Monty?...with all those vulgar Hollywood types..." He knit his brows, then raised them, "Not our class dear..."

"Forget the dramatics Jarvis!"

Jarvis Engleton couldn't stand Jews and knew he'd be faced with the prospect of social niceties towards some of them this week in Capri.

Well, at least Capri was a place one could escape with all the grottos and secret hotels…Monty did know everyone and it was stimulating to be with him, listen to him speak to the world from everywhere and then print the damn thing.

All people really wanted was publicity and would wine and dine Monty.

Gossip, that was the trend today. Society was dead. Now it was all *parvenus* who didn't know one thing about art, antiques or music… pushy Jewish Yids seeking "the best" who wanted their mug shots in magazines...the worst are Russian oligarchs who boss people like me with their money, thinking they own Jarvis Engleton! Me, a connoisseur, to select their antiques and clothes so they will look like they knew better. Better than what? They still have confusion at table when they pick up a fork. Monty didn't but he'd trained him, poor Monty coming from the other side of the tracks, but he had a good prick and that smile when they did it and the people they did it with…Yes, thought Jarvis, content with his control over Monty. Class wins the day. Good we met. It had a lot to do with Zofra. She kept her mouth shut, lesbian guts quiet and who could blame the three of them? Monty produced a fun lifestyle. Wasn't life all about having fun?

All those years being shy around women, thinking of becoming a priest, closeting myself, masking homosexuality! Thinking I'm a gay man stuck in a lesbian life. Even today having to be straight every now and again, like my priest friends. This was so much more liberating. Bless Monty…and the debauchery we have with bum boys everywhere.

I'd do anything for him…probably not anything but as long as the perks continue and his dick is hard…yes, as long as that …but when it goes….he goes too. That's what relationships like this should be. Open. I can afford somebody more classy, younger….and she, common as a street rat but the Hungarian shellac masks it.

Zofra's just as much an actor as we are. We're all actors. This is a travesty…this isn't life. Life is too raw, too real, too sad. This is better. I feel like a rich Emperor, like Tiberius must have felt and Monty Daniels is my catamite. It will be a piece of cake to impress those pigs from L.A. if only I don't make any slips with anti-Semitic slurs. Funny that. How many generations ago did my Great-grandfather shed the Englestein for Engelton? A fact not a soul has to know.

The manicurist finished buffing Nigel's nails. His thoughts wandered to Monty Daniels. "I owe him. Damned good of him not to do that kiss and tell on me with Lady Montagu. God that would have toppled this life of mine…but I don't like the feeling of that hanging over my head. Maybe this week I can come to terms with Monty."

Esmeralda entered his room.

"Nigel, Mark's just called from Rome. He's so excited, sounds like a ten year old to be invited, his first time in Capri."

"Which girlfriend is he bringing?"

"Who knows? We must be tolerant, he's important. I do hope you'll behave."

"Yes Esmeralda I'll behave like your Darling Nigel."

Mark Levy and his Girlfriend

"No one, I tell ya, Cat, no one arrives like Mark Levy!" He pulled the hand of his girlfriend hard, shoved his large Cuban cigar in his mouth and moved towards the helicopter stuffing his body in first having her trail behind.

"I'm scared Markie…"

"Forget it. Close your eyes. People pay a fortune to arrive like this. No one does it better than me! I'll show those smart assed European creeps how someone does it in style…American Style! Buckle your belt. We're off…"

"I'm afraid I'll break my nails. You do it Markie please…do it for me."

"Look don't be a dumb broad. If you are, zap. You are out of here like a shot. Got it? Understand?" Levy buckled her belt and huffed.

"Yeah..."

"Good. Now look at this. It's a book I bought ya...on how to eat. It's called Eddiket. You don't have to know the woudes. Study the pictures. 'En whateva you do, don't talk too much. Got it?"

"Yeah."

"For Christ's sake! Don't say YEAH. Say 'yes.' One more yeah outta you, it's back to LA and you can hussle your ass! Got it?"

"Yes. Markie is that betta?"

"Yes and don't call me Markie...Call me Mark. More professional sounding. And for God's sake! Stop chewing that god damned gum!"

Cat obeyed Levy continuously, making him feel in control of their relationship while she dreamed of a staring role in a film or better yet marriage. To be a spinster with disillusions about life was not her idea of happiness. This is how it is in Hollywood, she told herself, grab them while you can and maybe...I'll get what I want and change Mark Levy with a Cinderella ending.

Levy's pilot steered his 'copter from the helipad at San Felice Ciceo. Within minutes they were headed to Capri. Mark Levy couldn't believe his luck - all was coming together as he'd hoped. That's why he was Spotlight Films. That's why he grossed 237 million clams opening week on the last film he produced and everyone in the blasted business was at his feet. Let them be. This was his time, his world, his dream. Let everyone fall all over him...It separated him this success...God it felt like shit being at the top sometimes but it felt the same at the bottom of the heap. That he knew. This was better.

Producer Mark Levy was neither an angel or devil. He was a hard-core workaholic who knew his limitations and would never accept second best even if he had to be a sonofabitch. Early in his life, he promised himself money and fame would be his and today he achieved exactly what he wanted.

Money gave stature, respect. Yeah, respect from those crumbs who thought I should wipe their ass. The banking details for this next flick would be a cinch. Ricci had a good track record, his babe, Stella Gregotti, tough talented broad, but he, Levy would rewrite things, she'd give way to Levy - the master of what makes movies work. Enough with the art crap. No art film grossed 237 million. VARIETY wanted to put his name in lights b'Jesus. These Italians and the English. Forget the French! Europeans?… don't know shit from *shineola*…only America can make films. Do distribution, glitz, know how to market the whole *smear.*

As he commiserated with himself fidgeting with his oversized diamond Rolex, he watched his platinum blonde replica of Barbie trying to read the book her pressed upon her.

Vesmere…what I have to put up with and this dumb broad Cat Renoir.

I should have told her to change her name. Doesn't matter. These fools owe me, not me owe them. They need me, I don't need dem. OK the story is great, Ricci is great but I'm the boss!

He pressed his heavy thigh to Cat's slender leg. He was sweating even with the air conditioning at full blast. He felt his old nervous twitch returning to his face, that fuckin' ugly face of his with its double chin and his left eye that twitched when he got excited. He couldn't control it and the sweat, always the frigin' sweat.

He grabbed the hand of the doll he had dragged to Italy. Cat was good looking trailer park material and dumb as dishwater but that was better than someone smart. What was the saying that famous screenwriter once coined …*You can lead a whore to culture but you can't make her think*• Who needs her to think? If she keeps her mouth shut and smiles, looks like he told her to look and God knows she bought enough Versace, he'd make them all think she was a Hollywood lady, a starlet. Some starlet. Couldn't memorize *Three Blind Mice.* OK she's good for fucking, not that he wanted to fuck her and ruin his energy but when that lusting for fucking provoked him, she was good for inn'ercourse. If she stepped out of line, nothing's lost, she'd be replaced. Hundreds like her waitin' in line.

He wiped his perspired, beefy hand on his trouser and then removed a handkerchief from his breast pocket soaking up the sweat from his face. That damned twitch! He'd arrive looking cool, in his $8500 Brioni pinstriped suit, feeling in control. That was the important thing, to feel in control of the whole thing. Intimidate the whole crowd.

A man like me, Mark Levy they don't meet everyday! He pulled his Blackberry from his jacket pocket, ignited it, viewing the list of names he had to convince to throw their money in the pot and the others, well the others would open some doors to him, some doors closed before, doors of class. That's what he needed, just a little more class.

"You know Esmeralda, I'll be something to see all these people interact."

"Variety, Nigel, the mix will be dynamic."

"Hope no surprises happen. A group like this, well, you never know."

"Your set is included, that should put you at ease. We've got an important film to launch and if we keep that the focus…"

"Well, this whole thing wasn't my idea."

• Dorothy Parker's original quote was "You can lead a horticulture bur you can't make her think."

"Be open minded, Nigel. You just might have fun..."

"Easy for you to say…"

"Easy? Nothing's been easy for me, Nigel!" Esmeralda gave him a frigid stare, walked out of the room, closing the door thinking ...maybe this film will change my life.

Nicky Viscounti

"Another ten minutes and I'll start to move." Nicky Viscounti spoke to his masseuse. "Work the trapezium muscles. All that tennis, I should do more swimming.

Strange how things happen. If I'd gone on that catamaran with Albert and the rest of the crew from Monaco, I wouldn't be going to Villa Pina. This is not my kind of scene, the people will be too old but I like the idea of the film, investing in something from Hollywood."

He stirred enjoying the sybaritic pleasure of pampering his virile Latin body. "So Esmeralda has a shortage of men for her dinner party, funny that. If I didn't have a nose for money I'd forget leaving Sardina for Capri, but instinct tells me this is going to be a surprising weekend... if it doesn't work, I'll turn around and come right back to Paradise."

Nicky Viscounti was a young friend to Gianni Zianni who followed polo but never participated in the game. They moved in the same circles, shared interest in lucrative investments and Nicky looked to Gianni as one would a big brother. The shock of his death grieved Nicky for years who still couldn't trust anyone enough to marry.

Yet at thirty-seven, he was tired of the razzle-dazzle social scene… one event turned to ten, then twenty and when the number reached beyond fifty it was all routine, too boring for words.

So Nicky spent his time between his various houses in Italy, collecting art, being a sportsman and good son to his parents who were not pleased with his bachelor ways. Neither was Nicky. The irresponsibility of his peers including their addiction to cocaine didn't impress him. When all was said and done, what did they achieve? Notches in their belt and rehab centers, a slew of phone numbers he didn't want and visits to physiatrists all over the globe.

The more time went along, the only hype Nicky got out of life was investing. With his adroit knowledge of money markets, his fortune tripled from what he inherited on his twenty-first birthday, sixteen years ago to being on the International Rich List. That was an achievement but money left him cold.

How many cars could he own? Trips could he take? Paintings could he buy? It became a continual rerun like an old video, like bedding women. The dialog didn't change. He wanted something deeper, something lasting, something that had no monetary value, some heart to share life that could be true and it eluded him. Maybe, just maybe something remarkable will springfrom this weekend at Villa Pina. Nicky showered, ordered his crew on his dock at Colpe de Volpe, "Have my amphibious plane ready for takeoff," and went to meet his destiny.

Dame Naomi Griffin and Rupert Davidson

"Rupert, no trouble to fetch you from the train in Naples, then we'll take the car ferry to Capri."

Rupert telephoned Naomi in Tuscany hoping his voice would produce this reaction. "Brian Korthorpe, will be there."

"Are you sure?"

"Positive."

Hearing the news, Naomi flushed with excitement. A dozen years had passed since she'd seen Brian Korthorpe, the love of her life.

As Rupert droned on about old times, Naomi was distracted, assessing herself in the mirror. Everything was wrong. Her height had not changed, still tall and rather straight, but her sagging neck!....her sun-spotted English skin looked like a roadmap, wrinkles were everywhere, her legs were full of cellulite not to mention veins.

Rupert's words evaporated in thin air.

The mousy color of her hair was disgusting, late life Judy Dench...I look like a shipwreck. Was I ever sexy? her senior approach to the catastrophe made her wonder. Maybe streaks in my hair, something drastic, change what I see. But how can I alter my stomach? Far too big!...not that I drink too much, but a half a bottle of wine a day shows....or was it just a half bottle? She stabilized the wanderings of her mind, maybe it was that double shot of whiskey before bed to ward off insomnia so I can sleep without a 'dream bar'...Too many thoughts collided...

Why evaluate all this when there wasn't time to do a revision and appear as Brian remembered the woman who enflamed his desire! Naomi churned this over. He'll either still be in love with me just as I am, or he's not worth anything! Oh the joy of being sixty-seven and having a sense of self! Maybe my reclusive life will be injected with vitality. Decent of Esmeralda or was it Nigel to invite me? Nigel would do anything for security. Rupert was different. The two might have lineage in Debretts' hundreds of years but the differences between Pembrooke and Davidson was the way they thought. Rupert had an aerial view of life, Nigel, like Whitney lived in his own world.

To Rupert it made little difference to receive peerage, he'd never sell his soul for the life Nigel embraced. Rupert's financial circumstances catapulted to zero after the family inheritance was squandered and everything went to death duties but Rupert Davidson, now forty-six, accepted reversal and lived in gentile poverty between his rudimentary flat at the Albany, Piccadilly, and the last remaining acreage of his family's estate in the Cotswolds. Educated at Eton, he met Gianni Zianni, (a Harrovian), when they competed at cricket, polo, then rugger winning over Eton and finally rowed against each other. Rupert, was Gianni's closest friend, best man when he wed Esmeralda.

Now he would be visiting Villa Pina, a second home to Rupert, yet this time it would be different. This time like a reshuffled deck of cards, Rupert would not have the joy of Gianni's company but the company of his wife, Esmeralda, married to snob Pembrooke, who discarded his first wife with alacrity as soon as he knew he could move into Gianni's territory. With the match, Nigel Pembrooke basked in the luxury of Zianni money.

It wasn't in Rupert's nature to be judgmental but...that one word *but* always changed everything. Nigel designed life around percentages, stupid dick.

None of the Zianni family would be present. Esmeralda had eradicated them from a life once theirs. A disgrace, certainly. Nigel could be so cheap, he once sent a bill for the *foie gras* consumed at his house to his friends - that was, of course, before he married Esmeralda. He used to mark his liquor bottles, short changing us as he poured, always topping up his glass. Then he'd feign, "Oh, chappies! I forgot to offer another glass," and horde booze, like his pornography collection, keeping choice stuff for himself.

Those who judge by money - what you had, how you spent it, gave an identity to people, they were the herd. Rupert couldn't stand herd mentality. I've known too many sheep. Enough to last a lifetime. What he referred to had a dual idea: the family's immense land in Scotland raising sheep opposed to those with artificial dignity he met in society. Let me be a black sheep because I can't do things a person manor born is supposed to do. Sod that. If that's the way to have a fan club, I don't want the fans. He didn't need the stately manor house, the town house, the suits from Savile Row, hats from Lobb, guns from Holland & Holland..

Deluded Nigel did who relished the parade of status. Nigel - Lord Nigel!...but his twin became Lord...and Nigel stayed Mister!... Strange that. One act of Fate changes the mode of living.

Rupert's thoughts wandered to Naomi. Wretched husband disgraced her with vile tactics in the City, double dealing and insider trading. Even first rate Englishmen have flaws and his were great, two-timing bastard too. Naomi should have divorced him and married Korthorpe. That was a true story...but look at how it turned out. Married to a bloke who screws the marketplace, puts a Lord's daughter into the position of having a jail bird for a spouse, shaming that gorgeous daughter...what he did to his family is a disgrace plus all the tarts he had holed up between Bayswater and Ebury Street brothels! Utter slime.

How Naomi ever managed to write such profound poetry has to be one of life's miracles...and to be acclaimed as Poet Laureate this year, marvelous achievement, for a woman! Rare for England. God it will be great to see her!

Packing her beat-up Mercedes to leave her home in Tuscany, Naomi thought American women would cart Rupert off to Palm Beach for his title, manners and charm. I saw them over the years at the polo grounds fawning over him. If he were older, I'd have an affair with him! That's a hoot! Me - having an affair! Haven't been to bed with a man for twelve miserable years. She buttoned her oversized cardigan wondering if it was just as damp in Capri, poured herself a goblet of Chardonnay thinking how inertia had been her armor to delay any rendezvous with Brian. After so much has happened, it's right we should come together she thought with giddy excitement, engulfed with emotion. She snapped to consciousness. "I must call Elizabeth.""Darling it's good of you to join the group for the weekend at Villa Pina. I know you would prefer to be with younger people, but this will mean so much to your Mother. Brian Korthope will be there."

Elizabeth MacKenzie, Daughter to Naomi

Elizabeth, a student at Rome's Belli Arte Scuola, wanted to please her Mother, who'd done everything to secure her happy life. This was such a small favor to ask, stay the weekend at Villa Pina, where she used to go as a child. It must be a dozen years or more since she'd seen the beautiful island and exceptional villa.

We've come a long way, Mummy and I. Daddy's made a mess of his life. I want to emulate her. How exciting to tell her Prince William and Harry have asked me to Highgrove to meet their Father and Camilla. All things come if one's attitude is good. I don't want a disgrace like Daddy did to us. I want to marry the man I love just as Gianni married Esmeralda. To keep myself the pride of the family is what I want, no disgrace but to be like Esmeralda when she married Gianni. No matter what they say about her or motives, she never brought disgrace and Gianni did what his heart told him to do. She loved him. That's more than most people. That's sacred.

Elizabeth combed her long, straight hair, slipped her young body into jeans smoothing the denim on her slender legs, packed her suitcase and headed for the train that would take her to Naples, two hours later, a boat would transport her to Capri and she would enter another world.

"Sanjeev, please call the staff together....and...what about the mandolin players?"

"A half-dozen will arrive any minute, Contessa. The first guests will hear '*O Sole Mio'* as they enter the garden exactly as you planned."

"Thank you, Sanjeev. A good way to begin." Esmeralda was sure she had thought of everything as her drama was about to unfold.

"Set the scene, Esmeralda. You amaze me....next thing we'll do the tarantella with tambourines and revitalize the past."

"Nigel, is that a compliment?" Esmeralda eyed her husband waiting for his response. Instead he blew her a kiss and walked towards the loggia as her staff assembled.

"I want to thank all of you in advance for the effort you've made. This week means a great deal to me. I couldn't do it without you."

She studied her ten servants several of whom were too shy to meet her eye. They'd been trained by her late Mother-in-law and now served her.

To achieve what she wished was impossible without good people who understood her insistence for excellence.

These individuals, a mix of Italians and Sri Lankans, were important. They'd never betray her. Over the years, she'd listened to the problems of each of them and paid handsomely for their loyalty. To a large degree that loyalty and service was instilled in them by her *major d'uomo,* Sanjeev, a person Esmeralda viewed as saintly for his devotion to the Zianni name, and now to her and Nigel.

Esmeralda graciousness put everyone at ease. "You'll all be rewarded in a week's time when everyone departs and things return to normal. Then we'll take things easy. There's always something with an event like this none of us can predict. Remember there's no reason to rush unless some ghastly thing like a fire would occur. That, of course, is not going to happen. Thank you from me and Mr. Pembrooke."

Like a Queen, she smiled at each of them, and like loving children, they smiled back.

When the brief meeting finished, Esmeralda turned her thoughts to the guests to the unaccounted guests: Naomi Griffin, Poet Laureate, her young daughter, Elizabeth and Rupert Davidson, Gianni's closest friend.

One of those three, someone she'd least suspect, would alter Esmeralda's life forever.

Nigel spotted the gardener sweeping the walk at the front portico in the remaining minutes before everyone was to arrive. The central fountain was sprouting water into the fishpond.

"Luigi, is it my imagination or are there new fish in the pond?"

"Questa volta l'idea della Contessa era di avere tanti pesci. Chissà Signore, ...fantasia delle donne?"•

Nigel tried to fathom what he meant, smiling kindly watching one of his his Labradors pee all over the fountain. The two men laughed. Luigi quickly washed away the urine.

It was close to two, the hour guests were to arrive. Being English he liked punctuality, always punctual himself. The idea of adhering to formal time was unheard of in Italy and certainly in Capri. "Ridiculous to think people will be on time in Italy. It'll never happen. No one will arrive by two."

A degree of angst consumed Nigel. He crisscrossed the veranda as a hundred thoughts went through his head with a hundred vacant ideas. It was always like this like waiting for the curtain to go up as in the theatre, but this was the theatre, his wife's theatre and the show was about to begin.

Time ticked away...

On everyone's mind was the niggling question: How will this week develop? Who will be crucial to Esmeralda? Who will betray her? Moreover, will anyone love her? Or will Nigel's private desires out distance this marriage?

• This time it was the Countess' idea to have many fish. Who knows, Signore, the fantasy of women?

Hearing Nigel call her name as he mounted the stairs, Esmeralda took one last glance at herself in the mirror, "Strange, I keep feeling a force of destiny, akin to doom…I won't dwell on that or *déjà vu* or anything negative. This week will be extraordinary!"

Nigel entered her room for the third time today, eyeing her as noted earlier, this time speaking of the goldfish... and in her excitement with the omen and a myriad of details swirling in her head, she didn't hear a word he said. She only felt more keenly this week's activities would change her life forever.

This sets the initial part of my story.

This contingent will ignite world history on the serene island of Capri.

III

Véronique Joulin, Clairvoyant

Circumventing the cliff to Villa Pina, Véronique studied the unforgettable vista. Twenty years had passed since she was brought here to meet the Zianni clan by her fiancé, Argentine polo player, Pancho Ratucha.

It was in London when Véronique first met Gianni Zianni. The Parisian Joulins, not wealthy but privileged, had relocated to Britain for Véronique's father to assume Directorship of Cartier. During the firm's first sponsored polo event at the Guards Polo Club at Windsor Great Park, Véronique met Pancho and courtship followed.

Polo was a sport she knew nothing about, learning later it was the oldest team sport, a 2000-year-old game originally played between warlords in central Asia. Her Persian friends claimed it originated there and the first recorded game took place in 600 BC between them and the Turkomans. Some said the game was from China, Mongolia. Whatever, her Father's involvement with the game made her privy to the elegant parties and fascinating players of the day.

From the beginning the polo clique were inseparable: American Whitney Jameson, UK's Rupert Davidson and Nigel Pembrooke, (who always wanted centre stage), Gianni and Pancho were the international ones. The group contained a silent bond yet once married, Pancho's horsy friends stood by Véronique when he was found *flagrante* too many times that brought divorce. They introduced her to Javier Garcias, her second husband, from Montevideo, whom she shed within the first year. That marriage was a Latin replay of the first.

Véronique, a free thinker, turned to the occult, esoteric study, alchemy, and astrology to comprehend her Fate; once these nuggets of understanding were paired with her philosophical mind, she achieved what she'd been searching for, becoming a professional advisor of astrology, acclaimed today at the height of her profession worldwide. She understood the difference between psycho-analysis being one thing and astrology another, additionally, she was brilliant at analysis and clairvoyance.

Her Internet site had 500,000 hits daily, she wrote books, appeared on CNN weekly, advised celebrities, the secret service and statesmen. Several called her a 'witch' - her physic power was that astute. Charmed circles wanted her at their soirees. Dramatic, chic, Parisian Véronique brought excitement to any party. Whether one believed in the science or not, what she could previse no one could foresee.

"Véronique!....after so many years!" Esmeralda was ravishing, meeting guests with her soft-spoken voice as Véronique approached the vestibule. Kissing her hostess hello, Véronique was disarmed when Esmeralda drew back at arms length. "Remarkable...you look remarkable." The double-entendre and distancing put Esmeralda in control. It was her way to set the tone.

Wrapped in a lemon pique dress and Buccelatti jewels, Esmeralda was more beautiful than Véronique remembered her. She marveled how Esmeralda carried herself, as if on a cat-walk, her posture was as exceptional as her bone structure, sculptured mouth and turquoise eyes that met yours continually. Whenever Esmeralda appeared in a room, everyone's eyes were on her and when she exited, all seemed a wake...or perhaps best described, a tsunami going out to sea. There was an arrogant superiority to Esmeralda, nonetheless, Véronique detected her hostess was out of her depth with all her trappings of wealth.

"Remarkable you say, Esmeralda? Not as remarkable as you! What's your secret and where's dear Nigel?"

"I say gorgeous Véronique here I am dying to tear you away from everyone!" Nigel entered the atrium, doused two kisses on Véronique's cheeks and roared like a hyena.

"Nigel your charm has not dimmed! I was delighted to be included."

"Included? Nonsense. No way to have this happen without you! Esmeralda began this guest list, didn't you Darling?...and agreed we simply must have Véronique, Ahhh...what you can read in the stars! Véronique you bring life to the party, any party..."

"Nigel, you gush! How many years do we know each other?"

"Twenty?'

"And I see an interesting future for you." He loved her immediate response. Véronique said nothing more knowing his stars were keyed with the equinox and his life was about to change completely. Besides, his zodiac and gregarious persona, Véronique observed his elongated cupid's bow accenting razor thin lips, that told another story.

Nigel was a cynical wit and rapid talker. His experience throughout worldwide polo circles as the commentator on the game, the history of the sport and thoroughbreds, made him an 'oracle' in the field. Sportsmen valued his opinion. Accolades went to his head when he was at the height of his fame, thought the clairvoyant, but this marriage changed that. Some believed him cocky which meant nothing to Nigel who'd declare, "I value being a snob. We're not all created equal ducky!" Then with infectious laughter, his barbs made history; television and radio fans adore him to this day, thought Véronique, and what a life awaits him!

Nigel admired the spotlight. He wore clothes with dashing style, blessing his tailor who concealed his weight around the middle. English flair, inherited from ancestors, (all of whom dressed to be noticed), was Nigel's imprint, whose presence - like his wife's - dominated a room. GQ named him a *'trendsetter'* and a *'hall of fame'* dresser. Judging from his garb today in lime trousers, multi-colored shirt and ascot, he was. His silhouette was made complete by impeccable grooming and his superficial relish of gaiety and society. On exceedingly rare occasions, Nigel could be profound.

Being a Libra, he battled the flocculation of his scale; he was a rare character with a sharp ability to cut to the chase, fearlessly tackling any repartee that came his way. Véronique knew Nigel's flaws and put him at ease. Swiftly, he took her by the arm guiding her to the library away from the commotion in the front hall.

Véronique was the type of woman men never tired of speaking about amongst themselves; the type of female who brought a lasting elixir to life. Nigel never had the distinction to be one of her lovers, yet a chemistry ignited whenever she was near, what with her French accent and clever mind, thought Nigel.

Guests, in the meantime, assembled, greeting with the usual uproar of initial salutes in the atrium while servants hovered to escort VIPs to room designations.

Esmeralda noticed Véronique and Nigel exit the scene thinking, wouldn't you just know Nigel would go off with Véronique whispering about something just as everyone's arriving! No doubt she'll feed into his ego. UK's polo expert to a point. I hire trainers to do that.

"Do be a Darling Véronique and don't mind if I pick your brains… this group is a potpourri…sort of a hodgepodge, well it is not as it used to be at Villa Pina…but we have to be democratic with this movie to launch and…"

"What can I do for you Nigel?"

"Check the guest list before the dinner Saturday night and advise me. This mix of people, let me put it this way, in case you should surmise some clash of personalities or something tacky - tell me. The next few days will be buffet so anything goes, but dinner's another story… The last thing I want is some *faux pas* - a time bomb to fall and ruin the results for this…"

"Nigel do you have a sixth sense about the future?"

Nigel beamed at Véronique's remark wondering, what does she mean?

"Nigel you never change. There's something important riding on this visit for you and Esmeralda..." Véronique paused.

Nigel beamed again, this time inflating his chest, posturing himself to stretch his full height of 6'4" knowing that put him at an advantage and gave him a feeling of power. It must have been God's gift to make him taller than most men. "Yes, Véronique," he lied. "The buzz of glamour. There's vibrant energy making a film, being a part of the cinema, experiencing the excitement of show business after all the society stuff."

"You lie speaking of the buzz of glamour..."

"What the hell Véronique, I'm bored out of my mind. Do you know what it is like to be as bored as I am? Esmeralda is tiny in size but believe me she is as powerful as a grenade and I'm no rocket scientist. Look at me!" Nigel commanded and poured himself a full goblet of claret. "I'm not the personality of years ago, age sets in...but Véronique time doesn't allow me to have a long chat with you. Here's the list of the guests. Seems Rupert's detained, won't be able to join us 'til Sunday."

"Isn't that interesting."

"Something out of the blue, family matter, he said. I managed to have everyone's birth dates using a foil, saying it was necessary for Italian security. Maybe some of the women lied about the year they were born but..."

"That's fine, Nigel. There'll be a change with the moon but I'm not here to do in-depth astrology charts on your guests. I'll study this and am happy to advise which people will be more *simpatico* for seating arrangements."

"I just don't want a catastrophe to happen."

"Anything else you'd like?" Véronique met his eye not divulging that was exactly what would happen.

Nigel's fox-like eyes looked back, mystified. He rubbed his bald skull, reminiscent of Humpty Dumpty, diverting the intensity of the moment, "Yes. To kiss your gorgeous lips..."

"Not what I had in mind. "

Pembrooke passed the list of guests to Véronique. "I'm not too old to desire you...and Véronique, I'd love to have my chart read."

"Consider that done before I depart…and Nigel…."

"Yes…"

"*Sopra vivvre*…that's the Italian word. In English we call it 'to survive.' The Italian meaning is 'to live above life.' "

Nigel gulped his wine, stupefied that she would even suggest he had to survive, and kissed her on her forehead. "I'd better go greet everyone…" he exclaimed, exiting the library.

An ormolu clock ticked the hour of two thirty. Just as she knew, lunch would be late. Véronique looked at the list, making a mental note to include Nigel and Esmeralda on it. Nigel's Leo ascendant was evidenced in his bold script that took up the entire sheet of paper, a sign of immense ego. A smile came to her lips as she raised her head viewing di Chirico's paintings of the seasons in the hushed atmosphere of the library. The paneled room, filled with mountains of antiquarian books, made Véronique's mind percolate with one idea....all this wealth with no issue for Esmeralda…*"Not so,"* came her physic voice. This sensation, more powerful than she anticipated, brought Véronique to contemplate could Esmeralda be with child?

Both Véronique's marriages had been childless, the problem resting with her, undaunted, she enjoyed the attention of distinguished men, appreciating solitude not wanting to remarry. "Two husbands are enough for anyone, especially if they're Latin toy boys who disappoint," she'd proclaim at fifty, looking years younger. As Voltaire, Véronique believed freedom was the highest of all treasures.

Véronique made a mental tabulation of birthdates on the list and a chill went down her spine.

A day later, Nigel found Véronique in the library alone.

"*Sopra vivre*" boomed Nigel entering with a broad smile…" Oh those Italians with their words! I've been thinking of it, Véronique…."

They walked to the adjoining terrace overlooking the magnificence of the Amalfi Coast. The past hectic day gave the old friends little time to talk. Naomi entered, "Have I interrupted anything?"

"'Course not, Naomi….care for a Gin and Tonic?"

"Yes, thanks." Naomi moved to the bar, fidgeting with her drab linen dress that did little for her pallid English face.

Nigel enthusiastically mixed drinks as the women fixed their gaze to the sea.

"Heaven to be here, away from everyone." Naomi confessed. "Lovely of you and Esmeralda to ask me and Elizabeth. It did come as a surprise to see Brian."

"Esmeralda's idea of romance. Hope that suits you…" Nigel grinned.

"It was a surprise, but yes...."Naomi confessed.

"Véronique and I have been bantering about the phenomena of being alone, being bored…surviving…Naomi you're a poet, are you ever bored?"

"Interesting Nigel coming from you to pose that question. I'm less bored than most I believe, or fool myself to believe. I don't need people continually…and you?"

"The two of you know I've always been a people person." He smiled as if he running for office, handing them drinks, glancing at himself in the pane of glass of the Queen Anne secretary, adjusting his ascot.

"Nigel the extraordinary extrovert." Naomi proclaimed.

"Yes…*Extrovert Extraordinaire*!....the circus I create is my guise, my mask because of the fear of being alone, being bored…for I am alone with all the ostentatious life Esmeralda relishes, studying nature, contemplating life, boredom terrifies me."

His two friends regarded his candor.

"The clowning around I've done over the years is to distance myself from the real me, too intense with isolation." Nigel poured himself another drink. "I've avoided the whole bloody thing!...the fear of being with myself. What a fucking monster, knowing yourself and loneliness!"

"It's good Nigel to hear you voice something without the sham…"

"I can speak openly with you both. You've studied me over the years with my pompous narcissism!" Nigel laughed arrogantly. "The accolades, fame, the money has a boomerang. It separates me. I am more alone now than ever, and in some ways I want this aloneness. I want to hide, believing no one understands me. Then, like an addict, I thrive on the clowns, being one myself and throw myself back into the arena called 'living' to disguise the void."

"*Sopra vivre,* live above life! Naomi's achieved that with her poetry"

Véronique's calm state of mind had it all figured out. "The reality of life is one is always running from self, the alone self. Nigel, you finally recognize with all these people you're alone…like all of us, perhaps like Naomi when her artistic soul fails her." Véronique paused reminiscing, running her fingers through her mane of hair. "Think of the Zianni family, the cohesiveness of Italian closeness, the penalty independence brings of raw loneliness."

"…Yes, and when a marriage disintegrates," Naomi injected.

"Gershwin had it right with Summertime." To their surprise, Nigel burst in song, *"One of these mornings, you're gonna rise up singing, then you'll spread your wings and take to the sky..."*

"The greatest courage is to live alone – and like it." Véronique spoke,

Nigel tipped his glass to her as she expanded this remark. "Loneliness and boredom are everyone's malady, semi-curable, like an infection that can be modified…"

"Modified?" Nigel questioned, raising his voice a pitch, wide eyed like an owl.

Naomi snapped from concentration.

"For some, financial status, in your case Nigel with Esmeralda, your boredom and loneliness is taken in a grand style." She watched the other two, "Hence Nigel's remark yesterday when I said 'These people are using you for your houses and connections.' "

"And I responded, "Who's using who?" Nigel flippantly added, "I'd go mad if we didn't have guests."

"We all have guises. Outings to the theatre to divert attention from the self is another method to assuage the malady...here is where artists, perhaps like me, a poet, have a responsibility to entertain, enlighten... with our vanity, mind you.... I need to do this and survive loneliness whose side-car is boredom."

"Well said," injected Véronique, "for when loneliness and boredom collides, the human condition creates its own antidote, changing things..."

"Yes... divorce...." said Naomi sadly.

"Moving on with another woman, buying a house, selling a house, changing friends, a job..." Nigel began to smoke watching the ash of his *cigarello* as one watches dying embers of a love affair.

"In my case, countries," confessed Véronique, "running from the plague from one country to another...calling it living." Véronique moved about the library as the other two studied her spin the oversized antique globe resting her finger on South America.

"Double challenge, Véronique, you're bohemian and patrician." noted Nigel.

"I'm no different from most. When a kindred soul is discovered life's sweet!...How one wishes to keep this joy!"

"It can never be kept." Blurted Nigel.

"Never?" questioned Naomi..... "Fix me another G&T, Nigel... make it an aphrodisiac."

"You jest Naomi! The effects of gin are quite the opposite but I'll join you in a stiff one, just the same...Véronique you too...?"

"No thanks. Partnership eradicates these things, a radiance comes to face and heart."

"Love alive! My Dear Old Things!" scoffed Nigel.

"Yes, Nigel, Love alive!" answered Véronique, inquiring, "Do you think giving love is ever a mistake?"

"It depends," countered Nigel, stirring the drinks while Naomi listened. "With experience I've become increasingly reticent who enters my sphere of intimacy …vulnerable fool that I am…latent desire pounding at my door…"

"I agree with Nigel," Naomi took a cynic's view. "Nothing lasts forever. Love vanishes!" She looked to Vesuvius, "Emotional eruption burns, fire ignites like a volcano, then the aftermath with a rupture too painful to cure."

"Without touching one's core, what does one have?" Véronique's voice commanded, "So the heart is broken – big deal! It mends. It takes time. Trust is another matter more difficult than loving."

"Trust? Dear Véronique, sometimes I don't even trust myself!" And, another thing, speaking frankly, people can't stand honesty. " Nigel drained his glass "…makes them look within. My Dears! Everyone lies. Or keeps their mouth shut and suffers in silence."

"Secretly lying to themselves," said Naomi.

Nigel gulped his G&T "People all move in the field which they want ladies! What serves them, where they're comfortable. They can whine about conditions, wish for better but move a centimeter of that comfort gage aside and all hell breaks loose."

Labradors sat at his feet. "See these chappies? We should learn from these beasts. Actions are the only means we have to judge. Instincts never betray you unless you choose to be deaf to your instincts." He stroked his pets caressing their long ears.

"Spontaneous action. Nothing contrived," chimed Véronique.

"No one can change another's actions. You can mirror their image and let them see their reflection. If you want to, Christ! I'd never want to mirror Esmeralda!"

"And if people hurt you?" questioned Naomi.

"Turn the sting back on them! Let them crawl on their bellies, get scurvy, be bored! Jealous!…What a lovely thought, revenge!" Nigel downed his third drink.

Naomi's charm was disarmed unveiling thoughts confessed to herself, "Too many poor souls spend their life licking some wound from the past, hurt beyond proportions, locked in yesterday, not giving birth to today…I speak from experience."

"Death shakes you out of that frame of mind, Naomi," Véronique responded. I will not feed into negative responses. I must move on, time's too short."

"Couldn't say it better," Nigel mused, "Stagnation's death."

"My best advice," spoke Véronique, "is give LOVE!"

"Even if the hurt others inflict is vicious?" Naomi defended herself.

"It will rebound on them. Be there for those you love - when – not if – they return."

"Ah," Nigel relaxed in a club chair, smoking again, "Forgive and forget! Turn the other cheek! Jolly Good!...but can we?...all those nasty little grudges we carry around add flavor to life. "

"All this emotional trauma!" Naomi's response was immediate. She thought of her reticence with the drama of Brian Korthorpe re-entering her life.

"Fear is a phantom...." spoke Véronique. "Quit fear. It has no place! Love's a privilege! ...The joy of love entering your life is vibrant after years - you're petrified thinking what will happen should it vanish?

Nigel was silent but only a brief second. "Love drives everyone mad. I myself have avoided it for years. Esmeralda too...and see clearly why many court bad company, bad jobs, bad situations diluted with alcohol. Better, perhaps than the mockery of love or the void. Yes, that's me. No D.M.R."

"D.M.R.?" asked Véronique.

"Deep Meaningful Relationships. I treat you two better than most people. But don't get it wrong. I don't trust anyone! That includes my wife. Dante had it right. It's all a comedy. This life's a *Divina Commedia.* Cynical me lives by percentages. Screw the next guy before he screws you."

"Machiavellian?"

"Nigelvellian! Better than the mockery of love or the void. Marriage is a quid pro quo, not a bad trade-off. There's always something in exchange."

"Nigel! Such negatives! Véronique raised her voice, "A waste of time. Live in the moment! LOVE! We all die. We all have a destiny charted by our stars that can't change."

"Stars are a waste of time! I can control life!" Nigel bellowed.

"Control life?" Véronique raised her voice an octave, "Just try and it boomerangs..and controls you."

"Right, Véronique," agreed Naomi.

Nigel gulped his gin, voicing his mind in the next instant, "A person can make their own breaks! Decorative people! Give me decorative people to assuage my banal boredom. My Stars! Véronique, Fuck the Stars! I don't believe in them. That's fine for you women. Material things distract me."

Véronique and Naomi watched Nigel pace the room unburdening himself. "Take this art collection! Take our centre court box at Wimbledon! The horses at Beaumont Manor… Ascot! The Opera Board! This movie! The theatre! Shakespeare said it's a stage and I agree!"

Nigel exhaled with one of his dramatic sighs, answering his question, not waiting for a response. "Submerge myself with something or someone! A mistress! Any mistress! Drink! Questioning - what? To abandon Esmeralda and all this?…and do what?" He peered at his friends with a Cheshire-cat smile, pinpointing his next remark. "I ask - and you wonder." Nigel relit his *cigarillo* knowing he had a captive audience.

"Nigel. Change your attitude… !"

Naomi clinked her glass to Véronique's. "Fuck Mediocrity!" Gin had loosened her tongue.

Momentarily, as comes to intense conversation, everything was stilled, the three sat in silence reviewing their thoughts.

"Solitude can be my finest hour. Loneliness quite different, a demon to avoid." Véronique rose from the divan addressing her friends. "Good fortune and ill fortune falls upon us all. Enough whingeing! Enough philosophy! My bad fortune is everyone's bad fortune. Accept the present while Fate lurks around the corner. "

"Who said 'Life's a Bitch?' " Nigel sparked.

"You did," said Véronique. They laughed.

"Enough of this." Nigel stood tall and ran his long fingers over his forehead. "Time to dress for dinner, begin *bella figura* - and tolerate each other. Amusing group, isn't it girls? And I will call you 'girls,' provocative women though you be!"

Nigel laughed, "This ridiculous holiday with a film is an excuse to escape the real world - it distracts me with trivia." He kissed his friends and exited to rejoin the masquerade.

Real world? Véronique spun Nigel's words in her mind…and her skin prickled at the thought what was to come. She said nothing more, smiled at Naomi and the two women went to dress.

At that time of late afternoon, *merenda* the Italians call it, there came a monotonous hoot of an owl, who saw everything and spoke a language only birds could decipher. He positioned himself, hidden in the ramparts of the roof, his continual HOOT HOOT seemed a warning of imminent danger. The place he lingered was covered with bougainvillea and intoxicating honeysuckle that made his constant sound heard by everyone in the Villa....

He wanted to make his existence known.....HOOT HOOT....was it a signal? A message?

As the last beam of sun set, the owl's profile could be seen on a crumbled column by the sea. HOOT HOOT...HOOT....

By midnight, he flew off, stretching his wings to the sky, his silhouette was spotted a brief second against the half-moon. Perhaps the mermaid, Circe, called him where he wanted to be. The gentle tide murmured and like the wind died down as a bevy of starlings swooped in a magical dance between the pine trees at Villa Pina. Then, all was silent. Even the cicadas and that haunting hoot of the owl was never heard again. Silence like this one can only experience in Capri.

Nature sends mystic messages to this isle in a strange way. On this night, as a canopy of stars twinkled above, before life was to arrive at dawn, bliss descended on this paradise.

Never could one imagine the secret that was to come. Within hours havoc would descend on Villa Pina.

IV

Gianni Zianni, Heir

The portrait of Giovanni Zianni, nicknamed, Gianni, illuminates.

His family roots were Roman; their fortune acquired in pharmaceuticals. For centuries every marriage in the family had been a merger for financial, social or proprietary interests thus creating one of the most impressive dynasties in Italy with Medici, Sforza, Borghese and Agnelli families. Zianni relatives were everywhere.

Male members exited Italy to seek education at Harrow or Le Rosay, moved onto Oxford, Cambridge or Harvard to claim degrees and eventually a position at one of the headquarters of the family firm. Daughters attended the Sorbonne or fashionable universities in Italy or America.

Gianni was the only grandson of the Chairman, son of the President of Zianni Pharmaceuticals International, and maternal grandson of Florentine Federico Alessi, the world-renowned polo player and *bon vivant.* Born feisty in the Eternal City, ready to seize the world, a king would have received the same adulation bestowed upon dimpled cherub, Gianni, heir to the family fortune. His grandfathers, as different as night is to day, prayers were answered with his birth and although both avoided religion (as most Italian men do), their appearance at the Vatican was an occasion of significance when Pope John Paul I christened the baby

Giovanni one week after his birth in a ceremony at his private chapel with ten cardinals in attendance.

The family compound on Gianicolo, the grandest hill in Rome would always be home to Gianni where he took his first steps at the family's Villa Multifiore. There he learned to ride his pony going from one part of the property to another, and glimpsed at history from the unparallel panorama of Rome. Primed for the world he would inherit, Zianni Pharmaceuticals, his formal education began at home from masters received into the family to teach Latin and Greek before embarking on an international path of study. From his erudite Father and Grandfather Gianni was taught the responsibility to continue the success of the firm.

He grew to be unspoiled, six feet tall with a mass of hair, black as timbre. Cat-green eyes from his Neapolitan grandmother, the Marquessa di Sirilani, set off a manly complexion, akin to a Greek god.

The abundance of life was his birthright inherent to aristocrats, yet Gianni remained focused on global business and his ultimate responsibility to Italy.

Worldwide tabloids relished news of the advantaged family to no avail. Reared in a structured existence of religion and formality, ingrained by family members with their message to be his finer self, diminish ego and stay focused, journalists were *persona non grata* typical of true society.

When Gianni began his post at Harrow, (the school that educated future kings and Prime Minister Winston Churchill), they advised, "You're nothing special. Prove your ability, meet competitive assignments and have a social conscious for humanity." His Headmaster was stern, "Then, if these benchmarks are met and you excel in studies, beat Eton at games, you may win a place at Oxford or Cambridge." The school's zeal to produce the best in him brought pressure of this magnitude making Gianni long for time away from the Victorian complex to be with his sportive grandfather - who had a devil-may-care attitude to life and taught him the rudiments of polo.

Riding to the hunt in Tuscany, freedom to sail from Posillipo to Capri every summer and stay at Villa Pina were his to enjoy. There, his grandmother, a mixture of *maga* and sage, recounted stories about the family who'd never accept the mundane. While they strolled in her lush terraced gardens overlooking the Bay of Naples, Gianni held her fragile hand indulging in the slow tempo of Italian life. "Don't be caught in the race of life, Gianni. Reflect on eternity in comparison to earthy existence. The race of life, Gianni...has no time for true values. Take time...*pense bene,*"• she moved towards her pergola, "Be careful with those seductive lips you inherited from me." She laughed.

"Bella Nonna!" He kissed her hand and bowed as he'd been taught; she'd go to her chapel on the eastern side of the garden and later take a *penacella.*•

Thus the affection and vitality of his family formed his character and true to Italian principles, tradition put family before friends cultivated at school. These were invited to Italy to sample *la bella vita* during holidays.

Gianni's social life sprouted riding to the hounds, playing polo, parties with daughters of family friends, concerts, the opera, the theatre, lavish débuts and weddings to attend. Sensual stimuli necessary to satiate his strong libido was on offer with those of noble birth hoping for a merger.

By eighteen when Gianni entered a room all noticed. He had no arrogance and disarmed everyone. His ram rod straight posture highlighted by an engaging smile lit his face, displaying warmth and an astute mind. Everyone was comfortable who came within his range because he was comfortable with himself.

Gianni radiated optimism. His aquiline nose, angular face and muscular body set off broad shoulders and long legs making him appear as a film star.

More importantly, he kept his Italian emotions in check, chose words precisely in a cultivated voice from the wealth of vocabulary he knew speaking in addition to his *madre lingua* flawless English, French, German and when called for, Greek.

• think well

• a nap

He never forgot the duty he had to the family, to excel - and one day take the reigns of his forbearers and steer Zianni Pharmaceuticals into decades of progress with lucrative results. By Gianni's twenty-eighth year he was working in the Milanese headquarters with a degree in science from Cambridge, and master's from Oxford, meeting scientists around the globe. His enthusiasm for miracle drugs to cure deceases made him the pride of the Ziannis, who brought ether to Italian operating theatres in the 1800s. He sought gifted individuals with inventions, never renouncing the impossible, dreams of tomorrow, to believe in and be funded.

Fear held no place for Gianni who had the foresight to encourage brilliant innovators of every conceivable cure from Alzheimer's to cancer, hair loss to loss of libido and present their work to the Zianni board.

When Doctor Robert Gallo isolated the AIDS virus Zianni Pharmaceuticals had the distinction of being instrumental to his work, and Gianni never forgot Dr. Gallo in his laboratory at the National Institutes of Health, outside of Washington, D.C., when he visited the brilliant scientist as a young student of biology.

Pharmaceuticals were Gianni's world. Medicine, skilled scientists, laboratories fascinated the scholar turned biotech businessman. He would have been a workaholic had it not been for his grandfather, Federico, "Break the vigorous six-day a week schedule! Head for the polo fields!"

Gianni was a strong international player and British friends urged him to be part of their team competing at Windsor. "What in the devil are you doing, old thing, wasting your youth with those scientific principles?" Nigel Pembrooke with his flawless King's English pestered him to renounce the world of work for the field of play. Nigel announced, "They named me spokesman for the games with the team at Windsor. I dare say, we need some of that Italian dash for the team to thrash those bloody Argentines!… Get yourself here."

"We're working on a new pill, Nigel…to make impotence impotent!"

"Bring your miracle pill this weekend. I'll be delighted to roger some women and be a guinea pig!" Gianni rang off leaving the roar of

Pembrooke's resonant laughter reverberating in his ear. Nigel with his magnanimous personality intrigued Gianni, viewing the prospect of playing at Windsor in England again. Knowing he had nothing to lose, Gianni dialed Rupert Davidson in Gloucestershire.

"Rupert, Nigel Pembrooke's just rang encouraging me to be a part of the international team at Windsor - are you involved?"

"Wouldn't miss it, ponies arriving from Subia, Sheikh Makkum's stables, with that gorgeous niece of his, Shabadiba, coming from Emir to pay her respects to Prince Charles. Parties everywhere! Jameson from Boston's with us, he's gone wild with the chance to compete. An extraordinary team. Come aboard for God's sake!"

"Sounds impressive."

Never one to force an issue, Davidson imparted, "If not now, when?"

That call changed Gianni's life. When the polo coach placed the call to Gianni all was confirmed, London's social whirl ignited, Gianni was as the most dashing, accomplished newcomer of the polo players from abroad.

Simultaneously, Samir Redat, an Egyptian surgeon ten years Gianni's senior, presented his heart inventions to the board of Zianni Pharmaceuticals in Milano. Redat's devices of artificial valves replacing arteries and veins, little boxes called 'pacing' were the keystone of new medical practices. Instinctively Gianni recognized they would be the most remarkable inventions of a lifetime revolutionizing surgeons' techniques, saving cardiac patients. He patented them for ZIP, Zianni International. Pharmaceuticals. Gianni sensed the thrill of discovery, exactly as it had been for his Great Grandfather when he launched insulin in Italy for diabetics eighty years before.

Gianni took to the brilliant, humble Samir Redat immediately. Their work presented a unique chance to delve into the extraordinary – Samir and Gianni's mission in life. He pressed forward with ideas for the future with Redat, and other scientists; one year slipped into three, then five as Redat and he became friends between sessions in London when Gianni would dart off to take part in polo matches with former classmates in the royal circle of Prince Charles.

The flock of people Gianni was meeting were astonishing. His world consisted of high intensity medicine, pioneering inventions, bio-technology, entrepreneurial pursuits and board meetings coupled with dramatic international sport. The world of glamour mingled with scientists whose abstract thinking astounded Gianni devoted to the genius of science.

At the same time, Gianni met with Brian Korthorpe, his learned former professor, at Trinity College, Cambridge, given a chair for his work on Alzheimer's and dementia. The intellectually respected society of dons and peers, the Apostles, accepted Gianni (Korthope's candidate) into the prestigious selection process. Zianni Foundation funded Korthorpe's cognitive neurological studies at Gianni's personal request. Prince Charles urged him to consider alternative medicine and the effects Zianni Pharmaceuticals would have in producing a range of miracle herbs.

To no avail, journalists, in pursuit of stories about the private life of the dashing heir apparent, gained access. Gianni remained silent. Women seemed everywhere wanting to meet him, diverse types, (some planted by the media) with tricks to have Gianni in a compromising position that resulted in zero results.

From his privileged circle, Gianni dated Stella Gregotti occasionally for years. His full agenda was such Gianni didn't devote time to relationships and remained very much the bachelor who squired several women about in Italy and England distancing himself from commitment. Although the vibrations of love didn't manifest with Stella, both understood their match would keep a tradition, the usual Italian contract of *marriage Italian style.*

His only sibling, Serena, worked with him at the headquarters in Milano, sharing the family duplex that overlooked their garden and swannery after a love affair of hers turned sour. Marriage was expected of them and one evening playing chess they spoke candidly watching the spotlighted birds glide below motionless on the wide pond below.

"In a year Stella will be the right match for you," Serena began. Gianni knew she was a conduit to the family's ideas for wedding plans.

"That's not what I want."

Serena made her move knowing her brother's ability at the game seizing her chances. "The idea of marriage..." Serena began again.

Moving his knight, bemused, Gianni looked at his sister...."Is marriage is a long development... a contract, like business you're going to say..."

"It must have continuity. What does some flashy sexual encounter produce after a time?"

"Has your mind gone cold, Serena? Have you been around our parents too long?"

"Lifelong companionship as they've known has merit...not that sex isn't important. " She paused and gazed at swans who'd coupled.

"You mean tradition, the habit of togetherness is more important than some injection of sexual excitement."

"Does sex ever endure?" Serena questioned. "Love does, I suppose.

One must be careful not to mix sex with love."

"Or security with love." Gianni sipped his Grappa.

"Love seems impossible. A man can have a spasm of orgasm, walk away and leave a woman. Can he ever know love?...emotion?"

"So that's why you're here. You broke with Ernesto...remain in love with him and preach to me questioning do men fall in love?"

"Not to preach to you, Gianni, and, by the way, he broke with me, men compartmentalize feelings."

"You have this cold idea not to go forward in a union that is passionate choosing something more businesslike for marriage." He took a long look at his sister raising his eyebrows in disbelief, saying under his breath, "Questioning if men fall in love!"

"Women can't compartmentalize. Men can. Women's love endures with sacrifice, pain. "

Sipping his Grappa, Gianni looked at his overly dramatic sister, "Compartmentalize you say?"

Serena looked up, "Nature pushes us into things but perhaps the true secret of a happy marriage is not with sex but with ..."

"Serena you're brainwashed. Men fall in love. If sex isn't good in the bedroom you might as well be in the boardroom! And you speak of women knowing about love! .....Ha!"

"A double standard exists. You'll live *marriage Italian style* with a mistress on the side." Her curvaceous body posed, lit a cigarette and she confronted her younger brother. "In my case the double standard will never apply." She took an extended inhale on her cigarette. "In my case, I'd be promiscuous taking a lover, you merely a husband who needs outside stimulation." She smoothed the hem of her Chanel skirt crossing her zaftig legs, once, then twice.

"To have faithfulness in a marriage seems unobtainable, but one can hope - one can try..."

"Gianni you're more naive than I thought. Do you really think you could be faithful?" Not waiting for him to finish, seized with straightforwardness she continued, "I wager you'll take pleasure outings and keep them secret. The idea of a marriage, the way the family sees it, is a possibility."

"Perhaps you're referring to *your* life, Serena. Stella is a great friend, but I want love or nothing." He looked at her tenderly. "You DO know the difference...?" Serena's eyes linked with her brother. "Accomplish what the family wants, Serena. Maybe in my lifetime, I'll change my point of view. One never knows how life presents itself."

"Life is..."

"Short, Serena. *La vita e una volta!*• Now, I want to do things MY way. I've done enough to please everyone."

He moved his Queen into her field, knowing he would win on the next move sizing his strategy three moves ahead. His discourse delighted him.

" I know what you're going to say...you men are seed spreaders on the prowl..."

"Maybe you don't know what I'm going to say... Serena do whatever you please, be a hypocrite. Keep bloodlines in order and have a flirt

---

• Life is one time!

whenever you want as long as you return home like a stray cat when it's over. Don't rock the boat. Keep investments secure, the family intact. *Bella figura!* It isn't my idea."

"Be careful Gianni." His eyes caught hers, distracted, "You're on everyone's list as number one catch." She moved her knight, taking his Queen, blocking his King. "Be careful you don't get a gold digger."

"Me?....Ha! You jest"...he viewed the board.

"Check Mate..." said Serena winning, "And, I'm not joking."

Years later this halcyon evening would be regarded as an omen.

With an eclipse of the moon, when this conversation was void from memory, Gianni entered Annabel's, his eyes met the image of Botticelli's Venus Lightening struck...*Coup de foudre.*

This beauty stirred life by her very being. He never experienced anything like this sensation before.

"MINE! She must be MINE!" reverberated through his head.

In that fashionable din of music, conversation, strobe lights and smoke, taking her in with one gaze, feeling her hypnotic cool turquoise eyes meet his, Gianni's movements froze. Watching her move away as if she forgot he was alive, turned his blood to frenzy. He remained mesmerized memorizing this minx with porcelain skin, a flowing mane of strawberry-blonde hair. It was a miracle! Botticelli's Venus came alive.

This exquisite Goddess with her unmatched face and perfect body moved in perfect rhythm on the dance floor. She took the arm of a man Gianni knew from Rome, Stefano de Gesu, the Sicilian diplomat, (known as a roué escorting the best looking women in the world). Gianni became distracted, forgot his friends, moved in de Gesu's direction to cut in and dance with the stranger whose first glance was ineluctable.

An earthquake entered his life. *Terramotto.....*Love, that sly emotion he feared in the past, vanished. Women by the dozen he'd experienced. Her force was electrifying, rendering him with a one track mind - I have to have her!

de Gesu saw him coming, whisked her off the floor before Gianni could make his move, there she was!...*Nouveaux riche* Franco Lemma, the *burino* industrialist from Milano, put his arm around her. Shocked by the alacrity of how his usual smooth persona diminished, Gianni motioned to Rupert Davidson who'd entered the nightspot with him and a retinue of friends. Forged with courage, Gianni advanced to approach this inaccessible *femme fatale,* spying a large diamond ring on her left hand while Lemma began to dance with her. "It can't be. She can't be engaged to that swine!" The shady business deals of Lemma's and how he'd crash Zianni parties into society made Gianni detest him but now this! His mind raced heightened by her cool manner and indelible impression.

"Rupert, you know everyone!" he blurted. "Who's that woman!"

"That's the Baroness Esmeralda Beck, a divorcée." Rupert beamed, "Got a yen?"

"Find out whatever you can! Don't ask questions!"

Esmeralda entered Gianni's life three weeks later. As all men in love, Gianni knew what he wanted. Nothing would stop him. Esmeralda became his obsession. He learned everything about her, put obstacles in the path of her engagement, had her break with Lemma and won her.

V

The Ambassador Stefano de Gesu

Mezza Luna Dinner Dance

"Queen Elizabeth! Your Royal Highness! May I present His Excellency, the Ambassador of Italy to the United Kingdom, Stefano de Gesu!"

It all seemed a dream, a dream he dreamt, lived and dreamt again continuously. Stefano de Gesu, spent from swimming twenty laps, sprawled on the sun lounge at Villa Pina remembering his great souvenir. The memory of Buckingham Palace, presenting his credentials to England's Queen, was the finest moment of his life...but there were other moments...

His indecent bathing trunks tightened around his groin as he closed his coal-black eyes and began to relax. The tempo of his breathing matched his emotions, smoldering emotions ignited, deep sensual emotions revived. The sun penetrated every muscle on his body. Thoughts raced. His member stirred awakening a sensation that was marvelous. A smile came to his lips, feeling virile. He wanted to be still, savor this interlude of desire, his private world. Then he sensed someone near, approaching from a distance, stalking him like a cat, tiptoeing closer. Stefano de Gesu rolled over to feign sleep wanting to fuck the creature that entered his fantasy.

"Mind if I join you?" That was how it began.

Hours later, after a nap, before dinner he took pleasure in nostalgia, how many years was the first time with her? Perhaps twenty. Still marvelous - better because maturity gives a man a certain sense of himself. This time his body didn't wilt as it did now and again. "What lovemaking! My best!" Stefano was revitalized.

His forte was the chase yet how divine to lie back and be ravished! His expressive fingers ran along his body, caressing it as she had done an hour before....those drop dead looks of hers, that voice! "I want to eat you in small, little bites....." Her perfume filled the air, gardenia... jasmine. This was turning to be a delightful vacation at Villa Pina, full of surprises... a turning point in life.

Dressing for dinner sometime later, he heard music wafting through his room from the balcony. He stepped onto the terrace looking at the lights across the sea in Sorrento. "Perfect weather, perfect moonlight, stars and now this, marvelous Cole Porter music played at its best.."

Tonight was a dinner dance, *"Mezza Luna,"* the invitation read and the moon obediently lit the sky as darkness claimed the evening in Capri. The invitees were international movers and shakers chosen to view the first rushes of ESCAPADES, the film Esmeralda and Nigel were backing.

There are certain things that mark an epoch of life, meeting the Queen for one, an unforgettable party another. Truman Capote had his Black & White ball, Esmeralda has this event, an important debut is another, a wedding, a birth, only the uninvited will speak badly of these occasions, thought de Gesu. The greatness of this party will rest on what stems from this evening ...not the diamonds, *haute couture* or cuisine. This is a once in a lifetime party where the hostess will achieve fame and when I think back to this night, varying conversations with an assortment of accents will be called to memory.

"Esmeralda's living in a time warp wanting all to dress in black tie and decorations in Capri." He fastened a medal onto his sash, "So be it. After eighteen years as an Ambassador, second nature."

de Gesu was a man of inordinate charm, a libertine, a man other men placed in their trust. "Amazing life, this saga of mine! Buenos Aires, Saudi Arabia, the United Nations and at last London!" That was the plum, England ....again and again the words he would remember the rest of his life were those heard as he entered Buckingham Palace bowing to the Queen.

He glanced in his mirror studying his face carefully, combing his black hair with its chalk white sideburns. Looks helped. He couldn't deny that, nor could connections. His stately presence was elegant, that of an Ambassador.

"Levy from Hollywood would say I was sent from Central Casting." He laughed slipping into his Belgian patent shoes.

"Stefano de Gesu," he thought aloud appreciating his macho image,

"You're 61 ....and achieved all you wanted!" He snickered. "An Italian diplomat of the highest echelon, handsome, divorced, witty, articulate in several languages, including Arabic, I may add,..."

He began inserting his studs..."without serious means due to divorce, although dear Mother's family had ties to the Lazard fortune, Father's – De Beers...." He couldn't get in the last piece of sapphire jewelry, "...once a stud, now with pacemaker, but you preformed admirably today, BRAVO!

Surprise that. The vigor of yore returns! A climax like that I thought could come only with some pixy thirty years younger. Proves I'm still the man I was twenty years ago......a lady killer!"

He laughed at himself, knotting his black tie. "Some Lady Killer! A misogynist, name dropping, parsimonious, oversexed connoisseur of women, wine, and let's not forget lover of history, maker of history!...a Jewish boy smart as a fox who wangled his way to the top knowing how to grease axels in high places!" He stopped, put on his smoking jacket appraising himself in the full-length mirror.

"Ambassador de Gesu, you Sicilian kike, you never looked more handsome!" He amused himself laughing again, shook an Hermes foulard into his breast pocket, checked the time on his gold watch and exited, delighted.

The scene from the top of the circular staircase was hypnotic. As he descended the long flight of marble steps, an expectant buzz among the exquisitely attired guests added to the excitement. A wondrous atmosphere, scented with lilacs, tuberoses, lilies and jasmine, permeated the air of the gilt reception room below. To his right, a Monet hung next to a Modigliani, Rodin's *Eros meets Venus* stood on a pedestal at the landing to his left, Brancusi's bronze sphere and Giacometti's *Man Alighting* below threw supernatural shadows on the frescoed walls from candelabras glowing everywhere. The art collection alone was a spectacle to behold at Villa Pina.

Hundreds of sparkles competed for the eye's attention from the diamonds on the guests assembled to the immense Murano chandelier dangling above the vaulted cathedral ceiling. Ecru silk Fortuny draperies, cinched in silk, accented French doors open from floor to ceiling with the spectacular view beyond framing the setting.

As he neared closer, the combo sounded like Peter Duchin. 'It probably is Peter,' thought de Gesu, and indeed it was. Esmeralda had learned society's lessons and was at the peak of her form. "If today's romantic romp is any indication of tonight, this is going to be phenomenal," he thought, knowing his presence was noted by all, entering the scene as one would a stage and this was Act One.

As he walked into the reception room, before he said 'hello,' to the array of people gathered, he clocked the upper class English with their polite, pompous old school talk, who had clocked those of middle class ostentation whether Italian or otherwise, blazing with jewels, the Russian on point who used Swiss francs to buy whatever he wanted, a French intellectual in the throng, an American loud mouth, a Spanish on the make, an Arab wheeler-dealer and the Swedish Grand-dame whose villa next door dimmed by comparison. All were here....the brightness and dullness of their assorted lives found favor tonight being included. There were those who lived far beyond their means, relishing their *bella figura* this night and there was Levy who'd never forget this evening. A leap to prestige with this party had been his tonight, as the Hollywood power broker Producer, the grandson of a cobbler, son of a butcher, a baby boomer from WWII that belches when he eats - knowing his name is glazed on every important cinema in the world.

"Ambassador may I present our guest of honor Rudolf Nureyev."

Esmeralda beamed as the Russian dancer bowed to the diplomat. It was common knowledge Nureyev acquired the Galli Islands off the Amalfi coast and a coup for Esmeralda that she'd managed to present him at her party, "A" list in every detail.

"May I compliment you Esmeralda on the choice of your guest of honor, and the magical ambiance you've created tonight." Esmeralda held her dainty hand a moment longer than necessary as de Gesu bent to kiss it. People had to lean closer to Esmeralda to hear her soft spoken voice and although a highly feminine trait, this remoteness, Stefano often wondered was how she controlled people in her company.

Tonight she was dazzlingly beautiful, sheathed in a Dior dinner dress of white crepe de Chine, bias cut that accented every perfect curve of her sensuous, slender body. Her swanlike neck unadorned, had a wisp of strawberry-blonde curls meet her shoulder that displayed a Morganite diamond broach encrusted with cabochon rubies, matching her bracelet and glistening ear clips. Her skin was untouched by cosmetics, or so it seemed, and her long sable eyelashes set off exceptional rare turquoise eyes. Her voluptuous glossed pink lips smiled, conscious of her standing and social success. Earlier today she confessed, "I prefer London. The Italians," she stated, "except for you, Stefano, never trust me." It didn't matter. One sensed immediately the snob in her, no matter how she disguised it. Esmeralda had reached the pinnacle proportions tonight laughing at the audience she craved as if proclaiming, "Look at me! I arrived in Italy seven years ago and I'm more influential than any of you in this room tonight." There was triumph in her, she used it well, and to those she wished, patronizingly.

Conversation with Nureyev ensued, the two men having met years before in New York when he danced with Baryshnikov at the

Metropolitan Opera's Salute to America in 1986. Princess Shabadiba in beaded lace joined the group, her coiffure swirled atop her heart shaped face drew attention to raven eyes and a rare set of unforgettable emerald gems.

"I understand your plans are to build a ballet conservatory on Galli, Maestro."

"Rudi will tell you all his plans, Stefano, but I must steal him away to meet other guests," Esmeralda's eyes flashed with the joy of her success knowing even the half moon of September contributed to the perfection of her evening. She moved like a hummingbird in flight with Nureyev close by.

"Tell me, Darling," murmured Shabadiba in her throaty voice as Stefano lit her cigarette, "What do you make of our hostess?"

"Shabadiba, she has a certain allure, all the more appealing, because she will never be mine." Their eyes met in a secret merriment, as they clinked flutes and moved to others in the immediate vicinity.

de Gesu viewed the event with its fifty peacocks and doyen of society clustered together as the usual mix of socialites and plutocrats who spent their life fixed on people, parties, places and position. Krug was passed by white gloved Sri Lankan waiters wearing butler's jackets laced with gold braid, Duchin kept the mood light tinkling the keys, smiling from his perch on the marquee dance floor, candles flickered and diamonds glittered.

Stefano with his sharp focus, worked the room by rote, knowing when to bow, how to graze a hand with a kiss, speak to women longing for attention wanting to swoon. More importantly, how to look intently into the eyes of serious men he could engage in conversation of importance and not drivel after dinner. Having arrived at exactly where he wished to be in life, aside from making love, conversation was more important than anything in the world to Stefano. Then he could impart his wisdom and experience as the accomplished diplomat he was, offending no one while making a beeline to another circle, excusing himself momentarily from the hub of chatter to study the seating list posted on a side table of the loggia. It all was done effortlessly.

10 September 2004
Table One

Ambassador Stefano de Gesu

Olympia Sanford — *Naomi Dartworth*
Whitney Jameson — *Sir Brian Korthorpe*
Véronique Joulin — *Elizabeth MacKenzie*
Nigel Pembrooke — *Doctor Samir Redat*
Princess Shabadiba — *Stella Gregotti*
Nicky Viscounti — *Maestro Nureyev*
Zofra Zofany — *Esmeralda Pembrooke*
Marc Levy — *Marco Ricci*
Lynne Jameson — *Cat Renoir*
Monty Daniels — *Jarvis Engleton*

Jacqueine Redat

Regarding how Esmeralda positioned him, he made note Rupert was detained since last Thursday, returning to the centre of the room pleased with his position at table, eyeing Mark Levy, sensing how uncomfortable the American was. "You must be gratified to see everyone with high expectations to view the first footage of your film," he offered wishing to put Levy at ease discussing familiar territory.

"Wait til ya see da rushes! And did ya meet my fiancé, Cat?"

"Charmed," uttered de Gesu bowing as she reached for his hand and shook it vigorously, not understanding the European gallantry of a man's respect greeting a lady formally to brush a kiss on her hand.

"Now dis is not the exact way we do things in Hollywood, but I gotta hand it to you Italians!...ya know how to throw a party!"

"We've been partying over two thousand years," responded de Gesu bemused, moving away from the smoke of Cat's cigarette.

"Ya know I told Cat, I wish I had a camera crew here. Yeah, that is what we forgot to bring." Levy laughed at his remark. He pointed at his

Barbie doll. " She had so many Versace's to pack we couldhav packed a crew in her trunk and forgot the dresses!"

de Gesu glanced at Cat Renoir's costume, a black strappy skintight ball gown sprayed on her faultless body that reeked of too much scent. A tattooed heart that said *'Joy'* was obvious on her left forearm, her face was a fixed study in botox and rynoplasty not the highest caliber.

"Yeah the truth is we may know how to do movies, and you'll see tonight. That's Ricci ova dere, da star." Levy began waving his hands dramatically motioning the actor to come forth, "He's one hell of an star, smooth like too, no hard edges. I like dat. And not vain like all dose ego maniacs I worked with on my last flick. Ricci. Yeah. I like him, he's got..."

"So how's it going" said Marco Ricci approaching with his astonishing trained voice.

"Just sayin' you've got it, Marco. You're gonna get the Oscar for dis one. Wherz dat babe of yours Stella?"

"Over there, don't worry about her, she knows everyone..."

"Tell me Mr. Levy," began de Gesu leading the group to the balcony when Levy interrupted him.

"Look at dis view, spectacula! Da Bay of Naples with the half moon's shinin' da starry sky. Gorgeous Ambassador, dis place is gorgeous en call me Mark, like Marco here only de Americans pronounce it differently. "

"What I'd like to suggest is that we have a dinner for you, your stars, your backers at the Embassy when ESCAPADES opens in London."

"Thanks, damned nice of ya and da Queen will come too 'cauz we are negotiatin' for a Royal Command Performance. Did ya know that? en maybe the three countries, England with ha, you for the Italians and the Americans can do an event en stage it. Good idea, whatdaya think? Get some publicity, innerrrnational publicity..."

"Great PR idea." de Gesu turned to Ricci," Marco what about you?"

"I do everything Stella and the good producer Levy tells me to do." Ricci beamed knowing his slightest wish would be their command.

"Tell me, how do you guys know Esmeralda?" asked Levy curiously.

"You'd better ask Stefano, I'm a newcomer, only have known the elusive Esmeralda since Stella and I've been together," said Marco, the star.

"Ah yes. I had the pleasure to meet the beautiful Esmeralda when she first came to London. We all keeled over when we saw her for the first time and then she was greatly admired when she was on television."

"Television?" chirped Cat itching to be a part of the conversation.

"Yes. Esmeralda was considered the quintessence of English beauty. Harrods used her as their official model, which was a huge success abroad." The group stood non-pulsed. Wishing to continue the momentum, adding a little shock to the dialog, de Gesu continued, "Baron Beck, the mogul from Germany, was besotted with her photographs, flew to London and married her shortly thereafter."

"I didn't know she was married before Gianni." Marco 's surprise was obvious, imagining Esmeralda was the type of woman one could never discover. Was she divorced by Beck to marry Gianni Zianni - or vice versa?...always a big difference in that. And how many lovers were between marriages?...or did she dally once out of wedlock from boredom in the bedroom or boredom with life? All fascinating, considered Marco believing human beings should have every experience before Father Time enters the landscape.

"...and a model." Cat added considering her own aspirations starry eyed.

"Yes, a short-lived marriage she doesn't discuss but that's how I met her," de Gesu added quickly, surprising himself how his mind wandered to their true meeting and in a swift second thereafter, he contemplated if the Baron or Gianni had done a surveillance check on Esmeralda? Who was she really? Where did she came from before marriage? The notion passed his mind in a split-instant yet it registered as Levy interrupted, monopolizing the conversation.

"Quite a woman!" Levy swirled his champagne in his glass, "All dis was her idea" he took a heavy breath, "You know like a pre-bliz-party for backers en prominent people who'll add to the kitty, talk about the film. Not that we need it, or askin' you Ambassador, but Esmeralda wanted it like this, en she and Nigel yeah, you know dat's a team dat does things, like getting dis together, even with the ballet guy Nureyev en dat Stella of yours Marco, you two - too. Stella told em, Esmeralda and Nigel, like it is Ambassador."

Levy took out an oversized Cuban cigar and put it to his mouth. "And like, I mean, they all of a sudden wanted to be involved, yeah guys..so we got dem into a production company - dat's Hollywood.... en dis isn't for publication, but you wanna know the tax write off...?" de Gesu sparked his lighter at Levy's cigar that didn't leave his mouth as he spoke.

"Tonight with the rushes," injected Marco, "a modern day thriller with a Fellini touch, if I may say...will show you...."

"Say whateva you want Marco, you're the lead and your damned good. Carry the picture in my estimation."

"Yeah." Levy glared at Cat as she uttered this word as one would shoot a dart. "I mean Yes."

"Why I do declare ya'll standin' here together en I said to my honey of a husband, 'Whitney, I bet those movie people are tellin' the Ambassador all about our new production en I'm gonna walk right over en tell ya'll how marvelous it is to be one on the inside of makin a real honest to goodness blockbusta of a film,' Yes ya'll know it, this is gonna be the best film of the whole year, the whole decade, I'd say." Lynne Jamison decked in the glitter of her marquis set diamond necklace and dangling earrings made everyone believe her inventory of gems was limitless.

"Lynne, so interesting to hear you speak of the film as you do." Marco, at his best, smiled, as champagne glasses were exchanged for a fresh assortment from a passing tray. Nervously the bedecked fingers of Lynne fingered her garish diamond necklace and smiled at the star. She had that overdone look of purchase so unlike European women.

"En Cat, you gorgeous thing, why I do declare, dat dress es gotta be a Versahche en I just love those sexy things he does, or his sista does now that he's dead. Tragedy that was, but ya'll know how to wear that

Versahche an its somethin' I couldn't do but ya'll look mighty allurin' I'll say."

"Thank you Mrs. Jameson"

"Now ya'll call me Lynne like everyone else ya hear?"

Cat smiled nervously, Levy thrust his chest forward and Stefano de Gesu thanked his lucky stars he was not in the vicinity of these people at dinner.

He turned to Levy, "Your last film..."

Interrupting him, "You wanna talk gross?" and with that Levy began puffing his cigar and touting himself, his studio, his expertise. Marco Ricci, actor that he was, pretended to be called to another part of the room and departed. To escape Levy wouldn't be easy de Gesu surmised yet realized this influential swine of a producer could be utilized in some way, some time and to make this poor slob feel important was a ten-minute investment that could prove useful in the future. One would call it 'diplomatic niceties.' Levy didn't require interaction to keep his dialog running full tilt as he drowned on about commercialism and tinsel town. Cat listened with rapped attention and adoring eyes to Levy whom she saw as Zeus incarnated. Lynne's eyes, conversely, darted about the room evaluating everyone, determining how she could mingle with another group that would suit her fancy better than standing with a foursome she no longer wished to engage. One sensed her thoughts, calculating her next step, intent on seizing the moment.

"Ya'll forgive me please but I think I've just been asked to go over en see Mr. Nureyev." Without waiting for a reply, Lynne's pencil thin body pirouetted away through billows of peach chiffon shielding her wrinkled chest and arms from sight. Her practiced smile flashed once again accenting the artificial whiteness of capped teeth.

Marco from a distance threw de Gesu a glance that needed no explanation. It went over Levy's head.

From the garden three figures approached as dinner was announced. "Well if it isn't Mark Levy!" said Monty Daniels enthusiastically patting him on the back. "Want to get an exclusive scoop on ESCAPADES with all the details, my VIP friend…we're close-by at dinner."

"Hey Daniels! fancy lookin' ta nite!… en still workin'. I like a guy like dat."

Daniels motives were clear. "What do you think Ambassador?" without waiting for a response, he hurtled to his next thought. "Levy here is Hollywood's Ambassador, engineering in Capri the poshest international crowd possible…"

Levy's chest expand four more inches from its gluttonous girth with the accolade the society journalist planted.

"Daniels, I'm no Ambassador, but dat's a good angle…whatta ya think Ambassador?"

"Everything's possible." Smiled de Gesu too embarrassed to say anything more.

"Have you all met Zofra from Hungary? And my friend Jarvis Engelton, a New Yorker art dealer, sharp as a tack." Daniels offered.

"Charmed," de Gesu said gazing at the shapely form of the Hungarian whose intense eyes met his daringly, accepting his feigned kiss on her extended hand, holding a Turkish cigarette in the other. Daniels' slip of the tongue describing pink-faced Engleton amused the diplomat.

It was impossible for the male in him not to admire Zofra Zofany's pink mounds of breast spilling forth in her blue strapless creation with its cinched waistline. Here was a woman without taboos. *"Jo estet kivanok.. Magyarorszagrol jott ide?*•

"You speak Hungarian!"

"A few words learned while in Budapest when I had the pleasure to sail down the Danube." *Milyen szep ma este!*"•

"Men need beautiful women to look at but you see Mr. Ambassador women are pleased to look at other women." Her smile was immoral.

• Good Evening. Have you come from Hungary?

• How beautiful you look tonight.

This suited Zofra who prided herself making sexual innuendos to put a man off balance.

"Most provocative. Shall we proceed?" He gallantly extended his arm to escort Zofra to the dining room, thinking her a boa constrictor, nodding to the others.

On the isle where an exiled emperor once lived in splendor and met his Fate, Esmeralda was meeting her Fate with her unlimited means, in this regal setting. It crossed Stefano's mind there's always glory before a fall, as it was with Tiberius. What would all this mean to Esmeralda's future? This ruminated a brief moment not to be dismissed.

The dining room was theatre. Lavish tables were laid with ivory silk damask, emerald Sevres porcelain and incandescent crystal from Salviati. Epergnes gleamed of antique silver as did monogrammed flatware. Zimbidium orchids interlaced with stephanotis and vines that intertwined epergnes, candelabras and miniature statues by Carpeaux in Cararra marble of birds in flight. The marquee, adjoining in the garden, matched in fantasy with swaths of silk ribbon, harem-style, decorating the tent. From the balcony's niche, in the dining room, a harpist and string quartet presented the melodious sounds of Vivaldi, setting the mood for dining.

Place cards with the embossed Zianni crest had the name of each guest written in calligraphy etched with gold as were the personalized menus. Esmeralda had thought of everything, and de Gesu noticed, the menu of his dinner partner on his right, Olympia Stanford, was with vegetarian specifications. 'What a fascinating time this will be' had to be on the mind of all the guests as de Gesu seated himself unrolling his large monogrammed napkin.

For the instant he thought about monogramming and how people used it. Here, as in all fine Italian homes, the monogram was noted in several instances, the napkin, the place card, the flat wear and on the place plate yet the person who bore these monograms was dead and his widow was married to someone else.

Stefano's monograms were embossed on his white linen tucked shirt, discreetly near his waist, white upon white. Whereas Levy's clearly in view with his elbow on the table were the size of a postage stamp, boldly evident on his cuff in black letters. From across the long stretch of table one couldn't help notice the size of his diamond links, large as a dime matching his twin pinkie rings, worn, specifically de Gesu assumed, for this occasion. Women's costumes are chosen to make other women envious and men desire them. Tonight was no exception. While men in black tie, like penguins, have their minimal changes in formal dress. Those changes, as in the case of viewing Levy's ruffled blue shirt, gaudy diamonds and monograms, spoke volumes. Taking it all in at a gallop, Stefano appropriately was at the lead table of twenty-two, the others of fourteen each were hosted by dignitaries familiar to the world of arts and letters.

Nigel and Esmeralda sat across from each other at the large oval setting.

Guests alighted to their positions like thoroughbreds to a gate and dinner commenced. de Gesu glanced at the individual menus, his read:

Chatter was lightening sharp from guest to guest and de Gesu's eyes caught Esmeralda's and then Nigel's for a brief second as they seized every opportunity to view their spectacular, enthralled with its results.

"I wonder what each of these people are promoting?" passed Stefano's mind, a veteran to parties of this type, witnessing gaiety between Whitney and Olympia overhearing part of their conversation.

MEZZA LUNA DINNER

Prima Piatto ~
Spigola Geneovese ~ Pesto
Moulin de Duhart Domains
Barons de Rothschild (Lafite)
1990 Pauillac

Secondo ~
Pasta, Veneziana, Florentina e Sicilia
Romanée-Conti 1986

Amuse Bouche ~ Limone sorbet

Terzo ~
Capresi Quail ~ from the forests of Capri
Mignons of Lamb ~ cippolini, finoccho, sage
Chateau Petrus 1966

Fromage ~
L'époisses Bourguignonne, Grapes from Villa Pina
Chateau Pontet-Canet, Paulliac 1986

Dolce ~
'Mount Blanc' ~ Raspberry coulis
Château d'Yquem 1983

Villa Pina
10 September 2004

"Artists can seldom account for their own creations," she spoke freely, adjusting her white satin tuxedo dinner suit provocatively slit to her thigh. de Gesu caught Whitney's eyes focus on her cleavage as she prolonged her conversation, "Marvelous to speak to you about art, Whitney, you understand it, involved as you are with the Modern and the Tate." She babbled along spiritedly, "Whenever something springs from my hands that show genius, I consider it a gift. Critics categorize my work, as you know, but that's absurd. What they say with stilted jargon, all of them are not artists, mind you, well, they'll never get it right." She leaned over flirting, engaging him in laughter.

"Creation is intellectual, " he said resting his hand on hers.

"To a degree, the rest, and you must promise to visit my Studio," she daringly put her hand on his, "is instinct rather than ideas."

"Yes…instinct." Nervously, he cleared his throat.

Olympia's zest for life he admired yet she paid scant attention to de Gesu, then again she never gave him much time. He turned his gaze to Stella Gregotti and Redat locked in a serious discourse about Egyptian antiquities when Stella was not intent on every word Nureyev uttered.

Levy was delighted to have Zofra's undivided attention as he displayed abominable table manners while Cat stared blankly at the display of glasses, forks and knives checking other's use of utensils, hoping not to make a mistake.

A murmur of syncopated talk never stilled and as the quail was brought to the table, Nigel's voice carried speaking of Palazzo Inglese, formerly the home of the King of Naples who arrived twice a year to hunt quail exactly at this time of the year.

Lynne, her head-moving robot style not to disturb her hair, kept glancing up from her conversation with Daniels trying to read lips or hear something within range more interesting. Stefano caught a smile exchanged between Naomi and Brian Korthorpe but more importantly Jacqueline Redat and Nicky Viscounti and wondered if it was imagined or if something erotic was exchanged with their eyes.

A seasoned veteran to hundreds of dinner parties, just as a chimpanzee knows his turn to perform, Stefano knew his time had come as Louis Roederer Cristal Champagne was poured. He rose, glass in hand waiting for the hush of conversations to fade and for all to look and listen to what would spill from his lips. This was his own little drama with his own special panache to make all remember his words.

"Honorable Guests, Maestro Nureyev," he began capturing the eye of each person he beheld. "I wish to drink a toast to our dear and extraordinary hostess, Esmeralda, and our eminent host, Nigel," he held his glass high. "Tonight we privileged friends are in a wonderland, the wonderland of a couple who have brought Hollywood to Capri with such splendor that the esteemed director Franco Zefferelli would have a challenge should he try to duplicate this scenario." de Gesu turned his glance to meet the eye of the Italian director hosting a table of dignitaries to his left. Everyone laughed having been satiated by the epicurean meal and wines, enjoying the repartee.

Zefferelli chuckled, "Hear Hear!" respecting de Gesu's wordplay. All were at ease waiting for Stefano's next remarks. He would not fail Esmeralda. There were too many memories, too many years between them and as he eyed the crowd, he was sure he was the only friend she had in the room.

"I have had the privilege to know Esmeralda more than a dozen years and tonight, may I say, Esmeralda you have never been more beautiful. With your remarkable sense of style, timing and interest in the arts, you have brought together on this isle remarkable people from countries all over the world. Glory shines all around you." Words flowed. Stefano was singing for his supper as Marco had been known to say.

"We would have come at your beckoning whatever the occasion … nevertheless, to have the added allure to view a film written by my compatriot, Stella Gregotti staring another, Marco Ricci, artists Italy is proud to share with the world, is a unique occasion. This demonstrates your talent, Esmeralda, to mesh the best of Italy with the best of art and… and soon, the world! All extraordinary." Esmeralda glowed, as one in love, hearing his words for the importance of her standing as an international hostess respected world-wide was hers tonight, what she had set her life on. This would not escape the news media when Monty Daniels wrote his article. All sipped champagne knowing there was more to come forth from the eloquent Ambassador known for his *savoir-faire* standing tall being the accomplished circus master for the eager spectators.

de Gesu not wishing to elongate his remarks but wanting to stress the impeccable importance of the evening and Esmeralda's role in society continued. "It is possible for me to have all of you linger this evening expounding on the glorious courage of my hostess, but I will make my salute brief.

We are all aware of the exceptional circumstances of Fate that would have detained others from living and sharing life had they been given the challenges of Esmeralda." He halted dramatically for his words to have impact. "She's proven in the face of tragedy one can rise from the ashes and it is to Nigel Pembrooke's credit, an English gentleman of first tier, who has undoubtedly brought the woman known for her beauty back to flower as she does this evening. To you both, I'm honored to be your loyal friend." de Gesu held up his hand as applause was to begin. His champagne flute high, his voice distinct, "May we meet again, all of us, at the Oscar's!" He sipped his champagne and sat down elegantly.

Nigel alighted immediately, glass in hand. "To my beloved wife, Esmeralda," Her eyes met his giving forth a smile so convincing of a deep devotion between them that de Gesu was stunned by their intensity. Everyone lifted their flutes to the toast; women had tears swell in their eyes believing the Cinderella dance of life. Nigel remained standing, his articulate voice deepened using his most aristocratic English accent.

"Thank you Ambassador for your well chosen words and I wish to thank everyone for sharing this jolly good fun this evening with me and my wife who keeps me in wonderland." A gentle murmur was heard, Nigel chuckled, pleased with himself stealing de Gesu's words, as he continued. "We have the opportunity to view the first footage of ESCAPADES with you tonight that the guru of films, our esteemed producer Mark Levy, titian of the cinema, has brought from Hollywood."

He smiled to the boy wonder who was completely out of place. "After dinner in the screening room we will see the fruits of his labor and that of Marco and Stella's. And from there, I understand our good chum, Peter Duchin is going to keep our feet dancing the night away. Life's one time! *La Vita e Una Volta!* Make the most of it!"

Nigel drained his glass, looked to Esmeralda for approval and nodded to Levy, whose face was easy to read, thinking he had won the Oscar, died, gone to Heaven, and found himself seated with God at this dinner in Capri.

VI

Sanjeev, Major d'uomo

Esmeralda awoke viewing a cluster of notes, gifts and flowers in front of her bed. She tucked satin pillows around her, unmoved by sentiment and the exuberance of gratitude from guests at her *"Mezza Luna"* Dinner Dance.

Draperies and *persiani* were still closed, the room, in semi-darkness cast a dim light over her icy blue satin *douvet.* She was dazed for the instant, a gust of semi-consciousness seized her. Sanjeev's knock on her door broke the negative trance as he entered her room.

"Buon Giorno Contessa," Sanjeev proclaimed the Italian words he did daily. She could have had him refer to her as Mrs. Pembrooke but Sanjeev had been serving her breakfast in this room since she married Gianni and his sweet demeanor, never judging anyone, held a special place in Esmeralda's world. He put the breakfast tray before her and quickly opened the draperies and unlocked the *persiani* for her to have a view to the sea. He turned, standing a distance, at attention.

"Sanjeev, I wish to thank you and the staff for all you did to make the last evening a success," she took an envelope from her night table containing an additional contribution to his wages and bonus for the help. This was the custom of Count Gianni that she continued once he died.

The houseman bowed. "It was a privilege for me and all serving you, Contessa. It's not necessary to pay additionally. " He stood waiting for her to dismiss or engage him in conversation. She pressed the envelope to his hand. He knew what would come next.

"Sanjeev, as I've said before, at a function such as this, there's one person who sees and hears more than I do or Signor Pembrooke."

"Yes, Contessa."

"That's why I put so much trust in you. For several days I've had a strange premonition as I did once before."

"Yes, Contessa."

"Do you recall I was afraid when Count Gianni was going to play polo the last time…and then saw him die before my very eyes."

"Yes, I'm so sorry, Contessa, I do."

"Sanjeev, I'm afraid of something happening, another tragedy. I've not voiced this anyone. I wonder did you hear or see anything last night that I should be aware of to put me at ease?"

"There was nothing out of the ordinary. All the guests had a good time."

"I'm consumed with fear, Sanjeev."

"Please dear Contessa do not be alarmed. If I may say so, you're afraid because last night was so important . Maybe you think it a dream but last night was real. There's nothing to alarm you."

"Thank you, Sanjeev. But tell me what the guests said when you passed things, when you were about."

It was always like this. Sanjeev had been quizzed before but he was startled to see the beautiful woman trembling. Strange when she should be rejoicing, celebrating her success and good fortune with her new life. A worried expression (that he had seen only once before) etched her face.

"I saw something amusing, Contessa." He offered to ease her tension.

"What?"

"Before the dinner, Mme Jameson came and looked at the seating chart and tried to change the names so she could be close to Maestro Nureyev."

"Did she?"

"She did change the chart but she saw me and couldn't enter the dining room to switch name cards. I asked, "Is there was something I may do for you?"

"I'm just looking at the seating," she said, pretending the chart dropped and she was adjusting it. But she knew I understood her because for the chart to drop on its own was impossible, so she went away. When she left I made sure the names were as you'd organized them."

"Thank you Sanjeev, typical of Mrs. Jameson. She's harmless. Anything else?"

He stood before her and she read his mind. There was something embarrassing. Had Sanjeev been white, he would have blushed red to his eyelids.

"Tell me…whatever it is."

"Some things. The first is Mr. Daniels gave me $100 and told me that there was much more if I could meet with him today telling him secrets about the family. I gave the money back to Mr. Daniels and said I have been with the Ziannis thirty years none of the staff will betray you."

"That's wise and kind, Sanjeev. Thank you. I know you'd never betray the memory of my late husband or hurt me."

"Never Contessa."

"Any other things?"

"Some routine matters. The Princess had me bring her more cocaine this morning, but she's done that before, as you know…"

"Yes…"

"And Mr. Levy likes the Hungarian lady, Miss Zofra. He had me send flowers to her room with a note. He tips too much money every time I do anything. I told him it was unnecessary."

"That is quite alright, Sanjeev…and?"

"I overheard a conversation."

"Yes, go on..."

"Do you remember at teatime when you and the Ambassador went to the garden?"

"Yes."

"You said to those present "I want to show Stefano the view." And then you and the Ambassador went to the lower garden."

"Yes." She had begun to brush her long hair looking into her hand mirror. Sanjeev ceased to meet her eye, overcome with embarrassment.

"If you will excuse me, Contessa, but it was Mrs. Jameson again, what she said in front of Mme Redat, her husband and Mr. Engleton…"

Sanjeev grew timid.

"What did she say?"

"Contessa I know it's not true.

"Out with it, Sanjeev…What?" Esmeralda's nerves began to show.

"She said, 'Everyone knows Esmeralda is having it off with her former lover.'"

"Did she? Preposterous!" Esmeralda's eyes widened. The panic that seized her eased, yet the mirror she held slipped from her hands shattering in a million pieces hitting the marble floor. Sanjeev rushed to clear it.

"Dear God! Seven Years bad luck!"

"No Contessa…No…in my country it is good luck," he lied knowing she was not herself. He wouldn't let her panic over something as insequential as a mirror. He continued the conversation lightening the moment with a smile, "It was not my place to say anything to Mrs. Jameson, Contessa. The others didn't respond to her remark except her husband said, "Shut up," just like that, in front of everyone. Then he left the room. The conversation was changed by Mme Redat who spoke about how she would dress for the evening."

"Sanjeev you've settled me down, you've done well telling me this. I'm less anxious. What Mrs. Jameson thinks is totally wrong."

He held the broken mirror in his hand, "Anything else?"

"Not my place to say, I hear maybe more than I should."

"Yes…tongues wag."

Sanjeev's face changed expression grinning nervously with the interrogation thinking Count Gianni never would have interrogated him like this.

"Go on, this is fascinating. Look!….my trembling hands are still," Esmeralda thrust her hand out with her café cup holding it steady. He filled her cup thinking of her passion for respectability. "Sanjeev you're provoking my curiosity."

"The Ambassador's been enjoying the company of a woman but I know it isn't you."

"Certainly not! Thank you Sanjeev, you may go now."

The Sri Lankan left, advising, "Be careful of your feet on this floor until I've it cleaned properly, Contessa." With a slight bow he, opened the French doors to the balcony, blessing the fact that in Capri there was not a mosquito to be found and exited to collect the tray from Signor Pembrooke's room that he'd served earlier.

Pembrooke's head was concealed in *The Times*. "That you Sanjeev?"

"Yes Sir."

"Has the Mrs. Pembrooke awakened?"

"Yes Sir."

"It was good of you and your people to work as you did last night."

"Thank you, Sir."

"Mrs. Pembrooke will reward you, I'm sure." He crumpled the newspaper to his waist, "Tell me, Sanjeev," hear anything interesting last night serving all those guests?"

It amused the *Major d'uomo* how much alike the couple was.

"Nothing out of the ordinary, Sir, the guests had a good time."

"Cut the rubbish, Sanjeev, you must have heard something..."

"Nothing negative, Sir, it was a huge success."

"Marvelous. Take an hour off today and relax. The concert is tonight."

"Yes. Thank you, Sir. Anything else you require?"

"Walk the dogs."

"Certainly, Sir."

"Not at all, Sanjeev."

As Sanjeev closed the door to the outside corridor, he heard Pembrooke open the connecting door to his wife's bedroom. His voice resounded and the devoted houseman was mortified. He couldn't mistake the words, they were distinct.

"You Fucking Bitch! Having it off with de Gesu!" and once again one of the rows that had become commonplace in the villa reverberated with guttural talk that would make a tart wince.

The hour was eleven. By six the entire world of Esmeralda and Nigel's would be over

PART TWO

VII

Whitney Jameson, Philanthropist

Sunday afternoon…

Rupert arrived in Capri after the party, requesting a morning sail with Whitney. Idyllic conditions had the two meet by noon at Marina Piccolo where *The Other Woman* was moored. Whitney's crew raised the anchor and the two men relaxed, drinking bloody Marys, basking in the sun. Barbarosa's castle at the summit of the mountain caught their eye as they sailed out to sea.

"Rupert, with you, I don't have to be politically correct. Pleased you asked for this time alone."

"Good time to catch up."

Whitney Jameson smiled, leaning his tall, trim body back on cushions, motioning to his crew to leave them alone. "We Americans are the same renegades that left England on the 'Mayflower,'' he began thinking it wise to speak of history, then move onto important matters once the momentum of conversation began. Whitney was a man of structure even with a friend of long standing. No one appreciated this more than Rupert, his former roommate at Oxford.

"Renegades?" Rupert squinted, eyeing his friend, "Like Barbarossa?"

"Yes, Rupert, renegades…like that Ottoman pirate who made history not the propaganda Americans digest. 'Founding fathers' were upstarts not aristocracy. Had they been, they would have stayed put in England like your ancestors and not come to the new world. Glad you asked to get away from the scene at Villa Pina."

"Thought you wouldn't mind."

"Don't think me a bore, Rupert, but I want to return to my train of thought about upstarts, yuppies of yesterday wanting money, power, importance, greed motivated everything."

Jameson ran freckled fingers through his sandy hair; his face was one of privilege, a sportsman, the embodiment of masculinity. Lined grey eyes showed happiness and sorrow, his engaging smile was unlike his monotone preamble. "These ne're do wells mavericks, rednecks from England set the tone of America. Even that hypocrite Jefferson! God don't get me started on him!"

"Thomas Jefferson? I thought he was the most noble of men."

"Noble? Ha! He might have written in our Constitution, *'all men are created equal,* ' but he owned 175 slaves at the time trading them as lucrative commodity to buy wine, art and luxury goods."

"Are you sure?"

"Positive. Jefferson was committed to slavery, hostile to the 'interior race,' as he called it. He was the worst racist of the 'Founding Fathers.' He had, which is common knowledge, Sally Hemmings as his mistress, fathered a number of children with her, and in his Last Will and Testament, emancipated only five of his slaves that were her relatives, condemned 200 others to the auction block and although her children by Jefferson went free, Hemmings never had that privilege. She died a chantal, he was a racist even when he was six feet under. Jefferson spoke through two sides of his mouth. Some First Father! His criterion was ownership - exactly as it is today: money ruling. All this First Family business is American bullshit."

Rupert listened knowing he had important matters to disclose - the reasons he was late arriving at Villa Pina.

"Lynne's a racist like Jefferson - her mind has gone to flab. She's damned impressed she married me, a member of the Society of Cincinnati,

Son of the American Revolution, all the junk the Blue Book puts after my name. Fact remains, my ancestors, like all American ancestors, were neither noble by birth nor tolerant. Once we planted our feet in America, we stole it from the Indians and we were gentry."

"Whitney you have no delusions of your…"

"Delusions? Ha! I've wised up, Rupert. Not the innocent Whitney of years ago…but I've still got self-interest."

"Always a *but* to life."

"All these spent years, I was stupid to think my money would buy me into the electoral process, have an Ambassador title to some country, not too challenging, mind you…while away my years. No such luck. Others have done it, Rupert…" Whitney looked to the sea, "…but not with a wife like Lynne…"

The two friends knew the answer. No one spoke.

"For years I've contented myself with two things American. Firstly, not that I have to, I make money. Money is God in America. Goldman Sachs should be canonized saints, but they're Jewish!" The two sniggered.

"America is the only country in the world with 'God' imprinted on its money.

"Dealing with money is not what the privileged did or do, Rupert. Money matters were left to Jews like the Rothschilds. The traders, the merchants, ordinary types with quick minds…but I'm different."

"Anti-Semite Whitney?"

"Anti-Semite? Some of my best Jewish friends are anti-Semitic. I respect that religion, as I respect all religion, but then again when I respect a person's religion, race or place in life, whether Jew, Muslim or Hindu - do I need to respect his climb how he reached that pinnacle?…or his opinions that his wife's a raving beauty and his brats extraordinary?"

"If it weren't for the Jews," began Rupert, "and their contribution to the world, art, music, medicine, communications, I could go on and on….the quality of life we know today wouldn't exist. If you forgive me, generous as you are to charities, their philanthropy is without parallel."

"True, Rupert. I respect them for that but it goes against my hide when I see *nouveaux* with attitude, blasted ugly attitude, shoving their way into niches that once were more gentile without them – not all of them, but the majority …seeing their family parade, debasing WASPs, wanting at the same time to be exactly like us. Thinking themselves better, and we, a bunch of fools...and the clubs! with their hypocrisy - a token black, token Jews and people accept this and speak otherwise when in their own milieu."

"We English have an influx of new money - Russian billionaires, Muslims and give the Jewish and Muslim community more democracy in my opinion than anyplace on earth...we tolerate inter-racial marriages better than America, if I may say the USA is rooted in anti-Semitism, fear of Muslims ...racists....but it's changing, has to."

"The English are a breed unto themselves, much like the Jews. Maybe that's why you understand each other. Yet there is an undercurrent of exclusion against blacks, Jews and Muslims throughout Europe."

"To a degree, Whitney, not to the extent in America. It's not the Jew per say or the Arab or the black. It is the company he brings. One on one, like most races, religions, nationalities there are the stars, the dullards, the pushers and cravers. Believe me, everyone is prejudiced...even the English can't stand the English! The 'lower orders.'

"Jews have their own bastions of society where Christians are prohibited entry."

"In my opinion…"

"You English and your opinions include a contempt for Americans and American money. You can pretend but investigate…you'll find something else. The English realize how important their opinion is to America. Not just their opinion, their style, their attitude, Christ even their voice! Nigel could make a fortune if he went to America broadcasting like Alistair Cooke. Ralph Lauren got it right, making millions with his English look-alike school, look British, think Yiddish."

Rupert turned his face to the sun taking in its rays. A conversation with Whitney was always like this, his overview of society feeling pushed aside by more liberal thinkers. The last time they had a discussion of this nature was about the National Rifle Association and how it dominated the electoral process in the States. The cowboy mentality of *"the right to bear arms,"* both believed overblown and misinterpreted by lawmakers whose coffers were lined in gold especially each time they witnessed a mass shooting happening with frequency in the land that had *"the right to the pursuit of happiness."* On the gun issue they agreed. Usually, Rupert, a tolerant man, didn't scrutinize society as Whitney. He was patient and took life hoping for the best.

Rupert's body had once been firm, today he was out of shape yet still retained an English handsomeness with an aristocratic face, deep set brown eyes, high cheekbones and a balanced mouth that contained teeth stained by tea, as is typical in Britain. Rupert moved his robust body slowly feeling pain from an accident at a point-to-point race in Buckinghamshire years ago. He was a bear of a man, six feet tall, at ease on the settee, shoving pillows to support his back and long legs. He wore aged docksiders, no socks. a frayed shirt showing a toned, bronzed chest. Trousers were turned up at the ankle, sailor style, with tattered ends. Tossed over one shoulder was a moth eaten cashmere sweater - all adding to the impression of English 'shabby chic.'

"Brits look to America, Rupert, for their militia to protect them and God knows we have, but the contempt the English have for Americans stuffing their values down the throat, seeing themselves always as the exclusive victors of democracy."

"Are you referring to the Gulf War?"

"Begin with WWII...then, the first Gulf War proved George Bush's undoing. Talk is everywhere Papa Bush, ventriloquist style, prepares his son to follow all the ideas he failed to do. Same footsteps! Seems 9/11 happened 'cause Papa got it wrong the first time. I've a broader sense of the world. We Americans are failing and the populace is brain washed with commercialism, consumption and ideology America is the only country in the world who knows what's best – for EVERYONE! I can't stand that."

"Within twenty years, the aura of America will not be as it is today," replied Rupert.

"Hell our deficit shows the world owns more of us than we own of ourselves! China will crush us with economics, not to mention the Middle East with oil. Interesting how things turn, Rupert, like my kids, cold hearted snobs like their Mother. You can't buy another country's respect, your friends, or the love of your children. You can cram your money down their throat, do everything to control them to gain whatever it is you want…and they, the takers, take, walk away and do everything as they had intended never looking back."

"I agree money doesn't buy affection, loyalty or change of culture. Wasps Whitney, can be the most depressing of people, stoic and taciturn, without the color of life like Italians, Spanish or Jews...monotonous, like English churches - cold, plain, without passion."

The three-mast yacht was in full sail as they glided past Prochida's coastline.

"To a degree America rules the civilized world today, yet only to a degree."

"We are despised for our money, Rupert. In America, those revered are the ones like me who deal in stocks and bonds. Professions Jews made. And, don't get me started on journalists! That Daniels, who always hits below the belt for scandal, syndicating himself, courts those who foot the bill - Jews who control the media. Daniels will scrutinize anything of value to debase it, sell papers and eradicate the betters of this world. To make a living out of the private life of another, Rupert, has to be a sign of low culture. That's what America wants to read and journalists comply. Can you call that a profession?

"British tabloids are no worse."

"Professions of shylocks built America, changed the world. I've devoted the last twenty-five years to being in that arena where gentleman are few, knowing I'm selling my soul, fattening my coffers because that's the American way. I didn't have to achieve position or wealth. I was born into it… Lynne thrives on it. She'd tattle to the press as fast as a mongrel goes after a bitch in heat to see her name in print. The power of being able to ring up anyone – 'network,' the saying goes is easy for me. But Rupert, what comes easy is never appreciated."

Jameson stopped. "In a sea of sharks, I am not strong enough to be a pariah. The intelligencia of this world are artists. Outside of two or three good friends, you can't trust anyone, but artists. Priests forget about. Monks bowing all over the place, not doing a blasted thing except parading in robes are no better. God I love! but forget religion. This brings me to my last point." His face took on a glow, "Artists!...live in their own world, want to be left alone, free thinkers, not concerned with religion, politics or the almighty buck. True artists. I've been doing it wrong, Rupert. I question the direction my life has taken."

"Stop being so hard on yourself. You've got plenty to be proud of! On the board of the Heart Association, Tate, MOMA, the Opera..."

"Permit me to interrupt. Philanthropy pays for things. Let me tell you straight …that's the way it's done in America. One is never appreciated for the second million you give as when you gave the first." Whitney shook his head, cognizant his philanthropic days were coming to an end.

"Whitney, I'm broke. Our circle is dwindling. The British in the last quarter decade revere men in the City emulating America....but they always have. However, incredible as it sounds, in less than forty years, the Chinese economy will reach $123 trillion, three times the economic output of the entire world today. The prestige of military heroes, is finished. Respect's shifted. England is no different from America worshipping money but we are more subtle. Our monarchy exists, so aristocracy exists. European aristocracy lives, but in more cases than few, the titled are impoverished. Dignity, breeding, intellect abound and there will always be class difference. In fact, everywhere. The masses can try to eliminate it but once an individual - any individual succeeds making money they want two things: Fame and Class."

"It's all about education."

"Not all but close. What was once was impossible is now possible because of education. Oxford and Cambridge are no longer exclusively for the elite, same with our clubs." Rupert paused. His friend listened intently, "Finding oneself labeled is stamped upon every single person - Brits are no exception. I daresay class is much like age. It shows. People try to pooh-pooh the idea but one judges immediately what 'class' a person comes from."

"And achievers?"

"Today the young, high achievers maneuver everywhere, altering the course of tradition. Ours is a whet society in England - afraid to stake our ground that some terrorist will blow up St. Paul's - taking in new people who cannot speak rudimentary English. Serfs of the commonwealth have returned calling upon their Mother Country demanding 'rights,' and what arrives is usually not brainy, like the Jews of yore, but colony's kids demanding entitlement – the influx of Muslims and their culture has changed Great Britain. Low fertility rates among natives, massive immigration totting swarms of children has changed England and I dare say, Europe."

"Rupert, I'll say the world."

'With the influx of all this and high tech making the push-button-life of robots rule our every day, the world we knew is over. Queen Victoria never envisioned peons from remote conquests would make our present Queen deformalize the tenor of her voice to sound less regal."

"Whitney rant all you want…to no avail. Pedigreed souls scrape by with the weight of taxes. Mavericks get degrees jostling for positions once denied, stepping over anyone who stands in their way. Thousands seek asylum, get rubber stamped immigration approval, and suck off our welfare system. A new Britain! The country's tiara is changing and I, like you, question is it better?"

"I'm out of place, Rupert. I'll fight to a degree without having to hear the cheer of the crowd if I win, or the moans should I lose. Suffer in silence, like a WASP gentleman. The bounder wants it all, centre stage with all the cheers, pomp, public relations. Regrettably, look what's happened to Nigel....he's become a bounder!"

"Nigel may drink like a fish but never in all the years did I ever see him step out of line, he remains always at least the facade, the perfect English gentleman."

"OK not like journalist Daniels who tries to be well mannered, knowing the importance of weaseling his way into drawing rooms with a brash *bella figura,* emulating socialites to get a 'scoop.' Second agendas - wanting money and the spotlight."

"Balderdash! You can't compare Nigel and Daniels!"

"OK Nigel's straight. But how can I respect someone whose life is so different from mine? I can pretend, but in the case of Nigel I'm disgusted. Call me judgmental! Nigel sings the hymn of public applause, the same as a prize fighter. God he's vainglorious! Wait till this film gets off the ground! What he and 'vanity fair' Esmeralda will do will astound us."

"You're investing in the film aren't you?"

"I'm investing in it, a sure winner, but I'll be a silent investor much to Lynne's annoyance. I refuse to blast my name I'm involved."

"And publicity with Daniels?"

"Daniel's with all his homosexual disguises will poke around me or Lynne for some morsel of gossip for his column. A heterosexual can only go so far with a friendship to a gay, who parade about in "Pride Parades" looking for some snook like me to congratulate them!

"Gays probably believe they can only go so far with heterosexuals,"

"Nigel, sold himself to be in Gianni's kingdom."

"Aren't you lumbering on a bit? Enjoy yourself Whitney. Live and let live! Expand your views…"

"Call me narrow, if you like, but call me honest. A gentleman - whatever his background is - doesn't want to be in the company of a bounder, an ingrate or a phony anymore than a Jew - and believe me I know great Jews, like de Gesu for instance, doesn't wants to be with a Yid. And that Yid surely doesn't want to be in the company of an illiterate black or a weasel like Daniels who would choke if he was forced to sit beside a redneck who can't give him a scoop. I agree with you - we're all prejudiced, He who denies it is a hypocrite."

"What happened at the party last night?"

Whitney slumped back on his deck chair, his mood changed entirely. "You missed quite a shindig. Things have happened to change the entire course of my life, Rupert."

"Much like me, Whitney. Glad to have this time alone."

"Enough on all this pontificating about race, religion, money, homos! I've probably bored you to death."

"Never!" The two clinked glasses. "I just can't stand all the hypocrisy! In all ways I've more respect for artists who don't give a damn and an ill-bred like Levy who tells it like it is, without all this *bella figura* crap the Italians like. A bunch of monkeys, the Italians! Levy's honest. He goes through the motions of climbing the ladder without disguises. His act is in the open, loves the movie business and isn't tainted trying to be someone he's not."

"And when he gets what he wants?"

"So help him! I hope he retains that crude honesty. I hope he doesn't try to be what he's not."

"Much of what you say I agree with in part."

"Part? You English are cocksure." Jameson grinned at his loyal friend enjoying sparring. "An American with an English will always feel inferiority. Maybe it's the language, maybe it is your reserve where we're candid. We can become accustomed to each other's lifestyle but it takes an eternity to move into foreign territory and feel comfortable. "

"So what's happened?"

"I'm moving into foreign territory. I've fallen in love with an artist! She's English and don't capsize the boat…she's Jewish! And you called me an anti-Semite!"

"Whitney, I'm overwhelmed. Anyone I know?

"Overwhelmed? Me too! It's Olympia! Rupert, I finally had the courage to look myself square in the face and stop being afraid I'm too old. I'm going to stop being an American hen-pecked nerd whose balls have been busted. Frig Lynne when I announce I want a divorce! She'll go ape shit exposing this to the press."

"No offence, I never took to Lynne...but....Olympia's dynamite!"

"If you - with all your manners couldn't cotton to her, imagine the others! And me - alienated from my kids because their Mother - who should stop shopping and join AA, puts her mighty climb up the social ladder before them…showering reproaches to us all while declaring she's always and forever right!"

"What news...but isn't Olympia engaged to that Korean?"

"Ton Won? Don't give him a second thought. After my initial shock of finding myself alive again, in the last twenty-four hours, all illusions about my wife are erased. The strain on my face that I've had for years has been eliminated too." Jameson stood and stretched to the heavens. "My future is going to present a whole new set of ideas, Rupert, I'm not going to sit back anymore with the god damned American idea of staying in a country I don't agree with, in a toxic marriage without love, courting the wrong people, for the wrong reasons - remaining in a life that's wrong with the wrong wife!"

"Well, that's a start!," Rupert beamed as his friend resumed his relaxed position on the cruise.

"Rupert thanks for letting me get all this off my chest…you're the first to know. I'm ready to sign a fucking check made out to Mrs. Lynne Whitney for $40 million and get her out of my life!" He smiled, feeling the weight of the world removed.

"What's with you? Never married! Am I mistaken or did you sign the Declaration of Independence?" He laughed at his jab. "Why weren't you here Thursday?"

"I was detained because of a surprise meeting. There's something important to speak about. It concerns Nigel and Esmeralda and the reason I didn't make the dinner dance."

Jameson's attention sharpened hearing the change in the tone of Rupert's voice, seeing his smile vanish. "By the way, Whitney, if love is contagious, I'm in love too!"

"God Damn! What the hell have you been waiting for? This calls for a drink! Throw the bloody Marys overboard, let's open champagne!"

Whitney motioned the crew as the boat dropped anchor off the coast of Procida, the sleepy island close to Capri. It would be an unforgettable lunch aboard the private vessel moored where no one could eavesdrop, a time that would change the course of their sail, their lives and the lives of others.

"About the matter of the heart I've been gun shy too many years, waiting for 'the right thing,' and at the same time avoiding it." Rupert looked away downing his drink. "Love's a subject that always left me tongue-tied. You're a philanthropist, Whitney, and in another way I am too," began Rupert. "People are in your debt when you give. No matter how you give, open handedness without an agenda doesn't exist."

"Hell you're right. Even Mother Theresa expects!"

"Whitney, even now, I'm in Gianni's debt. He rescued me and that's my business but knowing that, I have an obligation to him, to his family and can't stand back seeing injustice. If I don't do what I must - because of what I've learned...not attending the "*Mezza Luna* Dinner Dance..."

"This sounds serious...."

"It is. I need you as my confidant because of what I've learned ."

"Whatever you need, whatever it is…I'm with you."

"You speak of money. This matter is of utmost urgency. It has nothing to do with *your* money. It has everything to do with Gianni's."

"Your voice sounds grave."

"It is." Rupert began to recount what had happened and where he'd been since last Thursday when he was to convene at the Naples train station, meet Naomi and come to Capri.

He began methodically with the facts. It was four thirty, the sun was beginning to make its descent.

"Esmeralda will not go quietly."

"Nor is Nigel."

"You're telling me? Best I text the old chums, inviting them to a private sail, fill them in on what you've told me."

Hours later after their swim, never wishing to interrogate his respected friend as to his love interest, Whitney found his curiosity peaked. "We've shared a lot today, my good friend, but you haven't told me who's the lucky woman."

"I've loved her for years, Whitney. I'm in love with Serena Zianni."

"Gianni's sister! My God! What a shock! This calls for a celebration." Whitney embraced Rupert bear hug style. The startled Italian crew couldn't understand the two *Inglese,* usually they were cold fish. Joyously content, the two friends lingered at sea, ignoring the roll of the waves, not wanting to race back for the Sunday concert that Esmeralda programmed for the evening.

VIII

Dame Naomi Griffin, Poet Laureate

Simultaneously, Sunday afternoon…

The music conservatory on the northern ridge of Villa Pina was reached by a serpentine path edged with oleander and moss coloring the terraced garden. Braided trunks of fichus marked the walk boasting an arboretum's foliage to cool the ambler. This afternoon, the clear sky was luminous forecasting tonight's weather would be magnificent but more important, was the performer, Oleg Kurezmakoff, the brilliant virtuoso from Russia, (acclaimed at the Rachmaninoff Piano Competition in St. Petersburg by Evgeny Kissin and music critics) would reproduce the concert millions heard on air waves throughout the civilized world. Tonight he'd include French composer Debussy's preludes from the first book, No.5 *"Les collines d'Anacapri."* Naomi was to recite poems, entertaining one hundred guests. A reception would follow in the marquee.

As Naomi approached the white stucco conservatory, reminiscent of a villa from Pompeii, millions of notes claimed her ear. Kurezmakoff was practicing; the young genius would be disturbed by her presence. No need to intrude, introduce herself and interrupt him until Oleg took a break. Interspersed in the garden were ruins from the time of the Romans and bronze statues of the Renaissance. All this Gianni shown her the first time she visited Villa Pina. They were students then, mutual friends of

Nigel's. It was a glorious time, and much like this, the sun was making its descent. Soon the flaming palette of red would burst forth the Capresi sky signaling the day had completed its cycle.

Naomi eyed Brian Korthorpe watching her from the gazebo below. He caught her eye and looked away, reading.

Brian didn't have the means to invest in a film, nor was he interested preferring classical theatre, but when Nigel introduced him as "the genius in our midst" expanding the remark "one feels insignificant in his company." "Please Nigel," Naomi heard Brian reply, "I'm no 'genius' and no one is insignificant. I'm still adventurous. In the end, love will conquer."

"Oh you've gone romantic on me," choked Nigel.

"My finest hour is yet to come. When it does, I'll be in full bloom." Gales of laughter came from Nigel; then Brian asked to escort Naomi to dinner.

"Life begins at seventy-five!" he said extending his arm. "We've met again."

He had aged, certainly, like she, and the photo she cherished did not resemble the man she saw tonight, a little stooped, wrinkles around his eyes, the neck withered, his hair completely white. How she respected him and his life's work Addressing problems of the elderly, publishing papers for grants to continue scientific research on dementia linked with Alzheimer's. Esmeralda had cut Brian's designated funds yet Brian held Esmeralda no grudge. He appreciated what they'd accomplished and was not a man to force anyone.

It was a pity when Naomi's last conversation with Gianni was how keen he was to erase "senior moments" from life. How many times had she'd caught herself unable to find a word, the title of a movie or book thinking she might be giving way to Alzheimer's. Or, enter a room looking for something forgetting why - then her mind raced back to Brian and his devotion to this work and suddenly, from no where, the name she couldn't recall would spring to her lips…or like magic, she'd instantly remember what she wanted to do - the mind going in and out rarely - yet although she wasn't victim to the dread disease, she, along with all her friends over sixty, worried if they would fall prey to losing the plot. Her Father broke her heart when he proclaimed, "I have the name of that disease when one loses one's mind. What's it called?" It struck her hard, as hard as when her mentor, Iris Murdoch, died not remembering anything having given thousands of thoughts to thousands of people and departed for paradise with the void of her own blank mind.

Thus when Brian penned his last book on neuroscience and consciousness, "The Quest to Eliminate Alzheimer's," (achieving the best seller list internationally), Brian's cognitive findings astonished the medical profession, dons at universities, scientist and an audience who understood his evaluation of the evolution of neuron development from the largest brain on record, that of Oliver Cromwell's neural tissue to Tom Thumb's. He unraveled his thesis: Size is not indicative to intelligence of physical flaws of Brain Development, correlating physical structure with personality. The Rockefeller Foundation dilated his findings on tobacco related hypothesis to lend a cure to Alzheimer's and his innovation for 'brain chips,' seemed revolutionary.

What a tragedy Gianni died suddenly and Brian's work halted not having funds necessary to complete what he foresaw. Gianni never would have wanted this, but what good would it do to tell Nigel, and for him to ride herd on Esmeralda? From what Naomi knew Nigel was like a dog on a lead, with a stipend...then again there are as many different types of marriage as there are people.

She glanced to Brian again, his head was turned towards his book. I remember we met at the dinner given in his honor Gianni had at Spenser House. He had won the humanitarian award for neuro-scientific research. We both were married, our spouses reneged on the invitation. There we were in a crowd of three hundred learned individuals, he was called to the podium to accept his well-deserved honor, a round of applause followed, the duration of which was longer than he'd expected. His speech struck me uniquely. His voice undressed me. His tone and diction faultless. He spoke of science and I thought how I would love to feel his body close to mine.

My marriage had been so unhappy, foolishly I never strayed. I was a woman of forty with a sudden lust for a scientist that didn't know if I were dead or alive, in a room of strangers, attending a dinner at the request of a treasured friend. As Brian's words echoed through the microphone, I was caught by the brilliance of his thoughts, his life's work and lack of vanity.

Before me was a self-effacing man dedicated to science, adroit beyond measure, twenty years my senior, tall and dignified with a determined, intelligent face who wore oversized clothes as a scholar. I was erotically moved to want his touch. This force was compelling, at one point, his speech dissolved in thin air and I was drawn to the man, not the scientist.

At the close of the dinner, I remember walking in his direction to congratulate him and depart. All went well until he looked up and our eyes met. There was a link to our first glance "Do you have to leave?" he asked.

Within a fortnight we were lovers.

Married people cheating on spouses was not the future we wanted. The force between us was unspoken. We moved in the direction of that force, there was no sin. I knew we would be together somewhere, sometime, somehow and used the word forever believing it fantasy. Now here we are, with a chance to reunite.

His lovemaking last night had not changed. He was hungry, a man on fire who was in love and selfish. In the past on two occasions only he spoke of his emotions, then buried them away never wanting to open the subject again. I recall how I wanted his love and reassurance, petting his naked body to rouse him, anticipating the hour to depart from one another, always with the fear of our spouse's questions to be answered should our trysts be revealed. He lay fast asleep, satiated and safe. I kissed him to speak of my needs and desire. In a stupor like a baby, he'd wrap me in his arms, my breasts beat close to his chest. I turned wanting, expectantly, and nothing but a sweet nuzzle would happen. He'd return to sleep, satiated, wake a bit later, thrust his sex inside and the hour would come to part.

How different our needs - for him physical desire held prominence without having to endure the longing to be reassured. Towards the end of our love story, I wanted another rendezvous to speak of this but he remained aloof. To open a closed corridor of his deep emotions was too painful. Sex was easier. Stinging letters were exchanged. Did he understand anything about me? Then silence. Terrible silence.

Better he never knew all the details of my bankruptcy. Whatever he read was stilted in the press with Jake MacKenzie's name and mine splashed all over the papers. I needed Brian so much then but I was so ashamed. To go to a man needy is when they turn away. I'd pushed him aside trying to keep the remnants of my marriage only to learn later Jake had been with innumerable squalid women, squandered so much of my inheritance, mortgaged our house in London and the family home in Gloucestershire. Jake had an magnanimous personality for everyone except his family, Elizabeth and me. We were the ones crucified as he manipulated stocks and insurance portfolios to pay off debts, robbing one to pay the other, wire fraud, his firm closed with all his clients jumping ship, dubious dealings with whispers about a Ponzi scheme and money laundering, thinking he could get away with it. And then his one lie stung when he was called before the Financial Securities Commission. The avalanche followed, the accusations denied, the court, the journalists, the invasion of privacy, the bank calling in notes, the whores calling in blackmail, the threats of fathering children by these women, the real estate vultures yanking my property from under my feet, the Sheriff literally at the door, pounding for entry to demand taxes, the auctioning of Dartworth family possessions, our name tarnished in the backlash of his deeds, the scoundrel - my husband, Jake, fibbing his way through the entire catastrophe!

What followed was the divorce when everything burst and I couldn't bear it any longer. Why had I waited to be sent to slaughter before eliminating Jake MacKenzie from my life? What regret that I have lost my way in life…ruined my life to this degree.

Gianni was there without once asking if I needed funds but giving with his enormous generosity. I survived because of him. It wasn't courage, it was because of the unspoken benevolence of Gianni Zianni and the love of my daughter whom I managed to keep in school because of Gianni paying all fees - and to have some assemblance of what her life was meant to be.

Gianni underwrote Elizabeth's education from fourteen to his death. And then, like a miracle poems began to spring to life - just as Jake was beginning a prison sentence. All England held a certain pity for me and respect. I never once gave into smut of an interview to add another iron to the fire the tabloids blasted to ruin my reputation linking it with Jake's evil deeds and the good name he'd dismantled.

When the *Literary Review* spoke of my work, when the Queen penned her invitation to visit Buckingham Palace and speak about my poetry, it was something I never expected. Since the debacle of Jake, thanks to Gianni, I managed to open the house in Gloucestershire to the public, keeping it in Dartworth's hands. Daddy would have been turning in his grave otherwise. Elizabeth would never have the chance to be in the circles that are hers by birthright if there wasn't the setting of Dartworth Hall. Amusing if people knew a dozen rooms were vacant of furnishings; Christie's auctioned the lot. *Bella figura.* What does it matter? Finances are my only problem. Elizabeth and I survived our struggle. She's a credit to me, the Dartworth name and now to be here with Brian...

Taking his eyes from his book, he spied her once again this time her head was turned, looking to the sky above. 'How beautiful she is! I should tell her. She'd want to hear me confess what I've hidden for years: my life was meaningless until I met her. How often I've thought this. Naomi understands me better than anyone. I've never been able to verbalize a truth of this nature, difficult to express my emotions.... so many years ago when, to my disbelief, my heart blurted "I love you!" That one and only time, and I said it again, like an echo, immediately thereafter, hearing myself, knowing I finally spoke the truth. I gave vent to what I'd concealed. It sprang from my soul, without my wretched controlling brain thinking about it. It shocked us both. I bolted leaving her on the doorstop, not knowing what this truth would produce. I was never taught to speak of feelings. How many times have I wanted to tell her things too deep within me? How many times have I been too shy?... or better - have I been too selfish?

He reminisced about those daring years when both escaped stale marriages to yield to feelings. Their kind didn't do this. They were afraid and yet fear gave passionate fire to the thrill of adulterous love. Lying together, bodies yielding as one - separated because of marriage to another, only to have the want to stay together forever. Theirs was a perfect tryst until emotions flared. Emotions and the upshot of their spouses' dramas convulsed.

Maybe now I should let her know what those memories meant. I've been trained to be on guard against the very emotions I need.

So this is how we came to this point. Too many years have gone by, twelve frosty years. We never met again to link with the love we knew. What blasted fools! Years slipped away, talk became stilled. Time, I thought, would resolve everything. Time has its own way of orchestrating life. With my inadequacy to express feelings, I believed I should expect nothing more. She, reserved as I, was timid to speak of her fears. It was the man's place to return or I'd call her aggressive. Pride, all hideous pride!

How could I pretend to be able to speak as a lover? Those were words in the theatre, literature – for Latins. To develop the dialog was foreign. I'm a scientist after all. Seeing her, it's clear, nothing changed. She's the only woman who's meant anything throughout my life and to be alone without her is a result of my inadequacy and pride.

Over the years, he convinced himself it was better to be alone. She had her own tormented life with a husband he wished dead. What he read in the media was horrendous. That did not stop his desirous heart from aching. In time, he let fear instead of love rule his actions. Long after his wife died and Naomi divorced, he believed his years of existence were to glide into his seventies then perhaps his eighties - pretending he was fulfilled with his work and life as it was. He tended his garden, met with peers putting on a brave front, published papers, sprouting one story or concept or another, going to a stream of parties as an 'extra man,' believing his obituary close at hand, rewrote his Last Will and Testament ten times, went to his club, ignorant to the want of her heart and the need of his own.

He accepted the cruel choice he'd made calling it 'Fate' living in denial, frozen in his tracks. Courage was a virtue he no longer contained. Is that what age does, he'd question. The fear of rejection overruled any thought of a reunion. It was only a surprise opportunity to reclaim love, this September at Villa Pina....Esmeralda had given him the chance....it was up to him to see what he and Naomi might contain.

His heart was suddenly carefree and never would he question why Naomi went away, not to return or recoil in fear. This chance was too good. Something wonderful was happening and this time, full of emotion he knew, I don't want to ruin it.

Naomi lingered listening to Liszt remembering every detail of last evening. Brian, moderately abstemious, made a toast to me as we were leaving the dining room to view the film. His eyes twinkled, "May I have the honor to be beside you this evening and ask for the first dance?" The smile I returned was my answer.

After the dancing had stopped, fireworks ignited and guests withdrew for the evening. There we were suddenly alone, the look in his eyes signaled something I thought dormant. Words were not exchanged yet when he accompanied me to my room, love sprang to passionate kisses and our fingers touched every part of each other.

In frenetic foreplay, something I believed was over and done with in my life, how jubilant! I remembered subtle touches that aroused him years ago as my body went afire with passion. Brian swelled with the slightest touch of my body near. It was as if he'd waited for me an eternity to return.

Erotic kisses descended all over my body. Exchanging one embrace for another, passion reached explosive pitch when frantic to be joined, we stripped naked. His arms had not lost their strength when he lifted me to bed. All his want was to penetrate me, rapidly, instantly, immediately. Primal passion flared, his engorged penis inside me without a moment to pause was his alone, fucking me - not understanding he was rupturing my tissues, as if I were a virgin. I screamed. He put his hand over my mouth, afraid we'd disturb the Villa - and continued hell bent to his imminent need, to explode sizzling sperm within me to satiate himself or was it to be sure he'd sustain potency?

I don't recall kisses. I bit my lip holding back a scream as he, panting, thrust his juices again and again into me. My legs were raised above my head to make his entry easier as he tore at me. He'd not prepared me with foreplay. It was a rape, without emotion; my vagina too dry for pleasure. Too many years without sex! Waiting for him all those years - and now this, a sexual disaster!

Never did he speak of our years apart, or his desire. All that consumed him was hunger. Perhaps, a dozen years of anger sprung from him. I would be lying if I said it was wonderful. Nothing was as before when an orgasm put me on some delirious plateau - where I remained until our next rendezvous. This felt accelerated, inadequate and what was worse he continued like a savage. He had to know my pain, yet no apology was forthcoming. I'm completely disillusioned. Years of waiting for this one man...Korthorpe! He's a beast!...but I crave that beast.

When his orgasm came he was overwhelmed with it - thrilled he had satiated his desire. A man of certain age receives his own accolade when he performs outwitting himself. Macho intact, he felt glory. "You could kill me," is all he uttered when finished. His entire body that attacked me, and once exalted me...all those years when sexual unity had been supreme – all the years of waiting and dreaming to renew our love, were the past.

He lie beside me, a limp, sweaty mass of flesh, exhausted. How I remained so close...dazed, unsatisfied, hearing his heavy breathing, without any way to reach him, I don't know. Where was love? Tenderness? There was not a word from him whatsoever. Something made him eventually rouse from his narcissist slumber, he sensed me near, held me briefly letting sleep take him once more. Words didn't exist. Or a kiss. He was in his own world, asleep within minutes, snoring. Hideous snoring filled the room!

What I thought would be splendor was the act of an animal. The nature of men is so unlike women, here was a prime example. This sex business! We mortals, complicate things. Before the first light of morning he alighted from the bed without any touch or words of endearment and went to his room, closing my door as if I didn't exist.

He hadn't changed. He was a genius for scientific theory but his deficiency of warmth was imbedded in his character.

Age had attacked me everywhere!

Why does he look at me like that from the lower garden? Is he as disillusioned as I am? What a waste of years!

How can one guess what is on a lover's mind? Am I not allowed to know? To ask? Is it his secret to keep and for me to keep mine? What fools we've been! I've made a horrible mistake coming, not understanding this could happen. Everything is ruined. I want him to be with me now and never let him go! My body betrayed me. I feel like a *putana* and act like a librarian! …I'm a sexual disappointment! The damned sly body wins in the end tormenting us.

"I will not go without a roar!" When I raised myself from the battleground of a bed that had seen wild, passionate, terrible action my first thought was: I don't want a finale like this, we can rekindle youth that we lost somewhere in the tedium of life.

Ablaze with pain from Brian, I'm not too old to change, dilute him until he cries in ecstasy and rants "I'M IN LOVE WITH YOU!" Let him drown in his emotional blockage with my wild caress. He can change too...words can flower...the fuel - the flame - the mystique.....

In every relationship there is the sadist and the masochist. The one who wins in the end is the optimist. My eyes met my reflection in the mirror all day, I've smiled and laughed aloud as a woman for the first time in twelve years. "Fuck it! I will seduce him and the next time be the woman he wants, the woman I was, the woman I am!"

All these thoughts flooded back in the stillness of the garden as Kurezmakoff finalized the last notes of Liszt's Hungarian Rhapsody. Later Naomi found courage to speak to Doctor Samir seeking his advice as he was going for a swim. "Nothing to worry about, Naomi. Your mucosa has dried. Use this cream," he said professionally taking a prescription pad from his vest pocket penning something she couldn't understand.

"Don't worry dear friend, it's easy to remedy. The pharmacy in Capri will fill this." His sweet face smiled full of understanding.

"Imagine what it is to be trapped in this body of mine."

"You aren't trapped, just out of practice." He stroked her shoulder and walked towards the pool. "Be foxy," Samir winked and moved quickly along.

"I will change," thought Naomi. "Be like men. Be randy. I've let too many years pass! Stupid wrench, living like a recluse. All the poetry in the world cannot compare to one great climax. Now I'm thinking like a slut. In some ways I am. Loose women are smarter about the basics of life than some high faluten' poet.

Naomi greeted Kurezmakoff and in her most elegant voice began reciting two of her poems that she would dedicate this evening. One to her daughter, Elizabeth, the other to Brian Korthorpe.

IX

The Movie Mogul and his Disciples

Simultaneously, Sunday afternoon…

"Sorry to keep ya waitin," Mark Levy burst into the projection room flatfooted, fidgeting with his oversize Rolex. Journalist Daniels was conferring with Stella Gregotti on the script.

"Had somethin' urgent to tend to." His smile gave him away. No man grins like that unless he's been tasting Hungarian caviar, thought Stella and Daniels. His attention to Zofra Zofany had not gone unnoticed.

Today his Marcel wave was darker without a trace of grey, slicked with pomade sending forth the aroma of Vitalis. His abundant arched brows were the exact hue of his small rodent eyes that dominated attention. Levy prided himself that his eyes didn't miss a thing, although wrinkled from his puffy face that twitched now and again.

After fifty, the corners of his abundant mouth gave shape to a meaty opening composed in a downward horseshoe design that set off "Hollywood teeth." Whatever costume he wore, his shoes were always the wrong shade. Levy studied too many Italian movies and believed it smart to put beige shoes with dark blue or black trousers. The beige was the color of Dijon mustard, too yellow for 'a gentleman of style' dressed entirely in Armani black. Daniels wondered if Armani made sizes that large.

"Mark, you have a masterpiece!" began Daniels. "I'm bowled over! ESCAPADES will out score anything ever produced in Hollywood. You've got to give me first option on the scoop!"

"Daniels thanks! Glad you liked our flick." He winked at Stella. "Dis Stella of ours has given us an original. No remake crap with legal reasons to halt what Mark Levy and the world wants! You can quote me on this. Des is a press conference, right…?"

He pulled a long cigar from his jacket pocket, licking the tip slowly; his mind wandered elsewhere for the moment, then he caught himself, adding, "No law suits on this one, straight from that brain of Stella's! Fabulous imagination. Talent like your's Stella, …windin' a story, knock out, it's like like what I wanna say, blockbusta stuff." He lit his Monte Cristo inhaling deeply. "En she gave everyone a voice, a violent voice, sly voice, anguished, mockin' voice, then she puts up a smoke screen," a bellow of smoke was released, he waved it with his beefy hand, "ya know like Hitchcock, she knocks the hell outaya with the dialog…en…Marco his film…start to finish…..what a star!....by the way, where the hell is Marco?"

"Monty interviewed him this morning Mark. He'll catch us later."

"Being photographed on Viscounti's amphibious plane for VANITY FAIR." Said Daniels. "We've got it, might as well use it."

"Nicky didn't mind." Added Stella.

"Mind? Are you serious? Nicky's in on the take. Told me last night, nice surprise, $10 million Euro. Smart like a Jewish boy, that's Nicky… you got dat from the horse's mouth Daniels…."

"So now tell me…"

"Ya wanna talk movies…?" Levy began tapping his fingers on the table anxiously.

"Mark, I…"

"Monty, let me tell ya' dere's no business like the movie business, if I can coin a phrase, making 'a film to rememba', yeah, that's what I wanted and Stella came along with this screenplay. It knocked me over. Punch! Pow! Right in the face." He gesticulated to add to his remark. "The dummies who will pay to see this film, you know what I wan em to do? Those zombies who can't tell one movie from anoder? ESCAPADES...... yeah great title, donya think? ESCAPADES is gonna entertain the pants off dem, and let them think about the whole *schmere* when they exit the theatre...I'm tellin' ya' its gonna be like this, I donhavta do publicity on dis one...wurd of mouth is gonna sell this movie, the critics will piss in their pants, b'Jesus!...the Censors are gonna love it, 16+ dat's it! En the best part it's the kinda film like Hitchcock used to make: dere gonna come back en see it twice."

"Pardon us," Jarvis Engleton's weedy voice was heard at the doorway. "Sorry to disturb everyone but I just wanted to tell Monty that Elizabeth and I are going down to the *piazzetta*."

"Wait a minute. You got Elizabeth with ya?" called Levy.

"Yes, I do, Mr. Levy."

"Elizabeth commere for a minute, sweetheart"

The trio watched as the bashful English student approached the group. Levy fingered his large long gold link chain around his neck that accented his double chin. "Elizabeth I'm gonna talk to ya Mother. I thinkya should have a screen test. I don tell this to everyone, right Stella?" He looked over to the screenwriter. "Now ya studin' art ya told me last night, en I know I'm a rough diamond but Elizabeth, you're the real McCoy...you've gotta have one hell of a pretty face, another Grace Kelly - betta in my estimation den her and forget that puss of Paltrow's"

"Thank you Mr. Levy." Elizabeth looked down shyly.

"Don't mention it. Hold ya chin up, Elizabeth en don be shy around me, we're friends of Esmeralda en Nigel, remember dat. Tellya Motha if you're interested. I don't do this everyday. She can come to Hollywood to be with ya. I think I see somethin' in ya face. Whatdoyou think Stella?"

"Yes, Elizabeth, your beauty is clear, fresh." The chic screenwriter was the essence of everything Mark Levy was not.

"Thank you Contessa Gregotti."

"Call me Stella like everyone else."

"Thank you Stella. We're going to Mass now. It begins at 1:30, the last one today we can't be late...afterwards I want to take Mr.Engleton to the Carthusian monastery. Imagine," she said enthralled by history, "after the pestilence, by Catholic law, everyone who died had all the possessions revert to the monastery. That was 1656..."

Monty Daniels stood by mute, completely bewildered. Jarvis was an atheist. Stella's eyes met Elizabeth's briefly. Childless Stella remembered it was her choice not to conceive. Marco had begged her to have a baby. Seeing Elizabeth again she wondered if she'd made the right decision.

"Say a prayer for me Sweetheart, Stella en Daniels" Levy winked, "... en don forget da screen-test Elizabeth."

Elizabeth, leaving with Jarvis, looked back and smiled, "Thank you," she didn't want to tell anyone except her Mother the last thing she'd ever want would be a screen test. Those women always went the wrong way, like Daddy.

She and Jarvis hurried down a corkscrew path to meet the driver who would take them to the *piazza* for Mass; thoughts were of her future. I have my art and the chance to be a friend to Prince William and Prince Harry. What an honor to have either of these opportunities blossom. I'd be so proud! This weekend has been exciting, even the attention of the older man, Nicky, nice but much too old for me. I hope we make the *piazzetta* in time for Mass. Her thoughts were full of her ideas for her future. Seventeen years between me and Nicky, that's a lifetime! Oh I would never want that! It's good to see Mother happy and all these people but I can't wait to return to England. The odd pair rushed to meet the fringed-top limo and go to the centre of Capri.

Jarvis, on the other hand, had different thoughts. What am I doing going to Mass with this girl, what's a hoot! Well at least they'll read the New Testament. The Apostles had it right, so much easier to understand than the overwritten Old Testament. Elizabeth has class, more than I can say for hypochondriac Lynne Jameson! They both think I'm straight. Elizabeth is innocent, like a niece, the other, a nag, hasn't left me alone since we met, always talking about her antiques, her contemporary art, her affiliation with the Met, but this Mass thing. Well, it's killing time. Elizabeth tells me there are some interesting paintings in the crypt, she has knowledge of art, thank God for that. Yes, a little time away from Daniels whose 'cell date' is finished, devoting all his time to Levy and that A-sexual Princess who won't give anyone the time of day. This has turned into one miserable holiday!

He scampered along to keep up with Elizabeth, thinking I can't see how I can work anyone to my advantage except that cow, Lynne, an excellent social source, taking her to things she says Whitney never wants to go to in New York. At least she understands Louis XV from Louis XVI, that's more than I can say for most. But that rouge and lousy highlight job. "I can't begin to believya," she said clutching that damned Bible, "that ya Faberge collection is anything close to my pieces from Russie's at Sherry's." What a snob, contaminated with hate for her husband! He's not bad but of course he's straight as they come.

Levy turned to Stella, "Sweet kid. Ya don find dat kind everyday. Da face is good…the babes in L.A. lost it…look like a bunch of Stepford wives…dumb broads, a bunch of silicone mannequins, fixed smiles, botox'd, lookin' and the lips! Inflated fish."

"What about your gorgeous female lead, Antonia Ivani?" Asked Monty Daniels.

"Stella here will tell ya'…perfect match with Marco…donya think?"

"We'd been casting for months without any luck. Nureyev was having a ballet recital on the Galli Islands, Marco and I were invited. (Mark reveled in her telling the story.) "We walked into his conservatory, there she was in his troupe. A diamond. It was all unbelievable! I spoke to her, never believing she could act."

"Daniels wait till ya hear..." he puffed his cigar, thrilled. "Vittorio Gassman, was ha Godfather. Antonia's acted a littl' in Rome but ha ballet's ha passion."

"Wonderful story," said Daniels jotting down everything.

"That's how we found her, lovely discovery, lovely story although it took convincing to have her leave ballet for film work," noted Stella liting a cigarette, passing the lighter to Mark Levy whose cigar had gone out. "The screen test confirmed her face was outstanding on a wide screen. Everything fell into place from there."

"Why isn't she here at Villa Pina?"

"Dis is off the record, OK?" Levy re-lit his cigar flooding the room with smoke.

"Sure. You'll have right of copy when I hammer out the story," assured Daniels.

"Good. Dat's the way to keep it, then you get your scoop and we're gonna give you a big one, Daniels. The Pembrooke's didn't do this for me for nothin' …When Esmeralda chose you as de only journalist, let me tell ya, we're talkin' exclusive."

"I appreciate that," said Daniels, pen in hand waiting. "So Antonia?" "She's doin' a ten-page spread with VOGUE celebratin' Valentino's fame …did all da clothes wid us for ESCAPADES en on location where we shot the film in outsida Rome in his house on Appia Anika…..she'll be here tanite' wid him for sure if those damned fools don't screw up the schedule. Publicists! Dey screw up the schedules den da film comes in over budget…."

"What about Antonia and the talk about her and the first Director T.J. Ferrante? They say he and she…"

"I don wantya to print anytin' about dat...so promise me, dis is between us, understand?"

"I'm with you, Mark."

"Ferrante couldn't keep his hands off ha. It was so hot en this innocent Antonia, well, let me put it this way, Ferrante was outta line. We couldhav had harmony but he was hungry. Saw Antonia en I wasn't about to lose the picture fa him. It was a time bomb, tough shoot with heated arguments every frigin' day on the set, typical with an ego like Ferrante."

He puffed his cigar, motioning Daniels to come forward for a secret. "Ferrante's into some kinda mid-life crisis, so whattif he won an Oscar two years ago? I called it as I saw it. He'd be hanging around Antonia's trailer yet if I hadn't stepped in. He was leadin' her en I didn't like where it was goin'. He didn't learn the cardinal rule."

"Cardinal rule? What's that?" questioned Daniels eagerly.

"A.P.L ...Always Please Levy.....I can't take all the credit, but in de end, the whole crew was fired up. Lightin' people, camera crew, Marco, the whole shebang en Stella too. Dis is the moment da Producer steps in and calls da shots. "Ferrante," I told him "Cut it out," he didn't listen, so I told him nice like a second time, a therd, en he thought he was some Messiah," Levy extinguished his cigar. "Then I canned him and pulled in the big gun from London, Brigham. We swept the carpet clean. No scandal not the Levy style ....So you got your scoop. Frig Ferante."

"Tell me about the endorsements."

"You wanna talk endorsements? *60 Minutes*? Int'rnet? Ralph Lauren? HBO? DVD? Valentino? Bulllgari? Call my publicist, Joey Johnson at ICI. Knows it all, speaks for me but shove it past my lawyer so you don't libel me, OK Daniels?

"Right."

"From the minute Brigham stepped in, de whole red carpet treatment started with harmony, yeah I'm a guy who likes harmony. We have Stella and her top script, and a babe like Stella you don't fool with de rewrites. She listens to me en Brigham - en even Marco and once to Antonia. Stella's a honey not cauz she's sittin' here, she knows what it takes, knows the craft, da language."

Levy was in awe of Stella, whom he viewed as an intellectual genius, and she intended to keep it that way - to control him as best she could. "Stella knows howda listen en then go forward. She's gotta have the speech perfect, even without wurds, she holds back the wurds, wurds what every otha writer wantsta stuff down ya throat, she keeps a silence." Levy put his 'index finger to his mouth, "'shhhhsh' ...." He wished to add drama of his next phrase. "Tell me, what screenwriter writes silence? Dats genius!" He gave the thumbs up sign.

"Stella's got a callin' for dis stuff. We gotta front runner, Number One en Marco as best actor for the Golden Globe already. Dis is not like the Oscar, but what the hell, it'll be a rehearsal, our foot in da door, at da Globes, chance for everyone when dey see what we've done. We've got one hell of talent ridding on dis one, one hell of a film."

Levy droned on, Daniels was patient to listen. He was getting the slant he wanted, maybe he'd get lucky with something jucier.

"Now look at last night, a trailer shot with some footage what did we get? Standin' ovation. That's nothin' wait until the finale…there'll be flowers, gifts en everyone will get drunk. We've got a deal set up with Google to knock the socks off everyone en arounda wurld, plus Facebook's negotiatin' like quick fire, dat's me inovatin' and once we get the Globe, en Daniels, it's the cuttin' room…don't be *mashuga* on me, cauz at the end the cuttin' room can killya. Da way I wanna edit dis, and Stella will be dere beside me, believe me, we'll get 8 Golden Globes…a sure thing, we'll sit and wait for the Oscar. After dhat, take if from me, Marco and Stella will have da two damned statues, en maybe Bigham en I'll have the biggie Oscar sittin in my house en everyone's on easy street." He reached for another cigar in his pocket. "I tell ya Daniels…watch this ESCAPADES" he began pointing his index finger aggressively at Daniel's face, "watch de distribution, the Command Performance with the Queen en watch it do dis: out run every film eva on the gross. I'm telling ya…."

"Fabulous! Mark. Truly. To give this story I'm doing a personal slant, Mark…tell me what do you drive? Where do you live? You're dream present…what would it be?

"When you come to L.A., you'll be my guest…when ya see my house, 55,000 square feet of house en I live dere up in the hills near da Getty Museum…believe me, a showcase, not like dis Villa Pina, but it ain't bad. Guaranteed. I gatta chauffeur, 'natch but a big guy like me? Whatdaya think I love? The Porsche Carrera GT and Ferrari 7430. Yeah…dream cars…like I want Julia Roberts in da front seat." He puffed on his cigar and laughed at his joke.

"Da best present es da Oscar, basically like its that, but I mean a present - like I mean somethin' to spoil myself? Well, da Ferrari does 130 mph in NINE seconds. Big deal. I said to da dealer. You know da latest? Give me one, yeah Stella you en Marco can give dis to me…! Dat's how much I believe in Stella ova here en my star. Da new Bugatti. 800,000 pounds not dollas. You know what dat is in dollas? The fastest car in the wurld. 250mph twin engines 2 V8s… Dats talking fast. b'Jesus! 100 litres of fuel in the tank with this speed - empty in TWELVE minutes… dat's class, real class.

"One last question, what about you and Cat Renoir?"

"I'm a guy who falls in love with the *shikas* of the wurld. Cat's a nice girl, believe me, sex for me is like hunger pangs…when you're hungry ya eat, right? When you're not, ya don't…I'm in love in Capri en when I get the Oscar in my hands I'll tell ya all about it. Now, no more questions."

"Is it true that…"

"I said, no more questions. Common' Stella I wanna run through some things with ya."

Levy was coarse, crude, corrupt and calculating. No one could dispute that or accuse him of being ineffective, or when roused, to have the temper of a mongrel. He knew his turf. He smelled victory. He had outdistanced every producer in Hollywood and the world of cinema. What's more, Levy knew it, loved it and was getting exactly what he came to Capri for, backer's money, further acclaim, adventure and his idea of class.

X

Canzone del Mare

Simultaneously Sunday afternoon…

To the extreme opposite of Capri's Marina Grande is Marina Piccolo. Thousands of years ago, two landmark chunks of mountain separated from the mainland, split into the sea creating what the Italians call, "*Faraglioni.*" The phenomenal setting is a short distance beyond Gracie Field's former residence Canzone del Mare, on the mollusk coastline where Churchill, Hitler, Sophia Loren, Farouk, Cary Grant, Marlon Brando, Marilyn Monroe, JFK, Elizabeth Taylor, plus scores more were entertained. Today, this is a semi-exclusive enclave for swimming and dining, popular with the chic set who haunt the island believing mermaids will enchant anyone bathing in the waters, thus it's name, "Song of the Sea."

As one approached the club this sunny afternoon, a photographic shoot of Marco Ricci in Nicky Viscounti's amphibious plane was underway. Tourists in the vicinity congregated on boats spying the star and from the one elegant restaurant, (with the privileged willing to spend $80 for a plate of pasta), all gaped at Hollywood in Capri.

Nicky watched at a distance from the terrace of the club, as the camera crew positioned Marco to sit in Nicky's pilot seat. *Paparazzi's* lenses resounded like time bombs. Marco loved the attention. Ogled spectators shouted,

"Marco Ricci, I want you!"

"Fly me to the moon, Baby!"

"Ricci you know how to fly that thing?"

"Take me higher, Lover Boy."

A private plane swooped overhead with a banner advertisement for ESCAPEDES. The hum made all look up, click, click, click, snap, snap went the cameras and within an hour Marco's task to publicize ESCAPADES was completed. Waving to fans, he exited the plane, swarmed by autograph seekers and was ushered forward by security guards. Once free from the aura of star status, he walked towards Nicky, who waited patiently sipping Campari and soda, relaxing at a secluded table under a large umbrella.

Pleased to be away from his demanding public, Marco exhaled a deep sigh. At last he was at ease, speaking his *madre lingua* with Nicky, away from Villa Pina where English was the exclusive language because Nigel never mastered Italian. Marco took a joint from his tight jean pocket, Nicky lit it, not accepting his offer to join him.

"I hear you invested in the film," began Marco.

"It can't fail. I don't invest in anything out of courtesy."

"Good boy."

"So what do you think?"

"Of what precisely?" Nicky was always guarded.

"Of the hoopla at Villa Pina."

"You want the truth?"

"You know me. Give me the truth baby or shut up." Marco inhaled his weed.

"What the hell's going on?" Nicky queried.

"I'm not complaining, why should I? Esmeralda heard about the film through Stella barking off about her extraordinary screenplay. "Talent like mine," she proclaimed…"and you know the rest, Nicky. Stella doesn't need a press agent. Cool it," I told her but never in the history of my how many years with Stella has she cooled it? I'm not counting, Nicky…never once has she ever listened to me so she wasn't about to have me, Marco Ricci, who is not an Italian noble, or wise ass like herself advise her what to do. She went to Villa Pina when I was on location in England, touted the film knowing the impact she'd have on Esmeralda and frankly has always wanted to put Esmeralda off guard, using her talent as a device. As you are well aware, years ago, Gianni chose Esmeralda over Stella, as his choice for marriage."

"It was never a love story with Stella," noted Nicky "Gianni gave Stella a Caravaggio guache to ease the so-called heart-break."

"A typical Gianni move, yes, I know. Nevertheless on this day Esmeralda saw an immediate entry for her into the world of Hollywood glamour, piggybacking on Stella's dynamite film that was already locked in production. Esmeralda insisted she wanted to back it. Financially it gives her tax write off with a production company no doubt about it."

"…and Nigel?"

"Nigel follows whatever Esmeralda tells him, laughing all the way to the bank."

"Lost his balls."

"Right…….. that's the story, he married for money, could have been worse."

"And Gianni lies in his grave."

"Not lying, rumbling." Marco took a long drag on his weed tapping his foot. "Dead. We're all going to be dead. So what's all the excitement about? I've decided to take this ride - yes Nicky – LIFE, the ride of life - for the best…Frankly, if it weren't for escaping every now and then on a spiritual retreat - yoga, not talking, the whole cleansing scene, detox from society and the scenario Stella thrives on, believe me, Nicky, I've gone India-a- go-go on this"

"It works?"

"Everything works. The film. Me. My life with Stella. I sit here at peace, energized, devoted, working, full of ZEN, drinking Campari, smoking good grass."

“The simple life.”

“Right....Look at this gorgeous landscape, Nicky, and expand to some aesthetic plateau that makes dreams come true....”

“What do you know about Elizabeth MacKenzie?” Nicky asked briskly.

Marco made a low whistle, “Too young. Jail bait. Went off to Mass with that queer Jarvis. Interested?”

“She’s the only one last night I’d like to know better.”

“Going for them twenty years younger these days…?”

“Seventeen.”

“She’s lovely, innocent, what a pair of legs!…her Mother watches over her like a hawk. She inherits a title via her grandfather’s title, no money, 100% class. That’s what I know.”

“The other two, Cat and Zofra, real tarts, and the rest too old.”

“Too old for you, Nicky. Not for others. The problem with you Nicky, like our pal, Gianni Agnelli, you’ll never be faithful. You only can have a feeling of sexual security if the woman you’re bedding has her suitcase clearly in view, packed to leave. So, what do you think?… are you in love with Miss MacKenzie?”

“Hell no. But MacKenzie is interesting if only for her freshness.”

“The face isn’t bad either.”

“Or the body.” A smile lurked on Nicky’s lips.

“OK you’ve taken inventory. What are you waiting for?”

“She’s not interested. Told me last night.”

“A non starter?”

“Yes...with a virgin or quasi-virgin mentality. With Elizabeth it will be…”

“Let me guess…two hours and fifty-five minutes of dinner at the Ritz to convince her to have sex and the whole thing will be over in five minutes.”

“I’d feel a sense of obligation and so I’m going back to Rome before the concert.”

“Don’t. Antonia Ivani is coming. She’s unattached. You may like her.”

"Sick of it Marco, the whole honey trap."

"My heart bleeds for you."

"Truth is I don't like being in Esmeralda's company. Never felt comfortable with her. Never trusted her. I'm still close to Serena, Gianni's sister."

"I didn't know Esmeralda was married before Gianni. Stefano let it slip…"

"I knew but neither did anyone else until she was days from marrying Gianni. Some old Baron forty years her senior. The only reason I'll stick around is the old crowd is going to have a lunch tomorrow, Gianni's pals, otherwise I'd ask you to join us. Nice to see them again. Maybe I'll get a chance to have a second talk with Elizabeth."

"Good luck, pal. She's going back to London tomorrow morning."

Marco noticed Nicky's surprise. "Now let's see what we're going to eat." Marco picked up the menu and began studying the specialties. His left foot pounded the flagstone terrace in some unknown tribal beat. A waiter hovered near. Both men, dark haired, skin the color of Etruscan statues, were in excellent form, Marco being of slighter build and wiry. There was a diverse sexuality about each of them with macho Italian virility oozing from every pore. Marco, some years older, with street's smarts that outdistanced any baccalaureate, had the wiser look with piercing eyes, furrowed wrinkles in his tawny face, sunken cheeks that fell exactly where they benefited his sinister star quality, his resonant voice matched a dark Machiavellian appearance required in ESCAPEDES. Marco was an accomplished thespian, and enjoyed his marijuana and his partner, Stella in that order. Contentment was his having mastered the art of self-discovery.

Nicky was taller, his nobility emphasized by his silhouette, akin to Michelangelo's David, pristine hygiene, clothes cut from the finest cloth and Italian tailors accented his muscular body. Nicky's movements were those of a panther, sure and steady. His observant shark eyes saw everything. He was sophisticated, kept his composure and smooth soft-spoken voice level at all times, not at monotone but at metronome. There was nothing about Nicky that wasn't smooth through and through. He was born, like Gianni Zianni, with all the accoutrements of the seriously rich and never displayed anything to announce the fact. His presence exhibited, much like Gianni's, one who has complete sense of self without conceit.

Nevertheless, although Marco knew Nicky's demeanor was one of high breeding, he sensed aristocratic Nicky could make one phone call, control any situation and cause an earthquake - much like his a dynamite prick that fucked like a Roman Emperor. (Or so it was rumored.)

Nicky was precise about his life, his mind, his food. He ordered without a menu explaining politely, "Scampi grilled, two cloves of garlic, teaspoon of olive oil and some parsley." Then he sat back amused watching wire thin Marco continue tapping his foot nervously, smoke his weeds and devour twice what a man like Levy could consume while staying slim as a rod.

Antonia Ivani meant nothing to either of them. Nicky had met her before. Beautiful, yes. Deep? No. Although he was diametrically opposed to involving himself in anything except financing a winner of a film, he'd go through the movements because something told Nicky the get-together Monday, would be an important day to be with Gianni's friends. It was unlike Whitney to text him to leave Villa Pina for a cruise.

Marco continued, "If I'm not asked to this inner sanctum meeting, Nicky - neither is Elizabeth bet's that's why she's off. I'll chat her up before she goes, see what's on her mind. She'd be nuts to ignore a catch like you!"

"Very kind but forget it. I can speak for myself."

"Just offering."

"The lunch will be on Whitney's yacht, sailing over to Ischia. Hang around the villa, Marco. See if you hear anything strange. I've a weird feeling something's going on."

"Since you're paying for lunch, paying to invest in the film and I like you, that's fine by me." Marco grinned lighting another joint feeling deliriously happy.

"Marco, How in the devil do you stay with a feminist who doesn't appreciate you?"

"Nicky it's like this. We have total openness in sex beyond the bullshit. Our two entities are one."

They ate a delicious lunch giving no notice to time, sipping café, enjoying the sun beginning to set and the last of the bikini clad beauties take their final dip in the sea.

Nicky's mobile rang. Someone was reporting to him, a man speaking rapid Italian. Curious as he was, given to eavesdropping, Marco couldn't grasp the angle of the call. He only saw Nicky's expression change dramatically and heard one response, "*Subito.*"•

"Sorry Marco, must dash."

Within seconds, he left the table, alighted two steps at a time up the steep incline to the exit, in a frenetic rush to meet someone. Marco took it in stride relaxing, inhaling marijuana slowly.

Something happened. Nicky's pulse was on powers that be. One hell of a drama thought Marco. He drew another drag from his weed, Zen illuminated....*he who can sit still can conquer the world*....Marco gazed at the sunset.

• Now

XI

Tennis Game

Simultaneously Sunday afternoon…

Before Stefano de Gesu left London for Villa Pina, a game of tennis with Nigel had been scheduled. They played singles well together and had done so for years.

It was two-thirty. They met on the lower terrace before it sloped to the dependence sipping lemonade steps from the court. Off in the distance, the grape arbor hid the court from sight.

"Wonderful party," de Gesu began. "Right to the end, the fireworks were unexpected."

"Liked it?"

"Your best as far as I'm concerned."

"Your toast was most revealing." Nigel curtly replied with friction in his voice.

"Revealing?"

"Yes." Nigel seemed to jeer not wanting to mince words. "I daresay made me wonder."

"Wonder what?" de Gesu questioned, astounded Nigel was not proclaiming the toast he made last evening was exactly what he and Esmeralda wished to hear.

"Forget it. Let's hit the court." Nigel didn't make eye contact, they walked in silence to begin the first set. Once the game began, de Gesu, (who knew Nigel's talkative style), couldn't help sense Nigel's silence and the way he hit the ball. His serve was wicked, the volleys impossible and he cursed more than ever. Nigel had always been foul mouthed, his forte in a way, but this was not the friend de Gesu knew.

Stefano couldn't understand Nigel's mood. End of first set. The same behavior ensued the second set. de Gesu challenged Nigel as best he could. The rage made Nigel's game better and the growl in his voice provoked the Ambassador who made it a habit to be exceedingly diplomatic whenever he was in the presence of someone this tense.

'He's got his Mother fuckin' Wop horns coming out of his head, God damned Satyr,' spun in Nigel's mind.

While de Gesu thought, 'He must have had a row with Esmeralda. Unreasonable jerk. He's throwing knives at me with every shot.

They broke after the second set and took another lemonade from the bar.

"Some problem, Nigel?"

"Problem?"

"You seem uptight, angry in fact."

"Angry? You dear old thing, me?" His eyes went wide owl style.

"Yes. Angry."

"Putting it bluntly, it's extraordinary to me…in my prudent opinion…" He peered at de Gesu.

"What'?"

"We Pembrookes…the way I was brought up…" Nigel always liked to announce his lineage.

"Out with it…" de Gesu looked at Nigel trying to control his Latin temper.

"The very idea to think that under my very nose, my roof!…a chappie I thought was decent, a friend I revered I see now is a poacher."

"A poacher?"

"Yes," he sneered…."shagging my wife."

"That's what you think?"

"Know - not think."

"And you think it's me?"

"None other, my dear fellow." Nigel threw one of his glassy expressions in de Gesu's direction.

"You're implying I'm a cad." de Gesu's tone of voice defended him.

"Right."

"Bloody that."

"I beg your pardon, M I S T E R Ambassador. You are on MY tennis court."

"Your tennis court? Fancy that and your Ego-mansion I suppose... I'll tell you what you want to know."

"Please do." Nigel stretched his height to its maximum. He always did this once he knew there was an imbroglio to spark. His height gave a certain power, four inches taller than de Gesu. "It's no secret Esmeralda and I were lovers many years ago, 'way before she met Gianni...or you."

"No news there."

"And I'm a lover of beautiful women."

Nigel waited, seething.

"Nigel, I did try to put the moves on Esmeralda when I arrived Thursday. So I confess. She is at the pinnacle of her beauty, lucky you..."

Nigel stood rigid, his eyes looked through de Gesu like a cobra ready to attack. His mouth grew taunt, fangs compressed.

de Gesu continued "Would you want to know her answer ?"

"I do."

"'Her answer was, 'Aren't we past that Stefano?' "

Nigel sharpened his stance.

'I cannot afford to dally with you as I did when we were young. My energy is not for sex. Please, Stefano,' she said, 'I did that. I want something more ....' this, Nigel, is exactly how the conversation went."

Nigel stood rock still.

"She said 'I want something more, Stefano, I want power.' And that was the end of it. My dear friend, you have nothing to worry about. Your wife is true to.......her power."

Every muscle in Nigel's tight expression was relieved. de Gesu had extinguished his raging jealousy.

"It was Lynne spreading the rumor." Nigel said looking at de Gesu.

"Lynne? That dim wit at the dangerous age of menopause! Screw her!" Shot from de Gesu.

"Who'd want to?"

"I won't deny I wouldn't have loved to lay Esmeralda. So would every man I know. She doesn't want any encounter to soil the throne she sits upon today. The scandal would kill her plans."

"I know. "

"Sorry, Nigel."

"Blimey. I was sure it was true."

"No. It's not."

"Sanjeev told her you've been having a woman in your room. Bloody lucky! Who is it?" Nigel was envious, his words cantering. "It can't be Zofra, she's too cheap or that call girl of Levy's. Olympia. It's Olympia!"

"It's someone I've loved a long time."

"Love did you say?"

"Yes, Nigel. The woman is Véronique."

Nigel was stunned. It all returned to him, when Véronique was engaged to her first husband, Ratucha in Buenos Aires, they were there, he was a spokesman for the game and there was rumor that Véronique had dallied with de Gesu, who took an interest in polo, was involved with the socialites, posted as Italy's young Deputy Chief of Mission, twenty years ago. "You couldn't have chosen better."

"Thank you, Nigel. I know. Shall we have a third set?"

They played until just after four in a jovial mod. "We deserve one hell of a brew," said Nigel pouring gin into glasses for a G&T. They told some obscene jokes while the sun made its descent and retired to their separate rooms.

XII

Doctor Samir Redat

Simultaneously Sunday afternoon…

Véronique tried to fathom the last half hour. She had a brief lunch with Nigel before he went off steaming mad to play tennis with de Gesu. He never revealed he had a score to settle and she found it odd he cut her short. He took scant interest when she advised a complete change in his life was taking place as the half moon turned full with Mercury aligned in his zodiac and Pluto's seventh house this very day. He grumbled, "Get on with it Véronique, you know I don't believe this shit." She retreated promising Nigel a fuller reading when he wished.

Nigel was an interesting man. Basically, he was good, yet he betrayed himself in both his marriages for financial gain and procrastinated about his many talents that he devalued. Now, seeing Pluto collide with Esmeralda's transept, Véronique was certain, Nigel was in the middle of a catastrophe that was imminent. Matching his chart with Esmeralda's for accuracy, whether she was born a year earlier or a year later (considering her vanity, or place of birth which Véronique questioned), startled the astrologer. All was grave, the couple doomed, communication snafus, misunderstandings, confusion and deception were forecast as the Sun quincunxes Jupiter. Mercury turns retrograde, too, with indecision causing problems thought Véronique. Neptune then turns direct making it difficult to separate fact from fiction.

The Sun quincunxes of Jupiter are an aspect of social discord. Véronique's work was precise. The Scorpio Sun is powerful, secretive, intense and wants to transform existing conditions. Everything will be in an upheaval. Jupiter in Gemini is interested in ideas -- witnessing two different universes with nothing in common. Some of the people here will try to strong-arm others into believing what they believe; others will seek ways to bridge gaps. Either way, when Mercury turns retrograde, misunderstandings are plentiful and these guests will be confronted about ethics, morals - who's right and wrong.... I must caution Nigel to weigh pros and cons before making decisions or signing contracts. She cross-referenced charts. Look at this! Neptune changes direction, logic vanishes and imagination is emphasized. Neptune rules dreams, fantasies and illusions. Not one of these people should accept anything without double-checking facts...they will all be vulnerable to deception with the dramatic lunar eclipse in Sagittarius.

The phenomena of the Pembrooke's stars, how they cross linked with the lives of others gathered at Villa Pina was a marvel Véronique had never experienced, paring the twenty guests' zodiacs. The charts astonished her. In the short space of time, viewing Esmeralda's astrological picture in particular, Véronique was seized with diabolical facts, much as she saw her own forecast with another message soon to be reality.

Years ago, there was a certain chemistry between Véronique and Stefano, a man filled with undisguised passion and that force made her betray her fiancé, twenty years ago, a fact only she and de Gesu knew. "After him," Véronique acknowledged to a stranger "all was prostitution."

Oftentimes she wondered if she would be his wife when her marriages and his failed. It was no consequence. de Gesu married a series of times unsuccessfully and never recovered from Véronique slighting him as a suitor choosing Ratucha. Now this coincidence, the two of them at Villa Pina, wise because of age and their stars forecast the future.

In all the years apart, so different this relationship from the icy silence of Naomi and Brian, diplomatic Stefano never built a wall between himself and Véronique but a bridge was the communication he developed with the woman he found, to this day, a woman to love. She understood him, didn't judge him, was warm, feminine, and every aspect of her reached his heart, though no thought of marriage was brought to fruition and then friendship sprang to passion yesterday.

Véronique was selfish to take her due. Stefano would be sent into a tidal wave of emotion within the next few months, that was evident in his stars, all because of her and yet, in this instance she was self-seeking, so unlike her. To give him the very essence of her being, long denied, was a joy and a curse; now it had found a home in him alone. She went to his room yesterday, this morning and would do so tonight and tomorrow.

She closed her charts and moved poolside. She had promised Samir to speak of her physic predictions for him as she did each year. He, an Egyptian, had a fine appreciation for astrology, unlike his wife who didn't wish to know her future - like Nigel, afraid to know. That was fine with Véronique, less people to counsel with insecurities.

Samir was swimming as she approached the sun deck. His energy matched that of Stefano's, both over sixty, strong, masculine men who achieved what they wished professionally, respecting themselves and those around them. She moved to the chaise lounge next to Samir's, slipped out of her sandals and serape, taking in the sun waiting for Samir to appear. They'd planned to enjoy an hour or so this afternoon with many guests dispersed in other pursuits. Samir exited the pool and came to join Véronique expectantly. He reached for her hand and put it to his lips.

"Good to see you. How are you?"

"Let's talk about you, Samir. I have a remarkable predication for you."

"Ah! a good one I hope," he said drying himself.

"You must concentrate on this. Question yourself when things begin to happen as the full moon appears, "What does this mean for me?' Take this selfishly. You are going to be drawn into a web, a web that you must be careful to guard. In some ways it will be an altruistic gesture. It may make you circumspect. Don't be unsure. Stay above the debris that will wash upon your shores within the next fortnight - and beyond, but be benevolent."

"Please tell me is there a problem with Jacqueline…is she faithful?"

"She'll be beside you. This will solidify you. She's your best partner and asset. Your family is not a part of this, or your profession. This goes into another realm. Ethics into the life of Nigel and Esmeralda, more Esmeralda I see. I am sorry to be vague but I see your seventh sun is directly posed on her Jupiter horizon. You will arrive on a steady course helping someone, someone you least expect. I believe it to be Esmeralda.

"And…"

"I cannot say more at this point." Véronique took out her papers with the geometrical signs of his chart crisscrossing in a myriad of directions showing them to him; Samir couldn't fathom anything. He trusted Véronique and all she said in the past had been an aid making difficult decisions, a fact they discussed often, with his compounding problem of insecurity.

"Does death have anything to do with this?"

Samir was fixed on death, like most Egyptians, since the history of their civilization. He had the hieroglyphics of Imhotep painted on his office wall in London whose précis on medicine 2500 years ago was profound for its landmark theory on longevity. Samir's family had come from the same small village on the Nile near Luxor, a village known to have people live the longest on earth. For this reason, his patient, Gianni Agnelli, sent his personal physician to inquire all he could discover about the mystery of life.

If Michael de Bakey and Viking Bjork were considered the fathers of modern cardiovascular surgery, Samir Redat was their younger brother. Some called Samir, "King of Hearts," because of his inventions, surgeries on more than 20,000 individuals, his scientific articles changed medical practices, translated throughout the world, his volunteer efforts forming the first hospital on the front in the Gulf War in 1990, and saving the life of the Emir in Subai.

Redat, like de Bakey and his colleagues Bjork and Yacoub had been honored countless times by reigning Kings, Princes, moguls and the Emir, the Grandfather of Shabadiba, whose life expectancy increased once he performed delicate operations. He remained modest. That is what first attracted Gianni Zianni to Samir years ago.

Journalists never failed to report the number of lives saved by Samir Redat's inventions or the fact that his mother had taught him how to make his first stitches wishing him to help her, a seamstress, in a derelict section south of Luxor, with her needlework. He was short listed for the Nobel Prize this year and unless people knew this fact, he would be the last to amplify it. Rubbing shoulders with the jet set of Europe didn't put him at ease, being more comfortable in the emergency room in Cairo's General Hospital. Discussing medicine with Brian Korthorpe was one of the reasons he came to Villa Pina for their dual work as pioneers in bio-medical engineering had teamed them at worldwide congresses dedicated to extending the quality of life.

Yet the thought of death determined the course of Samir's thinking. In all respects this is why he chose his field of heart research. The Egyptian, like his countrymen, concentrated continually on death and the preservation of the body post mortem. It was inbred, a country once renown for innovative thinking, today living in the world of memories.

Samir's being was Muslim but his philosophy of life vastly diverse from the Princess. Véronique knew he had divorced two wives who wore the veil, housed today in appropriate style in Luxor on the Nile, the same house he acquired as a young doctor. His initial wife, mother to his first children, knew her fate seeing pilings erected on their second floor, fully visible, haunting her, fore-telling the demise of her marriage through the steel girders. It was only a matter of time until Samir would divorce her and she would be another victim of the Egyptian tradition of housing both wives together for family unity and economic reasons. And so it was. As with all prominent Muslim men, it was understood Samir would have more than one wife. With the simple words, "I divorce you," all was accomplished without any attorney or fanfare. He honored his responsibility to his first family, rebuilt the flat on the second floor for his second wife who produced another child. Throughout this, the two wives lived in the same edifice hating each other and then accepting their destiny.

In time, his life work was recognized in London and then New York with the Zianni family funding his inventions. All became richer and Western life suited Samir, shy as he was. In Neuilly, outside of Paris, at a key party with other Egyptian friends, libertines - two years into his second marriage, he was held spellbound meeting French Jacqueline, destined to be his third wife. A former Ungaro model born in Marseilles, her flaming red hair and wide set blue eyes aroused the dark Egyptian. The French woman's supple body and flirtatious personality made him relinquish any thought of having his Muslim wife in Europe. She was quickly given a one-way ticket to Egypt, she was his world of yesterday and Jacqueline was eager to be his trophy wife in his world of today.

His French woman vamped him, sang and danced to entertain the love struck Doctor, who divorced with rapidity, beguiled and inspired his fantasies were satiated, taking his French beauty into his important circle of friends. It was a wise choice as Jacqueline's needs were met with jewelry and real estate, permitting Samir to have the occasional conquest without pangs of guilt.

The union, blessed by twin boys, gave Samir youth. French nannies reared the children while Jacqueline cared for the needs of her husband as one would an orchid. She never gave him too much attention, the spark of uncertainty grew in a man whom she knew thrived on insecurities. She understood how to control her sweet-hearted doctor.

"So you are sure about me and Jacqueline?"

"Positively."

"Good. Very good…and you? What do you see for yourself? After our last talk in June, I'm concerned.

"I see, of course, my stars, my future."

"What do you see?"

"Samir," and Véronique paused. "I wish you could perform some miracle."

"Your health Véronique, how is your health?" Samir's eyes met hers.

"I see my stars," she began, halting her voice, "If I were to read this to someone who asked me to tell them the truth…"

"Yes, Véronique…what?"

"I see my death."

"No!"

"Yes within a year, at best eighteen months. I'm certain. Keep my secret please. Honor me with that."

He took her hand, "*Maşallah*, you know I will," and anyone seeing this would have surmised they were lovers.

So it was uncanny when Cat Renoir, who had fled the bitchy scene at the spa, entered poolside, walkman in her ear, seeing Samir whose wife had bragged moments before how happy her marriage was that he was holding the hand of another woman.

"Sorry…am I…I am.."

"Come. Sit down with us," Encouraged Véronique warmly. The young woman was typically American in naiveté, thrust into a complex scene with its relationship from years past. What to say confused Cat. She couldn't string together a smart sentence and had no idea how to give words the impact she wanted. Véronique patted the chaise lounge next to her. Cat, as a child obeys a parent, sat on the edge of it, uneasy.

"Samir and I have been friends more than twenty years," began Véronique sensing at once Cat's appraisal of the scene, removing her hand from Samir's. "I have just completed his chart and we were discussing medicine. And you, Cat, are you having a difficult time with all these personalities at Villa Pina?"

"It is, well, I didn't expect, some of the…like I mean to say…you know, basically…" she began without connecting the sentence.

"You know Véronique is an astrologer," said Samir sensing the girl's confusion.

"Yes. I always read my horoscope in the papers, even on the Internet."

"Your sign, Gemini, is most interesting, the baby of the zodiac."

"You know my sign? You say baby?"

"Yes, I know your sign and you are wishing to communicate with those in Los Angeles. Do it, make the calls. You feel isolated here," said Véronique knowing the girl's vulnerable state. "Don't worry about anything. There are two sides to a Gemini. I promise what you least expect will happen and you will look back on everything you thought was a problem without regrets. You're too pretty to let me see you so glum."

"Thank you, Véronique."

"Tell Véronique everything." said Samir giving the young woman a broad smile, and he dove into the pool.

"I've heard so many things in the spa, I mean like vicious things and I think that, like, I want to say, you know, basically these guys, I mean these women gossip, but I have no one to turn to."

"Tell me whatever you like. It will stay between the two of us. Samir's not interested."

"Do you know Zofra?"

"Only as well as you do."

"I think, in fact, basically, I mean I know that she has…" she halted looking at Véronique. Cat Renoir had little education but in the ways of love, she was as educated as the next woman and knew Levy was cheating on her. He'd used her, brought her from Los Angeles but she had let herself be used, and now where would she go? Levy had given her the glamour of all the things she dreamed about as a star struck girl who came to Hollywood from a trailer park home in Idaho wanting stardom. Now this.

"Zofra has made a pass at your boyfriend?"

"Fiancé, he calls me his fiancé, so he has to be my fiancé, right?"

"Yes, I suppose but be wise, Cat. Zofra is a woman with more experience than you have and if you and Marc are not to be, I will look at your stars and speak to you about what I see for you, if you like."

"I would love that. I didn't want to ask."

"Have no fear. I was just telling Samir about things I saw for him. That's why you saw him holding my hand. What you see and what is reality are two different things. Now let's get some sun to look beautiful tonight. I promise I will see what I can for you."

Cat took Véronique's hand. In this setting of wealth that she had never experienced in her life there was one person she sensed was real. She put on her dark glasses to hide her eyes. In the midst of paradise, she was having a miserable time. Could something at Villa Pina have some meaning, any meaning beyond being hurt by the likes of that guy, that pig Mark Levy?

XIII

The Spa

....Sunday afternoon...

"A Turkish harem," Shabadiba remarked, entering the spa. Settling herself, taking a snort of coke in front of women who would mark her as an addict, she slipped naked into the Jacuzzi. Groucho sat close by.

The spa, adjacent to the outdoor pool, was an oasis of peace, resplendent with blue-green Arabic tiles sent to the Ziannis years ago as a gift from Shabadiba's family in the Persian Gulf. The design lent an atmosphere of tranquility. The Princess close her eyes to listened to the prattle the 'bees,' as she called them.

"Isn't this fabulous!" gushed Cat entering the premises. "Where is Esmeralda?"

"Esmeralda's detained," offered Olympia watching the pedicurist foliate her feet.

"Better that way, we can speak freely without having to pay homage," Shabadiba's candor was appreciated by all except Cat who viewed Esmeralda as a Goddess.

"Eva wonda what's detained ha?" Lynne questioned.

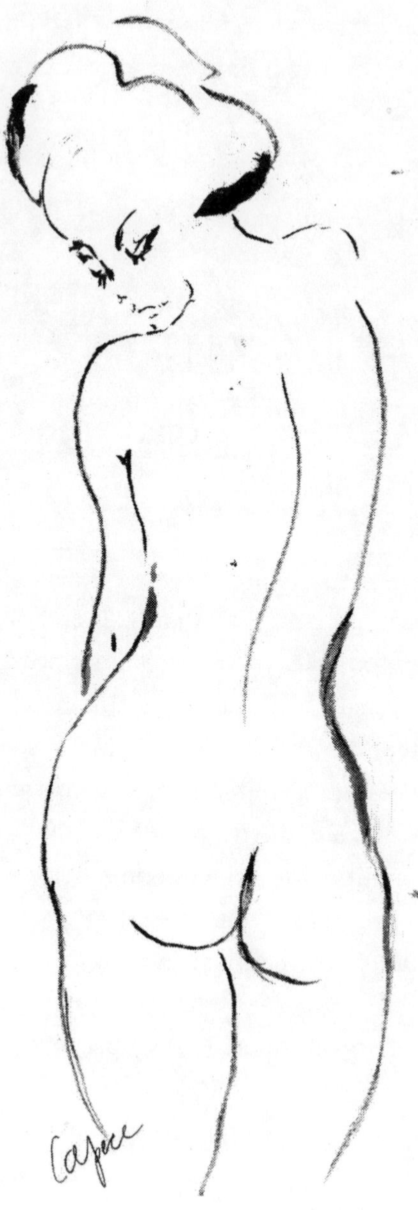

"Naomi's at zee conservatory in rehearsal with zee pianist for tonight." Jacqueline Redat called from the massage she was having. "En zee men? Here en zhere."

"Stella's working with Mark on rewrites for the script," said Cat with her nasal twang waiting for a seaweed wrap. "Monty Daniels was interviewing them."

"En where do ya'll think Véronique is?" asked Lynne, her tongue feeling like a powder puff from last night's drinking. Her swollen feet were raised on a settee as a Reflexologist eased her pain from standing too long last night in stilettos. Chin hairs were plucked by an Electrolocist. "My guess is she's with the old crowd, always livin' in the past and then she talks about the futya. My stars! She predicted a whole change fa me but she said she had no time to divulge it all."

"She's reading Nigel's chart," offered Zofra, "I heard them speaking about that at dinner."

"Well, I do declare that was some dinna en the music, en the flowers, en the movie, en Cat you better hold onto that fella of yours," she eyed the young woman knowing full well Zofra was moving into Cat's territory. "I tell ya honey ya neva know when there is someone about to pounce and I do mean pounce on your man." She threw a dagger of a look at Olympia who kept her English reserve magnificently.

"How wise to offer Cat advice, Lynne, as you are certainly old enough to be her Mother." Olympia jeered

"Why Olympia, I'm lookin' afta this little girl Cat cause we're investin' in this film en Cat's been already knowin' me in Hollywood en in New York when my ever lovin' Whitney en I had a dinna for them at the River Club. I have a sixth sense about these things....ya'll learn that readin' the Bible."

"Do you?" retorted Olympia, with an unexpected charm, loathing the woman who would ultimately be her rival when settlement time came.

"I surely do. In fact, I don't know about you Jacqueline, cauz ya'll been married to Samir ten years...but it's been donkey years for me en Whitney. Life isn't like it was. Now with a lot of single women around snaggin' men en men being so easy to be tempted at every turn. No scruples, I tell ya'll today the women have no scruples…en on top of that, courtin' money, lookin' for a tycoon."

"You should know," Shabidaba said, but Lynne who talked incessantly, whether drunk or sober, didn't stop long enough to hear.

"When I was wed, we were sweethearts so innocent…en life was lovely, I mean lovely with the respect a man should give a girl. Nowadays, well nowadays everythin's topsy turvey en my children! Don't get me started on my children! Too independent. Havin' Whitney give them money behind my back, en trust funds well, that doesn't help any…and fa all I know with that kind of money the two of them are temptin' the wrong people…"

"Temptation's the spice of life, we say in Hungary," Zofra commented in her seductive voice.

"I like that Zofra," responded Shabadiba, holding a dog biscuit to Groucho.

"Well, make sure Cat, that Mark makes some sorta financial provision for ya'll …unless he has already…has he honey?"

"A lot of girls in Hollywood do that but I really love Mark. He would never hurt me." Cat spoke guarded.

"Ya know Cat men love to subja-kate ya en when I'm depressed, en of course that doesn't happen very often, but the best remedy for anything like that, sugar is take yourself out en shop…the best shoppin' is for diamonds en shoes - put a big tab on your lover boy's credit card and never wear the damned things for him." Pleased with herself, Lynne smiled at all, "I do it all the time to Whitney."

"You do?" asked Cat which brought Lynne's next advice.

"Well, I'm sure Mark wouldn't intentionally hurt ya but ya'll know men en itz vicious out there en ya neva know what a fella will do… 'specially if there havin' a mid-life crisis.' She let out a huge sigh as her toes were massaged, "Seems to me, I'm the one here with all the marriage experience. In my case, Whitney knows I would take him to the cleanas if I eva caught him strayin' from our marriage vows, I'd scratch his eyes out."

“Jealousy is an enemy of freedom. It controls you and you should be controlling it. Jean Paul Satre said,” Shabadiba, made her statement to amuse Lynne.

“Thank you, Princess. I don’t think I met Satre last night but afta all, I gave Whitney two children en believe you me, Whitney is not an easy man to be lovin’…Fact is, we just put that to one side. We have no more of that, you know girls, once ya are married for a long time, I’m just tellin’ ya’ll sex is not important.”

“You really believe that?” Zofra amazed by Lynne’s candor.

“Ya’ll a young single lass from a foreign country en I don’t know what men do in Hungary but let’s face it there aren’t rich men in Hungary ‘cept George Soros and he lives in New York. I wouldn’t set my eyes on anyone who didn’t have money. Life just isn’t worth it.”

No one replied.

“‘Go for a nice ripe boy from en importan’ family with a nice ripe purse,’ that’s what my Mamma said tellin’ it like it is. We weren’t white trash en I am not gonna be like any colored girl en flaunt myself. Neva have en neva will. I like my Southern prejudices and keep em and I don give a hankerin who kows about it.”” She pulled the sides of her face towards her ears contemplating another face lift…“findin’ a man is like Mamma said, isn’t that so Jacqueline?”

“Zee men are all alike. Zey like ze sex. I do too. I am French but I am a woman who has to have Samir all the time. He likes that. It is why we made the twins. I like to have him desire me. It makes me feel…ah…feel like spring…”

“But honey ya’ll know Samir must have other women. Doctors always do, a bunch of cowboys pullin’ the trigger en the trigger well ya’ll know what that is…. Did ya’ll eva catch him with another woman…a nurse or somethin’?”

“I keep him zatisfied en we have a real bond. Maybe you do not have zis with Whitney, but we do…I am all his and I never think to the money. I think to the sex. To the life, to the family.”

“Sounds wonderful to me,” Olympia remarked. “Being engaged to Tong is interesting, he’s the same age as Whitney’s, and for that reason

I disagree with you Lynne. Men hit fifty-five, sixty and they become oversexed. What's the saying?"

"Zee older men make zee better lover like zee vine."

Olympia continued, "It's interesting Jacqueline because you and Samir are different in many respects, Egypt and France, when one considers the cradle of civilization and the inspiration for art, came from Egypt… Egypt is not as Middle East as other countries, agree Shabadiba?

"In the key cities, to a degree, yes and certainly about art."

"I do not believe I will go forward and marry Tong, our culture is too different."

"Culture…." The Muslim beauty with her pale Arab skin and sharp black eyes raised her chin high, "I'd never take the veil. I thank the day my Grandfather sent me to be educated in England."

"I'd love to hear about your country," nasally offered Cat exciting the sauna.

"I'll tell ya'll about our Princess 'cauz she's too modest." Lynne, loving the sound of her voice, claimed the floor.

"Our Shabadiba is the granddaughter of the Emir, the Sheikh of Subai. Now ya'll be a askin' where in tarnation is Subai…it's a boarderin' Saudi Arabia, an independent kingdom…en when the Princess' Granddaddy died," she rambled at a louder pitch than necessary, not giving Shabadiba a chance to get a word in edgewise, " she's the Crown Prince's daughta, I can tell you this, there was mourning at his death for forty days, like Jesus in the Garden, en the whole world came to tell everyone in Subai how sorry they were."

"Are you my Family spokesperson?"

"I'm tellin' it like it is, Shabadiba 'cauz I must be knowing ya'll about twenty years en we went, of course, when this happened but we weren't interested in the fact that the Sheikh or you call him Emir or Your Highness, well girls, he had when he died the largest oil reserves in private hands, I'm tellin' ya private hands for more than 300 years en the balance of oil my Whitney told me was more than $90 billion dollars. Whitney knows all that 'cauz he was handlin' his investments…Now I ask you that's talkin' money en the horses in Sheikh Makkum's stables! Why honey lambs ya'll neva believe it..."

Without pausing, Lynne rubbed her red eyes, having indulged in too much claret from last night, and continued, "En with all those billions, en I've neva eva seen anything like that palace, this Villa Pina, well, it's like an out house compared…I'm tellin' ya'll that man waz a sweetheart. He was a quiet listener en Shabadiba is just like him. En imagine…with all the money in God's kingdom, en he was Muslim, of course, en had many a woman, but that doesn't matta to me caus he was Muslim," (to delight in analyzing others was Lynne's specialty), "with all that money, honey you know what he did?" She looked at Cat, Zofra, then Olympia, "Why that man never indulged in anything! He neva eva drank en was satisfied with a little yoghurt and bread and prayed a whole lot believing in his karma."

"Awesome…. Like a fairy tale…" Cat was entranced.

"Cat honey, it was the truth en no fairy tale about it en he was important to the whole Arab world 'cause how he treated his women. Shabadiba was sent to London to study. En just last year, why honey he gave all the women the right to vote en this was neva done in that parta the world…a humanitarian, a real humanitarian who wanted women in the office and I do declare he was royalty. I mean real royalty…" The treatment on her chin was finished. She paused, changing position, sitting up with the reflexologist continuing to minister to her feet,…"en rich, ya'll know Cat it all depends on what ya'll call rich. Honey, there's rich, en then there's rich en then well honey, then there's serious money."

"You forgot two things Lynne." Shabadiba was incensed with the bantering of her family from this faded South Carolinian who'd tricked Whitney into marriage being three-months pregnant.

"Have I Shabadiba honey?"

"Yes honey-chile as you say, Granddaddy married twenty-three times and had forty children and I was his first granddaughter. Let's set the facts straight even if, much to my displeasure, we are discussing my blood line in a spa of all places….and by the way, Lynne, he detested ostentation. That would be foreign to you."

Olympia's antennae were tuned with Shabadiba's remark, "What money can do is always quiet when given sincerely, I agree Shabadiba. Whitney, like your generous grandfather, is a philanthropist for the Metropolitan Museum, the Modern, the Opera and now this film, not like Tong who's so conservative and doesn't do one blessed thing to support my art. Any man who does that, well, I can live without him thank you very much."

"And to think you have to have sex with him after he ignores your art, your one passion, gifted as you are..." Zofra voiced her opinion.

"Well, uncircumcised Tong isn't exactly a sex god!" laughed Olympia.

"I don wanna get personal or anything, but how much does Tong like to have sex? I'm meaning how often...?"

Her question was ignored and to distract herself with the sudden silence, she looked at her claw like hands with their translucent veins, like the veins on her legs and between her breasts despising the fact age had come to claim her. She was envious of these younger women. They were a continual reminder life would be insignificant if she didn't have her husband and his money. Alone, she would be in the throng of bored, rich women, drinking too much, drifting, hating what life had become.

"Men, men, men...all alike and maybe they say the same thing about us!" Cat chirped youngest in the group, afraid to commit herself to any opinion.

"I'm telling ya'll money is what makes me stay with Whitney. Sometimes we don't even speak fa days, en belive me, he's cold as ice. I've done everythin' to be lookin' gorgeous with all the best plastic surgeons in New York en he neva notices anything. Just for en example once got a porn movie to turn him on, en ya'll wonda what happened...well I was wearin' a sexy little slip from La Perla ya'll know La Perla...sittin' on the sofa with him en said, 'ya'll sit at one end en I'll sit at the otha en we'll see who moves first.' En Whitney looked at it one little minute. "I'm disgusted," he told me, sittin' there with me wantin' some nooky. "Lynne ya'll vulga," en walked out of the room...frankly I was turned on not by those men but the women..."

"Women turned you on?" questioned Zofra taking in the skeletal form of Lynne wondering who would ever want to see her naked.

"Just being truthful when I saw that one film en one time tryin' to do all I could to fire up my husband who'd ratha be writin' all those books no one eva wants to publish."

"Never try zo hard, Lynne," said Jacqueline coquettishly, winking at Zofra.

"Whitney's not like warm Samir....Whitney doesn't need sex...en that's fine with me cause I neva took to a man always usin' sex," She moved to the manicure table "...bein' honest with a group of women we can trust. Ya'll know ya own is what I say. Whitney's plumbin' doesn't work anymore...en I do fine, mighty fine without havin' sex at all...en what I'm tellin' ya is not for publication..."

She put her hand to her head nursing her hangover, continuing without a pause. "I'm sure ya'll got a gander at that look last night between Nigel en Esmeralda. Do ya'll think it's love or money?" Lynne looked 'round. "I'll tell ya. It's money...not sex. I'll bet they don't have sex en it's all Gianni's money. I don care how gorgeous she is, Nigel is lovin' that money like a parasite."

The spa went quiet, except for Groucho barking who wanted to announce Esmeralda had entered the scene. Lynne's back was to the entry door. She didn't realize Esmeralda heard every word.

"Do you think so, Lynne?" asked Esmeralda cool as ice.

"Why Esmeralda, honey, I didn't no ya'll were here en don't ya'll berate me, I was just talkin' about men en money en in your case it's the woman with the money. Frankly let's be honest 'cept Shabadiba there with more money than everyone, well, you be careful Princess cause men will flock to you for nothin' but money..."

The spa was silent except for a stream of sulfur water running down hot coals creating a therapeutic shower and bath near the Jacuzzi.

"Esmeralda maybe that Nigel of yours adores ya'll but with men better make the best of the money. "

"You would know, Lynne, being as you were…wasn't it a nurse to Whitney's ailing father?" Esmeralda questioned.

The group snickered, waiting for a duel of words between Lynne and Esmeralda who'd succeeded thwarting Lynne's hypothesis on love, marriage and money.

To everyone who knew Whitney, it was common knowledge he was bored with Lynne and miserable. Friends believed he was reticent to part with a huge settlement. Society whispers questioned who would be the one to make Whitney wake up and leave a woman who had tricked him into marriage? To climb the social ladder amoeba fashion, Lynne attached with vengeance to everything Whitney could do for her wanting to gain the limelight in Manhattan.

On that turf she acted as if she owned the city. She alienated Whitney from any politicos she believed beneath her, thus he lost any chance for a presidential post. Her loud-mouthed outspoken theories about racial and national issues appalled everyone connected to the White House with her prejudice killing Whitney's aspirations for Ambassador. Her 'dear Whitney' endured it all, including her drinking which was out of control, much to his chagrin. Lynne didn't have a clue her husband had taken to Olympia. Soon her best friend would be her divorce lawyer.

Trying to bring some gentleness to the stinging dialog, Jacqueline rose from her massage, thanking the masseuse. "For me I am happy with my Samir. We have a good life. Itzz nice to be back here, Esmeralda. Thank you for zee party, everything was beautiful. I hope you zingle girls find a wonderful, warm man like Samir. You zee it is important to have things in common en be feminine. Why all this power? Ze men will give you ze power if you do not steal it from them. Zis is very Latin. Like Italian women too. We have our young sons, we have the love of France. We love to ski, to be with music. To hear me sing is good for Samir, we go always to concerts…and his work, this is our life too…" Jacqueline Redat was completely secure in her marriage, and being French did not hanker one damn if Samir strayed from time to time.

"What if he ever strayed?" asked Cat wide-eyed.

"Stray? Zhey all stray…like cats but come back. Zis is the smart zing. Maybe zhey stray to a woman, or a golf game, its zee same. Zink about the future en ze patience for ze men. Forget if they stray. Let them think you stray! This is zee secret!" She laughed and all joined in except Lynne.

"What about you, Zofra?" asked Esmeralda wishing to have all included in this female blabbing.

"Me? I'm looking for my Mr. Right like every woman…have any suggestions?"

"What about Nicky? I seated you next to him last night."

Under her breath Lynne said "Mista Right? Or Mista Levy?" All pretended not to hear.

"Too young. I prefer older men." Zofra, a cougar who adored women firstly and then rich male conquests younger than she, lied through her teeth, not looking in Cat's direction as she spoke. "A man who's arrived, experienced. I agree with Jacqueline, vintage is my choice. Then, one doesn't have to inflate his ego continually with flattery. But, I don't know about children. Do you ever wish for children, Esmeralda? Nigel isn't too old, and you're certainly not."

Esmeralda didn't answer, Zofra thought she didn't hear her, "Would you ever want to have a baby?" she asked again.

"I had a still born child after Gianni's death and it was all too much for me." Esmeralda's blood ran cold. "Let's not talk about it."

"Oh forgive me. I'm terribly sorry I asked." Zofra's tone was compassionate.

"You didn't know….What about Olympia?" Esmeralda wanted to change the subject.

"Esmeralda, I loved the party too, it was unforgettable. I'm sorry Tong didn't accept your invitation and enjoy all the lovely things you've planned. We have problems. My art is first and he always wants me in Asia with him, "I own you, we're engaged' he says. I can't continue this any longer. Drop everything and be at his beck and call. I'm a fool not to put my art first especially now…I'm ready for an exhibition at a museum that will change my life."

"I understand Olympia." Esmeralda said sincerely while the others listened to Olympia's outpouring.

"I'm independent, a feminist and not ashamed to be one especially these days when there is gender bias everywhere. I must achieve everything on my own. I don't want any man's money. It's pathetic how you view men and money Lynne!"

"Pathetic? Why don't ya'll say that to me! Ya'll just wait until ya'll are my age believe me, ya'll be thinkin' of the money. When dere is no more lovey dovey en ya'll singin' the blues, ya'll think about security - even you feminists. Ya'll 'cept Shabadiba en I feel for ya too 'cause there aren't a lot of men you can choose from…I mean men with ya'll title en that."

"Thank you Lynne. I shall remember your kind words like a slipped disc." Shabadiba looked up from the Jacuzzi.

Olympia moved to the massage table, Jacqueline had a manicure, Cat didn't feel comfortable with these older women. "Excuse me, I'm off to the pool."

Shabadiba meditated turning the valve to high while Lynne admired her painted nails making a mental tabulation of what was said. I know I'm right, always am, after all. Why if Olympia dares go near Whitney, the worst, unexcitin' man in bed, the world will see a different Lynne Jameson! I haven't lived to Whitney, with no sex for the past decade, makin' me throw energy to decoratin' houses en this social life, sublimatin' all the time for a little attention en pleasure….but Lynne couldn't concentrate any longer. Her head began to throb and she was disgusted how much she drank last night. Lately she'd become no stranger to the bottle, drinking privately to get through her circumstances, which she viewed as miserable. She closed her eyes delicate to the light in the spa, nursing her hangover….thinking…with all I've done fa everyone en now this bunch of conivin' women! "Can I have a bromide?" she called to the physical trainer, to quell her raging head, knowing she was the butt of everyone's joke, then, soon after reclined as a face masque was applied by an esthetician. That would keep her mouth still for thirty minutes, by that time the rest of the women would depart to their rooms to dress.

Esmeralda's hairstylist called her for a shampoo, Zofra sat unruffled having a pedicure realizing the entire catty spectacle was one she knew well. Her punt was already on the line. Within three days Levy who believed her ten years younger than he, would leave Cat and be on his knees to take his 'class act' from Hungary back to Hollywood and make her Mrs. Levy. He was that easy to seduce. She would pussy whip him and spike his libido. Last night he loved the hand cuffs she put on him, making him beg for kisses. Financial security and glamour he could deliver. Forget the rest. Life was looking good, Hollywood was a far cry from Budapest.

———

When Esmeralda returned to her room, a letter was on the silver tray on her dressing table. The handwriting looked familiar but she hadn't seen it for years. The time was four o'clock.

PART THREE

XIV

Serena Zianni

Last Thursday...

"Serena! Serena! Serena Zianni!" Through the pandemonium of Eurostar trains arriving and departing in mass confusion with hundreds pushing and shoving valises, back packs, baby strollers and wheelchairs, Serena heard her name. "I must be hearing things," she moved quickly to Track 18 at Stazione Termini in Rome for her express train to Naples.

"Serena…Serena!" The voice was clear, English. It couldn't be, Serena turned around. There before her, short of breath was Rupert Davidson. Her face flushed, then beamed, as he gave her a bear hug.

"Rupert! What a shock! I didn't know you were in Italy! I'm rushing to take a train to Naples in five minutes! This is unbelievable!"

"I spotted you a minute ago and have been running to catch up. I'm on the same train, Track 28."

"No! Mine's 18, the Express."

They looked at each other amazed. "Hell with Track 28! I'll board the Express!" Rupert took her suitcase beaming, and quickly entered the more expensive Eurostar to be with Serena.

"This is Chance!" Rupert said, the two darting like thoroughbreds as the conductor's whistle blew, sending an all clear signal to the engineer.

"We made it!" squealed Serena, grasping Rupert's arm with affection. "I can't believe this!" Out of breath, the two quickly found the reserved seat of Serena's asking a fellow passenger to move so Rupert could sit beside her. All went well as Rupert stored the baggage overhead. "I was going to call you," they said simultaneously, then laughed.

"O.K., you first." Rupert observed Serena's sparkling green eyes. She had the same tint as Gianni's. Seeing her, memories swelled in his heart. "Rupert, this is Fate! Why are you here? I've so much to tell you, we won't ever have time enough on this train!"

"Don't be offended, I must tell the truth, Serena," he began guardedly, "I've been asked me to Villa Pina." She was crestfallen. "I missed my plane to Naples, took the next Easyjet from London, knowing trains run frequently from Rome to Naples. Naomi's going to fetch me. She's coming, too, from Tuscany, a group of the old crowd." Serena froze. "It's the first time I've been back," he stammered, "the old crew hasn't been in Capri since Gianni was alive."

"So much has happened Rupert. So much that you'll never believe why I was in Rome and now – meeting you!…taking the train like this!"

"We've two hours."

"That's not enough for me to begin!"

"Well, it's a start. You know Serena my first loyalty is to Gianni's family. That's you."

"But why haven't you called? Kept in touch?"

"It's a long story. How's your husband?"

"Finished. The marriage is finished." Serena bit her lip. "The whole thing, a mistake, thank God that's over. It's been one thing after another, Rupert, a plethora of problems since Mother died last year…"

"Sorry about that. I wrote."

"Yes. You wrote. Thank You."

"I should have come."

"It was better not to. It broke my heart to lose her. Now, I'm the only Zianni in the immediate family. Cousins have been remarkable but to lose your whole family. Gianni so young and such a brutal tragedy…and me, thirty-seven last week and I spent my birthday with lawyers!"

"Divorce?"

"Oh no! The annulment came through last year just after Mother died. The lawyers are another matter." Serena gave Rupert an expressive glance, lowering her eyes.

"Pardon me. It's none of my…"

"Oh but Rupert I wish you'd make it your business…"

"This meeting couldn't have been planned. I need you. I've learned terrible things about Esmeralda! That 's why I've been with lawyers. We're planning to contest Gianni's Will. We have all the documents we need to win."

"That's unbelievable."

"Please Rupert, tell me…is there anyway you can detain going to Villa Pina? Can you come with me to the house in Naples? Be my confidant? I have so much to tell you...I need you…"

Her revelation surprised him, her voice implored with urgency, making it impossible to refuse.

"Of course I'll come." Those words silenced them both. She looked out the window unable to contain her immediate happiness. When she turned, Serena's face radiated the beauty he remembered since the first time he saw her, a teenager with braces, when Gianni introduced him to his kid sister. There was always a hero worship quality how she viewed Rupert, that immediately put him in the position to protect her. Her chestnut hair was long, twisted in a chignon with wisps of soft curls around her face today. Her defined nose had an aristocratic air as did the tilt of her chin and generous mouth untouched by lipstick in Italian fashion. She smiled a genuine smile, much like her brother's, and her laugh was authentic, everything about her was authentic.

Serena's clothes showed the curves of an hourglass figure that any man would admire not mannequin thin and unappealing. Everything about her appealed to Rupert. Femininity was her right, dressed in elegant fashion without adornment.

"How do you think we can postpone my visit to Nigel? How long do you think you'll need me to help you?" He asked sincerely.

"A legal team is coming tomorrow and Saturday to see me. If you can stay until Sunday, I'll make sure you arrive at Villa Pina in the morning."

"That's fine. I must call Naomi and Nigel."

"But keep this confidential!"

"Without question."

Serena took her mobile phone from her purse. "Use this. My English phone. We can speak about private things once home in Naples."

He looked at her intently. What she wished to tell him was of great importance - to question Gianni's Will was unthinkable. He didn't know how she could do that. He dialed Nigel and then Naomi, leaving identical voice mail messages, "So sorry to miss the dinner party. Unexpected family business. Will arrive Sunday early morning, last minute problems. Please understand."

They would never suspect he was already in Italy with Serena. The train's momentum raced south from Rome, the grandeur of Campania's southern countryside zoomed past. The two passengers spoke of the day's events, the world at large, the theatre, music, friends, trivial things in light of the fact that both understood something pressing was lurking, a problem waiting to be told, tackled, and resolved.

Rupert never knew Serena was infatuated with him since their first meeting as Gianni's kid sister and their expanse of years and his diminished circumstances kept them apart. His trust fund dwindled keeping UK taxes paid and that didn't leave leeway for a comfortable future. Eventually he was no stranger to the pub, heavy drinking took its toll, too much for his own good. Word went about he didn't have a love story because he drank too much and was impotent.

Serena didn't give a dash about what others said, she believed in his goodness and in time learned he had put drinking aside and lived on the last remaining acres of his large estate in his family's hands in Gloucestershire. She was too preoccupied to think of anything else but believed a stroke of luck happened this day - incredible serendipity - she'd go so far as to say a Higher Power joined them together this day and now he knew her marriage was broken and maybe a new chapter, a future with him could be possible.

It would be impossible to think his feelings for her were anything more than platonic. They had greeted without a kiss. This thought went through both their minds. They sat without touching hands. She had loved him and he, her. The power of that love rose above her feminine romantic notions and his yearnings as a man. They had touched each other in another way, a serious way. From this meeting to his departure on Sunday everything would finally reflect on a future together. There was an aura about this meeting, the odd sensation that Gianni was there with them. This twist of fate intertwines us, Serena thought, as the train rumbled towards Naples and Rupert analyzed the situation.

Extraordinary thought Rupert sitting next to Serena, feeling her so close, so dear. This meeting, extraordinary. Extraordinary! This will be my greatest moment, I feel it, this is the reason I was Gianni's closest friend. Instincts told him what he'd hear would be catastrophic, not a failure for him, or for her, but something important was about to change everything. Extraordinary! Extraordinary! The word kept going through his mind like the rhythmic sounds of the train's wheels. What will she tell me? Little Serena we used to call her and now here she is!.... in control, mature and beautiful with something compelling to bring me to her....how remarkable the way we've met! Destiny's looking us in the face.

There was no way I could have approached her or the Zianni family, to ask her hand in marriage. I didn't have the means. That stopped me. It had to be done in the old fashioned tradition, the Italian way. I understood the line between aristocracy with money and aristocracy without. Respect held my dignity in check for myself and for them.

Zianni family pressured her into marriage with Gianfranco and now it is over. Finished. No children. Annulled. Why annulled? She'll tell me everything and Rupert's heart burst with happiness knowing she was a free woman and anticipation sensing the meeting of their minds as the train continued it's non-stop speed towards Naples.

Extraordinary! Extraordinary! Extraordinary! Extraordinary!...to see Serena is...and then Rupert was lulled by the movement of the train, beside his beautiful Serena knowing they were going home.

It was.......e x t r a o d i n a r y.

XIV

Esmeralda Pembrooke, Imposter

Sunday afternoon....

The time was four o'clock. The concert set for seven. Esmeralda stared at the letter on her dressing table. The inanimate object demanded attention. The handwriting registered, it was from Serena, her former sister-in-law.

Strange, after all this time, correspondence from Serena, hand-delivered on Sunday. A current of fear ran through her body. Like a cat's paw, she touched the ecru velum moving her fingers across her name. "Mrs. Pembrooke." "Urgent & Confidential," was etched below. It was sealed with wax bearing the Zianni crest. Esmeralda's heart beat faster.

A letter can obliterate. When one opens the envelope, the subtle drama begins, like lifting the receiver of a telephone, its message can change the course of one's life. Esmeralda knew instinctively this communication would be the second letter she received in her thirty-seven years that would transform her existence, the first being from her Mother when she was six months pregnant.

The two letters were linked inexplicitly one from the other. She dropped to her chaise, grasping Serena's correspondence, recalling her omen and *déjà vu*, while memories haunted her.

Nervously, she tore the seal, glanced at the first sentence and broke in a cold sweat. After that, her skin prickled with panic.

Esmeralda,

Six months ago your father, Danny McSweeney, was released from prison in South Africa and contacted the Zianni family searching for his missing daughter, Essy. He demanded money. He wrote of your early life history that bears no resemblance to untruths you conveyed about your background to my family prior to your marriage.

Private detectives were immediately dispatched to Johannesburg to challenge Mr. McSweeney's information. We continued investigating your past. Confidential records and substantiated testimonies are indisputable. Everything your Father wrote is true.

We plan to contest my late brother's Last Will and Testament. He was uninformed of your status prior to marriage and bequeathed the family legacy he acquired as heir primogeniture in its entirety to you should his infant son, bearing the Zianni name, predecease you.

We allege the infant whose death certificate states 'still born' one month after Gianni's tragic death is in question. We require documents of the baby's DNA and cause of death. You have robbed my family of what is rightfully ours and disgraced our name.

Tomorrow the Zianni family will denounce you as an imposter. Fraud has been perpetrated. You will be arraigned before the Court to answer criminal charges.

Justice will prevail.

Contessa Serena Zianni,

Posillipo, Naples 11 September 2004

Breathless, she read the letter twice, with a lump in her throat. Panic seized her. No solution came to mind except suicide.

Four-fifteen chimed from the *piazzetta* below in Capri as the sky streaked with scarlet and sun began its decent. "An incomparable sunset, an incomparable life is over…." Her blood ran cold.

Everything Serena wrote was true. Her past had come to claim her. No solution was possible only a multitude of chilling thoughts about yesterdays. She steadied herself. Her world was crashing upon her, her private earthquake. There was no way to stop it.

She heard Nigel enter the adjoining bedroom. She'd used him and despised him for being so weak. It was her determined mind to marry him and continue the dignity Gianni had given her, thus continue in society with *bella figura* - and Nigel, easily bought - auctioned himself.

She couldn't command her voice to speak, as if she had turned to stone and knew any words she spoke now had to be chosen precisely. No more mistakes could be made. Everything was too deep, too raw.

She betrayed Gianni, the only man she ever loved and now his sister was poison. Gianni's ghost returned from the grave to haunt her and ruin all she'd set in motion. How she had arrived at this point was beyond description. A pinprick of shame stung and then she translated it to another language - the language of survival. Her mind raced.

To free myself from bondage, I yielded. Lie became lie. We are all trying to survive, in a brutal world. I overstepped all bounds of propriety living my code of ethics. I will be stripped of everything.

Her eyes beheld the spectacular view of the Bay of Naples. Somewhere in the north was the Court, the Judges, those who would dissect her and make the final tally. How could she explain it? Details were too sinister, too vulgar to ever dismiss, forever in her mind. She struggled with feelings that erupted in torment. Her hands shook in self defense wanting to blame someone - anyone! Always the guilty wants to blame another...a fact she understood as her Irish temper flared and evil thoughts contorted her mind. It was that death of Gianni! My dead husband cannot rule me from the grave! This crisis will pass. I'll make it pass! I'll win! Hire lawyers! The best in the world!

Esmeralda paced the floor of her Belle Époque suite adorned with Guido Reni's paintings of angels and demons. Nigel will not abandon me. He offers little but we must stay united. He and I are unworthy of this wealth but evil can conquer good. It has and it will. de Gesu will help me. Her mind began to focus...pouring herself a whiskey, downing it quickly.

Gianni and his family must be forgotten. I must survive. Stop this righteous Serena trespassing into my past. I came from hell and have built a future, not to be eradicated by shame. I will conquer this! I lived it. Now I will deny it and conquer the consequences! They will not destroy me!

As thoughts combusted, her turquoise eyes went cold, darting wildly about her magnificent boudoir moving towards the adjacent bedroom. Nigel took note her surprising entrance, glancing at her from the corner of his eye, not raising his head, wondering what brought this on. He remained the picture of contentment, as she paced his room like a cat, while he relaxed, sensing her panic, reading *The Times*.

"Nigel…look at me. There's something we must discuss." Her face was ashen containing an expression he'd never seen before. She was commanding with rapid movements, pacing his room then sat beside him on an ottoman lowering herself, looking into his scrutinizing eyes. To see her humble herself in this manner, amazed Nigel, immediately observing her hands shaking, hearing her delicate voice crack as she spewed forth how she received a letter from Serena and then, like a sewer overflowing, with revelations of her past - her secretive history that overwhelmed him. It was a tsunami of shit.

Esmeralda was a woman he'd known for years, he'd divorced his first wife with alacrity to marry her three years ago. Everything he heard was contaminated, his heart and his lips compressed. His peering eyes never left her, listening to every word without interruption in awe and disbelief. The gushing confession was a sensation and the first time he ever heard her be so candid. Their marital chats in the past ended in a sea of fog, making his remarks guarded. Now he was able to speak as never before.

When she finished and waited, wanting his reply, he answered as a man of power.

Controlled as only an aristocratic Englishman can be, his sonorous voice began. "Esmeralda," he rose from his chair, locking his eyes to hers, "I am not the man you think I am. I do not intend to make this a dreaded scene and be washed amuck with your sins. You want me to be a party to your lies and protect you. This outpouring of bile stinks. I always knew you weren't honest, but I didn't expect this deception. You cannot ruin my life, the memory of Gianni, his family and believe I will stay with you. No, Esmeralda, you are wrong. I will not be coerced or manipulated."

His voltage turned to maximum yet his controlled British character was kept in check. He loathed her, this superficial marriage and what the last three years meant to him. "I will keep a cool head and a cold heart." He went to his liquor cabinet, poured a scotch, and turned to look at her; the vein in his left temple pulsated.

"You mean nothing to me. I am refined and you…disgust me - street trash, worse, in fact, hearing this. Do you think with your revelation I could ever look at you?"

He drained his scotch and poured another. He spoke methodically as if he'd prepared this exit speech in advance, completely sure of himself.

"It is said a woman reflects the character of the man she marries. Both Gianni and I, fortunately, do not bear a thread of similarity to your wicked, disreputable character."

Nigel walked slowly across his room, coolheaded, enunciating every word. Esmeralda didn't take her eyes from him. "Do you expect me to step into your *'Inferno?'*" He laughed mockingly, a deadly serious laugh as a raven would do, signaling the hour of doom.

"To remain with you and alienate myself from the decent and privileged social links of my lineage is not my idea of a future. You cannot fall back on that. I can. You're an outsider. I'm not. My kind will tolerate my mistake marrying you. Your behavior they will not."

Everything he said held impact. Life knifed her in the back. For the moment all was still.

"Nigel..."

"Please! If I may finish." He took a deep sigh seizing his next words. "Don't look for anything from me, Esmeralda, except divorce. And, My Dear, I intend to initiate one immediately and will expect a settlement."

She couldn't believe his words, never bargaining for this. He took one of his *cigarillos*, with utmost care, taking time, inserting it into a tortoise holder, as one would finger a switchblade, igniting the tip, inhaling the smoke. Then, with iced emotion prophesized, "With all your ceaseless vigilance to details," words chipped away at her, "didn't you ever consider your past would leak out? Gossip mongers will mutilate you." Nigel's strides grew broader, then he stopped. His control was that of an animal preparing to claw his victim.

"Nigel, please..."

He put his hands up halting her words.

"Do you believe I want to be there when vultures pick at a woman I was foolish enough to marry? No, you see Esmeralda, I will state you duped me, like you did everyone else. I will declare that I left my first marriage with a heart full of love for my beloved friend's widow who bewitched me with her grief, disguised herself to be someone else, wanting my social protection as a spouse. The world will view me a romantic, a cavalier, a hero who met guile at every turn with your venal personality. You have played me for a fool, but I'm no fool."

Nigel curled his lip, taking a long inhale from his cigar, smiling a fictitious smile, watching the smoke curl in the air. Every word he spoke was a nail in her coffin. Her blood froze. His voice was articulate, without rancor, deadly in its detachment and delivery.

"Over the past years of this superficial marriage, I've strayed from any ethics a decent man would revere. It's been a bitter experience being married to you." He stretched to full height, standing over her, domineeringly, "and if you expect me to turn a blind eye to this evening's confession about your past life - or shall I say the *edited* version of that life - and how you manipulated Zianni funds thinking it makes no difference to me, you've failed to understand my character. Esmeralda you are madder than I thought."

"Perhaps when Serena has her way with you – and she has ever right to dissect you in Court and make you destitute - you should plead insanity. But how can a person, who has manipulated life as you have, be insane thirty-nine years?"

"Furthermore, Esmeralda, you have no remorse for what you've done. Your soul is blacker than I imagined." He poured another stiff drink. She knew it best not to answer. He had made his judgment. His voice had finality to his decision. It was a schooled voice, one that he had used on television, radio and for events when he was the famous BBC Broadcaster. A perfect voice tonight with venom for words.

"Now go to your room, lock the door to me, as you've done countless times, and think about the gravity of this situation. And by the way," he said his eyes fixed on the grandfather clock in his room, "The time is 5:30. The concert begins at seven. There's a movie to be launched which will succeed and be part of my settlement."

Nigel stubbed out his *cigarillo* giving the impression that was exactly what he intended to do to Esmeralda. Draining his whiskey, he didn't look at her. "This conversation is finished." Nigel went to his bath and turned on the shower.

In a trance, struck wordless, Esmeralda did as she was told for the first time since she was married to Nigel. She hated him more than she believed anyone could hate another human being. He premeditated his exit! Had he sniffed the deceit she lived with?

The cold, calculating Englishman I viewed as a dolt outsmarts me with his mercenary mind, ran through hers piecing together the last twenty minutes. Bit by bit, as she revealed her past, Nigel turned to ice. The more he took it in, the more he distanced her with every phrase. Never had she expected him to abandon her.

His stinging words were the prologue to the inevitable disaster caused by her guilt. Time - brief time would make everything crash -- all she knew, all she had was to be relinquished - the money, the art, the houses, the trips, the jewels, the yacht, the plane, the world of respectability she built for herself, her selfish evil self.

I challenged everything, even Nigel's loyalty. His plan to survive is divorce before the axe falls. The god damned pigeon-hearted beast outfoxed me. How I underestimated scheming, heartless Nigel!

She passed her mirror not meeting her reflection. Her movements jerked. First she paced the room, sat down, stood rigid, paced again looking to the view, her heart pounded, the clock ticked. The moon was full and her mind was that of a lunatic, in frenzy.

Crazed, she cackled, "Society's knifed me in the back," reeled in her disturbed mind. The first blow from my coward of a husband. God knows how he will merchandise this! Not just privately between lawyers, but with news stories to guttersnipe journalists paying him to puke facts. He'll salivate with every detail! When I was plotting to marry him, I never dreamed to have him sign a gag order to protect my privacy.

The indigo sky set, streaked by one massive bolt of red the vibrancy of which seemed like hell, painted by the Almighty. She became numb, the pressure was too great, collapsing on her four-poster bed, dazed. "Let them destroy me," she whispered, "rob me of everything. I have rights, I must have rights from marriage to Gianni …people forgive, people must forgive this life of mine...a dung heap of hell - and survival." Yet, gritting her teeth, clenching her hands, she knew there were things no one would forgive and with all the years of a hardened heart, tears ceased to fall, just an excruciating tension drained her voluptuous lips dry, producing canker sores throughout the interior of her mouth. Now even her looks would betray her. She'd lost everything.

This crucial hour hung in the air, minutes moving ponderously. Suddenly, it was five-fifty. Seven was the concert. She alighted from the bed, moved to her secretary taking a stiff ecru card. "Contessa Zianni" was engraved stationery she hadn't used since her marriage to Nigel. She scrawled

"Stefano I must speak to you URGENTLY
Come immediately to my room. Esmeralda"

She rang for Sanjeev. "Wherever the Ambassador is, please present this note. Tell him it's urgent."

"Contessa, are you all right...?"

"Yes, Sanjeev. Do this quickly."

She closed her door, panting. Her hands gave her away with their trembling, her nerves ruled, out of control. She tore open packets of tranquilizers and antidepressants, downed both watching the clock. *Déjà vu* had been a warning. Her scheming mind churned.

It seemed an hour but de Gesu presented himself within minutes. Without speaking, Esmeralda passed Serena's letter to him.

Over the years, Stefano surmised Esmeralda's past was too mysterious to discuss. She never gave him precise facts about her life, the art of concealment lent an air of intrigue to her. Nevertheless, he'd studied his once lover, a dozen years and never trusted her, beautiful as she was. It had dawned upon him once that perhaps she was involved in espionage, foreign intrigue, she might have a false identity – be a foreign agent - a double agent, do something sinister. These thoughts he dismissed believing her not intelligent enough or that he judged unfairly, exaggerating an elusive quality he'd always found in Esmeralda.

Last night's premonition gripped him. He read Serena's letter carefully and as he did, she studied his eyes, moving from word to word. A stern expression arrived on his handsome face that held no compassion. He put the correspondence to one side and looked at Esmeralda.

"Nigel knows everything." She blurted, "I told him minutes ago. He says he will divorce me and will begin proceedings immediately demanding a settlement."

He listened intently as she began, "Stefano, my dear friend," she pleaded, knowing once her secret was told, she'd be a pawn to those who knew it. "Time does not allow me to speak in detail about these accusations ...but ...after all our years...."

He, the essence of good manners, for the first time in their friendship, interrupted her. "What do you expect me to do? You're a victim of your deeds, alone in a world of unreality. Wake up, Esmeralda. Whatever the reasons be, you've done wrong, you've lived a lie. Incognito. You've created this Esmeralda, you must live through it."

He wondered what conscious she had for a serious allegation of crime committed to be at the core of Serena's letter. "Does the end justify the means?," he asked not wishing to know her answer. "Call me whatever you want but Esmeralda, I will not side with you and be a party to this. Nigel's stance is correct, for him...for all of us who revere ethics, truth and dignity. You've betrayed everyone. Don't expect me to be swept into your debris. It's not my game." His words pierced.

Stefano, in a duplicate pose as Nigel, stood coolly in front of her, detached. She hated men who took aloof masculine power with lack of involvement, while at the same time ruled the vulnerable female victim, bonding together like a pack of rats.

"I cannot and will not accept any responsibility for what you've done. Nor excuse it. No, I'm sorry. I will speak about you kindly. I will say I never knew this, which is true. I will vouch for the fact that you, in my limited knowledge of the Esmeralda I knew, was a woman of quality. I cannot lie about the caliber of your character. It would take a magician to do that. No, Esmeralda, I cannot be weighed down with your sins. They are yours. You wouldn't take mine.

"Stefano…"

"Please." He put his hands up to stop her. Then, in a less menacing tone of voice, he said, "What I can advise is seek the best advocates you can. You will need someone in London as well as in Italy. This is only the beginning, the rupture of the volcano so to speak." He looked to Vesuvius, eighteen miles away, silhouetted by the moon. Stefano's back was to her, then, he turned 'round. "Let me repeat, Esmeralda, this is only the beginning. It will get worse. What you have to do now is wash you face, gussy yourself up for the mob you invited to the concert tonight and put on your best *bella figura*."

She observed him with his offer of advice, "Get through this holiday but alert your legal team immediately to be here tomorrow at the very latest. Make that call now...before the concert...and another thing...."

He stood in front of her, a man who had once seduced her, the only man she believed she could trust today "....have the lawyers squelch what they can. Kill the press announcement Serena's team will give the news media. Have them prepare a rebuttal to renounce what the opposing side will say. That is, if you want to fight this."

"Of course, I will..."

"In my estimation, lastly, I advise you to make truce with the family. They are not people to wash their dirty laundry in public. Settle this privately." He began to leave, "Devise something so lawyers and journalists alike will not pick you apart like vultures. Avoid prison."

The word prison made her wince. He took steps towards the door, turned, facing her, having empathy in his last remark. "Esmeralda, I am terribly sorry but I do not believe you are going to win this time. Nevertheless, courage at the critical moment is half the victory."

He turned the knob of the door to go but halted, for the second time, looking at her with compassion. "What I'm advising is beg – beg Serena Zianni to let you escape this wretched onslaught of accusations and legal issues, hand back the fortune rightfully theirs, leave Europe for someplace - anyplace - where you cannot be extradited."

"I want to keep this quiet, Stefano. Keeping up appearances is crucial....I made my entry into European society...I'm one of the upper class but...its' turned to hell, the American's would have treated me worse...they are more narrow minded than the Europeans..."

de Gesu glanced at his watch. "End your vanity. I told you what to do. You've over-reached yourself. It's 6:30, we must be in the conservatory for the concert in a half hour. I must go."

Twenty minutes later Esmeralda was dressed, coiffed to perfection, and poured a scotch from her cabinet gulping it down. There was a gentle knock on the door between her bedroom and Nigel's. He entered, his stance that of a peacock, impeccably dressed as always, his personality transformed.

"Are you ready for me to escort you downstairs, My Dear? We can't keep our guests waiting." Uxoricide in his pleasure, like poison, she held her own, tilting her chin upward, meeting his mocking eyes that knew everything. Those eyes were linked with hers forever no matter what was to ensue.

Marital secrecy made her vermilion, trembling lips lock as his unmistakable male gaze took in the body of his Goddess in Valentino red silk palazzo pajamas that skimmed her magnificent form. The male in Nigel wanted to punch her gorgeous face, throw her to the floor and rape her, he wanted to kill her but he wanted more than that to punish her and would do so by his ultimate vendetta, divorce.

Radiant and cool like the pearl and diamond choker that adorned her neck and matching earrings, Esmeralda sprayed herself with French perfume, prepared to play-act the scene and be escorted by Nigel downstairs, through the garden to the concert.

"Spray your mouth, Darling. You wreak of whiskey." Nigel spoke not as the man she viewed as spineless but as the victor; she detested him more than anyone in her life. This would be a new act, as hypocritical as the one before, but this time she was a loser and she knew it.

They walked in silence along the picturesque path to the conservatory at the northern ridge of the villa.

"Put a prance in your walk, Esmeralda," mocked Nigel, "and smile at me as if you meant it."

XVI

Danny McSweeney, Father

Johannesburg, South Africa

'How many years have passed since I saw her?' the deranged human being of Danny McSweeney questioned. Tormented by the moral quandary of his deeds, damaged by his desire, hatred, contempt and always his anger - his liquor and anger - toward every being he'd ever known made him like this, a savage animal with fierce, misdirected pride. He was the scum of the gutter - an outcast of society. Danny McSweeney, Irish convict, who once had a treasure and destroyed it, wanted revenge. To survive, he'd stoop at blackmail, an offence he did not view as evil.

On the outskirts of Johannesburg, the sleazy district he called 'home, he wrote his letter in front of an oil lamp, on a rickety table in his rat-infested, mechanic's shanty. Biting torn fingernails, pulling at the blackened cuticles, his rough hands told the story of sixty-seven miserable years, twenty-eight of which were in prison with menial work. Gritty with the stain of crime, McSweeney shook from the D. T.s, scraping for a living, surviving on scraps, guzzling cheap gut-poison called whiskey.

Danny was surrounded with broken belongings, a broken life and a broken heart. His was a knotted soul, garbled in misery prying into the life of his undefended daughter. His intention was razor sharp as his pen scratched words emanating from the depths of his illiterate being knowing he created the myth and it came at a price.

Hardened, unschooled, Danny McSweeney was ornery by nature; a run-away foundling, a laborer since childhood when he was not in trouble with the law. Cheated out of any existence of a life, living for most of his years without electricity or running water, he was inarticulate but shrewd. His anguish gave a sharper clarity to his plight. A lifelong quality of contempt for the human race and hatred filled his veins.

Danny's once taunt body had seen years inebriated. Shriveled, with a bloated stomach that hung over hand-me-down relics and filthy jeans, his shoes with mismatched laces and holes in the soles were much like him. His pilled, flannel plaid shirt resembled ragweed, sized for a man twice his measure; his undershirt bore the words, "Jesus Loves Me" wreaking of body odor.

A coarse beard grew helter-skelter all over his once fine-looking Irish face. Down his neck, shadowy copper hair protruded from his chest and wrists sprinkling the top of his hands. He was a slob, without any concept of rudimentary cleanliness. As he wrote, he shoved a grimy spoon of Shepherd's pie left from the day before into his hungry mouth feeling the mince on his chipped, agate colored teeth. On the table beside him, sat an ashtray brimming with butts and ash, adding its nicotine stink to the already sickening smell in the make-shift room.

A failed Catholic turned atheist, there was a sinister vivacity to his mind and that vivacity he'd use. Impecunious Danny squandered any promise for a life, embracing his bottle, talking to strangers, anyone who'd listen to his Irish yarn seeking attention, surrounded by bad company, castigating humanity and himself - always bitter with malicious intent. His vices outweighed any virtues had he been born to other circumstances.

He looked up from his writing seeing his reflection in the chrome fender of a wrecked car near the bedroom door, cursed in Gaelic and Afrikaans and spit. Bushy ginger eyebrows framed sapphire-blue eyes that once held sparkle as a boy, now jaded with deep furrows, cob-web style and moving down his long face, were hundreds of carroty freckles, "the Irish curse" he called them. His nose appeared as a road map with innumerable red capillaries from drink, broken more than half a dozen times in fist-fights. Once, it had been well positioned with even nostrils, now it was ill composed with a growing wart to the side where his larger nostril flared.

The negligent state of his person, (hygiene as foreign to him as this woman he was writing to in Italy), made him recalculate his message seething. Danny pushed himself from the table, moved to the iron ring in the front room, smelling burnt coffee, guzzled the dark brew sitting in the pot a day or two, picking at his hairy ears encrusted with wax.

He mumbled profanities. Outside of that noise, only his feet scuffed along irregular planks of wood, catching rusted nails protruding from the joining, and the scamper of a rat gnawing a hole in the garbage sack. The night was still, no one would come down his beaten path at this hour Danny reckoned, his thoughts would not be disturbed. He breathed ponderously, gulped a slug of whiskey from the bottle beside him, turning back to compose his words.

A silent euphoria foretelling victory passed his mind consumed by dark thoughts of despair. Despair brought him to this point. A life without hope twisted to inflict pain and take his vendetta that was his due.

He was of coarse Irish clay, the clay of his ancestors who bore life through rough times coming to this god forsaken country as prisoners "leavin' their Irish wit in Dublin," he'd tell his pub mates. They survived, he'd survive.

A sensation that he was about to create a catastrophe filled his heart giving power to what he wanted to do. This exhilarated him. Writing began to flow slowly from his tangled mind to his arthritic hands misspelling words with ill grammar not of any consequence.

"The decay of me life beginnin' in the mines….where fire burned for decades, sinkholes, deep at 98 feet, filled with danger en chemicals seepin' into groundwater, a polluted life with levels of sulfur surein' to make pennies to buy crumbs…then, jinxed from the Devil, a scandal all part of her history. She'll be a tattered doll like'in the one there on her old pillow I saved all these years."

No one could confuse his sick revenge fuelled by his pig headed Irish anger. "This time I'm within my bounds," Danny rumbled under his breath. Smugly, he picked at his teeth trying to find the next phrase to write enjoying the malignant pleasure of his deed. "To be paid for life's undeserved inequities is my masterpiece, surein, masterpiece!" The vermin of his thoughts swelled. Scribbling furiously, he pulled his greasy, coarse copper fringe that fell onto his eyes mad with passion. "Cheated outta of life, cheated outta pleasure, God damn the cock-suckin' Devil daughta."

Brutal memories stung with abuse. His heart pulsated. A murder had been committed in this room. It wasn't his fault, it was McSweeny taking the law. The Court crucified him, like she and her frigin' Mother, their crucifixion - excrement. He tore at his thumb-nail with his teeth until it bled, wiped it on his shirt and began again to pen words to this Italian woman whose name he could not pronounce.

"…S…E…R…E…N…A Z I…A N N I." He spoke aloud, taking time copying the name from a crumpled newspaper. "Luck of the Irish, findin' this wrapped 'round the auto part that wop Gargallo ordered... fuckin' luck..damned part from one of his ginny relatives, livin' in Italy. Fiat, wop car, Mothda fucker Essy married a wop..." he repeated himself, "luck'es with me, fuckin'wop comin' to me....so me, Danny McSweeney, could fix his frigin' ginny Fiat."

It all returned to him, unwrapping the small Fiat cylinder from Italy, that day, "hot as Hades, Jo'burg Hades, alone in this'in garage. Hatin' Gargallo for his money, his car cursin the Irish..." Danny never would revive from the shock that followed. Unwrapping the dirty Italian newspaper to find the cylinder, his heart leaped looking at the newspaper. "Surein the luck of the Irish," he told everyone he knew. Dumbfounded from that day to this, unable to understand the Italian words, before his eyes was an unmistakable photograph of his beautiful daughter, Essy, "who I hadn't set eyes on more than twenty years," he told his pub mates. "Therin the headlines - story 'bout a wop family Zianni."

Holding the newspaper in his clutches, his heart beat wildly. The paper's date was four and a half years ago. Danny was amazed he didn't have a stroke seeing the news the first time, another when Gargallo came 'round for his car a day later and translated the piece.

"Esmeralda Zianni," it read, "who lost her young husband in a polo accident at Windsor, England, October 3rd, 1999, has been named sole heir under the stipulations of Count Giovanni Zianni's Last Will and Testament. His entire fortune derived from the multi-national drug firm, Zianni International Pharmaceuticals, is valued in excess of £800 million pounds. The bequest is uncontested. The young widow remains in shock from the tragedy. She is seven months pregnant, secluded in bereavement, unable to be contacted."

Danny McSweeney was born with a larcenous streak, much like his forbearers, who left him at a foundling home unable to cope with the nasty bastard. Prospective candidates refused to adopt the fiery-red haired weasel whose identity was circumspect. Danny escaped St. Angelica's Convent Orphanage several times causing the authorities to beat him into submission and nuns to accept his erratic behavior and delinquent presence.

All came to naught except his escape at thirteen years of age living on the street, used by pimps, shining shoes, ironing clothes, scrubbing floors and finally working as a janitor, then an orderly at the Morningside Clinic in Johannesburg. There he met his only friend, Luke O'Brien, who toiled with him cleaning bedpans, disgruntled with themselves, mesmerizing nights in whiskey, dance halls and whoring. To ignite a brawl if anyone snickered at either one of them was usual or to make an occasional heist without detection in those Apartheid days where niggers were blamed for everything suited them just fine.

They were white, better than the colored race and that filled them with Irish pride. Stunts against minorities gave Danny, much like Luke, an exaggerated sense of superiority. They reveled in the killings and threats that permeated South African blacks, who knew only rampant poverty, punishment and widespread inequality throughout the land. White communities, whatever economic standard they had, were sure of taps that ran water, electricity and complicity with the cops. Whites were better than the 'uneducated inferiors,' with squalid quarters that went, much like crimes against them, unreported to the world.

"They vermin, easy to bribe en do anythin' for 2 1/2 cents." (This was especially true in rural impoverished towns nestled in the rolling hills near Jo'burg. Corrupt police (always) looked the other way; blacks were always the guilty party. Poor white trash like Danny had confidence knowing this and this confidence manifested for crude sex with ebony prostitutes lurking on back streets or squalid brothels that the hot-blooded Irishman would frequent regularly. To use the blacks was his power like so many whites. The forbidden enflamed his fantasies and erotic sado-masochistic wants revolved in his sex-fired mind wanting his white skin to penetrate a black bitch's sooty cunt whose scent was more pungent than any of the manipulating, run of the mill white women he met at bars, saw on the street or knew from the hospital.

In the heat of the African summer, clandestine encounters increased Danny's thrills as ruling whites segregated South Africa's blacks, punishing anyone who crossed colored lines. His bullying Irish nature demanded devotion from his women that white women wouldn't give, thus Danny preferred those whose lives were damaged, like his own, to rouse his libido and bring feelings of dominance, much like the ruling whites.

Ingrained forever was when the sun's fire clung to the humid night and he wandered about the slum passages, drunk with cheap wine lusting after a whore, his loins aching for relief, in the pitch darkness of dank solitude. The risk of discovery for Danny in the hidden brothels and secret meeting places brought the fury of sex with a strange Negroid female to a pinnacle. There was a violence in fucking, a consciousness of rape and immediacy that brought an unparalleled adrenaline rush.

McSweeney, as his cronies called him, would speak of these peccadilloes at the pub, swapping stories to outdo each other about forbidden sexual conquests, S&M orgies and getting away with everything short of murder against black women punishable under law. Life was macho irresponsibility, using his white supremacy, spreading seed everywhere to whom he wanted, without conscious, drunk on the elixir of sex.

One night, akin to an African blaze, he met Emerald whose burning heat matched burning coals like the color of her skin, hot as tar. Her lust satiated Danny as no other woman ever had. Her straight bitter chocolate colored tresses bore no resemblance to the kinky knots of the others just like her emerald green eyes, "from a jungle cat," she told him, inherited from her grandmother. Her type of woman bewitched and conquered Danny McSweeney. Emerald's voluptuous mouth drank him dry and in no time she became the only woman Danny wanted to conceal, to possess, and have her renounce whoring, the way of her Mother that was introduced to Emerald at thirteen.

Now seventeen, this pitch-black Goddess, with unique delicate features, high ripe breasts, long legs and tight Negroid ass, was his Emerald, gorgeous with a scarred life, that mirrored Danny's. She and only she aroused him to the epitome of sexuality.

Demolishing Catholic taboos imbedded from the antiseptic nuns in the orphanage, Danny believed the unattainable was his. He was intoxicated with love; this became a controlling force of pre-eminence for the first time in his life. Casting off every constriction, in his naiveté, he believed he could control everything, disregard law and society. That was until Emerald announced she was wiser, petrified of the authorities and saw the future clearly. There was no life for them together. This was South Africa. She didn't love him as he believed. Love didn't exist for people like her. He ranted mad with rage. Determined Emerald took her stance. "Ize gonna continue to be a prostitute. Ize gotta survive."

Unable to control his temper and to change her decision, Danny beat her to obedience and then fucked her. That did not change Emerald's mind nor did her circumstances. "Ize gone, en is yourz, Danny maybe five, more six months gone." She announced. The fruit of their love was not what she wanted. Emerald was illiterate but no fool. A baby born with his color, would put her in jeopardy of prison or death by the authorities, better to kill the baby. That happened in brothels with regularity, abortions commonplace.

"Gotta 'bort dis chile. Ize can't do it," she said bluntly. "No work nowheres with a babee. No one 'cept me or you, Ize beggin' ya Danny see life true, cut ya Irish pride give Emerald rand to abortion fa dis es a big mistake."

He refused. A convulsion of tears sprung from his heart, welled in him for all his twenty-six years. They didn't move Emerald, hardened to the street-world. Belligerently, he howled, "Have our baby. Give it to the orphanage, the good sisters – will accept a babe if white and if black they'll find a way. Don't kill our child!"

Danny pleaded, "Stay with Danny. Give life en birth. Don't leave me, Neva....."

Petrified for her safety, understanding the inequality of life better than he - her pregnant circumstances traumatized Emerald. She refused. In the darkest hour of Danny's life, terrified of his temper and the law, Emerald disappeared never to be seen again.

Three months later when all attempts to locate Emerald failed, McSweeney half-crazy, accepted the callous truth: Emerald aborted. There were massacres of black people shot by police regularly at that time, maybe she was one of them..

As his habit after work, after boozing himself half blind at his pub, he returned to his squalor of a shack unable to shake his anguish, void of hope, trying to forget the one person in his life who brought him happiness. Emerald was gone. The prostitutes bonded together afraid of any involvement with a whitey. Forbidding him to return to their zone or he'd be reported. He went elsewhere with white whores but nothing mattered. Entering his shanty he sensed something strange this burning night three months after Emerald left him forever. Drawers were overturned, his closet askew, chaos was everywhere. He'd been robbed of his few possessions, his cash gone…but there upon his mattress, wrapped in tattered blankets was a porcelain white newborn with a wisp of peach fuzz for hair, sleeping like an angel. Beside the blanket was a piece of paper with chicken scratch for writing.

> *Danny babee two weeks. Ha color shock me, Ize no choicee.*
> *mze people don wan Essy white trash likes you*
> *hav to leav Joburg 4 police git me*
> *police kill me en ize no money Es.....*

Danny McSweeney's life changed that night. He saw the remnants of ruin his cock inflicted. Yet the porcelain treasure, so helpless, innocent, beautiful made his Irish heart swell, gruff as he was, cradling his infant daughter weeping. That very night, in a stupor of emotions, he went to St. Angelica's Convent where his life began, begging the nuns to care for his child, saying her mother was dead.

Time passed in this wretched land of Apartheid with Danny going back and forth to St. Angelica's fifteen long years. Esmeralda was sheltered from life, living protected by the nuns and Catholic Church, in a privileged white environment; classmates were from conservative families that supported the Convent's private school, orphanage and the United Party who viewed nothing unusual about the white society they endorsed.

There was something outside Danny's miserable life, something beautiful to live for. In collusion with the good sisters (whom he told veiled truths) after a short time, the nuns, accepted the child as their ward, able to locate and authenticate Essy's birth certificate through the authorities finding Danny's name forever linked with his child and the space for mother left blank. "Surein she was dyin' en we tryin' to save the Mother, Sista we neva thought to put her name," the lies began in this fashion. With the help of Mother Superior, Danny changed this to the name "Esmeralda" (because he couldn't spell Emerald) and he gave the surname, "More"... the only name he thought of because it rhymed with whore.

"More?" replied Mother Superior, "like England's great Sir Thomas More?"

"Yes," Danny lied blushing with the lie, "How'da know these were my wife's relatives in London? Her death was so complex en da good doctor tryin' to save her en the baby, too Sister Mary Joseph, they failed me en neva wrote the name....thank you, thank you for helping me en this innocent."

Thus the myth Danny created began, baptising the baby with the sisters as Godmothers, noting in the Public Records Office of Johannesburg the exact details noted here. When Essy was old enough to understand, he told her "Your darlin' Mother – a fine lady of English blood - died giving birth to you." He viewed it as the truth for any feelings he had for Emerald died the day she abandoned him and their child.

Due to these circumstances, Danny found a cause to augment his income continuing to work days at Morningside Clinic and on weekend nights with rudimentary work at 'Oppenheimer's' in Kimberly, hours away, as the locals called DeBeers Diamond Mines that paid somewhat more than the clinic.

When he could, he'd repair things, perfecting the trade of car mechanic. Every cent he didn't spent on drink or whoring, he gave the sisters. He still frequented vile brothels and lived in a pig's sty but every Sunday Danny would scrub himself clean, wear a fresh shirt, shine his shoes and go to the convent to visit his daughter with present in hand, baiting his catch. The nuns thought him a saint, recalling his childhood when they prayed for his redemption.

Danny's prayers that Essy be spared for adoption were answered. He promised the authorities and the nuns he was working towards bettering himself to make a home for his child, to take her back one-day in his care. The good sisters, seeing his devotion, knowing him to be Esmeralda's legal father, appreciating any funds he gave to support her board at the Convent, rewarded his efforts with special love and care for Esmeralda, 'nicknamed' Essy.

The nuns assured the white families that the children in their care would never come in contact with the blacks endorsing racially segregated society. Theirs was a protected society, not like the blacks who had no hospital within fifty miles and lived in squalor. These spinsters of the Church, wed to Jesus, formed the mind of Esmeralda, instilling how fortunate she was not to come in contact with black people degradating them by the way they lived, spoke in a sing-song way that was completely ignorant of the educated tongue the students at St. Angelica's were known for. This education would allow the whites of South Africa to follow in the footsteps of their parents, ruling the country and the lower classes to submission to serve their purposes whether as servants at home or industry.

Early in life Esmeralda learned to be white was to be better. To have education, material means and be white like Jesus was high birth. God rewarded their kind "*the image of Christ.*"

Esmeralda, unique in her beauty, was a child who wanted to reign above her peers. The nuns attributed her early manifestations of grandeur as normal since the idea of privilege was instilled by her Father calling her 'My Princess," with extraordinary stories of her Mother's ancestry.

"Perhaps," the good sisters said, "Esmeralda will grow to marry royalty or be a famous, she's an exquisite child!"

The British Mother Superior, having been living in South Africa less than a dozen years, took pride teaching the child the King's English while formative. "We'll train you just as your sweet Mother would have done if she were alive." Esmeralda's retentive mind wanted to be satiated with everything about England, her Mother's country, including fine diction, turning a deaf ear to her classmates inflection of a South African accent. Everything far exceeded the Convent's expectations including that "You must speak proper Africaans. Never address the inferior race of blacks. They serve you but must be kept in their place. Yours is the race of God, Mother Mary and all the saints and apostles, the higher race with proper language, English diction distinguishes class, one from another, much like other languages, French, Italian, German. You'll see and you'll learn," said dear Mother Superior who voiced her bigoted views, enforcing them over years, every day to each and every lucky white student, brain washing her charges.

When she listened to tapes, and memorized puppet style the tone of voice from British actresses, Esmeralda demonstrated her intention to be the best in all subjects, smiling beguilingly at her Mother substitutes, the blessed nuns.

The school, open to white children exclusively, adjacent to the Orphanage, made no distinction between pupils attired in simple blue uniforms and oxfords. When questioned about her circumstances, Esmeralda would state what her Father told her, "My Mother was from a special family in London who died tragically when I was born." With simple words and ability to share her never ending loss, jealousy was extinguished from her peers. Compassionate nuns empathized with her sorrow and Esmeralda, successful at studies, became their favorite, going to Mass and communion daily.

St. Angelica's, funded by the Roman Catholic Church in Rome and South African State's mandate was clear: to produce the highest degree of competence from grade one to high school composed of children adhering to Catholic Convent standards for boarders and day students alike of Johannesburg's elite white families. Competition was the norm as was Esmeralda's aspiration to emulate the ways of English Mother, her namesake.

Viewing the zeal of Esmeralda's father to earn money and enlarge the coffers at St. Angelica's, even in his humble way, plus his expressed appreciation seeing the sisters train his daughter as a lady, Mother Superior's vanity expanded. "I believe in miracles from God," she'd say to her loyal sisters viewing the goodness of Danny McSweeney, "The former uncontrollable delinquent who escaped the Convent all those difficult years, is one of the Lord's miracles, with his complete change in life to a real gentleman." Pride swelled in their hearts.

In time, Danny with his twaddle how all the saints were blessing him and Esmeralda with the grace and goodness of God, dilating what

St. Angelica's meant to him, achieved what he wanted when pock-marked Mother Superior Mary Mercy brought a promise, (exclusive to the circumstances), acknowledging Danny's petition, to retain custody of his child when Esmeralda was sixteen. Her legal education would cease then and she could live at his home and become a day student graduating high school at eighteen. In this unique setting, Esmeralda came to love her Father as only one could love an idol, her only relative. He had done so much for her, never questioning his Irish imagination that embellished anew each Sunday recounting extraordinary fantasies about her beautiful Mother "Who tried to stay alive with the love she had in her heart for you, bonnie lass, but the good Lord took her, an angel, ya Mother was, to Heaven, en now she's a watchin' both of us…saint that she be."

Narrating myths as only a gifted Irish raconteur can do, Danny wove fairy tales on every occasion, thrilling the impressionable child. All had no reason to doubt the chatty Irishman's blarney when his eyes filled with tears, his voice slowed to a dramatic pace exclaiming with emotion. "All the photos of your darlin' Mother, exquisite creature that she was, were burnt in a fire many years ago." He'd expand further, "She was 'from her home country, dear England' not Irish like me, and, poor Darlin' had no family or friends in South Africa, a noble lady who had traveled here to study the Queen's domain to write a book, beautiful en smart that she was, sure'in she was, who came into me life like a Princess, marry the likes of me in a love story…. it was en then ta have the curse of the devil en the tragedy of leavin' us alone, dyin' a death during her blessed time with child, the baby girl she wanted more than anything in God's beautiful kingdom, to come to en end only the Good Lord in Heaven knows why, Angels came and took her…." Once uttered, he'd bend his head forward, wiping his wrinkled brow and no one dared refute his tragic tale.

The more untruths Danny spun, the more the turquoise eyes the child took in. "Her body was sent to London. buried with her people en the mournin' terrible for all." Nuns sat transfixed listening to the dramatic saga that became taller. Danny's every word was brought to their heart. Thus, he relived his love for Emerald in Essy, this love with a purity he never understood before, making all who witnessed him with the exquisite doll-like creature, delicate in every respect, express virtues about him that were non existent.

Some attributed his devotion to the fact no one ever listened to McSweeney the way his little daughter did. Perhaps this was true. Irish pride being no stranger to Danny swelled and finally the day arrived when Esmeralda would be going home to share her life with her beloved father - to care for him as he had for her, to help him while she completed her last remaining years of high school with the good sisters - tending his house and learning how he intended to make a lot of money in his mechanic's shop "to be able to take you, Esmeralda to England, en surein be with ya beautiful Mother's people. Love you en bring you into society she come from, dear Darlin' wife of mine and you were was meant for everythin' beautiful…fine people, pretty dresses en jewelry - right proper folk with riches like princes – who'll adore their Esmeralda 'cause you speak proper, like them, like your smart lovin' Mother who loved you like the Queen of all England with beautiful mannas en knowledge 'bout history, art en pretty things like your Mother, dear Soul, a beautiful girl, with the finest of everthin' in God's kingdom! Why you're Danny McSweeney's daughter, Emerald More's blood's in you, sweet lass, entitled sure'in noble people were your ever lovin' Mother's family. You entitled, intended to live in splendor God born by her…and how the good sisters at St. Angelica taught you."

All was glorious. Her every prayer blessed her father and mother, her mother's family and all the good in life. "A dream is going to come true one day very soon," promised Danny who sold the whole idea to Esmeralda, then to the devoted sisters who had no reason to doubt the man who had exhibited fifteen years of respectable behavior towards his innocent daughter and towards each and everyone of the religious group of nuns at the Convent.

They had a sixth sense about good people. They, dear sisters, devoted their lives to Jesus Christ, reciting the rosary attached to the belts of their long white linen habits everyday. They studied Danny McSweeney when he prayed on his knees in Church and took communion, devout in faith. He'd bring Esmeralda to England as soon as she completed her high school, they said among themselves, just as he promised and their ward, a part of them for sixteen years, would tell everyone about how she learned to be a lady under their guidance and good graces, their dear Esmeralda will have a beautiful life, the life she was meant to have as her dear Father told them.

Upon making the change of residence, fuelled with hope, Esmeralda was excited beyond words. The institutional life would be a world of the past; the freedom of a home hers at last. She'd focus her love and attention on her Father who sacrificed so much for her promising a future that she dreamed about continuously. Everything was never in question, her sheltered nature was innocent and trusting. A sad farewell came to all the good sisters who packed her small belongings with embroideries they made as gifts. Now their boarder would be a day student. Her life would begin a new chapter.

As they ate steak and kidney pie at his smoky pub, a cigarette burned beside his dinner plate. Esmeralda observed everything, most singularly Danny for the first time inebriated. Exiting, venturing down a long dirt path to her Father's jalopy, his talk seemed strangely different. Blatant braggadocio filled her ears as her own truth swelled, instincts ruling, fearing she would be brought into a life that she never envisioned, a life that suddenly illuminated before her.

Tall Irish tales, sweet in detail that riveted her to learn more about her lineage and beautiful Mother, suddenly in the new setting of living together vanished, bringing distrust. In a fraction of a second, she sensed her Father was lying from that first evening. It was as if she'd been hit by lightening. Poison entered her untainted mind - a consciousness of mixed emotions - the most vibrant of which that she was utterly alone. Separate from her Father, the nuns, her few friends and world she knew, mistrust grew from that moment at the pub before she entered what was to be her home.

The vulnerability of her life without any fragment of security except from this man whose carriage swayed beside her drunk, with a voice that continued to speak without any notion his daughter had distanced herself from him, brought maturity to Esmeralda, for the first time - a maturity called survival. She was frightened, an innocent sixteen year old virgin and believed her life had ended.

Up to now she had the protection of the Convent. She knew all who lived and traveled in Johannesburg lived in fear, spine-chilling fear. It was eleven at night when police guards patrolling the streets stopped their car, questioned them about their whereabouts. "Where you going on a night like this?"

She wanted to give herself up for their protection, to scream, to cry, yet knew it was impossible. "My worst nightmare, was my first night away from the Convent…" she wrote in her diary.

The patrol on the main road called out, "It's McSweeney and his daughter." The officer waved them through the hidden dirt path recognizing her father. It was her first time out in the night. Sensing a changed reaction in Essy, Danny believed it to be her first experience with police curfew. He squeezed her hand as they exited his Chevy, putting shivers through her at his touch. The dirt pitch of what must have been his drive was unlit by any moon or light; Essy was unable to see anything in the blackness of the night.

"I'm tellin' you, Darlin' Essy, not to worry 'cause our house isn't fancy. No niggers will harm ya….no guards in the area either since our place is remote and isn't the ritzy part of town but I'm workin' for our livin'."

In the darkness of the night, careful of her footing, they approached her Father's mechanic shop with a hovel for a house crudely attached behind it. "Ya see it's right off the main road, not too far but good enough…" he was saying as she stood frozen in her tracks trying to fathom this hell.

Danny opened the unlocked door, the place was in darkness but the stench of the interior wafted from the door consuming Esmeralda.

Garbling words, nothing was out of the ordinary for him. In her shock she couldn't take in what he was saying, repeating himself continually within the last twenty minutes. She believed him to be nervous at the same time and drunk. This is the way she imagined inebriated people to act.

She held her breath from the stench and peered through the grime that beheld her. Danny stumbled, "God Damned switch," feeling the wall to light the room trying not to show disgust, she wiped her feet on a ragged mat, the words "*Season's Greetings*," were its message.

"Fuckin Jesus!" he exclaimed, swaying. She winced. It was the first time she heard the Lord's name taken in vain. He cursed the switch again, moved towards a wobbly lamp catching it before it toppled over. "This is the back entry, sort of the living room en the front is through the shop, kitchen behind the parlor en our two bedrooms side by side with the bath 'cross the hall." The lamp cast a sinister shadow over everything. He carried her minimal belongings towards her bedroom, swaying.

To avoid being inside the room with him, she stepped aside.

Essy's education never explored the realm of depression. She knew instinctively this was what lives without hope were like. Lives separated from anything good. It was not just the filth - vile food she viewed left over in the kitchen with ants crawling on plates, stains were everywhere and the stagnant stench of decay. How could her Father live like this? Roaches scampered with wire haired rodents at the sound of their footsteps entering the place as light lit the scene. These vermin, thought Esmeralda, are the only creatures who could inhabit this hovel and share space with him.

"He lives in another world," Esmeralda was aghast by the first sight of the shambles, this shanty she must now call home. Seeing everything at once portrayed Danny's true persona and made her thunderstruck in anguish. She never expecting anything like what she beheld. "I'm nothing like him." She repeated over and over in her mind, the revelation eradicated all delusions of his hero status immediately.

This eventful night she knew the truth at last. In anguish Esmeralda vowed to escape and better herself like her Mother, a woman of quality and noble blood from London.

"Comen' en look at this, little Essy, why I bought you all these things, just for you. See this bed, see the cover, isn't it pretty, just like you. I bought it just for you...."

Danny started to close the blind on the only window of her room, "Now ya neva know little lass who might be lookin' in the window. Even though we live out here in the woods, but you watch me close this for you en always make sure it's closed...colored people, the niggers can escape ya know..."

Piles of newspapers and magazines everywhere, a broken television, antennas for radios, televisions, car parts were shoved in bookcases devoid of books, cello-taped batteries and motor parts strewn throughout the place. Grease was everywhere, infested with cob webs and dust, the incomparable stink was foreign, something she never knew existed. Something she never would forget in her lifetime.

"Thank you, Papa. I'm tired. I want to go to the bathroom."

"Certainly Essy, your house now. Do what you like. Mighty tired, like me."

Esmeralda moved to the rudimentary bathroom, a dirt infested cubicle where roaches darted to their secret hideaway when the one light dangling from a wire above the sink was turned on. A small window, covered with grime and an aged translucent oil-cloth curtain on top of it held up by a close pin was to the right. The toilet bowl contained his excrement and had not been flushed. Essy pulled the chain above the commode holding her breath, breathing through her mouth not to smell the putrid waste of another. The toilet seat was non-existent. Toilet paper was nowhere in sight. She had to put her virgin bottom on the cold, cracked ceramic bowl stained with urine.

She wiped herself with her hand, wanting to puke, and then washed it in cold water coming from the sink's rusted tap, cleaning the stained soap first. There was one threadbare towel to be shared with her Father.

The shower was blocked, its knob nailed shut - the basin, toilet and tub showed no sign of ever being cleaned, hairs were everywhere. To bathe she reckoned she would have to squat not letting her body touch the tub encrusted with pubic hair. From the shower rod hung wet laundry and a paper-thin plastic shower curtain.

The small chipped mirror above the sink splattered with toothpaste sprinklings let Essy see her reflection wishing immediate escape from the surroundings. In disbelief, she locked the door and promised herself at school to wash properly.

Essy moved to her small bedroom. An odor permeated everything as if the place had been washed in sewage. She closed her door and saw no lock on the flimsy bedroom latch. Scared, she placed her belongings against it fixing it closed as much as possible. As she undressed, she heard her Father in the next room, his door adjacent to hers. First came a loud burp, then mumbling and loud farts as he passed gas and grunted. A heavy sigh followed. When he collapsed on his bed was unmistakable, exhausted from drink, unwashed and within moments he was snoring.

Essy tip-toed to her bed feeling the dust of the floor between her toes and pulled back the lumpy coverlet. It has been used, like the sheets. There wasn't enough light in the room to check for bedbugs. There was a pillow, the case seemed cleaner than the sheets but as she lie down extinguishing the one small lamp near the bed, her senses sharpened. In that higher degree of sensation, her hearing, her touch tuned to any harm that might be lurking. The pillow was contaminated with the rancid smells of her Father's sweat. She wrenched holding back vomit knowing it would mean a fast exit to the toilet to relieve herself. Afraid to wake her Father and let him see her in pajamas, not trusting him for the first time in her life, sensing a fear too vulgar to imagine, began her first night, hearing his loud snore through the prefab wall that separated her room from his, choked Esmeralda with terror. She lay rigid in bed, knowing he presented a completely different version of himself to her and the dedicated nuns.

Tears streamed down her cheeks, disillusioned tears that any life could exist beyond this held no hope, only fear. "He's nothing like me nor is his world, this shanty, his life" she thought too terrified to sleep should he wake and enter her room. How her beautiful mother could have ever lived like this or loved a man who lived like a beast raced through her innocent mind.

All his stories lulled her into a false security, all those years of visitation - Sundays for tea cakes were a guise to have her come to this hovel and live with him as his enchanted daughter. How could her Mother, from British lineage, choose a man like this from the gutter? How could she have loved him in spite of their differences? She must have been an angel….. or, Esmeralda thought for the first time, were these concocted stories her father wove as a spider weaves a web? Would he do this to receive all my undivided attention? Her mind questioned her very existence.

Essy understood her beauty was rare, that validated how beautiful her Mother must have been. Not wanting to venture into any exploration of her parents, she chose to delude herself thinking perhaps one time this grease monkey Father of hers, Danny McSweeney, was a gentleman, her Mother loved him, like I did throughout my life for his kind and cheerful endearing ways. All I had to judge him by were visits, outings…. it was all too painful to understand. She wouldn't believe her Mother wasn't an angel. She gave her life and sacrificed death for her. Essy's heart broke in smithereens.

The darkness of the night was endless. Every sound in the ram shackled box of a mechanic's shop with its puny family dwelling behind echoed a thousand echoes. Wind rattled through the warped wood siding and rolled into the heavens. "It's all a hoax. God has betrayed me," she repeated and prayed knowing her prayers would never be answered because this was a betrayal but the first betrayal was to be separated from her beautiful Mother. Deceived to this degree…."I must promise myself somehow to escape," echoed through her, trembling with fear Essy put her head to rest on the pillow. Her neck was tense. Beautiful strawberry-golden blonde hair cascaded on the thin lumpy pillow with its stench to her sensitive nostrils. She immediately sat up, the stink from the pillow too vile. She took the only bottle of cologne she owned, one that he had given her on her birthday, and sprayed the scent on the case trying to fumigate it.

The cot-like bed creaked as she moved her light body that was less than one-hundred pounds. She was terribly afraid of everything including to have her smooth, porcelain cheek touch the pillowcase and naked feet reach the bottom of the bed imagining bugs coming to swarm all over her being.

She heard rats in the nook that was the kitchen looking for food. A cold sweat washed over her. "Where had he found this bed?... whose linens these were, who had used them before me?... they smelled of other bodies." Essy imagined a foul sexual encounter had stained the sheets, "II swear to God to escape this madhouse...... whatever way....as soon as possible."

In that maze of fear, sleep took her, the light of early morning produced a knock on her door, "Wake up Princess. time for you to go to school." The trauma of living with her Father never left her. One day seemed a year. Everyday he drove her to school in the morning and fetched her at six from the library where she studied. "There you'll be safe til I'm comin' fer you."

It was impossible for her to be immune to his drinking and squalor. Her Mother's death must have ruined him, surely that was the answer she sought to understand her circumstances. Asking the nuns if she could work on weekends as an excuse to remove herself from the bondage she felt being Danny McSweeney's daughter, Esmeralda was too frightened to confide anything to the sisters - petrified every night - hearing him walk about the house for hours. To escape was her only thought, run away, exit his environment, a Father whose obvious alcoholism was now no mystery.

Danny McSweeney had what he wanted and no longer had to impress Esmeralda or the nuns whom he didn't see anymore.

At the library, the only place she knew where there was a degree of privacy, she sat reading newspapers from abroad seeking a job or a ship that would take her far away. This became routine to no avail. She persevered, achieving grades, searching, always searching. Months went by ponderously, every day - a year passed, every moment with her Father was hell on earth, always on guard, always afraid.

This particular day from the corner of her eye she glimpsed a frail, handsome looking man (about thirty years old) sit across from her at the library table. Esmeralda didn't acknowledge his presence and kept reading. He was twice her age, white as she, a complete stranger in South Africa she could tell by his clothes. South Africa being unsafe made everyone suspect. He was writing something and shortly thereafter moved, giving her the paper, upon which he wrote,

> *I'm Graham Anderson, a photographer for the BBC, here on assignment, Apartheid '98 is the name of the documentary. The Embassy will vouch for my credentials. Tomorrow at the same time I'll be here and hope you will speak to me. You are very beautiful and can be a professional model.*

Esmeralda read the paper and read it again and again. Could it be her prayers were answered? It had been just over one year confined to the house of her Father. There wasn't one pleasant memory since leaving the Convent.

"If Father ever knew this man approached me or what he wrote his temper would flare into a fight," she deduced, wanting to keep the note but instead memorized every word, tore it to miniscule pieces, discarded it and waited at six for her Father to bring her home. Then she made dinner for him, washed the dishes and when he went off to the pub she went to her room to study and thin about all that happened this day and this year.

Excitement that her future could be changed made her heart beat fiercely. Could it work? Could it be? The next day, hours moved ponderously with expectation until class was dismissed and she left for the library, sitting exactly as she did the day before. There was no way for her to concentrate. Waiting was endless.

She spotted the stranger coming towards her after hope vanished, her heart pounded wildly. She never spoke to strangers. In his hand were several large books. She sat very still. He did not greet her but put a note in front of her books, *"Do you want to speak to me?"* is all it said.

"Yes," Esmeralda scribbled as quickly as she could on the same piece of notepaper.

Graham Anderson became Esmeralda's only friend. He was working in Johannesburg for a month. The BBC would either recall him to London or send him on another assignment. It was thrilling to think he came from the same town as her Mother. Within a week's time Esmeralda listened to his thoughts about her modeling career. She heard so many untruths from her Father but believed she could trust this well spoken, well presented man who confessed quite candidly that he was not interested in her as a woman because he was a homosexual.

Esmeralda understood the reality of her circumstances, anyway she could escape would be her answer. Graham was polite and kind explaining he found her face exceptional - one London would appreciate. How she would photograph under the lens of a camera was all that was required. She had little to risk. They would be head shots. Without trepidation Esmeralda agreed to let Graham photograph her in a studio close by to the library before her Father would cart her home.

Photos of her were air expressed to Graham's contacts in London and the rapid answer returned was "Bring her to England ASAP." Money was forthcoming but there were a million questions. How could she go? What about papers? She was a minor. How would she exist without her Father's support? He would kill her if he knew she would abandon him. What about the authorities? Documents? Immigration?

Undeterred, this was her chance of a lifetime. Esmeralda begged Graham, "Please come to the mechanics shop with the excuse of needing something for your car, see my circumstances and what confronts me to have a better idea how I can escape."

Every hour was devoted how she could get money for the trip, if it would ever come to fruition. All she could think of was to steal or to prostitute herself, revolted by both ideas. Was there any alternative? Her Father wanted her dependency, never accepting the notion she'd speak to a stranger. He'd never help her, never dreaming a life in London was her desire. If he discovered her motives to free herself from his clutches, he would be capable of the worst atrocity possible. Danny McSweeney believed the library was to enhance her studies, she was too naive to contemplate an independent life, she'd never leave him. She was his!

Terror filled her ever hour.

Graham located the dilapidated shanty the next day. One glance at the appalling conditions signaled the crusty son of a bitch McSweeney owned nothing of value except his daughter. A vile feeling of sexual perversity swept over Graham. Disgruntled McSweeney was under a pick-up truck tinkering with its carburetor, as a redneck stood idling close-by listening to rock music from his walkman viewing the malfunction of the wreck. McSweeney crawled out, choking up a lump of phlegm, spitting the yellow spittle on the pavement shouting at the redneck, "Repair this piece of shit, gone to rack and ruin!" Yanking his baseball cap on and off his sweaty head, "Cost ya. It's gonna cost ya." McSweeney's voice carried. A battered Studebaker was heisted on a lift, without tires that were left askew near the gas pump, where Graham parked his car.

As she was taught to help her Father, Esmeralda, acting her part, came out of the shop asking Graham, "What do you require?"

"Think I've got a busted fuse or something…I don't know about cars and this Mini is fussy."

Graham spoke guardedly pleased to tell her he had information about his next assignment; it would be London! They could leave together. Her Father stayed involved with the other bloke, hearing Essy speak to this man about her Mother's homeland. "Passin' conversation," he muttered under his breath.

"How in hell did ya find my shop?" he called out.

"Some friends told me about you," came Graham's reply, "Just need petrol today."

Quickly, Graham explained to Esmeralda he was transferred from one part of town to another, staying at a hotel directly across from Morningside's Clinic. BBC wanted him to document a story about life-saving techniques doctors developed for white people in threat of death, arriving from the jungle of Madagascar with meningitis and how they distinctly treated whites and blacks differently throughout South Africa. This was said loud enough for McSweeney to take it in without interest, returning to his original customer.

"Your chance to escape, I can feel it," Graham whispered. "Come to my hotel by next Friday at the latest, you've got six days. We can leave immediately. I've connections and will arrange all your necessary documents."

"But how? It's impossible!"

"Nothing's impossible. Journalists travel under a guise all the time. We'll fix your papers. Don't worry."

"But my ticket. My belongings…"

"Ticket's in the works. Don't worry. Forget your belongings. Please don't think I'm deluding you like your Father. I promise your ticket will be in my possession and I'll be reimbursed by the agency. I will free you from this rat hole."

"I can't believe we've met!…how I've found you!"

"I believe in you, Esmeralda." He caught himself for although his tendencies were otherwise, this innocent girl with radiant face moved his heart, he loved her as a sister. "I have only one demand."

She looked at him thinking the worst.

"I want first rights to present you to an important connection I have, a person I've worked for from time to time – he believes in my photos. Strictly business." Graham's British accent accentuated the importance of the connection. "His name is Al-Fayed, the owner of Harrods, London's most important department store. I've an idea to present you as the answer to his search for the perfect English face!"

All these were grand promises like her Father's. Graham could be a pimp, yet the idea about Harrods, a department store she heard about made her believe. Ambition gave courage to her dream: Get to London under whatever circumstances. Her life depended upon it.

Graham filled his tank asking in a rudimentary way, "Hey, sometimes this old Mini doesn't start….you could change a gasket, seems to leak, too. I'll be in Jo'burg some months, got to photograph doctors at a place called Morningside Clinic."

"I work there four days a week," came McSweeney's reply chewing on a toothpick, finding common ground.

"How long will it take to fix this car of mine so I can stop worrying about it always breaking down?"

"Come 'round next week," he greased the redneck's car sweating, "I'll repair it for ya."

"Think you can fix that Studebaker...?"

"Me specialty, fixin' classic cars...surein me life, inter'ested?"

"Too much money for me…but let me see it when you're finished."

"Hey guy, so how'da find me?"

"Like I said, I'm at the Clinic, one of the crew from Morningside told me you're the best mechanic in town," lied Graham.

Danny grinned, sizing up the stranger.

"How much for the petrol?"

McSweeney watched Essy go into the shop to pay as Graham entered wallet in hand; this was customary for Essy to tend the cash.

"Hey! Hurry up will ya?" McSweeney was distracted by the redneck's demand and the idea he could pawn off the Studebaker at a later date.

Graham pressed extra money into Essy's hand with details to meet the next day.

Seeing this odd-ball, perked the interest of the sly mechanic who didn't trust anyone, much less someone who spoke to his daughter in a fine tongue. The only redeeming factor in the whole thing was the guy looked like a poof.

Esmeralda's reverent Catholic beliefs had been chipped away with every passing day living with Danny McSweeney. God couldn't do this to her and let her still love Him. Taking her Mother in childbirth, having this wretched Father...it was all in question. Slowly she began to think of religion and the way it alters one's mind. Brain washing with all the tenants of religion was a part of all religions - yet for her, slowly, very slowly she began to question God, religion and all that she had been taught in the Roman Catholic Convent. Life wasn't as they say, life was different.

Danny McSweeney never changed his vile behavior. It wasn't long after Esmeralda came to live in a claustrophobic life with her Father that his love turned to desire. As Essy's budding breasts began to create a gentle curve in her shirts, often he would rub beside her (accidentally he said), stirring his penis. Repulsed, pulling away, made him roar with laughter as her denial increased his desire and Essy approached seventeen, living with him, those formative months of her life.

In the shack where they lived, sleeping with a thin prefab wall between them, he'd finger his prick, stimulate an erection, he wanted his due, his passion exploding his cock, larger than he remembered, he told his drinking buddy, that idler Luke O'Brien, the only Irishman in the vicinity who'd been busted like him and served time, "I hanker after a young one, Luke…one night I'm gonna have my due, rape her as I done ha mother."

"Sounds hot……….real hot," Luke's evil smile gleamed.

"En don't you eva put your hawk eyes on my Essy," warned Danny guzzling night after night.

"I like em young too, innocent, makes a man a REAL man, you can do what you want without a bitch givin' directions, tellin' ya what turns em on."

"Yeah..........fire your weapon...........POW!"

The men drank smiling at each other with a sinful glint in dishonest eyes. Both hoodlums past their prime had a low esteem for the opposite sex. Luke was a drifter. Danny had his mechanics shop, the garage turned into a small flat, neater now as Esmeralda, seething and helpless about her circumstances, toiled as a maid on the squalid premises cooking, doing laundry when she wasn't studying and watching the cash register.

Luke, a ner'do well, was, like her Father, a lecher, a part-time orderly at Morningside Clinic, where Danny worked shift basis when not tending his mechanic's shop. Danny's job at DeBeers was terminated one day with authorities asking questions about matters that never reached the ears of Esmeralda.

For extra money, Luke would swipe drugs from the clinic and sell them on the black market whenever he could, he'd come calling on Danny as an excuse to speak to Essy, recounting these episodes to give him excitement and weave a mystery hoping to interest the beautiful daughter of his friend.

Instead she understood how limited life can be. Luke hated himself, his mangy grey hair, overweight squat body, swollen from drink, the moles on his face, and back, the ringworm that appeared on his flesh, his dirty breath, but he liked young skin. His rodent eyes bulged when he'd see Essy as she grew older and more beautiful.

Utterly repulsed, afraid to look him in the face, nauseous when he spit on the rubble - whenever he exited or entered the isolated shanty, he'd tell her mundane stories. To appease him and her Father, who sat transfixed, she'd pretend to listen, making scant acknowledgements. Theirs was a prole mentality. She was afraid to go against them. The nuns had told her about the men of Johannesburg, "They rape young girls and babies. A rape happens every twenty seconds. Police are corrupt everywhere and in rural areas will rape girls, men take women by force....one in four girls are raped in this country, protect yourself," they cautioned, "Ours is the nation with the highest rate of rapes in the world, men are brutal." These men, her Father and Luke, were her only adult company except the nuns – a cause of extremes that was ridiculous and then Graham Anderson met her at the library.

Esmeralda's glow was pure, her waist length strawberry-blonde thick hair curled down her back like Botticelli's Venus. "You're reincarnated from the original model," said Graham, "like an angel." Esmealda's luminous skin turned red for the moment, embarrassed. She went to the library and studied Botticelli's masterwork. in a book. She loved what she saw and told no one.

Danny remarked always about her looks. "Delicate features from yer Mother." He said this in front of Luke that made Esmeralda blush causing Luke to exclaim, "You're the only innocent girl left, blushin' like that."

Luke never knew her Mother. He'd arrived as a wanderer when Essy was seven and visited the garage whenever he wasn't working. He became a fixture. Sometimes he'd appear when Danny was elsewhere showing off, stupid like a clown. Unlike Luke whose I.Q. was of a minimal, Danny's imagination was gifted in storytelling that would entertain anyone who'd listen. His best client, Jack O'Sullivan, (that rich stevedore turned gentry), who had an old Rolls Royce "got it doin' a favor," he said, went to plays in Cape Town even Dublin and would say, "Danny use ya senses, get educated! Write, like those other Irish playwrights, kin to us, that pansy Wilde - macho Pinter, ya life can be different. "

Danny would listen and do nothing. O'Sullivan would repeat at the pub, "Danny's like that Pinter, Irish bloke livin' in riches, who has a sharp feelin' about life lived rough, Danny you can be another Pinter. Imagination rich like that..." This presented something new. Danny would concentrate nights alone in his bed after drinking with the likes of Jack O'Sullivan who was more interestin' than Luke, his mind wandered how he'd sense something, how if he had his chance he'd write it down one day and turn his luck, write en be famous, make a play.

Sometimes he heard a shuffling of feet, in his imagination these days, they seemed big feet. Then he'd think of his play and then he'd be still, thinking. He'd wait until silence filled the garage turned cabin in the woods...thinking of his play, thinking of what he thought about for a long time. Evil thoughts would come in his brain and he couldn't control them.

They always were the same…maybe she would be better taken while asleep. Ravenous for Essy, he'd think and rethink his strategy. Those feet came and went and he imagined it was a prowler playing tricks with his thoughts….a wolf…he'd wank off, fall to sleep inebriated until the next night when passion stirred him waiting for the courage to write a story about sex or better seize his daughter and deflower her.

"Gawd she's the most beautiful creature!"

The night came. It was hot. The temperature thick with heat reaching towards 98o degrees, those shuffling feet had disappeared or had they returned? His excitement grew to fever pitch. The vein at his temple throbbed and with his hand on his cock he hankered for fucking. He made no sound. His breath was that of a dragon, he seized courage, wild with fantasy, his naked body creeping to Essy's room.

He'd find her, sleeping, explode with a tiger's force, unleash all his pent up desire that boiled for years in that pink pussy. There were those porn films he saw with Luke at the Adult Movie Room that advertised "Incest is best," arousin' him, always, always arousin' the likes of him. Now she would be his, what he longed for. Now he would feel the thrill of rape, rape of an innocent, his innocent!…he owned her..let her start giving back all he had given her, little bitch. He'd be her first. He'd teach her. Train her.

He opened her door slowly. All was dark. Suddenly there was movement. Just when he thought his path clear to take her by surprise, he heard a sound louder than what was produced through his paper-thin wall between them. He lost potency immediately, surprise swept over him. Then shock.

The moan of his daughter, then her scream excited him again…but then…a gruff moan – the moan of a man, a man, bigger than he. There was no mistaking this for his imagination. "That cunt's in bed with a man!" He threw the lights on. Before him was Luke O'Brien fuckin' Essy!..........Mother-fuckin' Bastard......Rapin' his Essy!!

Luke bolted. Essy's piercing screams filled the night.

Cursing, Danny went for his gun and the whip he kept in his room that he'd use when whores visited giving him S&M. His fury was insane. He'd whip the shit out of that two timing daughter of his, just like he had done to her no good Niger mother! And shoot the b'Jesuz out of O'Brien, fuckin' his property.

Everything happened in a flash. The loaded gun and the whip were stuffed into the wooden crate near his bed overloaded with crap he never used. The gun he found quickly on the top, the whip hadn't seen action for a year. Then he found it, cracked it and walked back to Essy's room to throttle her and rape her himself.

Let her see what her Father's juices were! His pecker, his mouth salivating to mutilate her with his hard dick, whip her to submission, make her vomit with shame and then be his, just as he'd seen in porn flicks, fathers became masters of bitch daughters.

He was afire, alive with tension, resolve filled his brawny hands clasping the whip in one hand, gun in the other. This was his moment, his time, his power and that god damned wrench of a daughter would pay for this, pay for the shame of her mother, lettin' Luke fuck her like a common whore, for her givin' her cunt and all his years of being shit on. No body shits on me! Profanities raged, fired from his lips like the monster he was. He kicked her door open again. The bed was in front of him, sheets askew and all was barren, vacated, empty, a blank canvas. Nothing but squalor remained of his daughter's room, this sty of a bedroom startled him with the shock that Essy fled with god damned Luke, the one true friend he thought he had, Danny's anger knew no bounds.

Esmeralda raced at breakneck speed from the house in floods of tears tearing herself away from the swine, Luke, carrying a beat-up rucksack - running wildly, her breath pounding with the beat of her heart like a drum….all hell….the horrible scene taunted her, she'd lost everything, her mother, her father, any family she dreamed of, her virginity, any idea for a decent life, running in the night, her innocence gone, the virginity she cherished stained forever by a beast who raped her, her mind askew, never understanding the strength of character she possessed, near collapse, alert, her heart inflamed, her exquisite silhouette leaving forever the thread-bear squalor behind. She ran like a gazelle, faster than she ever dreamed possible.

Hearing a train rumble down the tracks in the far distance, knowing escaping was the only way to survive, she ran down the long dirt road, clutching dollars Luke threw at her when she grit her teeth, without force to fight off his flabby body as he ruptured her hyman and raped her virgin body. Fear, shame, panic, it was all monumental.

Freedom was hers after a lifetime of virtue and anxiety - eighteen months living with her Father, in continually dread that the night would arrive when incest would be the scenario. She was consumed with remorse, raped by her Father's friend, petrified her Father would catch her and follow suit. She ran on, panting, racing in flight. Afraid an ambush would turn her back to a sordid past, her mind went in orbit. "I wanted to be pure, my first time....this horror!..." She felt blood between her legs, "I'm not a bitch. I'm not a whore! A new life! I will find it! I must! I WILL!"

Power she'd never experienced accelerated to a velocity she never knew she contained. The power to be free! Heartbroken but free! She expedited her speed with the momentum of extraordinary exuberance, a new found freedom was hers! Few could understand the spirit of her teenage courage; her sprint became a magnificent exit escaping hell. The release filled every pore of her body and exalted her mind. This wretched night would remain indelible. "God HELP ME! FORGIVE ME..."As she raced to the highway, tears falling from her eyes, with the impetus of flight - like a miracle - a car appeared, she flagged it down panting..."It's an emergency! Morningside Clinic PLEASE!" Shots in the air were heard as the car pulled away. Esmeralda never looked back.

His life, her life in South Africa was over. This was a life that she would never claim as hers, a life plagued by disadvantage. She would never return once she escaped and never, ever consider it home. All that awaited was London, the beauty of knowing her Mother's people, being the woman she was always meant to be - and, to be free at last.

Graham Anderson couldn't believe there was someone in the lobby calling from the front desk in the middle of the night. Two days earlier than expected, there stood Esmeralda. He rushed to shield her from the inquisitive staff.

Within twenty minutes Esmeralda was safe, in his car speeding to Cape Town for a flight to London the next morning with all documents required. The BBC helped, Graham had foreseen everything and knew they had to leave South Africa immediately.

Essy McSweeney was now his eighteen-year old sister, Esmeralda Anderson. Luke was pronounced dead. Danny McSweeney arrested for murder that night.

The violent tale made headlines throughout South Africa including the strange disappearance of Essy McSweeney, "a victim of racial violence," "Brutalized" said the headlines, "by Negroes who wanted revenge on Danny McSweeny, her Father." Her body was never found.

The nuns at the Convent were stunned and all went into mourning.

The good sisters of St. Angelica's Convent were further shocked, receiving a letter days later addressed to Mother Superior from a woman named Emerald with another sealed envelope enclosed instructing the benevolent nun:

> *pleas help if yu eva no wear my daughsta is..*
> *giv Essy ths letta so she no why Ize left ha.*
> *God bles yu. Emerald Jones.*

Mother Superior crossed herself twice, in awe, staring into space, speechless, never thinking she would forward the letter eighteen years later.

XVII

London

It was a damp, autumn night when Esmeralda arrived in London. Ochre leaves wet with dew decorated the pavements of Chelsea glistening from street lights like the yellow brick road to Oz. Settling into the ten-foot wide Queen Anne townhouse, a street away from Chelsea Embankment, the Lilliputian dwelling Graham inherited from his parents was situated midway on the miniscule one-way street. A Victorian lantern set off a luminous glow on the varnished front door with shiny brass fittings. The time was seven in the evening. Esmeralda was to learn London's weather changed at four, then at seven and finally at midnight. Her dream had come true.

"Your bedroom's on the third floor. You have your own bath," Graham said carrying two small cases.

Esmeralda's first glance at the diminutive sitting room, decorated tastefully with antiques, walls lined with books and two framed portraits of what must have been his parents, were as she imagined from British novels. The front room contained a undersized staircase to the right of the entry, further along came a dining space with a mahogany table and set of chairs. From the French doors beyond a pint sized garden overgrown with ivy creepers clung to the fence and adjoining houses.

The ceiling was low yet high enough for Graham's six-foot lanky body not to stoop. There was a crystal bowl of potpourri on a side table and random width oak floors, Persian carpets complimented oxblood walls and gleaming white wainscot.

Wide eyed at her new surroundings, enchantment came to mind. Peace was in this house, everything spoke of goodness, security and serenity. For the first time in her life, Esmeralda knew trust. The importance of this virtue overwhelmed her. It was perfect, perhaps the most perfect thing one could do was to trust, and in that trust was its twin, respect. She revered Graham, who had brought the two most precious components of life into her world.

Throughout her seventeen years, Esmeralda lived with anguish that at anytime the Convent would dismiss their promise and authorize foster parents to remove her from the institution, the only home she knew. Then, the delusion of her father's home was extinguished with the first whiff of stench seeing his hovel. Graham presented something entirely different.

Her new country gave a feeling of permanence, belonging - and to belong to a place, to a person had to be the most valued of all treasures – especially when that treasure came with peace of mind and an environment of tranquility. Love, she deemed was different. Love came as a bouquet with many species of flowers. One falls in love with a lover, one falls in love with a spouse, and one falls in love with a place: London.

Still in shock from the past few days of changing identity and escaping, innocent of mind although the vulgar smut of rape stained Esmeralda vilely, she instinctively understood to love another was the highest plateau in life. Without respect and trust, without peace, that was not love, that was passion - infatuation or something disloyal without a soul connection.

God never presented her with a brother, but now Graham was here whom she loved more than any human, he was her complete family. The miracle that this soft-spoken, calm English gentleman had rescued her from a pit of hell and would not abandon her made the barbed wire horror of Esmeralda's past fade; her secret never to be revealed.

Graham created her dream and would see it came true without any sexual connotations. He didn't expect payment in return; there were no conditions between them yet there was a line, a curtain, an understanding and her heart broke with pain knowing she would never have a future with this exceptional man.

Graham's sensitivity absorbed all of Esmeralda's thoughts, "I'll light the fire," he said shyly keeping his back turned as he did adjusting the gas coals, bursting with his own emotions. 'We will live as brother and sister,' mirrored their initial thoughts. It was the first time Esmeralda wanted a man in the most exquisite sense how a woman can desire a man and the profound message was clear. He was not her man and never would be.

"There are few people in this world," Graham advised, "who don't have something to hide. We all have secrets, Esmeralda. Be careful wherever I take you. A slip of the tongue can reveal your secret which would discredit everything."

"Please Graham, go over everything again."

"We have an appointment with the Director of Advertising for Harrods. They've been searching for a woman who'll be their exclusive model publicizing English products for their international market. You will succeed! I'm positive."

Esmeralda took in everything he said.

"It will mean substantial money for us both," he confided. "The marketplace is always hunting for a new look, a fresh face that will spark the public, someone to admire that conveys a message the reigning girls do not contain. They've over commercialized themselves." He continued as if it were a business meeting. But it was, wasn't it? "The initial shots I took are wonderful but Harrods want more. We will work like a team. What you must remember always: People will treat you as you allow them to treat you."

The next week at Graham's Soho studio were fifty black and white oversized blowups of Esmeralda everywhere. Graham had developed reams of film from photo sessions the past days. He'd bound another half dozen color prints on board and created 'her book,' he called it for presentation.

"These people don't care who you are. But they don't want scandal! Your name is Anderson, you're my distant cousin, not my sister as you were when we left South Africa for the authorities. No one will know the difference. Your passport reads you're one year older, eighteen, born in London and no one will question that. You don't have to say much. Better to be mysterious, let me talk."

"Yes." Esmeralda said memorizing all he was saying.

"In time we'll figure out every angle for your new identity. The way you speak helps, that's a give away in England, you sound like a right proper Sloane."

"Sloane?…What's a Sloane?"

"A Sloane's someone like Princess Diana, speaking the right phrases in a correct twang, learned from boarding school."

"How can I get away with it?"

"You will. The CIA, the MI5, and journalists all get away with it taking false identities. The Italians have a name for it "*bella figura.*"

"Bella figura," What does it mean? I like the way that sounds. Do you want me to speak Italian too?" "You will! And a little French!. *Bella figura* is what you convey, the image you present. It takes in everything from the top of your head to how you walk, talk, dress and move...also what you know and how you express it. It's façade this game of life, remember that Esmeralda. It's how you present yourself. That'll be your benediction or your downfall. You'll make it. I'm sure of it."

Graham arranged everything. The past weeks were frenetic with details to learn by heart, how to pose, walk, sit, stand, laugh. "I feel like Henry Higgins but he had to teach Eliza how to speak."

"Who's Henry Higgins and Eliza?" brought Esmeralda's response. Graham realized he was creating a fresh human being and it would take every waking minute to create Esmeralda Anderson. "They are characters from George Bernhard Shaw's play, *'My Fair Lady.'*"

"Oh I've heard of that show."

They'd shopped for clothes, took a thousand photos, spoke of philosophy, visited museums, art galleries, classical concerts, the West End's theatre. Graham took Esmeralda all over London. She never knew her entry into his life was a cause for him to live again but that comes further along in this story.

The Modeling Agency that produced funds to leave South Africa was anxious for Esmeralda to go under contract. Graham paid them off for the airline ticket out of his own funds and never told Esmeralda knowing he had to keep the country of her birth secret. He told the Agency he'd discovered her in Madagascar.

"Harrods is more important if we can get an exclusive. I don't want to see you pawned over by everyone in town. That's what a model agency does, overexposes models."

Graham advised, "When the Harrods contract expires in a year, and they get their 100% out of you, believe me, Esmeralda you'll be more mature and sought by everyone. You'll never worry about money again in your life." Graham began brushing her long strawberry-blonde mane, "Here's how I want you to wear your hair."

Esmeralda was Graham's fantasy. Her face, unique turquoise eyes, magnificent skin and perfect features were photogenic beyond his wildest hopes. He'd been waiting for a decade to find a face like Esmeralda's and knew others had succeeded and she would too, wasn't it his former colleague Rodney Barclay who discovered Kildine Mousson and the rest was history.

Sitting across from Harrods Board of Directors a week later left no doubt as the globular eyes of Mohamed al Fayed locked onto Esmeralda's with triumph. Behind large horn-rimmed glasses, which he took off and on, the quick notes he made, his decisive mind claimed the day. In less than two weeks, Esmeralda Anderson was the exclusive face of Harrods for their 1988 campaign. Graham the official photographer. The ante for Esmeralda sounded like a long distance telephone number, all of which was given to Graham as her business partner to invest carefully with his investment broker.

Thus the masquerade began.

They shadowed each other as Esmeralda started her rapid education into the ways London life. As it was when she was a young student, Esmeralda absorbed every lesson and every experience Graham introduced. She felt lost when he wasn't in her company. Everyone who met her was curious…where did she come from? Who was she? Did she have a lover? What were her passion…. who were her friends? Where did she go to school? What did she eat? Was she rich? An adventurer? Promiscuous? What did she do after photographic sessions? Why were the cousins so close, could it be a love story?

Esmeralda's art of concealment brought more interest. She'd learned the spirit of language. It was what she didn't say that appealed to everyone. Using her eyes, her smile, exhibiting her pedigreed class (that all believed inherent) made suitors of all ages desire the ravishing model who spoke magnificently, the essence of English femininity. Harrods adored her mystique and restraint not to seek outside publicity in a vulgar manner thus creating further allure to her extraordinary entrance into their domain. The Model Agency was promised an exclusive contract immediately after the Harrods year ran out but only if they never divulged in what city Graham had discovered his Venus. Legal papers were drawn up to secure this promise.

Graham loved Esmeralda with all the energy of his soul. To squelch gossip, he found a sunny flat two streets away from his house for her, yet moving from his home made little difference, the two were inseparable. Harrods contract included work in Germany, France and Ben-lux countries for the first phase, the Latin countries, Middle East and Asian would follow for the second. Traveling together brought the 'relatives' closer and in time Esmeralda relaxed. The fear that entwined her of being discovered for something other than she was, began to evaporate producing the pearl that had arrived in Graham's life from a rough shell of a wretched father.

Graham Anderson was thirty years old when he met Esmeralda. His parents had died from a terrorist attack by the I.R.A. in London fifteen years before. Broken hearted, it was just as well he believed for they never wouldhave accepted their only child was homosexual. It was easier for Graham to acknowledge his proclivity without unnecessary guilt trips like several of his friends at St. Martin's in the Fields studying art who contemplated suicide, one of whom succeeded. Those were still the years of concealment and homosexuals didn't advertise the fact.

Graham was financially independent and could pursue the forbidden. From his earliest days there was a bohemian quality in him wishing to shed posh English upbringing that was his birthright, not that he was titled, but his family had 'means,' public schooling began when he was seven at Whitafield's where he met his is first contact into the dark world of homosexuality. The photographic profession brought him into the realm of the theatre, hence he had a studio in the West End on a dank, stinking alley where beautiful women arrived with androgynous men, their stylists. The free love life of a homosexual was his, Soho being a mecca for promiscuity.

Making his mark as a photographer, complex assignments began. The BBC and *The Times* sent him on location for in-depth articles for documentaries or Sunday magazine supplements. He dreamed to be another Frank Capra squirreling himself in ditches clicking his shutter to produce unforgettable photographic journalism. Exotic travels produced freedom as the latchkey and a string of sexual encounters ensued, homosexuality being no stranger to orgies. Graham never knew where it happened but Morningside Clinic days before he met Esmeralda informed him he was H.I.V. positive. The prognosis was he had less than three years to live.

This left no doubt in his mind to be Esmeralda's 'guardian angel' when he saw her dire circumstances. He had played with gay lust and before him was his ideal, had he been born female. She would come to understand all this in time; that's why he openly announced his homosexuality the day they met. Their bond was a strange mix of unspoken love and misery. Both knew the other was sexually unavailable. This produced a friendship of love known only to those who have undertaken the same path.

With experts in the beauty field and the finest theatrical coaches in the entertainment industry Graham, (her 'Zvengali), formed the life of Esmeralda. In time twenty months of charade were accomplished. Harrods renewed their contract for another year and al Fayed recommended Esmeralda open the famous store's annual parade and sale, announced in the past by Goldie Hawn. Everyone was entranced with Esmeralda, the woman whose image invoked Harrods aristocratic clientele. Mohammed al Fayed was ecstatic as were his customers.

Nevertheless with a future set before her as an icon, in a brief time Graham was suffering at Chelsea Westminster Hospital with AIDS. Esmeralda's donned gloves and a sterile costume daily to be with her beloved Graham, containing her grief. His face had turned to a pallid shade of white with violent tones under his eyes and sores everywhere. He sweat like one who had run a mile, his bowels were uncontrollable. The man she loved the most in this world was dying before her eyes and she was unable to save him. She was nineteen, twenty by English standards and Graham knew she was to be alone in the world. His love for her swelled as his departure drew near.

They discussed everything everyday knowing days were numbered and soon she would be alone in her charade, vulnerable to everyone. Graham wanted her protected. He wanted to have someone come to take his place and in time the someone he wished for materialized.

XVIII

Herr Baron Martin Heindrick von Beck

"In all my years I have wanted for happiness. When I saw you, the first time you were on television in Munich, you said some English words about visiting London. I stood spellbound, I came searching for you... that's how it happened for me. And, for you?"

"My dear Baron," Esmeralda began in her gentle voice looking into the eyes of the kind soul beside her, his podgy body moving closer, his large grey droopy eyes akin to a basset hound were aglow, "I'm flattered with your words, and thoughts unspoken that I know you contain but..."

"At my age decisions are made with intensity." His heavily accented German voice was kind. "Please, Esmeralda, do not refuse me...and do not say the word 'but' please...Esmeralda...consider what I have to say. I beg you."

Baron Martin Heindrick von Beck was not a man to be refused. He'd seen her image on television and that was all he required to tell his butler "Order the plane. Call al Fayed, arrange a meeting with the woman I cannot erase from memory."

This night, hunched over with tasteful double-breasted suit, a rotund cranium that produced a face of like dimension, with wisps of white hair circling his bald head in corkscrew curls, sat Martin Heindrick von Beck, besotted. A stout yachtsman, wrinkled from the sun, with a devilish gleam in his eye that left no doubt as to his desire, his straight nose was large for his face but not unattractive, his ears oversized, close to his head that set off a sagging jaw, punctuated by a seductive mouth that had seen a billion kisses from far too many women.

He had been a Casanova, married five times, extraordinarily rich and had no children. His rogue-like humor was without parallel creating the illusion he was far younger than his years. Esmeralda knew he was the answer to Graham's prayers.

She sat back on the plush velvet banquette of Claridge's dining and listening. It was late. They were the last guests lingering in the hushed ambiance of the dining room. A waiter stood hovering in the shadow, respecting the distance, should the generous Baron, their esteemed client, signal him.

"I am forty-five years your senior Esmeralda and I'm in love with you. I know you do not love me but I can give you everything your heart desires. I will protect you from everything." His hand held hers." This is not my ageing fantasy. You're hearing my heart speak. You will make me sublimely happy if you accept my proposal to be my wife." His eyes were unmistakable in their sincerity. Baron Martin Heindrick von Beck was a man in love.

She smiled. She couldn't help but smile. "If I am to marry you, aren't you afraid I will take away from you all that makes your life worth living for?"

"Your presence in my life makes all life worth living. We will go forward and I trust in time you will see life from my perspective ...With time perhaps you will love me. My wish is that you will."

"Baron…"

"Esmeralda I'm so glad you didn't say 'but'…but you must say Martin.... You see, Esmeralda, with you I will have a reason to live, a life to be enjoyed, traveling everywhere, giving you whatever you…"

She put her soft, porcelain fingers upon his aged, spotted squared hand. She'd been in London three years, her one true friend Graham Anderson lay in a hospice dying of AIDS. Together they'd transformed her into the most important symbol of English beauty under exclusive contract to Harrods. She didn't take to the fanfare of celebrity - afraid of exposure - and blessed the day Graham refused modeling agencies to overexpose 'his cousin.' The London party scene with its superficiality, women discarded like cards as a new one emerged, without love, commitment or responsibility, she'd witnessed.

Sentiment seemed to have left her persona after the nightmare of leaving Johannesburg. Only Graham had her heart. Now the Baron wanted it. Esmeralda confided in Graham about everything... Beck's intentions and his fascination realizing with Graham's passing there was no man in her life who'd want her other than for a sexual conquest. Beck wanted the security of marriage and in that security would provide protection. Graham was the man she would love forever. Never in the way it should be, his devotion to her was unique as he lay shivering with blankets and a hat to shield the open sores on his head.

"Don't be a fool," his voice struggled to speak that afternoon, "If he asks to marry you, do! From there the world will be yours. Beck will die soon, his fortune will be all you need to do what you wish. You're still very young…"

Those were the last words Esmeralda heard Graham utter. He died in the middle of the night while she was at Claridge's with Baron Martin Heindrick von Beck.

To please Graham she would accept this withered, overweight, sweet, bulky man whose height was three inches less than her own. To please the Baron and to please herself….she would be his Baroness, his protected Baroness. Graham will die in peace with me acquiescing to his last advice and I will never be afraid. She reflected countless thoughts.

She studied the Baron as they ate *frois gras* then a la carte specialties sipping Romani Conti '72. Men have pawed me all my adult life except Graham. It will make no difference to have this man in bed and give myself to him. This is not love. This is charity. He will give me dignity and security. I will be his final passion. Let me take this chance, a golden chance, I can always divorce. He will give me his name and this will solidify permanence for us both. I will play act as Baroness. I can smile, as I do on camera, and with the incognito identity of my life, his title will shield my past more than anything before...

...Martin Beck will safeguard me from life. He will use me, everyone has used me but Graham. Martin Beck is willing to have me use him, and I will. I will accept the Baron's proposal.

She listened as Martin spoke of life together. He speaks of love! Oh this game of life is a farce! Love! He means lust! Possession! If Martin knew where I came from, would he love me as much?

"Baron would you like me to speak of my background?"

"Nothing is important to me except we are together," he replied understanding, more than she realized, she had something to hide. She was far too young to know the depth of the Baron's tolerance, intelligence or devotion; his only wish was to have her rekindle his life. That's all he wanted.

Thanks to Graham my secret will be taken to his grave. Her mind wandered as Martin confessed his heart's longings.

There's magic and mystery to disguise. One should never tell everything. Certainly I never will to anyone. Esmeralda thought....no reason I ever have to! Martin Beck is marrying the woman he saw on television. I have been reinvented and prefer this me. This is 'the me' I was born to be! This is what the Italians call *bella figura*. My Mother would adore this! Father can die in his prison cell consumed in his stench. There is nothing in me like him.

"My sweet Martin," her voice whispered knowing she could wound him, and would never want to, "is this the place to speak of such matters?"

His pleading eyes rested on her glowing. They were easy to read. She stroked his hand slowly, his meaty mouth was open like a large fish, yes, she thought, Martin is a good catch. Esmeralda smiled provocatively, "Why don't we go some place more private." The tone of her voice was velvet. With this phrase, her consent was assured.

The Baron kissed her hand with what seemed like a hundred kisses, the two left the banquette, his heart aflame with desire.

Baroness Beck eloped with her nobleman within a fortnight just before her twentieth birthday. He believed she was twenty-one, he believed everything, as a man in love does.

With Graham dead, it was better for Esmeralda to be away from London, away from everything, giving up any thought of a career, mourning the loss of her beloved friend.

Enshrined as a Baroness in Bavaria, Paris and Cap d'Antibes, Martin brought a fantasy world to Esmeralda, one she could profit by not exclusive in riches alone. He was the seventh Baron of the von Beck family dynasty whose lineage linked with the Hanovers thus they were invited to drawing rooms of the inner circle of nobility throughout Europe. Her modeling career was put aside.

Their castle outside Munich was a towering edifice that made her think of Rapunzel needing to let down her long hair to have a lover enter her chambers by the ramparts. The vastness of the castle built in at the time of Ludwig II of Bavaria's reign, reminiscent to a miniature Schloss Neuschwanstein with its towers and moat, frightened her with its enormity, intimacy being put aside for grandeur, which the apartment at the Ritz in Paris contained. That was a duplex, gilded as Versailles, Esmeralda enjoyed ordering *haute couture* clothes from the finest establishments in a city full of fascination and the French language.

Spoiled by her husband who remained in rapture of his *jeune* wife, the joy of his existence!...she received whatever her heart desired.

She never felt alone in Paris as she did in Germany for Martin would encourage her to view the galleries and never permitted her to venture alone. If he couldn't be with her, his chauffeur accompanied her everywhere like a bodyguard. It was Martin's possessiveness certainly but this endeared him to her until his domination became stultifying.

The pristine villa in Cap d'Antibes behind its electronic gates was located juxtapose to Hotel du Cap around the bend in the road, out of sight from the tourists with an overview of the Mediterranean that left her breathless from its beauty.

In this position, Esmeralda studied the rhythm of the sea with its currents and drama sensing the power of life giving full respect to nature, having the puzzles of her life begin to fit a pattern as she digested the drama of her circumstances. These thoughts were private where her husband couldn't trespass. He respected her retreat inside her solitude viewing it as youth, overwhelmed with the glamour of her new life, and like a sculptor, tried to chip away at her hidden chasm in his quest to possess all of her, including her every thought. This was his own battle of wills, the need to possess his bride entirely, which fired the love of the Baron in his pride at having his exquisite wife by his side as his ultimate trophy.

The glamour of the international elite became second nature to the deprived girl from South Africa whose breeding was never in question, polished as she was to the ways of beauty and society learning new lessons in life from patient Martin who enjoyed every moment together teaching her the ways of aristocrats.

From the vantage point of the Cap, they would cruise on his luxurious yacht, *BUTTERFLY,* languishing over gourmet cuisine and vintage wines escaping to nooks on the coastline where the Baron could indulge in fucking his wife on a strip of beach unable to be reached by anyone lost in erotic passion for the tall, cream colored, Goddess, soft spoken Esmeralda.

For her, there was this or the other choice, his circle of friends as guests clamored for invitations from the munificent host, her husband, the Baron. The trouble was outside of the Salzburg Festival - when they would go to Bayreuth for Wagner's Ring, staying at the Sacher - all the guests were always the same elderly people with faces like pugs or bulldogs. Their endless conversations spoke of monotonous details: money, politics, health issues, which one of their friends endowed the most to the Mozarterum or Symphony, died recently, did they read the obituary, attend the service, and taxes and taxes and taxes when they were not complaining about their children, older than Esmeralda, or some poor soul on their staff who incensed them and then they grew tired and they dozed off to sleep....

With Martin beside her she learned lessons Graham didn't teach, lessons of languages, society, equestrian sport, tennis and golf. Wise to detail, there were insignificant nuisances Martin recognized. His gorgeous Esmeralda was not from a well-born family, educated, perhaps, at an elite boarding school but not debutante material. What difference did it make to him?....whose plan was to tailor make his bride to his own specifications as his Baroness? It pleased Esmeralda to see herself as she believed was her birthright, her bona fide place in society at last!

I must never forget the memory of my beloved Mother. I feel certain she and I will reunite one day in Paradise, the rupture of my heart will mend. I'm comfortable in this ambiance. My blood is indisputably hers and she'd repeat again and again, "I was born to live a life as this."

In fairy tale delusion, like any heroine of a trumped up fable, Esmeralda's thoughts were of grandeur, graciousness, glamour, greatness and those positive messages propelled her brain with optimism that mirrored on her face. Those that eyed her saw the pinnacle of her beauty, beholding this ingénue who glided through life as the Baroness Beck without any hint of inferiority.

Nonetheless, Esmeralda in her confidential quest to locate the family of her deceased Mother, came to realize with all her connections she couldn't find a tie to her mother's family in England. She divulged this to no one. Strange, she thought, yet as years passed and she began to assume her own mantle, walk with the dignity and self-respect befitting her position as the Baroness Beck, with her own coterie of false friends who clamored to be in her ambiance because of her title and riches, she put aside her quest to learn about her Mother. Esmeralda understood that the life she was intended was hers, no matter how repetitive and artificial it was.

If the term 'friend' were to be used by her, she preferred weekend friendships as she had in London for her life, people who had no beginning or finale, without emotion, that were bought by an invitation and cut without qualms to eradicate any emotional tie or last scene.

"Perhaps life is artificial," she told herself pondering discontentment for perfection while her husband doted on her every whim wherever they went in the world.

His was a fortune from real estate that turned investments into numerous activities including the last hundred years as brewing magnets, a business run by conglomerates that held scant interest for the multi-lingual Baron, a man who validated the idea to delegate his wants to those in his entourage as the only means to have business succeed.

Martin Beck didn't require reassurance from professional sources as to his acumen. He hired and dismissed staff with adroit skill always in control, choosing to delegate, out of the vulgar picture of business. At this point in his life, he preferred to sail, participate in coaching with nobility, his expertise was four in hand, ride, ski, parade 'in season' to parties of noteworthy people his age, besotted with pride, showing off his bride and fucking her by day and night. She went along with his fetish to have a hidden camera in their bedroom at the Cap and take her naked in 'fuck me' stilettos or high boots of every colour and description, sex from the front, from the back, in the mouth, oftentimes surprising him with erotic play, like his wanton whore. He had trained her in every dimension and his private life was the most crucial part of Martin Beck's existence.

There were the round of habitual parties with people speaking German that Esmeralda had no desire to engage although she came to understand the language of her husband to a degree, French was much more melodious and the Baron gifted her with a French tutor, Jean Olivier, who resembled Voltaire in his failing years, an expert in conversational French.

"Your words must chime like the finest clock.... *voulez vous....*" the discipline was self improvement, something she would always have as a souvenir of the marriage, she reckoned and thought her life would eventually be one as Martin's widow.

The thought of infidelity never crossed Esmeralda's mind, young as she was, for all her sexual experiences thus far had proven to be mechanical without a glorious, higher passion she read about in books.

Martin was a generous lover wanting to please continually but his touch and kisses wet from his drooling mouth left her uninspired. She retained her desire enclosed deeply and days followed days, months and soon years, years - suddenly they'd been wed five years. Five boring, monotonous years of dressing, traveling, spending, eating, smiling, listening to Martin day in and day out, to his friends, to his enemies, to everyone in his circle who rattled old as Methuselah and to him - every night grinding his teeth, snoring throughout the night, seeing him age before her very eyes, a sight that held no fascination for a ravishing creature of twenty-six.

Everything she could want was hers except true mutual love and the easy enjoyment she'd known in London with Graham. That was finished and never to return she told herself. With Martin she was protected from the onslaught of suitors who were not interested in her as a person, he held a certain type of love for her, if it was not just a conquest type of lust. Or need, great need for she extended his life by her very existence as his spouse.

Some nights as she lay awake unable to lull herself to sleep hearing his night noises from impaired indigestion of eating too much rich food, she would examine her own philosophy about her marriage. I was the child he never had, the nymph of his fantasy, she'd think... And he?...is the man I envisioned to protect me. Yet I'm skeptical with this pretence of a marriage. Have I've prostituted myself? If it weren't for his proclamations of love and the exceptional way in which he treats me, I would be living in shame. But Martin loves me. I know that. And I love him in my own way more akin to a family, or good friend...not a romantic love...my unreciprocated love eats away at his heart and fires his passion. For him, love has become deeper than lust, yet for me.......hours would pass and she'd find herself saying 'he loves me' and sleep would come and she was protected.

She'd kiss him, stirring him like a child, "I love you Martin," and in many ways she did. She consoled herself that with time something would change, light would suddenly appear or his sudden death, a baby or perhaps a wild love affair with a person whose fire would ignite all pent up desire and imaginings she concealed like her identity.

To select clothes, nail varnish, shoes, perfume on a daily basis brought her mind to the epitome of tedium. Martin would become jealous if he saw her reading a book inquiring "What is it?" Her life had little privacy. It was only when he went away on shoots for men only in the hinterlands of Hungary for wild boar or grouse in the remote moors of Scotland, when she was alone (with the staff somewhere in one of the houses). She'd do as she pleased, to a degree as the servants were left explicit orders to look after her. She viewed them as phantoms serving her every need, never permitting solitude. Those hunts where women were excluded and her obedience to her husband's wishes prevailed, curtailed any thoughts she had to venture into London solo.

The Baron didn't fancy London as much as Paris where she had no friends, his conversely were preparing for God's waiting room, dull and quivering, morose, with whistling false teeth, snobs of extraordinary proportions, spending money on injections to stay young and trying to hear because it seemed to Esmeralda they all were deaf. If not deaf by age, deaf by the way they listened and thought like Martin who could have black moods rambling on with horrid pessimistic thoughts of death as age reared its head and his desire for longevity threatened with each passing ache or pain.

Esmeralda examined her face, now twenty-six and wondered if she was beginning to show signs of the telltale void existing in her marriage. Could there be a sour line by the corners of her mouth? Was it as beautiful as before? She didn't smile as she used to and now rarely. She went to her chaise lounge taking her enlarging mirror scrutinizing her porcelain skin if a wrinkle had appeared realizing at her age it was preposterous. She opened her long stain peignoir, admiring herself odalisque style, fantasizing Lucien Freud to paint her, enjoying the site of her exquisite nakedness, touching her high firm pink breasts, her magnificent derriere, raising her long legs, opening them wide, fondling her Mount of Venus. Yes, she was rare, wonderfully rare and the thought of having a child repelled her considering it would be the Baron's issue.

"I want to impregnate you, I love you as never before, you must have my child" he would plead touching her everywhere. She let him have his way with her. His continual expressions of the depth of his love left Esmeralda detached with less respect had he presented some mystery. She believed a man should refrain from showing all his emotions, thus creating an uncertainty to fire a woman's heart. Martin Beck couldn't disguise emotions if he were a starving infant wanting to suckle at his Mother's breast.

She used every precaution of birth control fearing pregnancy, lowering her gentle voice, dropping her eyes, beguiling her spouse, "Darling I want you as my only baby. You need so much care and attention." She would move her slender hands towards his legs stroking them close to his groin and he forgot any notion of children thanking the Heavens Esmeralda was his alone to enjoy.

Dreams would arrive about having a tryst as her English girlfriends told her they were doing. Hers would have to be exotic, terribly handsome, dangerous and young. She would have to be madly in love to threaten her prized security with Martin....if he ever found out, he would be torn to pieces. She contained a degree of loyalty towards him after all, yet the idea of having him alone as a lover and no one else in her life infuriated her! Martin Heindrick Beck could live forever! The idea of an affair began to sprout. At times being so alone emotionally and then in company when everyone spoke about illnesses and investments, producing intense monotony, Esmeralda's ennui would dilate giving way to keen imagination, wandering to thoughts of the perfect stranger who would steal erotic kisses and devour her sex. Somewhere mid-conversation the old hawks would view a smile playing on her voluptuous lips believing she was listening to their every word, loving her for it.

Weeks dragged into months with counterfeit passion from Esmeralda and unwanted gifts from Martin. The routine was same: uninspiring people in their circle - never a new face to be seen, with butlers who served champagne at seven and breakfast at ten and every shopping spree became an empty journey to nowhere with nothing to do except look magnificently beautiful and longingly into Martin's droopy eyes that swelled with love whenever she came near.

People need the company of others when their marriage is vacant, thought Esmeralda and perhaps Martins' friends filled a void she couldn't bring forth to satiate him with his trusted circle of noble friends. None of them filled her void producing a gaiety in her life, they were in the winter of their lives and she, in spring. Throughout the estate in Bavaria and the Cap, Esmeralda would take walks alone befriending her long-haired dachshund called 'Sister Mercy,' remembering the kindness of her former Mother Superior, telling him everything, blessing the fact he was the one soul to confide in.

It was during one of these times, she was moved with emotion and decided to write to the old nun saying briefly she was happily married to a Baron begging the sister's silence to never divulge her correspondence to her Father or anyone. She explained she wanted the good sisters to respect the life that they had prepared for her. A life where she'd finally found security expressing how she appreciated all the intentions of the good sisters and what they had done for her throughout difficult years that she had no wish to remember. She appealed to Mother Superior to keep her letter confidential and not to answer but to remember her in prayer.

Esmeralda, wrote on the crest engraved stationery of her spouse, as was usual. She didn't include any address. In this way, her letter would go unanswered.

Studying her husband as she did from time to time, Esmeralda came to learn and respect her Baron was a man of wisdom with a sound mind, intuitive about people, set with certain Teutonic ideas, that once fixed were inflexible. As generous as he was to her, she saw that he could be as avaricious with others. His was a giving nature, like most men when loved and when they are on the receiving end.

Martin's 'other side' reared its head especially with adversaries who challenged him or were motivated for their own gain. She would take stock of these lessons respecting him as he taught her about his earlier life working in the Resistance, saving Jewish lives not wanting any acclaim for his deeds hating the Nazis, speaking of his philosophy of life, philanthropy, finance, believing one day should he die, all his treasures would be hers.

Nevertheless, the life force of Esmeralda to this point was never money motivated. Hers was a primary focus of love and if she could not have the love she instinctively knew was her ultimate aim, financial considerations, which were never her primary concern, would be the life she was being taught to understand by Martin. In his wisdom, Martin understood this but kept his silence. Protection and security were the core of this marriage, which arrived with trust and respect for each other, "loftier desires of her heart," Martin would say.

The young Baroness absorbed the generous and parsimonious lessons of her husband whom she relied on for five years of marriage that had no ripples of discontent for Esmeralda, realizing the trade off of keeping quiet about her boredom for Martin was more than giving about his promises to her.

Under Martin's astute direction, (his mind that of a financier), her money from her professional modeling days and inheritance from Graham's bequest, were wisely invested in securities in Switzerland. Martin generously added to her monthly allowance as his beloved wife from another account exclusively in her name with his bankers in Liechtenstein. She held another account at Paribas, Paris, hers to enjoy as she wished, and as all his financial gestures were exceedingly kind, Esmeralda came to view his openhandedness as another means to control her fidelity, which he had no cause to question.

When the Baron had patience to discuss his portfolio with his wife, he'd educate her to the artifacts of the von Beck Castle in Bavaria, the art collection in Paris and treasures in Cap d'Antibes. "One day all this will be yours," he would state speaking of investments and various advisors describing how she would be looked after by his retinue of advisors should death part them.

Esmeralda, without cause of alarming her dear, elderly Baron to any preconceived ideas that passed her mind about dissolving the match, or to her future should this marriage be destined for widowhood, would listen patiently to his counsel, something she didn't understand in the least. She depended him entirely, knowing she was protected without any cause of apprehension. Her sweet nature, as he spoke, was noted by the Baron, no stranger to the wiles of women, whose heart broadened idolizing Esmeralda, never a source of worry to him as his other mercenary wives had been.

She demanded little and received much, content in his opinion. He had made a wise choice selecting her as his last Baroness who would grace his home and give honor to his name perhaps one day give him an heir. Living with her pliable nature, Martin changed Esmeralda to a degree. He saw the subtle distinction between acquired and natural breeding that he had - in comparison to her nouveau knowledge benefited from education and what society gave Esmeralda thus far.

The two were completely diverse to what birth and nature bequeathed. 'I won't question where she's come from but one day, I will learn the truth. I've raised her social station, she is mine and it is my duty to protect her,' thus were Martin Beck's thoughts.

Esmeralda under his tutelage during the past few years had a richer identity, not exclusive of wealth but of aristocratic elegance. She'd become a Baroness to the Manor born, the light of his life but his own life was beginning to fade. There was no thought to disclose this to his beloved. His doctors diagnosed glaucoma, an inherited malfunction of the von Beck strain much like diabetes, which ran in the family, and he monitored both with pills.

Fresh warnings had arrived with his latest physical about his heart. He would sacrifice his health hoping it would not threaten his marriage and have the desired effect to produce an heir. That is all he wished for. He reveled in her innocence of youth and blessed the day she agreed to marry him.

Martin Heindrick von Beck was not a man who ever saw a need to question his beloved wife for her indulgences for they centered around couture and that pleased him seeing her beautifully presented on a daily basis. He was a sensual being who appreciated a woman dressing to admire, as an elegant Baroness, speaking of art history that she studied with interest she engaged him with higher ideas about aesthetic matters and in knowing these pleasures he was no stranger to the finest jewelers in Europe surprising his wife with exquisite gems. He was a man who appreciated a beautiful woman and Esmeralda believed him worth dressing for, speaking beautifully and her vanity increased believing it was love.

Martin Beck had a fine sense of art and antiques and it was to her learned Baron with his expertise who recognized his wife's appreciation of the Masters that he initiated Esmeralda's education into the field of the visual arts. He taught her how to invest and fired her passion to emulate him with visits to Christie's when they would acquire a fine painting celebrating an anniversary or special birthday. He surprised her with a trip to Florence so she could glimpse at the Botticelli painting, *"The Birth of Venus,"* understanding, like Graham whom he never met, he was living with a woman who bore the exact resemblance. He also mercifully read her mind as their sixth year of marriage was coming into focus understanding his pangs of jealousy and the monotony of their lavish routine, announcing magnanimously at breakfast one morning,

"We are going to St. Moritz. It is high time you learned to ski!" The thrill of a new sport and a place she had read about filled her with energy, which pleased the Baron whose intent oftentimes was to shield her from any spotlight afraid she'd be tempted out of his clutches. He was extremely careful presenting Esmeralda to new people not out of shame, heavens no!...but from his lack of confidence, always being wary that her head could be turned and she would leave him for a younger suitor.

She'd proven a good wife for five years, longer than his last two, and now the time had come to bring his undemanding wife into the world he knew from years before they met. The Palace Hotel was booked for a month. Esmeralda would to learn to ski from the best instructor there thus giving her a jump start to catch up with her sprightly Baron who began to ski at Klosters when he was three years old.

Martin whose love for Esmeralda was coated in presents glowed seeing the exuberance she contained as each day approached. Finally they were at St. Moritz and he had engaged the most wretched looking private instructor to be with her continuously on the slopes. Viewing her in ski gear befitting the woman who had captured his heart taking her first solo run, he sang to the heavens, "Thank God! The heart and quintessence of English beauty is mine!"

He had no worries about his Baroness, the pride of his life who regarded the lineage of the von Becks as her own. He'd ski his black diamond routes leisurely and they'd meet for lunch appropriately as he designated throughout the plush slopes where he was known to all as a devotee of the sport who hadn't seen him for several seasons.

The exertion of exercise and the fornication he wanted daily to satiate his once vigorous libido made Martin keenly aware of his age. He wished to remain blind to the fact the onset of sixty-nine years made him spent. The syncopation of everything his life entailed, dulled by years of repetition, had one stimulant, his goddess of a wife next to him whenever and however he wanted her. But could he keep her?

Her vagueness about herself gave him no cause for distrust, but he was shrewd, no fool to class difference. Women had crowned him and cursed him and as he viewed seventy years coming into focus, he understood his only two energies worth living for. His prick dictated his life and his need to possess Esmeralda was his desire.

With the intimacy of the marital chamber now transported to the surroundings at Palace Hotel, St. Moritz, Esmeralda viewed him one night as he came to pounce on her quite differently. He didn't look old or embalmed, he looked exhumed. She closed her eyes wanting to be in denial, listening to his proclamations of love as he pawed her, his effete penis limp unable to match the vigor of his mind. The sly beast of age had beckoned. He went down on her with ardor lapping her moist young gem with his thick wet tongue to bring her to orgasm. Although she could lose herself in fantasy, which pleased him and excited him in arousal, he couldn't sustain potency.

Unbeknown to Esmeralda, never wanting to show her the side of him that was failing, Martin's doctors warned, "Steer clear of Viagra. Your heart shows signs of early trouble if you exert yourself. You could have deep vein thrombosis or a clot." He groaned with the onset of senility forgetting too much yet understood for the first time there was no way he could ever hold his own again with Esmeralda.

A man his age couldn't be a sportsman on the slopes and one in bed any longer. The sly Devil was keeping score dictating the future. Martin's initial thoughts were terrifying for without satisfying his young Esmeralda, she would ultimately leave him. His ageing body betrayed him. He was in torment, afraid of abandonment, afraid of death.... this unforgettable night in St. Moritz, she turned towards him, pet his jowly face seeing his image in the candlelit room, devastated him with disappointment. There was no need for words. Speech would carry them to a different level, all had been unspoken for years. Emotion was something else.

'My true understanding of emotion has never been with my husband,' was her own private truth, now magnified. Esmeralda maintained her silent power over her aged spouse understanding if he couldn't perform in the confines of their private life, he could exhibit *bella figura* to his friends, with her as his Baroness validating his macho image. This pleased Martin who understand the world has a bias about age but he could take pleasure to torment envious aged friends venting double entendres that left no doubt his marital bed was secure aflame with lust.

"Lies, lies everyone lies to protect their image," he would say. Wealth couldn't turn back the clock and bring renewed testosterone and vigor. It was a matter of time, the wise Baron surmised in his stupor of impotence, when his twenty-six year old minx would want her freedom, and the married life of the Baron and Baroness von Beck would be over.

Different than her Baron, Esmeralda knew any exit from her marriage would be more than sexual. She had no intention to be thrown to the wolves. Martin's love wasn't perfect but it was real. Esmeralda would meditate on this idea as she painfully watched Martin become an old man, bald with dry skin that flaked on the pillow, snored like a freight train and slurped his food. He became deaf, couldn't hear and swore he could. He had a spirit that failed to invigorate himself some days moaning about impending death ad infinitum or socializing with old people trying to outdo his cronies that he would outlive them, deluding himself Esmeralda would be beside him forever to flaunt and pretend. Pretending was easy - so much nicer than reality. Let his male friends think he could still penetrate a young wife. Let those old women whose necks and hands looked like crows - who had turned him down when he was young be jealous.

With truths unspoken, the first ten days in St. Moritz presented a new chapter. Esmeralda, fresh with a novelty that abated her boredom glided into position delighted with her lessons and accomplishment to reach the next level of downhill skiing the second week of their trip. She would meet her kind husband whose generosity kept her in check making all view him as the luckiest man on earth. It was under these circumstances Esmeralda, alone for once, rushed to lunch to meet her husband by two, racing downhill at breakneck speed descending the piste and went out of control. Her skis collided into another skier. "I'm so terribly sorry." She said in French and then in English.

The young stranger, the essence of good manners, lifted her from the snow, meeting her eyes like a magnet, never realizing what she did was completely premeditated.

This was how Esmeralda met the esteemed Italian Ambassador vacationing from his post in New York, Stefano de Gesu.

After lunch while Martin rested, Esmeralda explained, "I'm going to the spa for a massage," taking her first rendezvous with Stefano de Gesu. He became her lover for the duration of the next two weeks. Stefano, the forty-nine year diplomat on vacation from his post at the United

Nations, in his prime, rugged with handsomeness captivated Esmeralda. He was besotted from their clandestine intrigue and the adulterous affair brought the twenty six year old to the epitome of her sexuality.

She couldn't live a lie. It would be impossible to remain in her stale marriage of terminal boredom with the dear, kind Martin Beck. Finally, too, his age took its toll on her. She still had a lifetime ahead of her and wanted to seize it. Within months, while de Gesu arranged trysts in whatever city possible for them to meet with the Baron engaged in business meetings or napping, Esmeralda took courage to ask for a divorce. de Gesu was not the reason for the divorce but although it was unspoken, he gave Esmeralda the courage to do so.

Her mourning for Graham had abated; her charity towards Martin was paid in full. It had become an obligation to be the Baroness von Beck. Serving his needs to keep a lifestyle that was more than she needed was crazy. One day she added the score, she had enough and didn't have any guilt or need to bestow anymore indulgence towards Martin. The final straw was when he asked a prune-faced aristocrat whose teeth clattered like castinettes to dine without asking her first after she had returned early from Paris. Esmeralda wanted a night to herself, not to hear the goings on of Munich's latest funeral or family squabble.

Martin's retinue of tedious friends had no vibrancy to life, they, like he, were waiting to see who was the next one to croak. Life can't continue this way was a phrase that returned to her too often. She was fond of Martin, even loved him in a special way but nothing more, nothing that was to bind her forever and see her life disintegrate in his old age. Freedom suddenly felt possible - and it wasn't frightening. There was only one place in the world she wanted to go once divorced, where she belonged - London. Stefano could go to New York. He was a lover not a husband, the last thing in the world she wanted was another husband.

"I swear to you, dearest Martin, there is no one else," she lied yet in a way it was the truth. Esmeralda was a gorgeous woman whose devoted husband reluctantly understood. He also understood her honesty was in question and more correctly understood her want for youthful years, her freedom and her lack of mercenary intent to wait for his demise and claim all his family's possessions. He understood these things because wherever she went, the Baron's ear was tuned to her every movement. He was shrewd. It came as no surprise when he tried to reach her at the spa in St. Moritz, he learned she had never made an appointment.

He understood further that finally the vast years between them was too much and theirs was a private matter without a torrid love story of a third party (or so he led her to believe). He appreciated the fact that he would not lose face within his circle. She would honor him with discretion. Yet more than anything, Baron Martin Heindrick von Beck understood he never wanted anyone as long as he lived - to claim his Baroness - Esmeralda Beck as a wife.

"This is a terrible, unsettling set of affairs in our life, Esmeralda. I am a tolerant man, who is broken and do not want anything to be threatening for you. Do you believe this decision of yours to be final?" he said dearly as their Rolls drove along the busy streets in Munich to divorce as one would go in mourning to solicitors to read a Last Will and Testament.

"My Darling Martin, yes, I do. Please understand. It's my youth. Thank you, thank you for everything." She kissed the palm as his hand, a gesture he loved to sense. His eyes brimmed with tears and, sadly he noticed hers were clear, clearer than he'd witnessed throughout their married life. Gratitude, she so willingly gave, weakened his intent to beg further.

"As long as I live," he began holding her hand, "you are the Baroness von Beck and always will be. Return to be my wife whenever, for that is how I love you, how I see you."

There were no further words exchanged.

Entering the private chambers of Zumwelden & Zumwelden in Munich's city centre, were a dozen men in long black robes who solemnity matched the mood of the appointment. With this intent, his legal advisors received instructions accordingly and for Esmeralda the German divorce was not in the least acrimonious as she had feared. In the legal studio, she was merely asked to sign papers in front of several witnesses as was Martin. Some of these solicitors Esmeralda knew from past appointments when she was brought to the impressive offices to sign her name on other papers in the past.

Somberly all watched as first Esmeralda and then the Baron signed a plethora of documents in front of them, which they, the solicitors, in a compendious manner, countersigned and stamped with seals. She, like a child being led by her devoted Baron, agreed to a substantial settlement from him not speaking a word to anyone about "arrangements," furthermore, everything was conducted in rapid German. She was fully aware, as were all who joined this meeting, of the death of a marriage. There was great formality and gratitude to her actions; it was like ice without any emotion whatsoever and because of that, more painful. She had broken Martin's heart. He was devastated.

Baron Martin Heindrick von Beck would provide for Esmeralda generously until she would remarry. His only stipulation was that she would agree to everything including the reason for of divorce as 'irreconcilable differences' and never divulge anything further. Esmeralda concurred moved by the extraordinary grandiosity of her dear, kind Baron who insisted all the jewelry he gave her, the paintings and investment were hers to keep forever.

Although their marriage came to a civil parting with his adored wife, the crestfallen Baron Martin Heindrick von Beck's love fired anew, astonished at her willingness to relinquish her claim on all his vast properties, holdings and investments.

With the doxhound he gave to Esmeralda, "Mercy," in his arms, bitter tears streamed down his face at their last farewell. His chauffer drove Esmeralda downhill the long, pebble driveway through the maze of topiary garden with all the withered leaves grey and dying on the Estate, brittle with winter in the von Beck's Bavarian forest.

Baron Martin Hendrick von Beck watched from the highest point of the castle, the tower. The black vintage Daimler slowly wound its way down and away the serpentine hillside.

"You will always be the Baroness von Beck," he choked the words, convulsed in tears, grasping the little hound. "We will be together again…we will...we will...." and then the car took its final turn and was out of sight.

The date was the first of February 1996.

XIX

The Divorcée, Baroness von Beck in London

Esmeralda was not a woman given to promiscuity. de Gesu remained her lover when they were in the same city. She didn't accept his invitations to meet in New York or elsewhere. That was not her focus. For the first time in her life, she experienced an extraordinary sense of independence. She was able to control her lust, emotions and spiritual link managing relationships pragmatically retaining her emotional power, taking any lover she chose only to a particular level. She understood men knowing the more she did for them the less she was appreciated.

There were few men who were ever satisfied, deeply satisfied. If she didn't give herself to a man, he was angry and went away. If she did, she had to guard her precious emotions for she knew innately that once all was given -- a man appreciates you less and less. It was difficult to achieve a balance with a man. Men always wanted it on their terms.

To be a love object as she'd been with Martin was not her want. Or to have an entanglement with Stefano de Gesu, a typical married Italian man cheating on his second wife, understanding he was not hers exclusively. And he, most probably on the prowl in another city.

She'd been spoiled with the love of two men who adored her: Graham and Martin. de Gesu loved himself. She would not play into his game and lose. Esmeralda's intent was to reposition herself, she had everything she needed including self respect.

The London scene with its buzz and glamour, stimulating conversations, black tie champagne dinner dances, sensational theatre, concerts, opera, country weekends and British sense of humor was a mecca of used bodacious women outnumbering pusillanimous men who had little hope to settle and marry. The players engaged in hop scotch, going one to another. Friendships ripened too quickly and died overnight.

Although a celebrity as a young Baroness, coupled with funds and the advantage of being remembered as the icon for Harrods, Esmeralda had the kind of beauty women envy and make men nervous. She was an outsider. She craved the isolation. In its loneliness she was safe from those who'd pry and exploit her, yet to be alone after the companionship she knew with Graham and Martin brought a huge void and emptiness to life that no London society man could fill. It was raw, cold, superficial. Gaiety from the crowd could mask that void but now and again it came to haunt her whenever silence returned, the lights went out and the music stopped.

Invitations were plentiful, 'supposed' suitors gallantly presented themselves, (some not so gallant), while she tasted the life of the well-heeled divorcée remaining unimpressed after rounds of events and house parties with easy sexual encounters. The Cotswold's, Glyndebourne, Isle of Wight, Mayfair, Chelsea, Kensington, Ascot, Wimbledon, Henley...they all produced the same insincere responses and second-rate scenarios. There were no delusions. Esmeralda saw through the new found acquaintances, "a carousel of glitterati" she'd call them. Questioning – always questioning: "Who are these people? What do they want? Where do they come from? What do I have to gain from them? What do they want from me?"

Her mystique fascinated those wanting entry into her realm. On cue, when one doesn't give into curiosity seekers - concocted elaborate fantasies about the beautiful Baroness von Beck percolated. 'Is hidden life best?' the Baron had once questioned her years ago realizing there was a private life to his wife that he couldn't penetrate.

"Yes," came her coy answer teasing him, raising her eyes to meet his knowing as Graham had taught her, the spirit of language was what one didn't say. Life without mystery was an open book Once read, people lost interest. Her single life would be as she and Graham designed from their eventful exit from South Africa, veiled in mystery.

There was no way she could have been bored in the stimulating city that she loved but Esmeralda wasn't satiated either. Watching others play into the game, London style, she recoiled. She was reinvented, perhaps they were also, but she knew the difference. There was a certain type of mentality required by 'movers and shakers' to stay on the fast track. It didn't appeal to Esmeralda. The Baron succeeded making her highly self assured, with all her disguises she was true how she viewed the falseness of society.

She'd experienced a remarkable transformation three times in her young life and although not born to wealth and privilege, she felt part of it having been reared a Baroness.

With sufficient funds, she settled into a notable townhouse in Kensington with a blue plaque noting it as the former residence of Isadora Duncan. The proximity to Kensington Palace would find her in the gardens where she would take daily walks imagining one day a house of greater proportions on the exclusive street adjacent would be hers.

Returning home in a downpour one afternoon without the luxury of a chauffeur, drenched to the skin, she blessed Martin's goodness, understanding her acceptance of that union was contrived. Now she was her own person who would achieve great things and not be beholden to any man. Conformity required to fit into the mould of what peers considered the epitome of a social life were difficult for her to accept. She had lead a lifetime in a half a dozen years. "I never wanted to be unique, but I am." That was the reality of it all.

She blessed the day her dear sweet Baron had seen to it that she didn't have to expose herself to another liaison out of vulnerability and she appreciated his financial kindness. At times she missed him terribly. They'd agreed to a clean break unless she wanted to return and reunite as his wife. That was not her intention. Suitors were plentiful imagining her with more wealth than she contained, pleasure seekers seeking pleasure. Superficial people the tabloids gossiped about always wanted to pierce her privacy, the watchers watching the watched. Individuals who lacked depth. Where was the meaning to their lives?

Esmeralda contemplated what would she do with hers. "If one more person tells me I'm beautiful I'll scream!" No one looked beyond that. She had a philosophy, could recognize a fine piece of music or superior painting. Poetry appealed to her, like good books - everyone overlooked her cultivated intellectuality seeing only her face. Modeling was something of her past, now a thing beneath her, the social circuit woo'd her to functions and committees taking her time boring her once again with the monotony of people with little to say and nothing to do. After a series of occasions with the razzle-dazzle glamour of London, Esmeralda searched for more. Love was her quest, Esmeralda wise to know she'd never find it in the circus of the crowd. However, it came as no surprise when the Milanese industrialist, Franco Lemma, pursued her, flattering her cerebral vanity for close to a year wanting marriage.

"You are a woman of breeding, intelligence and high social standing," he said asking to marry her.

"Yes, Franco," was her reply, "What can there possibly be between you and me?"

"Let us proceed and see…"

"Engagements are meant to be broken" came her retort.

"We are speaking of a life together, not a business appointment."

"I will accept your proposal conditionally. I'll not accept it completely. It is your choice to take the risk for I may leave you at any time."

With her youth, grace and beauty, unattached and comfortable, she captivated him easily. Her independence astonished him for all the women in his circle ran towards him making fools of themselves. Lemma was certainly not in the Baron's financial league or with any sign of a noble strain as she'd become accustomed; he was merely a dozen years her senior. He was determined to break her resolve, "To please you, my Darling, we will make our engagement conditional."

She questioned relinquishing her title, something of value in London, knowing she'd turned into a snob. When he pressed her for an engagement the fifth time she went along with it, telling herself he was a safe haven, postponing his demands for a wedding date, making the excuse she needed time to study his friends, family and lifestyle, not wishing to be swept into another marriage.

What she discovered about Lemma in the short span of time she knew him, made her reticent, realizing the respect, trust and goodness she'd enjoyed with Graham and Martin was what she wanted. Yearning for the impossible, seeing herself approaching thirty, she questioned if true love was a fantasy.

"Is it possible not to be some trophy?" She looked at her engagement ring, reminding her of its vulgarity – like Lemma. It was too big, gaudy. All flash, like him. Lemma seized the chance to place Graf's 28 karat canary diamond with two oversized baguettes of blue diamonds from their Bond Street window on the hand of his bride to be. The Italian industrialist paid cash, no questions asked.

"The quality of love I envision is impossible," thought Esmeralda as Lemma slipped the ring on her finger, declaring undying love. As he slipped it on, her first thoughts were: I know I'll return his ring and break this engagement. I will never see this out. He is too common. Oh for spontaneity! A spark! Her wishes were everything this future match would never contain. All the parties and fanfare seemed endless wishing for a miracle to happen, wondering at the same time if a life with Lemma was better than the continual round of suitors who wanted her money. He had means. Where he received these means was in question. Industrialist to a point but she sniffed dishonesty in him. Martin would have had him checked by a detective. She didn't care. Lemma wasn't that important and here she was engaged to him!

What she wanted seemed unachievable, a pipe dream...the clock ticked and she was thirty-one.

Then she met Gianni Zianni on the 3rd of October, 1997.

XX

The Wedding

Gianni waited in top hat and tails fingering his cuff links, greeting guests arriving in splendor for to him take Esmeralda Anderson Beck as his bride. She was thirty-one by European documents, thirty by birth, and he, ten years her senior.

It had been a whirlwind courtship.

Gianni plotted to have her break her engagement to his rival, Franco Lemma, but had he known she had her own misgivings, perhaps he wouldn't have pursued Esmeralda with such alacrity, but only perhaps. For Gianni was a man hopelessly in love with the woman he beheld as the most beautiful creature on earth who contained no guile and radiated intelligence and social graces inherent to those born, as he, privileged.

Her gentleness captivated his family and although they had worries about the scion of their dynasty marrying a woman who had already tasted five years of matrimony, seeing the couple together eradicated reservations. They were duly impressed she'd stepped away from the fortune of Baron Martin Heindrick von Beck, accepting the idea that marriage was more of a father figure situation as the dear girl was orphaned so young in life.

Furthermore, she had relinquished a modeling career, which would have displeased the Zianni family whose obsession for privacy was meshed in their soul. Then too she took Italian lessons and religious instruction to marry in the Catholic Church, born an Anglican as she was, and pleased the family wishing to have the sanctity of this union recognized by the Church and receive a Papal blessing. All this augured well with the conservative relatives who scrutinized Gianni's choice and quick wedding, jealousy being no stranger to youth, money or beauty.

Esmeralda noticed Gianni the first night at Annabel's and wanted to taunt him knowing the male animal aroused is easy bait for capture. Her objectives were finely-honed and should he be another candidate on the scene who resulted in a duplicate scenario of the others, she didn't want to waste her time. Her feminine nature understood by not acquiescesing to Gianni, she'd be his obsession. The more she refused to submit to his demands, the more he came forward.

Esmeralda was selfish and pragmatic. Her unstable life formed her in one respect and Martin Beck in another. She used the shield of self-protection to anyone who could prey on her hidden emotions, which, like her identity, were not for disclosure.

Although they had traveled in parallel social circles, Esmeralda and Gianni never met. When Lemma was out of sight, it took one question to former lover, Stefano de Gesu, to learn about the handsome stranger staring at her.

The next day when flowers arrived and Gianni telephoned, she was prepared. Their fate was sealed.

The wedding was everything both dreamed it would be. Gianni's family was in abundance and friends arrived from all corners of the globe, wonderful friends of diverse backgrounds, loyal to Gianni for decades, some of whom Esmeralda met during their courtship duly reported in the press as one that 'swept the bride off her feet.' Esmeralda's contingent was nowhere near as large as Gianni's, mostly friends from London or shared acquaintances from the social circuit who arrived at functions such as this to mingle with society searching for means to capitalize on any opportunity of grand scale.

His clan was completely the opposite united in bonds over centuries who made it life's practice to attend every important family function where all knew each other nodding their salutes while memories ignited who was who in the vast assortment of kin.

Esmeralda was the topic of everyone's opinion and they attributed her lack of relatives to her sad circumstances of the I.R.A. bombing that killed her parents, "and other relatives in London some years ago. Poor darling," they exclaimed, "An only child too, left tragically in the world without the immense circle of relatives Gianni has who love him!"

" We will take her in the fold of the family,"

"We will make it up to her."

"She needs to feel the warmth and love of our Italian clan," said another, and yet another, "Loving him we shall love her."

"From today she's a Zianni."

Esmeralda smiled beautifully to one and all secretly withdrawing into her shell feeling the suffocation of a vast, inquisitive family, never having had one, wondering if she really wanted to be a part of all that held their interest, losing her privacy. Typical of Italian families, their intent was to know everyone else's business. Gianni was all she wanted in this world. With time they would begin a family of their own. This glorious dream of being married to the man who would fulfill all her expectations was hers. That was all that mattered and she kissed her single life in London adieu.

Gianni was more than good, he was wonderful. Everyone sensed the supreme quality of Gianni and Esmeralda most of all. Her past had put her in a position to keep her antennae tuned to duplicity and she appreciated someone of Gianni's caliber more than most. He was her secret fantasy she had in her heart all her life, a man you could love, trust and respect.

Her future was turning and life was going to be perfect. The sun was shining on her from this magnificent wedding day and a rainbow was coming into view for Esmeralda. All her hopes would come true; she was overwhelmed to think of her past and view her present, marveling at the power of God to turn things right.

As she prepared herself to ride in the carriage to the Basilica at the top of the Campodoglio in *centro storico*, she blessed the day that through the Baron she had come to know the acclaimed diplomat whom she chose to gives her away in marriage. She explained to Sir Oliver Thompson, the British Ambassador to Rome, she wished to have him do the honor as she was orphaned and believed he represented her home country, the British Isles. The statesman was so bowled over at her request, realizing he certainly wasn't a close tie to the beauty, yet knew he couldn't refuse. By his presence, he brought dignity to her circle as the only prestigious Englishman appropriate for this distinction. The Ziannis were duly impressed. What they didn't surmise is that Esmeralda couldn't think of anyone else except Mohammed al Fayed and she knew that was absurd.

Glancing in the long gilt mirror in her suite of rooms at the Borghese Palace, Esmeralda viewed herself in the breathtaking bridal gown Yves St. Laurent designed. The texture of the French ribbed silk fabric accented the utterly simple design highlighting Esmeralda's the sublime lines with long sleeves and a square neckline that flattered the bride and dazzling diamond necklace Gianni gave her, presented at midnight as the clock struck the first minute of their wedding day, June the 1st 1998.

Her strawberry-blonde curls were swept up securing the two hundred year old lace veil Gianni's Mother wished her to wear. It trailed three meters from the hem of her dress. She was a vision of exquisite taste. It was as if an angel had descended on the world and the angel was Esmeralda. And, like a phantom from Heaven, she was utterly alone. Outside of her future husband no one in the world meant anything to her. She would take her vows to wed Gianni Zianni, without another close soul who could understand her joy. Bliss mixed with painful sadness as the excitement mounted.

The ushers stood alongside Gianni nervously joking, adjusting their dove grey double-breasted waist coats, fumbling with gloves, pulling the points of their gellets, fingering cravats, comparing top hats, preparing themselves for the exciting day having partied for the last several nights together at various events given for the couple.

Gianni's best man was Rupert Davidson, two of his cousins were chosen to be a part of the wedding party along with Nicky Viscounti, Whitney Jameson and Nigel Pembrooke, whose colorless wife, Catherine stood by waiting her turn to be seated in the Basilica wondering if the costume she wore was appropriate.

Violins of St. Cecelia began the musical program with the oversized organ, sopranos, mezzo-sopranos and tenors voicing melodious notes adding to the chorus of the Basilica's famed choir. All lent an ethereal atmosphere to the setting as did the thousands of white lilacs, lilies and wild flowers.

A general movement followed of stylishly attired ladies and gentlemen of diverse ages and backgrounds ushered to their seats. Whispered salutes began and eyes alighted everywhere to see who was in which position, who was wearing what costume, opinions of all details being on their lips, murmuring them to spouse, friend or foe, evaluating who was not readily seen and all regarding the exquisite event as unforgettable.

The voices of the guests took on a certain pattern like a musical score, and it was the wise listener not to be in the immediate vicinity of the 'brass trumpets' or the 'percussion ensemble.'

Scanning the group one could recognize the mongrel of an Uncle with the face of his withered Mother, the relatives with old names with links woven too tightly, the parchment faces and weathered Romeos of yore, the various expressions of emotions - happiness, agitation, nostalgia, envy, jealousy - all the drama magnified by the grandiose setting. As the ushers escorted guests to their positions, seating the most important members towards the front, asking, "Which side, the bride or the grooms?" they balanced the disparity with smooth elegance befitting manners and taste. All one viewed was perfection.

There were a number of invitees pleased with the match. One could hear the soignée, nonagenarian great aunt of Gianni, Zia Florinda, whose death was imminent and had nothing to fear from loss of inheritance conclude, "This is a merger of beauty and wealth, an exceptional choice on the part of my nephew considering young people breed." Thrusting her chin in the air to accent a diamond dog collar (the very one she wore at King Edward's coronation), she sashayed down the aisle in a grey Alencon lace costume. Her position was the second pew. Zia Florinda looked around smiling, pleased with her remark considering her ideas of propriety were expressed.

The expectant guests couldn't keep still, whispering. "Surprising she doesn't have a retinue of her own friends like Gianni."

"Leave it to the Catholics to create an extravaganza, not at all like a wedding in England,"

"Italians love this sort of thing," said Catherine Pembrooke offensively, "we do things differently at St. Paul's."

"Such an old title, she's fortunate indeed."

"Do you know her?"

"Not at all"

"She is very shy" answered another.

"Shy or did you say sly?"

"No one that beautiful has true friends" said another and that reason was the truth. Esmeralda didn't trust anyone. She had some male friends but no true friends in the sense of friendship. Stefano de Gesu, attended the wedding, a mutual friend of Gianni's and he was her friend with a unusual link (which both disguised).

It all seemed imagined, this mood of those assembled, magnificently imagined. The cohesiveness of the group held a particular rhythm of society flowing one into its own, recognizing pedigree and scrutinizing others. The mood, despite whatever the agenda, was congenial and expectant ready for the great event to signify a moment in the history of the Zianni family never to be forgotten.

There was a certain intimacy for this moment in time, when all became best friends, the wedding welded the entire group into a bond of togetherness, belonging - beautiful for the occasion they told themselves, to be together like this, in happy times with the knowledge that true love has conquered. (Much like a funeral thought others, together like this... wonder who's next?)

Yet with all the camaraderie, as can be imagined, some were suspect as suspicion mounted in their mind. They poked their spouse speaking under their breath of ill will at the alacrity of the courtship questioning everything, cynically believing love non-existent. There were others who made a financial tally of what this cost, what was Esmeralda's net worth before descending on one of Italy's great fortunes...did they have a pre-nuptial agreement?... how would Gianni react as a spouse? Would he relinquish his carefree days?... or choose to be wed Italian style with some fortunate mistress on the side?

Everyone in the throng had gone through their significant experiences, and now sitting, waiting with the magnificent music resounding, reveries stirred. There were those who wished to ferret every particle of information to hash over in coming months and years about the love story and event. These were relatives, friends and acquaintances invited, not the press in abundance who were denied entry to the Church. These vicarious individuals saw this spectacle as one of the greatest events they would attend in a lifetime and their wish was to give full reign to the excitement of the day and the drama how they digested the extraordinary occasion.

Some things were predictable, who sat with whom, who had false smiles, eyeing costumes in a glance as only women can do while men's thoughts were elsewhere. There was decency everywhere, understandable for the circumstances, and it crossed several minds if the bride could possibly be pregnant and that was the reason for the rapid marriage. "Interesting to see what will arrive," one could hear a dowager whisper anxious to spread gossip to the next person.

As the brilliant sun illuminated the attendees in costumes designed by Europe's finest designers, casting facets of light from the stained glass windows, a rainbow swept over the four hundred guests, resembling exotic birds in a perfect oasis. Viewing the entire ensemble from the choir master's point of view, one man stood out sitting alone, like a leper, to the rear of the church, on the bride's side, dressed formally, not knowing anyone. The choirmaster gave him scant attention as he took his position, baton in hand waiting to lead the throng in celestial music to consume the magnificent Basilica.

Gianni's parents took their place as the last seated and things progressed smoothly. Everyone exchanged civilities, giving opinions to the Mother of the Groom's costume. It was easy to read the plotting yet to come as men and women chose to view this an auspicious hunting ground where they would set their aim for the most attractive candidate of the day and move onto their future.

"Perhaps I'll meet someone,"

"He's here? Maybe we'll cut a business deal,"

"She's just left her husband"

"He could second me at the Jockey Club"

"His yacht's in Portofino"

"Her face lift is ghastly."

"He looks better than when his wife was alive"

"They're still together after all…"

"I wonder how much money she has?"

"So she's here with him," and so it went.

Soon there was a silent hush, conversation ceased and a silence commanded. One nod from the Cardinal standing in attendance at the altar for the Solemn High Mass of ten Monsignors and a dozen acolytes signaled the show was about to begin. Divine Grace shined upon the entire throng. A dozen trumpets announced the bride was prepared to grace their presence with her walk from the long white marble staircase Michelangelo designed for Piazza del Campidoglio in 1546, accept the name Zianni, and and wed the heir to the entire fortune of Zianni International Pharmaceuticals.

A dozen flower girls in Gianni's family led the procession, dressed in white, endearing Esmeralda to cousins wishing to show off progeny, looking angelic, followed by Gianni's sister, Serena, as Maid of Honor.

The cliques that had clustered prior to the ceremony, the relatives that arrived in limousines, the strangers who found themselves lucky to be a part of this - all the dressed up performers stood facing the nave of the Basicilia watching, waiting, praying and voicing their silent thoughts.

Time, and time alone would tell what these thoughts were. Esmeralda appeared, contained as only the actress in her could perform. Moving as in a dream holding the arm of the dignified tall, senior Ambassador whose presence she'd staged (as one sets about to cast a father figure for a play), was her magnificence.

From the throng of guests transported into this dreamland, hands were squeezed remembering their own loves, handkerchiefs appeared for ladies to avoid tears ruining their made-up faces and as the procession began along the thirty meter aisle, with the trumpeting of Mendelssohn's Wedding March, throughout was heard a hum ...

"My God, magnificent,"

"Unbelievable"

"Perfection"

"Beautiful, truly beautiful,"

"Mio Dio, An Angel!" and the service began.

Gianni's Mother was praying, "Please God let this be the beginning of another dynasty. May they have many children. May this love never end. I was wrong to question Esmeralda's background, she does honor to the family. She will do what all women do, take her husband's identity for her own."

Gianni's father, "What a lucky man my son is. Beauty like that doesn't exist. She must be marvelous in bed…She's a Zianni, and will give us an heir."

From Rupert Davidson, "Holy God I hope he isn't making a mistake,"

From Serena, "I know he's making a mistake,"

From Nigel Pembrooke, "I'd love to be in his place," from his wife, "She looks like a real bitch,"

From Lynne Jameson, "I wonder what that necklace cost?"

From Whitney, "Thank God. She's wonderful, soft and feminine."

From Nicky Viscounti, "I don't feel it right. There's something about her I don't like."

From Princess Shabadiba, "Another one bites the dust,"

From Olympia "I hope they like the painting I made for a wedding gift."

Standing beside her Stella Gregotti was with a fixed expression, "This was to be my wedding," while Marco's thoughts were different, "Look at destiny, Stella's mine!"

... and from Brian Korthorpe, whispering to Samir Redat, "Pity Naomi isn't here to see this splendor,"

"Yes, I am sorry her Father died," he answered, reaching for the hand of his wife, Jacqueline.

"Zes es something from Paradise, yes, Samir?"

"Yes, Darling...bless them."

Sitting on the bride's side together Stefano spoke to Véronique, "Did you see marriage in their stars?" while thinking, "God she gives great fellatio, lucky bastard Gianni,"...

... and she, "Actually yes" but thoughts ran through her mind and she touched his hand, "there will be darkness too."

"Extra sensory perception?" he asked but she didn't answer.

While others kept their silent remarks,

"One could devour her with one's eyes,"

"She's profiting by this merger,"

"Amazing there's no scandal, her stomach's flat as a board,"

"How I'd love to supplant Gianni,"

"Coitus with his Italian prick, I'm jealous as hell,"

"It was a natural, she has fine breeding."

"Gianni always wins,"

"What a romantic match"

"It can't be true, I bet she takes a lover,"

"I wish I was her lover,"

"They both choose status" and then the deep voice of the Cardinal was heard, "I now pronounce you man and wife."

Gianni kissed Esmeralda and the couple glowed with happiness, the campanile bells rang by the hundreds, gracious smiles reigned throughout the guests both good and notorious, rich and craving to be rich, the shrewd, the intelligent, the bitter, the calculating and the sweet as they all moved onto the reception.

XXI

Count & Countess Zianni

Entitlement came to the Ziannis as it does to all rich people. From the beginning, they had three homes. One in Rome, a 16th century palazzo in *centro storico* overlooking St. Peter's. Esmeralda's former house in Kensington, situated close to the Palace and after their Asian honeymoon, Gianni surprised Esmeralda buying Beaumont Manor, a Georgian treasure, in the peaceful English countryside of Whitshire, close to his polo friend's estates. On the endless stretch of grass, they planned to house the polo ponies Gianni boarded in Britain. An Arabian stallion from the stables of Sheikh Makkum, Sabadiba's Grandfather, had been a wedding present for the couple.

Villa Pina in Capri was used by the whole family, as were the apartments in Milano, Paris and New York. With all the trappings of wealth, a world of pleasure was theirs blessed with trust, dignity and the warmth of intimate love.

Picture if you will this setting of two magnificently matched mortals, in the prime of life, deeply in love where every kiss was high voltage inspiring the next embrace, with masses of money, position and all the accoutrements of wealth and social prestige. They lacked nothing. In this setting envy had its place, and one was wise to understand its worth.

It separated them from others and jealousy surrounded the couple on another plateau.

"Let's not be naive," Esmeralda said to Gianni one Sunday, lighting incense in their bedroom hearing the telephone suddenly go quiet. "There are few, very few who are true friends." She moved about the room in an open black satin peignoir, igniting candles and arranging a bouquet of lilies by their bed. Gianni pulled the robe gently from her body and she stood in front of him assuredly letting him touch her honey colored bush with his lips.

Her smooth long leg wrapped around him as she returned to bed beside him that afternoon.

"Do we need friends?"

"No, Darling…and the way you looked at me right now with those eyes makes me desire you."

"All my rivals are jealous as hell you're mine…"

"You did have some competition, Count Zianni."

"Ah the hunt of pursuit! My desire for you had become an obsession ….right now I have a marvelous impulse…"

"How lovely to be an obsession! I feel racy…" Featherweight kisses began.

"You bewitched me." Gianni turned her over caressing Esmeralda's splendid *derriere.*

"No one has your special talent, my vixen, my gorgeous minx!…" He wanted to stride her, "Your bewitching power." Saying these words, Gianni caressed his bride. "I want your special lock from another world, another century."

"Ah Cleopatra's gift! ….First, how much do you love me, my *amorata*?"

"Voluptuous kisses, here…your Mount of Venus….here....your neck... here...your toes...here...your breasts....here....." She loved it like this, his kisses everywhere until he was tasting her sex with love bites to make her wild with excitement. Here she was worshipped, achieving orgasm again....his power over her was at its peak.

"The best knowledge," he said smiling, looking up withholding a kiss …let me teach you what Italian men like…."

His magnificent masculinity soared, he took her in his powerful arms and slowly began penetrating Esmeralda, with all the tenderness, strength and love of his being. Their fluid bodies meshed to one achieving climax as the fever pitch of sexuality reached its pinnacle, treasured words were said to last a lifetime.

Sometime later, when Gianni brought her champagne, she asked, "What woman of passion would fail...to have... a burning lust for her adored?

"Women don't tend to be as honest as you, Contessa Zianni."

"This woman wants to have you never stop seducing her. I want to be everything to you…even your *putana*….lie back, Count Gianni let your bride make you alive again until your dynamic dick begs me to stop…"

Gianni fired by passion, laid back and let her consume him with her splendid voluptuous lips. sitting on his face, her jewel thrust to his mouth as he lavished kisses satiating desire. Gianni's sex appeal was all giving. He was the most generous man Esmeralda ever knew. It was not Esmeralda's nature to give but her sex dictated, her heart commanded and her soul was entwined with her beloved husband's. Theirs was a match of 'soul mates,' with the fervor of intense sexuality.

Everything else came second - intellectual pursuits and a common bond between them how their life would be, their friends, family, children, business and social life flowed together without obstacles. Those who were jealous were not a part of their entourage.

Gianni never surmised she had learned about the quality of life from Martin Beck. The Beck imprint changed the girl from the humble Convent in Johannesburg to the exquisite Contessa who was Gianni's wife today. Dear Martin Beck taught her about sexuality, not that she returned Martin's love as she did to Gianni, but Martin loved her and had given Esmeralda the experience she needed to satiate her passionate Italian husband. Now she and Gianni were designing their life and all seemed natural. Theirs was the type of marriage lovers dream to have - passionate lovers not with the give and take of good friends but with all the strength of true first love, for this was first love for them both.

"Ours is the type of love where I can spend an eternity with you," said Gianni. mirroring her heart.

There was a strength to this love that bonded them requiring nothing more, devoted to each other wherever, whenever. "They're too wrapped up in themselves," said close friends. The young Zianni's took no notice, their link strengthened daily, without realizing it, two had become one in every sense. Everything was shared with the first inclination on the part of both to do the best for the other.

Wherever they were their happiness spread joy wherever they went. Laughter filled the air and it was, as Gianni's parents agreed, a true love story. Anytime they'd call their own, as in this particular Sunday, they would remain in their bedroom, affectionate to each other, enraptured, reaching ecstasy until the clock chimed seven when they had to dress to join his family for dinner.

Twenty-one months passed gloriously for the couple who had a rhythm to their lives with annual events which included receiving communion semi-annually in a private audience with the Pope and being presented to the royals of Europe. Esmeralda managed decorating houses, entertaining Gianni's family and friends and smiling gently when his parents spoke of an heir. It was their intention to begin a family immediately and inquisitive members of the close-knit clan tip-toed around the question of pregnancy delicately. "What could be the problem? "It certainly can't be Gianni," they whispered never dreaming a Zianni unable to sire a child. But it was Gianni for all his ardor, his premature ejaculation did not help Esmeralda conceive.

Their voluptuous caresses often time brought climax too quickly. With patience, time and good counsel from their doctor making him swear to keep matters private, all stood waiting for some news from the gorgeous couple who would undoubtedly give the world another Zianni that would be equally handsome.

Most of all the desire rested with the couple followed by Gianni's Father who was diagnosed with terminal cancer. He'd been gravely ill and as was the custom, his diagnosis was shared by everyone in the family, the Italian approach to show undying support in their quest to strengthen the patriarch. Nevertheless, it was to no avail. The villa on Rome's spectacular hill, Gianicolo, Villa Multifiore, was filled with gloom. The prognosis was Gianni's Father, Roberto had at best weeks to live. Shaken by the doctors' findings, which he knew from pain and chemotherapy was inevitable, he took the liberty to speak to his son one evening before the ladies joined them for dinner.

"Gianni, it is none of my business..."

"I know what you are going to say. Have patience." Gianni bent over him and kissed his forehead. "Shall I fix a drink? Or would you prefer to wait for Mother and Esmeralda? They're coming shortly."

"I can wait."

"Let me tell you about a magnetic device Samir brought to my attention that we are importing from an old Egyptian remedy for arthritis." Gianni was enthusiastic changing the subject while his Father feigned an interest hearing what he had to discuss about business.

Although Roberto remained in name only as the Chairman of the Board of Zianni Pharmaceuticals, in the last six months, Gianni was completely at the helm. It was only natural he should be pleased about success and a new cure. As he began to dilate the pluses for the age-old Egyptian treatment sitting beside his ailing father wheelchair bound, the French doors opened and his Mother and Esmeralda entered, dressed in silk costumes for dinner. Their perfume filled the room and faces glowed changing the feeling of sorrow in the formal drawing room as they came round to kiss their men..

"Ah we were waiting to have drinks..." Gianni began and he looked at Esmeralda and winked. His parents noted how they'd flirt before and this pleased them as Gianni rang for Sanjeev, who, as always was the custom, entered with champagne glasses and a bottle of Krug wrapped with its cork to be popped.

"I'll do the honors on this, Sanjeev, if you please."

"Yes Sir."

Gianni began to twist the stuffed cork from the neck of the bottle slowly as all stood by, Esmeralda moved closer to him. "Father this champagne is for you especially!"

POP!

"Esmeralda is pregnant!"

Imagine the joy of this moment. The heir they had been waiting for was to arrive! Tears of happiness came to all in the room while devoted Sanjeev brushed aside his own. The news of the young couple restored bliss to Villa Multifiore and this occasion would remain, like the wedding, one of the greatest moments in Esmeralda's life, and that of her husband, and her loved in-laws.

New life would come into this family, and it wasn't without superstition the Italians in the room thought of the omen, "One comes and one goes." Soon Gianni's Mother would be a widow.

Roberto Zianni was loved by all. If he could have controlled his destiny he would have succeeded in willing himself to live wanting to see his first grandchild. Fate had other plans. Six weeks later, with Esmeralda's flat stomach now a secure tiny pouch, the couple was called to the bedside of their Father. He said his farewells, was given last rites and slowly dimmed his lights of this life for another.

United in death, united in marriage, united in life itself, Gianni and Esmeralda understood the weight of responsibility of this heartbreaking death. Gianni's Mother and sister, Serena, stood by devastated, grief written all over their faces, like Gianni, while Esmeralda tried to control her emotions feeling nauseas from her pregnancy.

Everything now fell to Gianni. He was not surprised with the bequest of his Father's Last Will and Testament. The stipulations were the act of primogeniture, as it had been for Roberto when his Father died. Gianni inherited everything. He was thirty-nine years old. It was the old fashioned Italian tradition and now it would be Gianni's responsibility to look after his entire family as the new patriarch.

The strain of the funeral was difficult for Esmeralda and as she was completing her first trimester, doctors insisted she have an amniocentesis to be sure everything was secure. Gianni was more in love than before knowing how Esmeralda was patient throughout the long process to conceive, never giving him any cause for anxiety. Understanding the depth of her love he worried how she could endure this pregnancy. Each grew more precious to the other knowing they would soon be parents. They spoke about names and shopped for a myriad of baby necessities for the nursery being decorated in each of their three houses. Gianni amused everyone with his jitters, wanting to attend appointments with the doctor wishing to be a part of the miracle of birth. All were in awe of his devotion and this happiness eased the pain of bereavement.

Esmeralda wished to keep the mystery of birth and didn't want to know the sex of the child. They were thrilled they could conceive and wanted many children. Gianni was terribly curious insisting upon all the findings of the test. The Chairman of the Board of Zianni Pharmaceuticals would not be put off with anything that concerned medicine or the miracle that would soon be his, the birth of his first baby.

The doctors adhered to his demand for factual data. When all results proved favorable, the mourning was broken by the news Esmeralda was carrying a son. Light returned to the family and Gianni, loved his wife as never before telling her he was making necessary arrangements for the future.

Although she had no knowledge about his business or legal affairs, it didn't come as a shock to D'Albora & D'Albora Avvocati to write Gianni's new Will naming his son, as primogenitor and Esmeralda Zianni sole heirs to his fortune and all his possessions. They would usher in a new family and she would be the matriarch once his Mother died. They would look after the entire family together, including Serena and anyone she was to marry with the same loving care Gianni's Father had looked after them. The death of his Father was a huge tragedy for Gianni but it was negated by the joy of his son to be born in January. He had six months to wait.

XXII

The Concert and The Interval

At this point in our story, we return to present events at Villa Pina.

Nigel was relaxed with the attitude of a winner. Giving way to bonhomie, a false smile lit his face, greeting guests, sipping champagne just before the concert was to begin.

Esmeralda studied those that were intent to annihilate her, the cosmopolitan, the famous, the infamous, the people who had a past and the ones eager to make one, the forgers of society, the phonies who counted money, the mad eccentrics, the timid traditionalists, the erudite, the stupid, the colony of malcontents, disinherited nobility, retired pensioners, widows, divorcees, gays, bores jubilantly kissing each other thrilled to be linked in some tribal rite called *society* here this evening at her Villa Pina.

Nigel's basking superficiality was the essence of *bella figura,* prompting a duplicate response from Esmeralda as they took their place applauding the piano virtuoso like performing seals.

"Ziz es ze greatest moment in my life," the musical wizard, Oleg Kurezmakoff, bowed, kissing Esmeralda on the hand, blushing. "Zank you my host and hostess for prezenting thiz premier opportunity for me to debut in Europe."

Stunned by events, Esmeralda held herself in check, wishing to forestall a panic attack. Kurezmakoff's touched the rare Fazioli. Instantly his dexterity ignited the room with Rachmaninoff's Eighth, *allegro* notes colliding in syncopation with the *adagio* score and what seemed a thousand fingers moved with alacrity, in perfect harmony.

Deep in thought, Esmeralda clocked her husband's arrogance. "The comedy of life, the drama- are all over...there's no music in my soul...." the sensation was increased when she studied Nigel further, the tilt of his chin, a gesture one learned early in life. His elongated nose twitched a little this evening, his nostrils appeared to sniff something indelicate, or was it his way to put Esmeralda off guard? Do I reek of liquor? She thought as his patrician hand rubbed the tip of his dominating feature and then smoothed his arched brows and bald head.

At one point his fingertips tapped the rhythm of the music on his long legs as if they were sending an S.O.S. Esmeralda had the unmistakable impression he'd already set his plans in motion. It all came down to money...Nigel was from a mediocre inheritance until I came into his life, she sneered inwardly. Pompous Nigel! Genealogically perfect but a spendthrift of the first degree, initially marrying his first wife for money and then me. Stupid me, who never denied his cravings for indulgences believing I could buy his loyalty.

To endure the first forty minutes of the concert brought suspense of what was to come. Esmeralda was panicky. Her mind rushed to the centre of heavy thoughts. Unable to concentrate, trying to appear a gracious hostess to the litany of a hundred guests whose eyes were focused upon her, a drama of hysterics churned. She had to organize thoughts, set her scheme in motion. Emotion can't shake me. Let me learn from this cold-hearted husband and pretend nothing has happened. I must win!

Her conscious spoke knowing she would never win. My purpose is to survive, she readdressed her tangled thoughts, her cool fingers dripped with perspiration, so unlike her. Sweaty palms would stain her beautiful Valentino costume. Important to keep up appearances, she told her vain self and then realized how ridiculous it all was under the horrendous circumstances.

Strange how the mind works injecting something mundane at the time of crisis. She cringed turning over Nigel's plans for a rapid divorce. He'd made it his business years before to be aware of her financial portfolio. I won't be controlled by him! He's not the central figure in this plot, he's a bit player, a pigmy as far as I'm concerned. Tonight he's betrayed me. I would sooner die than have him walk away with my money and the Zianni fortune. He's never been a husband. He's been an actor.

The gifted musician whose debut put butterflies in his stomach viewed the elegant guests this night at Villa Pina. His world of delirium was celestial, from here, my future will be guaranteed throughout Europe and America he thought, the group assembled is extraordinary. His agile fingers danced over the keys of the grand piano with a Liszt's masterpiece but was anyone concentrating on the music? Esmeralda's tension filled the air as a backdrop while the exceptional notes resounded, as all she could concentrate on was death speaking to her and suddenly the last notes of Liszt Rhapsody filled the conservatory and Oleg Kurezmakoff, lost in the world of music, completed the first part of the program and bowed.

Peering at Esmeralda from under his brows, applauding enthusiastically, Nigel questioned, "What are your plans during the interval?"

With cold distain and a smile to dazzle those who didn't surmise a thing, she answered, "To send Sanjeev to Naples with the speed launch and letter for Serena."

He nodded approvingly, "Very wise, my Dear, under the circumstances."

A callous smile crossed his lips as Naomi stepped to centre stage to deliver her poem, thanking guests for their applause, enraptured.

"My first poem is dedicated to a special friend," she said looking directly at Brian Korthorpe sitting in the front row with Elizabeth, "The Power of Love."

While her words delighted the others, Esmeralda took no notice and quickly penned ideas on the program how she'd phrase her letter to her former sister-in-law.

Véronique watched the scenario. She'd studied the astrological charts of her host and hostess hours ago. Catastrophe was at hand. She harkened back to her compatriot, La Rochefoucauld, with his philosophy imprinted on her young mind from lycée days in Paris, "*There is always something of a friend's misfortune that gives one pleasure.*"

Véronique couldn't mistake a devilish smile playing on the corners of Nigel's mouth. *There is no misfortune that cannot be exploited,* those words sprung to mind from the inspiration of La Rochefoucauld. Nigel will exploit things. I sense it.

Journalist Daniels sat completely ignorant of the enormity of the situation to come. He will have his own means to exploit this couple, thought Véronique knowing the power of the media. Her eyes gazed downward for the moment taking in Naomi's eloquent words to her ardent suitor who was returning his affection to his poet, beaming with love.

Classical music and poetry, so unusual for Cat to hear, made her mind wander to her future. Véronique predicted not to be concerned with a broken romance. It all was so terrible, sitting here, a complete stranger! All these highbrow people! Everyone speaking in Italian or British English! She didn't understand music like this, poems like this, people like this.

Marc Levy sat beside her as if she didn't exist. She watched his reptilian glance dart back and forth to Zofra without any sense of guilt. That hussy smiled at him rolling her tongue on her lips. Cat's resolve after speaking with Véronique gave her courage; she wouldn't be steamrolled as if she was a nobody. She had youth! She'd even the score if Mark Levy hurt her. Levy puffed away with his shortness of breath, overweight and overfed, uncomfortable on the gilt chair. Maybe, thought Cat, it would be better not to dedicate her life to a womanizer twice her age. Another group who will exploit things, Véronique considered. Zofra already had staked her claim effectively.

Véronique saw all the extraordinary predictions of the stars she'd scrutinized coming into view. There was no way anyone could stop what was to be.

Olympia was concerned. Whitney had stayed away from the concert without any word to her except to 'be on the yacht tomorrow.' Rupert was nowhere in sight. Could it be now when she and Whitney sensed an unexplainable magic between them something happened? An accident? She was worried about someone other than herself, turning around, looking towards the door, catching the piercing eye of Lynne who wished, conversely, something did happened to Whitney and that he was dead somewhere in the Bay of Naples and she would be a widow and inherit everything as she justly deserved. *There is no catastrophe from which someone cannot take an advantage* came to Véronique's mind viewing these women intent on what Whitney Jameson's absence meant to their future.

Levy could sense the agitation in Cat. Too damned bad. I'm single. I've found somethin' better, he calculated, while Jarvis Engelton looked to Lynne and then back to Daniels who met his expression in a blank way. *There is no calamity someone cannot bend to his own advantage,* reverberated in Véronique.

Meanwhile in Naples, Serena fit into all these categories. She would benefit from this misfortune with a fortune. This catastrophe, would make Rupert and Serena victors knowing all the cards were stacked in their favor, and to their credit, there was a self-effacing quality how they spent the evening, Serena with lawyers, Rupert quietly with Whitney.

Whitney had not contacted his wife but called a summit of the old friends texting:

> Pals ONLY Confidential.
> Be on my boat tomorrow 10am.
> Marina Grande. Sail Ischia. W

Shabadiba received the first text, then the others. No one had a clue what it meant. Plans were for Serena with her entourage of attorneys to meet them on Ischia. The rest would be history.

While Esmeralda made herself scarce, Nigel's charisma was vibrant, hosting the Interval reception completely at ease, sparkling with repartee as the tinkling of glasses was heard throughout the marquee and Beluga caviar was served. Nigel felt a lightness about himself, as though an albatross was removed from his back.

"Dear Oleg Kurezmakoff! Remarkable!" he exclaimed buoyantly, "This night is our night in history, my dear old thing! Let me introduce you to a marvelous chappie from Hollywood, Marc Levy. I'm sure he can use you in a film."

Nigel glided through intermission like Fred Astaire in a foxtrot all smiles, giggly with triumph inside, delighted to take his sinister revenge towards Esmeralda. He turned to Stefano, "Esmeralda will be here in a moment! Busy girl has a surprise I daresay…Yes…Something she least expected to do. You know how fastidious she is about organizing everything."

Nigel had no notion Esmeralda confided in her former lover, de Gesu. Their eyes met and in that one second, with Véronique beside Stefano, the three understood Nigel was lying through his teeth. The brink of chaos was threatening Nigel's life. Had they not known Nigel as well as they did, his acting was worthy of a superstar.

What they didn't realize until that moment, Nigel was going to reduce Esmeralda to rubble; his vicious topaz eyes gave him away. He had every right to be more at ease than his spouse. While she was dressing this evening, his solicitors in London froze her assets and began divorce proceedings, the papers of which would arrive tomorrow morning. Interesting when a law firm smells money how quickly they respond, thought Nigel. He'd also managed to put in a 'teaser' to Richard Kaye at the Daily Mail via his law firm without naming names. Tomorrow's tabloid would read, "*Who will be the latest British couple to divorce presently enjoying the 'dolce far niente' life on Capri?*" That will cause a flutter in a drawing room or two, thought Nigel preparing to destroy Esmeralda before Serena could do so.

Frantically, in contrast, during the twenty-minute time-period, Esmeralda raced to her room signaling Sanjeev, "I need you, there's an emergency. You must depart immediately on their motor launch for Contessa Serena in Naples."

Within minutes she'd give him a letter before the second part of the concert began. The music had concentrated her mind. Firstly, she rang her lawyer in London, Arthur & Porter demanding, "Your presence is of vital importance. Be here tomorrow." Her voice was stringent with grave commands. "Everything's at stake. Notify me what time you'll arrive, even if in the middle of the night."

"Are you sure, Esmeralda this is necessary?"

"Imperative. Plan to stay a few days, liaise with Italian counterparts, D'Albora & D'Albora, who must be in attendance." Her demand intensified, "It's a matter of life or death." Esmeralda was not a woman given to hysterics, she was never rabid. They'd never received a call of this nature. Her lawyers obeyed.

"Your husband's solicitors Baker, Baker & MacCloud have already contacted us. We've been informed a divorce is in progress." She gasped when David Arthur informed her of Nigel's alacrity. The prestigious firm had handled her legal affairs since she was the Baroness Beck.

"Yes," was her only answer, given coldly. "That's the least of my legal problems."

She closed the phone with five minutes to act before people returned to their seats. With jittery fingers she scribbled the most important letter of her life. She put down her pen, tearing the original paper to shreds knowing every word she wrote would be weighed against her. She thought it wise to reduce the size of her handwriting, chose grey paper then thought it too morbid taking instead a light blue velum, changing her pen using blue ink instead of black. Every step was calculated. This note would be her post mortem. Keep it brief, don't commit to anything crossed her mind and then there was only one word she understood. The one word that her only friend, that self-protective coward, Stefano de Gesu, uttered: Beg.

Dear Serena,

In the memory of Gianni, I implore you please do not to act in haste with the information you have.

I beg you ~ let us speak privately or through solicitors.

Esmeralda.

Everything she could control was attended during the brief interval. No one would suspect a thing. Sanjeev asked no questions and departed in haste for Naples. Becoming a messenger with a sealed envelope was highly irregular. Without formal education he understood what he held in his hand was deadly.

Esmeralda entered the conservatory looking beguiling and contained, the greatest act of her life was to begin.

Nigel with his affectations waved and smiled as if he was on the cover of PALM BEACH ILLUSTRATED. She returned his artificial smile. Although he never took his eyes off her entering the room, Nigel was thinking, I'm not going to make a public fool of myself, wisdom tells me let this be handled as a business matter, a business gone sour, I know how to survive....there's something to be said for middle age.

Other guests noted Esmeralda's arrival never surmising the anguished knot in her stomach tighten. How would she get through the dinner following this concert? She couldn't envision the play of events. Stefano caught her eye before the house lights dimmed and one look exchanged told him she had taken his advice.

Esmeralda sat like a sphinx for the second half of the program.

Let me return to certain surprise telephone call Nicky received at Canzone del Mare. What would make the cool headed Nicky leave Marco after their leisurely lunch in such haste?

And, what about the man at Esmeralda's wedding in formal attire sitting alone like a leper on the bridal side, who was he?

XXIII

Ischia and The Unexpected

The next day...

To all appearances, as the unsuspecting friends departed Villa Pina, the scene was one of informal tranquility.

Nigel spotted Whitney in the entry way.

"What's happening, old thing?" Nigel questioned.

"A reunion of the old crowd, polo chums meeting in Ischia," Whitney proclaimed speaking a half-truth, "They insisted we come for the day." Nonchalantly, he walked off.

"Interesting," remarked Marco to Nigel as he wandered near going to the pool.

"Yes...My dear boy…" Nigel said to Marco, standing transfixed in the garden.

"Thought you were a part of the polo crowd."

"Whitney…" he called out to Jameson, "What about me?"

"You have too much to do here. I'll tell you about it later."

"With everyone's carousing at Guericino's last night, aren't they wiped out…? What with the concert and all."

"You only live once!" Whitney called back walking down the steps of the veranda.

"Whitney..." Nigel called again, "The weather doesn't look promising…see the cloud over the sun, looks like rain..."

"Rubbish! I don't believe it. It'll blow over." Whitney waved and was out of sight.

As Nigel moved towards the house, he came face to face with Stefano de Gesu, packed and ready to go. "Nigel, I've received a message and I'm off." This came as a bolt without warning.

"Leaving? Does Esmeralda know?"

"I think we both know more about present circumstances than we care to discuss. A bigger scandal that we can imagine is brewing."

"Fuck the whole thing, Stefano. This is a bottle of scotch day."

"What?"

"You know when the weather stinks, so does your wife, and all these people - the only way to get through it is to get drunk."

"Esmeralda's told me you're filing for divorce."

"Survival, my dear old thing, survival." He looked at de Gesu. "So you're leaving a sinking ship?"

"Duty before pleasure, Nigel…and under the circumstances…"

"You don't have to explain."

"I've left a note for Esmeralda with Sanjeev."

Nigel watched the dignified Ambassador go off with a taxi and his luggage. Strange they're all departing at the same time. He opened his Grandfather's pocket watch dangling from its gold chain. Nine-thirty, I suppose he'll catch the ten o'clock *aloscalfi.*

His attention turned to Shabadiba, Olympia and Véronique coming towards him in the garden.

"Buon Giorno Nigel" said Olympia planting a kiss on his cheek, followed by Véronique and Shabadiba.

"Darlings! Don't abandon me!"

"See you tonight…" Olympia smiled. "the concert was wonderful."

"You've got plenty of company, Nigel," Véronique added, "lots to do." It was as if she read his mind.

"Have fun with Lynne," Shabadiba joked under her breath.

"Where are the others?" Nigel stood dismayed watching the women dart away.

"Nicky's taking Stella." Said Olympia. "Marco's with you."

"Samir, Naomi and Brian are coming in a minute with Rupert." Véronique called walking down the path.

It's all too strange this sudden evacuation from the villa, considered Nigel.

Being untrustworthy himself he never trusted anyone. No one knows about Serena's letter except de Gesu. He's not one to talk. Anyway, with those trumped up bunch of solicitors Esmeralda's expecting it's just as well. God knows I have enough to do with *my* lawyers.

"Nigel! We've been looking for you inside. We're off for a bit. Anything you want from Ischia?" Naomi smiled with Brian beside her and Samir hurried along from the library.

"I think you've picked a lousy day to sail."

"Wasn't our choice," injected Brian rapidly. "If you need us, call."

"Yes, Brian, you too." Nigel patted him on the shoulder as the couple departed.

"Look after Jacqueline, please, Nigel," Samir said nervously. "She's going shopping with Lynne." Saluting Nigel good-bye he walked briskly to catch up with the others.

"If things get boring here," Nigel shouted, "maybe I'll take a launch and meet you!"

"Do" said Rupert startling Nigel coming up from behind him, the last to leave the house. "Got Whitney's mobile?"

"Yes…but Rupert…what the hell's going on? The weather looks precarious. Who are you meeting?"

"Whitney's crew will be fine, don't worry. What's your plan for today?" Rupert was loathe to lie and turned the question back to Nigel.

"Besides getting drunk? Esmeralda's expecting people. There's personal business to attend with London. Really, old chap, I'm curious. In a way this exodus is a blessing but it seems strange with weather like this."

"Poppycock! Don't worry."

"There's dinner tonight, you know."

"Yes, we know…" Rupert met his eye and for the minute Nigel had the distinct feeling Rupert was briefed to the crisis. Warmly, he squeezed Nigel's shoulder, "Anything you want to tell me?"

Nigel clenched his jaw meeting Rupert's eyes. He sighed deeply, Nigel's trademark before giving birth to a large idea.

"I'm divorcing Esmeralda. Tell our friends." The shock Nigel expected from his revelation was non-existent. The conversation stilled, anything else would be strained and didn't flow to say the least. "What a cock-up! This fucked up life of mine!"

Rupert's eyed his friend of thirty years. The unnatural silence bonded the two. The toot of a horn was heard in the distance. Rupert put his hand on Nigel's shoulder again. "Everything has two sides, Nigel. There are better days ahead. Your friends will never betray you."

Rupert moved away quickly, not noticing cynical Nigel who had a wise remark for every circumstance standing alone, wordless, swallowing hard.

"Call for you, Sir."

"Thank you Sanjeev, I'll take it in the library."

Nigel Pembrooke walked through the atrium, scuffing his Belgian loafers along mosaic tiles to the library, one of his Labradors followed. "Sanjeev bring me café and today's newspaper." Few people called this early in the day. It was either his lawyer or the press.

"Pronto."

"Nigel! That you? Richard Kaye from *The Daily Mail*. Want to make a statement?"

"Statement?"

"Yes. We're running an article for tomorrow's paper. Do you believe this to be a caprice divorcing Esmeralda?"

"My dear old thing," Nigel said regaining composure, "Caprice did you say?" Holding the receiver in hand, standing tall, he looked at his naked left hand without his wedding ring, trying to switch the subject collecting his thoughts.

"Yes, caprice..." said Richard Kaye.

"I'll take you to lunch at Caprice when I'm in London next week."

"Haha….We're on. Do you want to make a statement?"

"How much will *The Mail* pay me for the exclusive?"

"Let me speak to the powers that be."

"How nice of you to call Richard. Keep in touch." Nigel closed the receiver pleased at Kaye's alacrity and that he handled him to his advantage. The tension of the morning made him collapse in the leather desk chair rubbing weary eyes. It wasn't yet ten and the house buzzed with activity, foreign to its usual peace. He removed a small key from his pocket unlocking a drawer. He shuffled through papers. Sanjeev entered with his café.

"Thanks, Sanjeev. I've some things that must go by courier this morning to London. Has the boat arrived with mail and newspapers? Has Mrs. Pembrooke awakened?"

"Yes, Sir she has. The boat's been detained."

"Is she upstairs?"

"No, Sir she left the house early this morning to meet people arriving."

"Must be her lawyers." Nigel mumbled. The devoted houseman waited to be dismissed. "Sanjeev, did she explain anything to you about some unexpected events?"

"She told me this evening will be a dinner of the guests at the villa and the new arrivals, giving me the menu, Sir."

"That's all?"

"Yes, Sir."

"Sanjeev we both need you."

"Yes Sir."

"Who's remaining at the villa?"

"There is Miss Elizabeth who is departing for Rome at noon, Mrs. Jameson and Mme Redat are having breakfast in their rooms and so are the movie people, Mr. Levy with Miss Renoir, Mr. Daniels with Mr. Engleton. Mme Zofany is looking after Princess Shabadiba's dog. Mr. Ricci is swimming."

"Excellent Sanjeev. Everyone's doing their thing. What time is Mrs. Pembrooke expected to return?"

"By six."

"Six?" Nigel raised his brows surprised, his mouth hung open for the moment.

"Yes, Sir. Cocktails at eight, buffet following at nine."

Nigel surmised correctly Esmeralda was seeing her legal team sequestering them elsewhere plotting survival. "She didn't happen to mention where she was?"

"No Sir. She has her mobile phone."

"Of course. That will be all, Sanjeev. Do organize the courier. I wonder why the boat's delayed. These documents will be complete in an hour, I want them to make the noon boat."

"Yes sir. Changing weather is predicted. Shall I return when you ring."

"Jolly good."

Guests on the three-mast yacht had their own thoughts. Rupert longed to be alone with Serena. Plans were to meet everyone by noon at Villa Adriana, the residence of Jacopa Zianni, a cousin, in Ischia. Everyone inquired why they were summoned by text message. A sense of secrecy lent mystery to the outing. The old friends' believed it strange to be led away from Capri at this hour, on this day when the weather was foul.

Whitney was the last person in the world to be cloaked in mystery. Yet, he called the appointment. This group trusted each other. Therefore, although anticipation consumed everyone, an air of good will surrounded them.

It was telling Stefano de Gesu joined the cruise. All believed he was leaving for London. No pretence was made that his attention was far from platonic towards Véronique. Duplicating the scenario was Jameson and Olympia. This seemed a good omen. No one failed to notice the chemistry that ignited at Saturday's dinner dance with those named and the poet and scientist, Brian Korthorpe.

Heaving grey waves swelled with intensity and white caps gave way to the morning wind. A sudden chill turned the humid air brisk as the undulating waves surged with the rise and fall of the rapid tide. Attentive to the sea's motion, Whitney's dexterous crew trimmed sails accordingly. Once on the open stretch of the Mediterranean, high waves and gusty wind made the women go below while the men remained on the aft or the stern pitching to and fro enjoying the vigor of a dramatic cruise to the nearby larger island, Ischia twenty miles away. Turbulence at sea appealed to Whitney yet one could sense the women's fright sailing on a risky morning. The sea matched the overcast sky without promise of sun.

"Perhaps it's too early," said Shabadiba to Véronique's "it'll clear."

"Whitney's not reckless," offered Olympia.

Samir was overly anxious. He recalled Véronique's words about benevolence and questioned once he reached Ischia if he'd know why this impromptu rendezvous came to be. Although born in Luxor on the Nile, the Mediterranean was something else, he was not fond of a chancy sea.

Whitney, Stefano and Rupert commiserated at ease. Brian Korthorpe was too enchanted with his personal life to consider anything but a future with Naomi.

Stella, meanwhile, was with Nicky in his amphibious plane taking delight in the danger it presented wondering why Nicky had insisted she come with him. Expectations ran high. Nicky would reveal something. Always closed mouthed, not like Marco, she didn't know how to play him. They'd known each other all their lives. In due time he'll spill forth what's on his mind.

He flattered her ego, he had invested in ESCAPADES. Italian money backing her efforts - even if Nicky bankrolled the project a fraction of what Esmeralda assumed - heightened her pride. His belief in the film, and undoubtedly in her talent gave a sense of importance to Stella. Professional plaudits were turning in her direction.

Her memories turned to Gianni. His destiny was to die young. What would she have done with all that money had they wed? or later, as his widow? Her mind would've gone to seed, not produced the competence of screenwriting she achieved today. She contained much more than she could understand, deep within her this was just the beginning she told herself. Some women like her are meant to soar and stand above the crowd. Her's was genius. Power. She was talked about for herself, not some legacy from a spouse or famous father.

Gianni's fortune seemed marvelous at the time, but Stella discovered something these years, her talent to be a screenwriter, revered in a tough business and no one could take that from her. Marco made her feel womanly, an intellectual marvel, whereas Gianni would have always been the star in the relationship requiring adulation....adulation she didn't intend to give anyone but herself.

Marc Levy and the others who challenged her in business were players she could handle. Tag her a feminist? Tough as nails? Out for power? Cold? Ambitious? Good. What do I care? Let them believe what they want. When I trot off with the Oscar, they'll stand agog singing praises to Stella Gregotti, carpeting my path with rose petals. I've courage to achieve what's out of their reach. Marco helped. God bless him! He knows how to let me fly my own chariot.

Nicky's engine zoomed to maximum, in seconds they were air-born. The exhilaration thrilled Stella.

It took one phone call, thought Nicky cruising close to the wind-swept sea, and I have the low-down on what this jaunt's about. My plan is set. Benefiting me. How I viewed Esmeralda years ago was right. Instincts are never wrong. A tail wind gave a surge of speed to the craft. Nicky's second nature controlled the scene. He bit his lips tensing the repercussions....what was to be announced in Ischia...

What a tragedy this whole thing is. That bitch put a curse on the family. Nicky felt in complete control. There's a boomerang to things and he had a front row ticket to the show...of course, Serena has her own agenda. If she wins, I wonder if she'll be prickled with conscious, think again Nicky...think again....

Lynne Jameson was beginning to see the light. Whitney had come to bed late both nights. Had he been drinking with Nigel? Or ogling over those two common tarts, Zofra and Cat? Just like a man, interested in trash when he can't even perform. Her accusatory nature didn't appreciate being excluded from the clique that had excluded her in the past. The old cohorts were a necessary evil all these years. A necessary evil. They kept Whitney controlled and that was sufficient in her eyes.

On the other hand, Jacqueline and Samir had spoken about the text and both surmised something important would happen in Ischia. Shopping was on the agenda in the heart of Capri, lunch at the Quissiana and an art exhibit in the afternoon at Princess Caravacallo's studio. If the others wished to join them, so be it. Lynne and Jacqueline were not friends after all these years but acquaintances.

"Make ya'self scarce, there's movie matters to discuss," Marc Levy told Cat Renoir and the insecure girl accepted his gold Visa card and joined the women shopping. This gave Levy the afternoon with Zofra while Daniels and Engelton joined Marco for an insider's romp slumming in Capri.

Nigel was left alone with calls to London, planning legal strategy to seize everything he could from Esmeralda. 'Asset stripping,' was his intent.

Esmeralda, in the boardroom at the Caesar Augustus Hotel, was pleading with lawyers to break Serena Zianni's resolve and confront accusations hoping legal craftiness would salvage the wreckage of her life.

Rupert waited for the sea to calm as they approached Ischia and called the women on deck to appraise everyone the reason for the sail. His mind was fixed on his three-day visit with Serena...how she looked with her high cheekbones and full lips, the fragrance in the air when she came near, as they entered the palazzo in Posillipo, the words she spoke unraveling details confronting them today.

Last Thursday when they'd arrived in Naples, she brought him up to date speaking of the large palazzo in Posillipo overlooking the Bay of Naples was where she lived now on the *piano nobile* floor exclusively. The four-story mansion with its expanse of terrace above was the past. Esmeralda's investment bankers arranged for American millionaires to rent the rest of the palatial home and Serena and her Mother's were shortchanged by Esmeralda's greed. Rupert gazed about recalling the upper floor's beauty. "At least you have this, I suppose you were able to receive the antiques prior to Gianni's death."

Serena had a gentility about her, amidst the setting that was commendable. "It's another world, Rupert. I know others have much less, but Esmeralda's an imposter. She's robbed us blind. The Zianni fortune, paintings, silver, diamonds, yachts, Rolls, homes that Gianni said we could share, she's stripped me of everything and basks in Zianni money." Her assaults were punctuated with smoldering smite that was understandable. "Insatiable greed knows no bounds. When I received the letter from her Father I was in shock, and then came an overwhelming desire to solve the mystery."

The set of events she dilated amazed Rupert. "She has Sanjeev iron Nigel's newspapers and press his socks! Our luxuries are few, my memories are great and Gianni must be turning in his grave. I must contest Gianni's Will."

"Esmeralda Anderson Beck was not legally married to my brother. Her papers are false. She's false. Everything's a lie!" Emotionally, she continued, "What she's done to Gianni's child, is a sin of catastrophic proportions. We can circumvent her, exhume the body, check DNA and find the cause of death. I want the Italian State to crucify her. We've been swindled."

He looked at her harshly. Serena's words were out of character. Yet, in her torment, she was ravishingly beautiful. "I am not cruel Rupert. I believe in justice. If I have to fight this alone I will. Go off!"

"I'm not going off. I'm staying with you." His tender smile melted her heart. He completely understood her rancor.

"If we hadn't seen Gianni die before our eyes at Windsor I would have sworn Esmeralda killed him. She used his death saying it was the shock for her miscarriage or 'still birth' as it stated on the birth certificate. That's been wrapped in secretly for years. Nothing rang true for me ever! With Danny McSweeney's letter, I question things entirely. I remember walking down the aisle at their wedding knowing it was a mistake."

"I had the same concerns, Serena." She looked at him and words were not necessary. This terrible tragedy joined them. They would never be apart again.

"I was so bereaved, as was Mother with Gianni's death, Father's death months before and then the baby! The depths of hell surrounded us. My brother never would have disinherited his Mother and me to the degree as written in his Last Will. It's an Italian Will the majority of aristocrats make knowing that the head of the family will honor ties and never give cause of insecurity to others. Mother died with her soul in pieces. No one understood the brutal change in Esmeralda. "Mother believed she'd suffered two tragedies, her husband and her baby and she forgave what she referred to as 'misjudgments.' I never had those stars in my eyes."

When all was spoken, once Rupert had met with Serena's advisors, seen documents, they parted without shaking hands, without a kiss. Three days brought them together with a rare intimacy without sensual force. As he hailed a taxi to catch the *alocalfi* to Capri, he kept a vision of Serena, remembering every detal of his time with her. This is what one waits for. He understood life at last. I have run in another direction, I've avoided what's best in life and kept my defenses. I told myself I'm too old, close to fifty, believing all love futile. To open my heart was frightening. Everything's changed!

Glancing at his watch he appreciated the newness of his being, the top speed that day when the driver reached the boat to Capri and meet his friends at Villa Pina.

Serena and I abandoned each other before - Serena with a marriage to a man of questionable sexuality and me, a man void of happiness all these years. Love conquered Rupert. Chance directed his path.

"Good weather," he said to the driver as they reached the boat to Capri in time.

"Si Signor, bel tempo." Yes, thought Rupert, it will be a beautiful time not understanding the driver meant beautiful weather.

That was three days ago, now it was Monday and he was well gone from Villa Pina. The flurry of brisk air felt marvelous through his hair, smarting his tanned face. A rare intimacy was achieved without the physical joining forces that day with Serena, he concentrated on today, he'd grown a mile.

Ischia is an easy sail from Capri. To maneuver without an engine depends on wind. Today the force was strong, the hour approaching noon as the sea calmed. A genial atmosphere came to the vessel.

Women stepped from below assured and all laughed believing themselves seasoned sailors, making room to sit together on the aft in cozy fashion. Rupert, rarely took center stage. He looked at Whitney. "You're all wondering why Whitney demanded this sail," he began. "I've asked him to." Friends chatter quieted, tuned to hear Rupert speak.

"I failed to arrive on Thursday because as Fate decreed, rushing to catch the train to Naples, I met Serena Zianni." A flutter of voices came from the women. "She was in Rome returning to Naples after meetings with lawyers over highly confidential matters. She asked me to bring us together. I'm dismayed to be the one to break the news but Serena has horrid facts she wants us to know. It pertains to someone we thought we knew well. It doesn't please me to speak of evil. Serena will meet us in Ischia with her lawyers and produce documents I've seen that none of you will believe." An interchange alighted and Rupert coaxed them to be still.

"Serena, has the soul of an angel; she was blackmailed by Esmeralda's father in South Africa. "

"What?"

"Can't be!"

"You can imagine her position. We all thought she was orphaned from an I.R.A. attack."

Everyone began sprouting opinions. Rupert silenced them again raising his hand. "She undertook an investigation in a precise manner. What she's learned is atrocious. Horrific details will startle you as they have me. Two of us besides myself know these facts today, I informed Whitney yesterday. Esmeralda informed Stefano. In the memory of Gianni, I beg you we must support Serena. Justice is at stake. I cannot abide by untruths."

"Neither can we," Whitney spoke for the group.

"That's what's bound us together all these years," offered Brian, "but this is so upsetting...".

The echoes amplified at sea. Rupert continued, "I don't want to expand things here, that will be for Serena and her lawyers. Suffice to say, Esmeralda's an imposter."

"No!"

"My God…"

"Unbelievable!"

"Is it true?"

"How do you know?"

The remarks came fast. Rupert urged silence and the friends, like the waves, stilled. Ischia was in sight and they would disembark in minutes.

"Nigel's another matter. I believe him to be broken. We must stand by our friend. He's asked me to tell you, he's divorcing Esmeralda."

Another uproar ensued. The contingent looked to one another each collecting data that suddenly came to the forefront of memory.

"But last night!"

"Saturday's beautiful dinner - they seemed so in love."

The friends wanted to expel whatever they deemed important seized each one. Unity commanded with a sense of allegiance to Serena including Stefano who had earlier defended his belief to have ethics and dignity reign. None onboard were vicious and none aboard aligned with Esmeralda; truth would prevail. As Rupert surmised the loyalty Gianni had given each of them would be returned to Serena.

As they began to disembark, a gentle drizzle descended and threatening clouds commenced, across the sky. The crew furled sails rapidly, tied them to the masts, lowered the anchor and adjusted the gangplank for the loyal mates to rendezvous with Serena.

———

"Stella," said Nicky taking her arm to come ashore, "I want to tell you something before we meet the others. We're going to meet Serena."

"Serena?" Stella exclaimed surprised. "It's been years since I've seen Gianni's sister. Why this strange appointment?"

"I don't know everything but listen to what I have to say." They walked to a nearby café before going to Serena's rendezvous taking cover under the canopy from the rain.

———

Over the past two years, seeing the sham of his marriage, Nigel shrewdly copied sensitive documents. Today those would be couriered to London by noon. "Liquidity for me. Financial ruin for her," he mumbled sneering. Investment counselors call it by other names," A foxy smile came to his calculating lips. He'd learned from a master. As her lure to have him leave his first marriage and remarry, Esmeralda said she didn't need to have a pre-nup as it never would hold water under English law and briefed Nigel about her finances and the monumental fortune that was in her command from Gianni's legacy. She needed his trusted companionship to alleviate the burden of the vast legacy, or so she said.

Once wed, her tune changed. Private investments were made with professional advisors, Nigel was totally excluded. Esmeralda was ruthless about disclosures to her husband, however, whenever he could, Nigel made it a practice to know every minute detail of her portfolio. This included eyeing mail and once in a while, when he was particularly devilish and hateful from her off handed behavior, he'd eavesdrop on conversations. Those moments became habit as their marriage deteriorated. True, he had married for money and saw his mercenary chances shrewdly. Money solves things, he philosophized.

His position on international turf, which dimmed as he grew older, his desire to renew the spotlight denied to him now that commentary days were finished were revitalized with wealth. Money talked. With a gold purse his, Nigel was well invited to the coveted set that dismissed him as fame declined.

After their first year of marriage, fawning over his gorgeous wife, the cost of auctioning Nigel Pembrooke, a kept spouse, was exorbitant. When he took inventory, he hated prostituting himself.

My wife is a conniving witch. She realigned Gianni's wealth for her own gain, dismantled bequests he would have made his sister and Mother, reduced my allowance and never gave me love, attention or respect as her husband.

He'd gone along with the charade, drinking, laughing at the funeral oration he'd receive with the final tally of living in luxury. With her extraordinary revelation yesterday, Nigel took the addition of his life differently, rewriting his obituary.

The score he'd settle would be divorce with alimony in his favor. She bought him to use him, use his position in society, to be secure with a partner who knew how to swim in circles she wished to retain. Nigel's presence furthered her ambitions. She manipulated an English aristocrat and he'd fallen for her witchcraft with his greedy soul, using her, wanting more than his due. He was contaminated, certainly, but she outdistanced him by miles.

Simultaneously, Esmeralda went to confront the solemn faces of her lawyers, men who had revered her in the past and now waited for her brutal confession.

Serena was in Ischia with another set of attorneys whose expectant faces displayed victory. The core of both meetings was greed.

Esmeralda wanted to salvage what she could and dared not to dream of a future where she would be thrust into a prison, as a common criminal, exposed to vultures of the world's press, face a jury condemning her to hell, striped of everything.

Serena saw the life she was entitled returning like a phoenix rising from the ashes. Her gentle nature had turned vindictive, wanting revenge on a woman who destroyed the respected name of Zianni, eliminated a rightful heir, robbed her and her Mother of possessions and made mockery of her brother's memory.

Mercenary lawyers saw fees, duplicating their client's objectives. The greed factor permeated everything. Those acting for Esmeralda deliberated what course of action to take, while representatives for Serena considered how to crucify her adversary. The differences were as clear as day. Esmeralda couldn't refute allegations. Serena held the winning hand.

David Arthur of Arthur & Porter, a man of bearing, wearing the decorum of his seventy years as a barrister, whose wise decisions and undisputed knowledge of the law placed him in the highest echelon of legal minds in London, sat quietly contemplating matters, waiting for his client. The roster he represented was "Who's Who in the United Kingdom."

His colleagues in the famed chambers in Middle Temple mirrored the Queen's Counsel's profile. He had arrived in Capri by nine to meet Esmeralda Pembrooke and her Italian solicitors from D'Albora & D'Albora, most notably Luigi D'Albora, known throughout the European Community as the mastermind who handled Prime Minister Andreotti's legal affairs.

David Arthur was not one to panic. In less than fifteen hours after Esmeralda's call, he departed London with a member of his firm, a male secretary who traveled everywhere with him.

Arthur, a divorced gentleman with an Oxbridge education and mellow voice was known to put clients at ease. This morning he dressed in dark grey, a suit tailored to specifications. Graying hair, combed to one side on his noble head framed a patrician face. His piercing blue eyes were made more intense by half-glasses that he looked over that rested on his prominent nose. He rarely removed his spectacles, although he didn't require them for distance, but they gave an aura to his face. Once removed, Arthur drew them aside dramatically to stress a point. His lips were ample hidden below a well-combed moustache accenting teeth that protruded crookedly like a message, he could tear a rival to threads.

Luigi D'Albora on the other hand was slender. His abundant mane worn in the style of Marcello Mastroianni, (a former client), gave the impression of well coiffed locks, too much for a British barrister, but dashing for a Latin, with the flair of a matinee idol. Furthermore, he was from the south of Italy and gallant in gestures. Viewing him one believed he was from the last century, marked by his trademark, a silver handled rosewood walking stick that he didn't require. Thick white eyebrows punctuated hazel eyes lined from seventy-six years that had seen every facet of the human condition.

D'Albora had an air of gentleness, a protective façade that could turn menacing. He required no eyeglasses having laser treatment years ago and took exceptional pride in his bronze complexion that showed no evidence of his botox shots, his idiosyncrasy being the want for eternal youth. The same was true of his bi-monthly testosterone shots. His hands were long and fingernails buffed, cufflinks of burnished gold as was his crest ring, worn turned slightly on his right hand, the other displayed his marriage band, which amused all for his mistress, Vivianna Nordio, was present more than his wife.

Luigi D'Albora arrived with one colleague, Elena, his forty-year old butch daughter, who sat in a dark black Armani pants suit, touching gelled short hair, considering the few facts David Arthur described.

All waited, respecting the credentials of the other in silence. The five legal minds sat at an inlaid marble table in the former suite of King Farouk at the Caesar Augustus Hotel. The thought passed D'Albora if Esmeralda would meet a similar fate to the late King, whose legal affairs he handled before the Monarch was poisoned to death. The imposing room with its Palladian windows and dark green marble floor looked to the Amalfi coast and was stilled this morning by a dreary light coming into the room from the overcast sky. The mood was funereal.

In all the years they'd represented Esmeralda Beck, then Zianni and now Pembrooke, the senior gentlemen had never experienced such an unsettled air of uncertainty.

Questions stirred: Why was a directive of this nature made in such haste?

What could be so urgent that demanded their unified visit? The Contessa behavior in the past was one of great elegance and poise. What made the reserved, wealthy client give an order in a demanding manner stating 'It's 'a matter of life and death?'

'Imperative,' that's the word she used and Arthur discussed with D'Albora. A divorce would not involve this degree of mystery. Nigel, they understood from the Contessa' innuendos, was of lightweight caliber, easy to eliminate.

The advisors were grave, attuned to private recollections of Esmeralda's financial portfolio memorized over years. Ominous thoughts consumed D'Albora who looked to David, mirroring his own. He tapped his slender fingers on the cold marble table, then removed his hand to his lap, not wishing to disturb colleagues whose concentration brought one thought: Deceit.

Similarly, wise juniors had depressing anticipation, adjusting laptops, touching Blackberrys, pencils and notepads, looking nervously to the encasement of antiques to the left and frayed leather volumes to the right.

On the isle of Ischia, Serena aglow with confidence from the display of friendship from Gianni's retinue, smiled warmly as the group arrived at the 16th century villa. Her cousin put the villa at her disposal however long it would take to resolve legal matters. A butler ushered the throng into a sapphire dining room that would suffice as a conference area. The terracotta cherry-wood floors shined like amber, as did oversized gilt Neapolitan mirrors reflecting a view to the sea. There was an air of serenity in the dark room, decorated with ancient tapestries on two large walls parallel to the long inlaid wood table.

Serena's advisors from the studio of Frederico Spiga in Milano and Rome arrived the day before. They stood when the group entered, putting aside rows of manila files tied with dark grosgrain, set out like coffins on the table. The manner of all was somber, polite, without a strain of stress. Expectation filled the air that a catastrophic change was to be announced and they, the spectators, were to have first knowledge of a secret long hidden, akin to an overwhelming archaeological find before the discovery is announced to the public.

As they settled into position, intermittent sun flashed through bleak clouds casting a light-works effect on the surroundings. This brought drama to the high vaulted room. Salutations were exchanged and café served while Serena thanked everyone for making the excursion without prior knowledge why they were abruptly interrupted from enjoyment at Villa Pina.

Spiga was their contemporary, a man in excellent form at fifty, in navy blazer and grey slacks. An open shirt showed his flair for informality. He preferred this meeting to have a non-threatening ambiance, nonetheless, peering at everyone, through thick tortoise spectacles, the color of which matched the whiskey hue of his hair and eyes magnified his eyes like a turtle. (who would win the race). He wasn't handsome with his olive skin, long nose, warts and slanted mouth that hid teeth no one saw when he smiled, but his persona gave rise to dynamic energy and quickness of mind with dramatic gesticulations His voltage was set permanently maximum sounding like thunderbolt. The alacrity of his movements seized the listener in awe, much like his ability in the English language. Some called him "Little Napoleon," behind his back, a bull terrier of 5'3" who venerated one word: control.

When he became excited, he'd rise from his chair, orator style with his encyclopedic brain speaking like Marcus Aurellius. Schooled at Bologna and then Cambridge, Spiga read law with several of their mutual friends. Seeing him preside with a serious countenance, the mood of the room changed notably.

"This is business. We're here to discuss classified information. Get your hankies out. It's going to be a melodrama." His initial words began, "The time for joviality is finished."

Véronique memorized the zodiac of all viewing among the most mysterious the 'eighth house', illuminated in the lives of the lead characters of this drama. The eighth house covers secrets, finance, contracts, sex and a profound transformation from which there is no coming back. She contemplated the strange energy of this. One could get lost for years if the transept remained lingering. The layers of relationship and oneself are always revealed with this transept.

In the meantime, with Sanjeev's assistance, Marc Levy had arranged a private car and vessel to take him and Zofra to Positano to lunch at San Pietro, the breathtaking hotel built into the precipitous cliff on the

Amalfi drive. Taking crisp hundred dollar bills from his pocket, he thrust yapping Groucho and money into Sanjeev's hands.

"Take this frigin' dog en don't tell anyone where we're goin'." They looked at each other, Sanjeev was speechless. "You're a man…en will appreciate, I got lucky. Understand…pal?"

"Yes Sir," The Sri Lankan uttered as Marc Levy in his rumpled suit and loosened tie, darted away for his tryst with his latest conquest, the Hungarian vixen.

The day matured. Each had his own agenda. What was the compelling force of these people whose past influenced their present?

Bella figura and *brutta figura* was at its pitch.

XXIV

Strategy

Earlier that morning as Esmeralda paced her room viewing no promise of sun, the table had turned. In the future she'd be the one fuming, waiting at each event. And what events? Her incognito mask disintegrated. The fake life, precisely constructed, as one constructs a piece of sculpture, was finished. Truth had won.

Serena might know some facts about South Africa, Esmeralda turned in her mind, but who can say they ever knew me? Only I contain the details of my life, why things happened and how I reacted to achieve what I have today. What's in my mind is more interesting than what I will reveal outside my mind. Once speech is uttered, like a gong giving forth, the privacy of that reflection is open to everyone, and like a boomerang, will return to wound me.

Could that miserable Serena have contacted Martin? He won't betray me. He loved me with intensity. The welcome she'd get presenting a dossier about me would not affect my dear Baron. It would be of no concern to him if I were born in the gutter. He'd view it as Serena's vicious jealousy. I must remove myself from fear.

That's the first point of my plan. When you're afraid people claw every aspect to destroy you. Fortunately, in my panic when I read Serena's letter and confided in that coward of a husband and then two-faced de

Gesu, I never gave complete details of my worst secrets. Those are mine and will remain mine. Everyone has a secret to hide.

To learn what documents are in Serena's possession and what slime my bastard Father has sworn to will be of interest. She's paid him off, that's certain. Let me take a lesson from the English and remain calm.

Esmeralda downed a Valium, attired herself as the splendid woman she presented to society, viewed the dense fog from her balcony window and prepared her mind for the crisis of her private life. She rang for Sanjeev to alert her driver she'd meet him momentarily and as she went through the garden at a rapid pace, caught herself, wise as she was to the techniques of stress.

She stood by the courtyard pond watching goldfish swimming effortlessly and inhaled slowly three deep yogic breaths. Nature is giving me a clue. First the fog on this misty morning, and she promised herself, I'll speak in half-truths and veil matters no one has to know. Secondly, these fish, full of gracefulness. "Beauty disarms people," she said aloud speaking to the orange colored creatures that changed her perspective. "Let me take a lesson from you."

Slowly she walked towards the end of the garden, wasn't it Wilde whose precept was, *"The first duty in life is to be as artificial as possible?"* She met her driver and the limousine drove to the Caesar Augustus Hotel.

Women like Esmeralda made it a point to have people in their control by letting them wait, today was no exception. Nigel had called her down for it in the past and she told him it added to the anticipation of seeing her. Her obnoxiousness infuriated him. Today he would no longer wait for her, nor would anyone else. Legal people she was paying. They could wait.

Not one of her lawyers stirred watching the clock tick past the hour of nine, then five minutes more, then ten. Suddenly, the French doors opened and Esmeralda stood like a vision, motionless, waiting to see what the reactions would be.

Everyone rose to attention as if greeting a Queen, viewing the slender beauty they'd advised through complicated legal issues for years. The senior attorneys speculated. The objective of the Contessa had always been financial matters. In the short space of six years the trusted counsels had seen her marriage, widowhood, remarriage and along with her investment advisors, marveled that the young beauty they beheld this murky, drizzly morning in Capri had become one of the richest women in Europe.

She appeared in an understated navy suit, low heels and a white vicuna serape extending her hand greeting them composed.

She spoke in her hushed tone making everyone seize each word she uttered moving closer to listen to her greeting, the ploy Esmeralda used all her life. This passive aggressive quality disarmed people who were distracted with her beauty and didn't realize her intimidating motives of superior control. Esmeralda had the type of personality she would now reveal. She would be deadly.

"Before we begin, I have written my own document," she announced removing a paper from her purse. Seated between David Arthur and Luigi D'Albora, she began. "It states no one in this room will divulge what I'm about to reveal. Before we proceed, it's necessary to have all sign in my presence."

"Very well," David Arthur without hesitation, extended his hand to accept Esmeralda's document. She sat pensively watching as each read the short statement. A gag order was going into effect. Fuck legal confidentiality. I've won the first round.

There wasn't a murmur in the room, only the scratch of Mont Blanc pen points as the five people's signatures marked the paper. Luigi D'Albora was the final name on the document. He passed it to Esmeralda, and the wise Italian who knew women and loved the guiles of the female realized in a brief flash the exquisite Esmeralda was of thick skin; a woman to distrust.

David Arthur judged her, too, as the type of woman, ageless in quality, with a voice of silver notes that on rare instances, when magnified would shatter glass.

"Thank you. I've been overtaken by circumstances and have called you here because of a letter from my sister in law, Serena Zianni, delivered yesterday. I'm on the brink of destruction." She stopped.

"My dear Contessa," Luigi D'Albora said seeing his client wanting to take command, yet ignorant to the law, "Everyone has a story to tell. It's a matter how one tells it. We're here to protect you." His melodious voice lent an air of security; she gave him a slight smile.

The light in the room darkened with a storm on the horizon from the mainland and David Arthur's secretary, Peter Evans, moved quietly around the room switching on lamps before Esmeralda began.

"Thank you Luigi. Please let us dispense with formalities, call me Esmeralda. I will narrate the story of my painful past beginning with Serena's letter."

"Esmeralda, dear, before you do," interjected David Arthur, "we must take notes. That's why I've asked my secretary, Mr. Evans, whom you've met in the past, to be present. I've interrupted because I don't wish you to be alarmed."

"Certainly. I understand." It was ten o'clock. "There are several issues that require legal attention. My life and fortune are at stake. The crucial situation is the Zianni family plan to destroy me. This merits expert dexterity of the law how I can be protected. That's why it was imperative to be here immediately with both legal teams. A separate issue, less complicated, nevertheless arriving concurrently, I will bring to your attention not to take precious time from serious issues."

"You've been briefed by my husband's attorneys. Nigel has begun proceedings for a divorce." Her voice held no emotion discussing her spouse. "He wants money. I'm not interested in an acrimonious ending. This divorce cannot distract me from the battle for survival."

'Sopra vivre' passed Luigi D'Albora's mind wondering if she could survive what lay ahead.

"To a degree, Nigel knows about my portfolio and his strategy is to gain from this rupture in our marriage. Between you, David and Luigi, devise the most economical means to pay him off and dissolve the marriage. Place a gag order on his vicious mouth. He will want to merchandise what he knows for international notoriety with the press. Kill his tongue. If I could cut it from his mouth, I would. But there are other methods. Pay him with funds in Switzerland, be judicious and present something digestible. I don't want him to touch Zianni money. That will incense Serena." Her voice never wavered with emotion.

"Make your calculations as one would skin a cat. I see Nigel through cold eyes. This divorce I consider a business gone belly up."

"Very well, Esmeralda," said David Arthur.

"It's unnecessary to discuss Nigel Pembrooke further except to mention we will dine with him this evening." She looked to each person assuring herself they would be at ease with this notion.

"Nigel will keep up appearances." Her icy detachment stunned the recipient's ears. "We have a house full of guests including Monty Daniels the society reporter, because of a film I'm backing. The producer, Marc Levy, is also in attendance. It's best to make a blanket statement you're in Capri pertaining to business. Nigel, with his avaricious tentacles, will concur. He's controllable wanting a fruitful settlement. To support me with your presence will weaken him. Are we in agreement?" Her evaluation of her marital life, was to annihilate Nigel and use money to do so.

Grim faces looked back to Esmeralda voicing their acceptance to comply nodding heads to the affirmative like toys from China with necks that dangle from wires of coil. Her aloof evaluation of her marital life left everyone nonplussed (except Elena D'Albora), yet this group was used to tyrants, Mafiosi, Russian oligarchs and relatives of the Queen whose dossiers had been restructured by their astute legal minds.

Esmeralda had no intention to discuss her Mother or the baby today. She needed time to consider what she would say. This was Monday, she'd pace herself. A monumental achievement had entered her life: to reveal facts about her birth, schooling in South Africa, how she was reared by bigoted nuns, housed in a Convent during Apartheid, why her past was like this, what type of surroundings she knew prior to going to live with her Father and after - and then exposing his despicable character. She would divulge as much as she believed necessary, facts no one knew except her departed friend, Graham. There were no reasons to elaborate on the smut of her existence at her Father's house or the stain of rape from Luke. No reason to say her grandmother was detained, then banished to a remote town of Tzaneen in the north where she was killed and thrown into swamplands from the slums where she lived. No one had to know everything. Be murky. Like the fog. Tell only so much.

Graham told me people treat you as you allow yourself to be treated. If they view me disadvantaged, that will be a life saving. If they view me as a whore, I'm finished.

"I'll begin at the beginning," she said softly looking to David Arthur and then Luigi D'Albora, "and speak of the convent in South Africa. It was Apartheid, the Afrikaans name for racial segregation, enforced from 1948 when my father was very young to 1994 after I had left the country. I was born in 1970, white supremacy time. There was a loss of moral authority, pervasive corruption was everywhere. Poverty, color and gender bias, religious bias made the doomed place. There was no dignity except for the privileged whites. Colored people lived bitter days without hope, deprived of citizenship. Sexual relations with a person of a different race was a criminal offence, women had no legal rights, malnutrition and sanitary problems created huge mortality rates. Filfth was everywhere. Rich white people lived as I did in the Convent in a guarded, gated compound with attack dogs. The poor in shacks, or used containers with tin roofs, rusted and leaking. The Red Cross avoided remote areas. To scrounge for food was a battle. Even today they tell me on a crowded street, no one brushes up against anyone of color.

In the years I lived there, television was not introduced in South Africa until I was eight years old dubbing English language to Afrikaans so that European thought did not influence the people of the country. Please keep in mind, as I explain my past, how could my delinquent Father, who has blackmailed Serena Zianni, be trusted? We need details from the other side to study testimonies because I'm at a loss to understand how this man - who I escaped from, petrified of his actions - could know of my existence - and to be put in touch with Serena Zianni."

"With your permission, Esmeralda, we want to communicate with the other side demanding an exchange of documents. We must study their findings and allegations."

"You have my permission."

Luigi D'Albora turned to his daughter, "Elena, send a text message and Email to Spiga, handling this. Esmeralda, in case you didn't know Serena's retained him."

"Yes, Papa." Elena D'Albora was hard, astute and calculated the reason Esmeralda sat in this room, doing a strip tease of her past was because some corrupt man - or men, robbed her of her dignity. Esmeralda didn't realize Elena D'Albora was more aligned with her than any others who would be privy to the past she was about to reveal. "God damned men," Elena's thoughts penetrated through her strong, sensitive mind, proud to be a lesbian. "Always men...always..."

The handsomely appointed suite hushed and Esmeralda's voice similar to the voice a priest hears in confession, began. The advisors had set aside two days to take Esmeralda's statement of facts and advise her. Today and tomorrow morning would be devoted to freeing herself from fine points of her past while they were in receipt of documents from Spiga.

Tuesday afternoon was time enough to question her about evidence the other side presented. Her financial advisors would be brought in on Wednesday and the initial structure of proceedings in place that evening.

How they would erect their defense was paramount. Would a settlement be in order? Counter suit for libel? Could this be a case, as with Andreotti, stretching for years enabling their client freedom to live in her present luxury? How much was at stake? What fees would be forthcoming?

David Arthur and Luigi D'Albora saw seven figures, without question. Then again they were men who didn't touch a paper clip unless seven figures were on offer.

Esmeralda's professional team would leave for London and Rome by Thursday contacting Switzerland, Liechtenstein and Wall Street brokers detailing legal hocus-pocus. As soon as Esmeralda began and David

Arthur and Luigi D'Albora heard her first statement, their task for their client would be impossible to salvage. She was a fraud. No magician could change that.

"Christ," said David Arthur, "this will hit like a bomb on the financial marketplace."

Federico Spiga caught the attention of the dozen people in front of him, much like he caught the attention of journalists when he represented the inquiry into the *ménage a trois* with the Swiss Guards at the Vatican some years ago. Standing at the head of the table, his compact form thrust a black shadow on the wall of large proportions. His diminutive size, and common birth, his Napoleonic complex intensified especially at a time like this. A good fight with the esteemed D'Albora and Arthur, men whose intellect reflected his own, he relished, achieving all he wanted in the end, after all, he was sure of a win. Spiga removed his heavy lenses, his pertuberous eyes glanced around the room, then he quickly covered them dilating findings, ready to charge.

"This is not a she wolf campaign to destroy another human being. Serena's not like that."

Everyone's immediate reaction was, Serena not...but you, Spiga - are.

"You are aware of the character of Gianni's sister, my great friend from Cambridge. We are dealing with an evil genius. Her name is not Esmeralda Pembrooke or Esmeralda Zianni or Esmeralda Beck but Essy McSweeney born of questionable lineage from South Africa."

Disbelief filled the room with comments one to another.

"Please keep remarks until I've finished exhibiting findings. We'll break for lunch and this afternoon before you depart for Capri I would appreciate if anyone of you have additional information, please present it to aid our case." He paused, looked about the table. "Several matters are at hand. If anyone had prior knowledge of this before coming today, please speak now."

"I knew of Serena's letter last night," said de Gesu standing immediately. His arresting nature and ease of extemporaneous speech commanded attention. de Gesu was a man torn with loyalties, understanding a tragedy taking place to dissect another human being known for years, who hours before gave each of them joyous hospitality was not his game. His affection for Esmeralda after so many years, so many memories had its place. Overriding this, Stefano was a man of principle that would dissolve sentiment.

He looked Serena in the eye and held that look making all aware he did so, then to Spiga, "Time was brief because there was a concert at Villa Pina. Esmeralda sent a note to my room asking to see me urgently. We had less than twenty minutes together. She wanted to take me into her confidence to a degree. Time allowed me to read what Serena wrote, Esmeralda announced Nigel was going to divorce her. She didn't elaborate what Serena knew yet asked me to side with her. My conscious couldn't accept that. Knowing Serena, I believed she would never have penned a letter with the serious allegations she made unless they were true."

Self-contained, it pleased him to say, "I bluntly refused to side with Esmeralda, ignorant of her past." He looked to his friends, "It was my suggestion, and I'm not ashamed to admit this, for I didn't know, nor do I know now all the ramifications of the facts but what I do understand Esmeralda is an imposter, the reason remains inexplicable."

"I'm unaware of any of the accusations in the letter except that I advised Esmeralda to implore you, Serena, not to amplify this horrific situation to the press. My belief was to have her lawyers advice as soon as possible, make an agreement with you not to exercise your legal right but to have her relinquish everything belonging to the Zianni family. In the limited capacity of my knowledge of the law and the depths of the seriousness of this case, I suggested extradition to another country with an order not to divulge this monstrosity to anyone." Samir looked to Véronique and understood the prediction of his astrologer.

"I left her, dressed and went to the concert with Véronique. I had no more contact with Esmeralda. As of this morning, I have officially left

Villa Pina. The Pembrookes believe me to be on my way to London. I didn't want to remain in their company. My decision to join the group is because I cannot abide by lies."

"Thank you, Ambassador." Spiga was on his feet again and looked from one to another, "Anyone else?" When he saw no one forthcoming he announced, "Now we shall proceed. Serena if you care to start from the beginning when you received Danny McSweeney's letter."

Unaccustomed to the situation in which she found herself, preoccupied she was publicly judging her sister in law, Serena began. Words came easily cognizant of her plight for justice to prevail. "Thank you for being here, all of you," she looked for a moment to Stefano de Gesu, "Thank you Stefano for rendering events from last night."

Assurance came to her as she began to unravel the mystery of discovery. "Imagine my shock six months ago when I found a crumpled letter from South Africa from a stranger in my mail box. The original is in the vault, but here on the table you shall see the photocopy. I was seized by the first words. In all the years I've known Esmeralda, and with the bond that we were 'sisters,' she was a woman I never believed I could take into my confidence, nor give her mine. Instinctively I sensed something false from the very beginning, but I told myself that was sibling jealousy for no one was good enough for my brother. She didn't marry Gianni for his money or his title, she had money and title and loved him, in many ways that makes things more difficult."

She controlled her emotions. "It will be for legal advisors to discover why we have reached this point." She looked from one to another. "What I do know and it's documented by private investigators and testimonies from South Africa, Esmeralda was born in Johannesburg not London. Her father is a disreputable, an ex-convict, a murderer who was a bastard child, coming from the dregs of society. Her Mother is in question. Mr. McSweeney has sworn testimony, but one must take his testimony guardedly, that Esmeralda's mother was a Negro." The room stirred with this revelation.

"This was difficult to fathom knowing Esmeralda's coloring. We have other issues. Mr. McSweeney kept the letter he says was attached to the baby's blanket when Essy, as he calls her, was left at his premises. I do not believe one could call it a home. She was left there in dreadful condition. He brought her to an Convent to be reared by the nuns of St. Angelica's until she was sixteen. You can view a photocopy of that letter. He stated Esmeralda never knew of its existence. As I say, one must question his testimony. However, we have other facts regarding this, a matter which we will broach as we go along.

The nuns that knew Mr. McSweeney have made separate testimony that he is Esmeralda's true Father. They have loving memories of a beautiful girl whose Mother, they affirm from what they were told by Mr. McSweeney was British, white, and died in childbirth. They have no further knowledge except Mother Superior, now in her mid-eighties, helped McSweeney locate the birth certificate of his daughter, a copy of which is here today. The Mother Superior received only one letter from Esmeralda after she left South Africa. It was when she was wed to the Baron thanking them for rearing her as they did, stating she was married, withholding her spouse's name, and asking them never to divulge her whereabouts to anyone. The letter had no return address. The nuns abided by this because her Father had been arrested for murder. They feared for the girl's safety.

Days later, after Esmeralda escaped South Africa (and the nuns thought she had met with foul play), a letter came into their possession asking them to pass it to Esmeralda. The person claimed to be her Mother. Imagine the sisters disbelief. A copy of that letter, the Convent has made available to us. This letter was never opened by the Mother Superior but kept for years until she knew Esmeralda's whereabouts. When she received the note without a return address - but with a crest on the notepaper, duty bound she forward the letter to her Mother General in Rome. Mother General researched the crest, sending the letter to Baroness Esmeralda Beck in Bavaria.

The letter remained sealed. By the time this correspondence, thought to be from Esmeralda's Mother, reached Germany, Esmeralda had divorced the Baron. The Baron was devastated by the divorce and one supposes, perhaps, out of spite, he kept the letter. Finally he sent it to Esmeralda at her home in Rome. We don't know if the correspondence was opened by the Baron or if he knew Esmeralda was pregnant.

The Baron refuses to give further details. One must read his testimony, presented here. It's impossible to know if the Baron believed in the childhood she presented to us. He never questioned Esmeralda background is what he swears in his deposition.

We imagine when Esmeralda received her Mother's letter, a Mother whom she was told died at childbirth, the shock of that may have brought a miscarriage. We have reports to the contrary," Serena's voice cracked with emotion, "I beg you all to please read the findings of our investigation."

"But Serena what do you believe will be Esmeralda's ideas about this?" asked Samir wishing to respect the person who would be torn to shreds.

"Ideas?" answered Serena, "she has no ideas. She has plots, plans but ideas?"

The commotion could not be contained. Spiga seeing his client halt and shaken, took control, continuing to divulge facts. "I know you're as shocked as we are, even now as we present this, six months after the initial letter was received trying to understand the reasons for this horrid deception." Serena had parried the interrogative glances and knew the documents to be viewed prior to lunch would create a diabolical discussion.

"Please let me continue," Spiga insisted. All hushed their opinions in their fervor to support what Serena had thus far revealed.

"Evidently, and this was remarkable how detectives uncovered the path Esmeralda took, she fled the country under an assumed name, that of Esmeralda Anderson, underage, aided by a photographer who, unfortunately sometime later died of AIDS. No one knows how she met this individual, Graham Anderson whose surname she acquired. Mr. McSweeney, a mechanic by trade, makes note of him briefly having seen him once at his garage believing him to be a customer needing a car repair. Nights later she fled, Mr. McSweeney was arrested for murder. The victim was his friend, Luke O'Brien. Graham Anderson, the photographer, bequeathed his legacy to Esmeralda, and launched her career as a model for Harrods, the famous store in London, and guided her life in Europe. This was not a love story, we've interrogated many individuals, more of an 'adopted family,' you may call it. He assumed responsibility for Esmeralda as one would a younger sister. As noted, she assumed his name and to a large degree the identity of his family, that is the reason she explained her family died in I.R.A. bombings in London, because, you see, Graham Anderson's parents died in those bombings. Not Esmeralda's." Another buzz filled the room as remarkable facts of the investigation became public for the first time.

"A plethora of photos from Harrods store files from the work she did for them, and to her credit she was the essence of comportment during her stint with the store is joined with documents. While under contract endorsing Harrods, their icon, she met Baron Martin Heindrick von Beck, a man eighty years old today whose testimony is astounding, this is also available to review. They eloped when Esmeralda was nineteen in 1989 and that marriage endured five and a half years of relative peace in the life of the elegant woman we know today. She never brought Harrods or the Baron disgrace.

You know the rest of this story, they divorced and she was in London, engaged to the Milanese industrialist, Franco Lemma, knew Ambassador de Gesu at that time and met Gianni in 1997. Within eight months Esmeralda was married to Serena's brother and became Contessa Zianni"

Serena resumed her remarks and Spiga deferred to her. "Twenty-one months into their marriage, she became pregnant. My brother died months later and the seven month old fetus, documents reveal, was born early, 'still born,' at the Convento di Santo Spirito in Taormina, Sicily. Esmeralda was there in seclusion suffering shock from the death of my brother. The date is November 17th, 2000. A midwife has sworn testimony, a copy of which is with the documents. The baby was left the entire Zianni fortune as next of kin to Gianni and in case of the child's death, it went to Gianni's wife. Of course this was made when Gianni thought he would live to a ripe old age. The child is buried in the Zianni mausoleum.

Thirteen-months later, she married Nigel Pembrooke. Esmeralda handled her financial activities through her people which included her acquired Zianni assets." Serena looked 'round the table. All were dazed by disclosures. "The race, legitimacy and death of the fetus is in question." Commotion reigned with a jumble of words. Spiga raised his hand to hush the friends.

"Now you can understand why I couldn't take this alone." Serena said. "As Fate would decree, completely unintended, Rupert saw me bereft last Thursday rushing to catch a train to Naples to be with all of you at Villa Pina. I had been with Frederico Spiga and his team who had completed their investigation wanting me to prosecute Esmeralda. It's been difficult to say the least to face all this compounded by deaths in my family and my own marriage annulled. Rupert came to my rescue wanting to see me through this tragedy. He was of the opinion that all of you would want to stand beside me. That's why you are here today."

Spiga took command. "Now you have the kernel of this extraordinary case. Keep in mind the law doesn't deal with emotion. Take your time and look through documents and securities. We have an inheritance claim worth eighty billion euro in assets." He looked at his watch, "It's close to midday, lunch is at one. Shall we break now and review things later? This will give us a chance to speak freely and maybe some of you will shed more light on the facts. All in favor…"

While on via Tragara in Capri....the shoppers distracted themselves with the Italian ritual, a *passeggiata*.

"Why Jacqueline, there's just no cashmere like the cashmere ya'll find here in Italy! Bless my stars, I'm so excited with what we found…en Cat…you feelin' betta?"

The two women looked at the girl in skin-tight jeans and boots carrying shopping bags from Valentino, Ferragamo and Prada. "Yeah, I mean shopping helps, you know…I mean it's therapy."

"Zis es very smart to zink to ze fashion ven ze men are not zo nice."

"Do you two really think he's, I mean I bet he's not, you know, he's like I think, well, Marc I bet is with, you know, Zofra…"

"Who cares for zat? Enjoy yourself. Look to ze other men, you are very young…"

"Honey, you did the right thing! Shop and neva let him see those things. Save em for someone else ta see!…com'on…let's go to the Quisisana and have a big lunch with lobsters en put it on Levy's tab!" The women laughed and spent their day drinking martinis and speaking of banal concerns wasting time while the grey sky and wind threatened showers in the late afternoon.

Marc Levy and Zofra were also drinking not martinis but champagne ignoring the weather in their Suite Azuro at the San Pietro eyeing each other provocatively. A waiter had delivered two bottles of Dom Perignon, '79 in silver buckets along with Beluga caviar and lunch under a silver dome that would be devoured later. Zofra, cougar that she was at 60 looking like 44, was too busy tantalizing Marc, a man of 50, undressing him to join her in the huge Jacuzzi in their suite. Beginning her seduction, she'd start letting him believe she was too shy to commence lovemaking. She wanted some erotic sex play to thank him for the necklace he bought from the Van Cleef and Arpels vitrine in the lobby. Although it wasn't diamonds, the gold was important laced with multi-colored precious stones, she had to train her Producer right the first time to suit her fancy for diamonds before she gave away *all* her charms. A good spanking would teach him.

Marco Ricci had been with so many gays on location and knew the thrill of the forbidden enticed them. This would endear him to Daniels and Ricci's name spotlighted when Monty Daniels article appeared about the film, ESCAPADES. He arranged a series of hidden places, taking them to a hideaway café, and opium dens where he pulled out a joint, Daniels joined him, the prude Jarvis declined while Marco mapped out strategic brothels the two should visit. He'd accompany them just so far then get lost.

"The gay scene isn't mine, but I know the best haunts." His open point of view appealed to them and Marco was pleased advising them, "One can do whatever one pleases in Capri," he remarked, considering the shenanigans at Villa Pina, he flashed his show-biz smile, shrugged his shoulders and began to leave the two entranced with the isle's dark side.

At the *piazza*, he was pleased to have time alone, ordered a Campari and soda considering Elizabeth was smart to take off for Rome. Nicky wasn't for her. Let the sweet kid do her sculpture and head for London, see the Prince and meet the future King of England. She doesn't have to be bothered to know '*la bella vita.*' She's the only person I ever knew who went to the Blue Grotto because Hans Christian Anderson wrote about its discovery in 1835. Smut like the scene developing here she doesn't need to know.

He sipped his drink pleased at the enthusiasm of Daniels trying to ignite a spirit in that snob Jarvis. 'To each his own,' Marco thought from the Tao di Ching. He glanced at a script he'd brought along. Shortly, he'd return to Villa Pina for a *penecella*. The gays could screw their brains out, what did he care?

Nigel had the peace he wanted. He went to the pool, removed his large towel swimming some laps in the buff, panting for breath cursing himself for being out of shape and collapsed on a deck chair with his mobile phone. He rang his lawyers in London and as he did the skies opened.

Quickly, he grabbed his towel, running inside for shelter telling Baker, Baker & MacCloud, "The courier took all documents hours ago on the noon ferry. Move forward immediately." He buzzed for Sanjeev. It was good to be alone after the hell of a night he'd had.

"You rang Sir?"

"Yes, Sanjeev. What's the program for dinner?"

"Mrs. Pembrooke wanted to eat *alfresco* but now that we've had this shower…"

"It'll blow over…how many are we?"

"Twenty five and it will be a buffet but I don't believe it will blow over if I may say, Sir."

"At eight for drinks?"

"Yes Sir, that's right."

"Wake me at six-thirty. Oh and Sanjeev…"

"Yes Sir.."

"If Mr. Baker or MacCloud call from London, or Mrs. Pembrooke needs me, wake me please."

"Certainly Sir."

"Thanks Sanjeev." Nigel walked the long corridor to the circular staircase considering which piece of art he wanted to make part of his settlement from Esmeralda. 'Best to take something Martin Beck gave her, this way Ziannis can't claim it back,' he calculated. He looked into Esmeralda's bedroom at the two Guido Reni paintings. One would do. He took his digital camera and photographed his choice. 'I'll send this to MacCloud by Email later.'

He went to his bedroom turned on the steam bath and unwound. After twenty minutes, he took a needle shower and collapsed on his oversized bed falling asleep instantly. His two Labradors snuggled on the Persian carpet nearby.

Hours later imagine if you will the violence of nature.

Esmeralda's car fetched her from the Caesar Augustus Hotel at five. She experienced emotional exhaustion and knew she required an hour or so to unwind alone before the onslaught of guests to entertain tonight at dinner. Sanjeev, seeing the questionable weather, would have the presence of mind to arrange the buffet to a seated dinner, a blessing he would handle things without direction. As the Bentley pulled to the drive and she exited the car, a whirl of wind swept the air, Esmeralda dashed into the house, her hair in disarray. A sirocco from Egypt began. Every year this happened but it seemed early for the storm this season. Pity she wanted to have an evening in the garden. She called Sanjeev.

"Please don't disturb me under any circumstances until six-thirty. Where is Mr. Pembrooke?"

"Contessa he's asleep. He said to wake him if you needed him."

"Fine. I need sleep."

"Signor Ricci, Miss Renoir, Mrs. Jameson and Mme Redat are resting, they've just returned from shopping. Everyone else is expected. I've set the dining room as you like it."

"Excellent. I'm exhausted Sanjeev. Wake me at six-thirty."

"Certainly Contessa." He closed the door behind him, Esmeralda took a hot shower, split a 'dream bar' in two, downed one and within minutes she was asleep.

Neither Mr. or Mrs. Pembrooke heard the ferocity of a storm approaching from the sea nor did the other guests asleep at Villa Pina. Howling winds began on a rampage.

A storm on the island of Capri is an unforgettable experience. Sanjeev had watched it coming all afternoon. Fog hung over the island, boats alerted each other with fog horns since four in the afternoon. *Aloscalfi* and ferries were nowhere in sight. BOOM!...............**BOOM!** suddenly the thunderstorm grew violent with torrential rain. The position of the isle made a tempest more dramatic. Two taxis arrived from Caesar

Augustus with Esmerald's legal team twenty minutes after her arrival, alighting from vehicles dashing for cover in the main portico.

BOOM!...............**BOOM!**

"The hotel thought it best to arrive earlier than we expected. Taxis are at a premium," David Arthur said to Sanjeev who took their wet umbrellas ushering the group to the library, a fire had been lit and the room had a soft glow of permanence.

BOOM!...............**BOOM!** Lights flickered.

"Mr. and Mrs. Pembrooke are resting and have asked not to be disturbed."

BOOM!...............**BOOM!**

"Thunderbolts from hell! Christ!" said David Porter.

"A gift from Tiberius is what the Capresi say, Sir."

BOOM!...............**BOOM!**

"Some gift! Don't disturb our hosts, my good man, but do you have some sherry? Whiskey?"

"At the cupboard in the corner," the *Major d'uomo* motioned, "Do help yourselves. Is there anything else?"

"No, we're fine," Luigi addressed Sanjeev, "actually we have some strategy to plan."

"Please call me if you require anything." He noted the button on the wall for his services, "Press this button to call me."

"This type of weather happen often?"

"Not often but...Capri, Sir has been a refuge. If I may put your minds at ease, never did Vesuvius eruptions penetrate the island. Although this island is less than four miles long and five and a half miles wide, Capri has been blessed throughout history, standing apart from history." As if he was programmed, or perhaps it was the jitters from the unexpected happenings, the shy Sri Lankan continued,"When WWII bombardments in Naples met within one year of Vesuvius erupting in 1944, Neapolitans desperate to survive, rowed to Capri seeking peace, shelter and food."

"I say!" remarked David Arthur.

"In earlier wars, when Anacapresi men had to fight and go off to war, their women were raped by Capresi men who climbed the mountain to seized what they desired (Anacapresi women being better looking than those of Capri)."

"Full of information, my good man."

"A storm here is dramatic but we're used to it, Sir." Sensing he'd spoken too long, he was embarrassed. "Please call me if you require anything." The phone rang. "Pardon me."

"Thank you, Sanjeev."

"*Pronto* Villa Pina..."

"That you Sanjeev, it's Whitney Jameson."

"Yes, Mr. Jameson, Would you like Mrs Jameson...?"

"Where is Mr. Pembrooke?"

"He's resting Sir."

"Mrs Pembrooke?"

"Mrs. Pembrooke is also."

"Mrs. Jameson is…"

"Forget Mrs. Jameson. Sanjeev do me a favor." He spoke very fast. Sanjeev's adept mind took in his orders. "Tell Nigel or Mrs. Pembrooke when they wake this storm is treacherous. There's no way we can sail back to Capri tonight. We tried to make the crossing from Ischia. The sea's a bitch. It's has taken a violent turn, a roller coaster ride to stay on course. Impossible. I can't endanger anyone. We've heard few boats are at sea.

"They're closing both ports here and in Capri, gale force of five, six and the forecast is to reach eleven… We're…" and the house phone went dead.

Electricity in the house flickered for the instant threatening a loss of power.

"Mr. Jameson…Mr. Jameson…" Sanjeev didn't try again. He'd lived on Capri thirty years tending the Ziannis and when a storm of this magnitude threatened, (as it did at this hour), it would worsen by eight.

The cock's crow would come with the dawn if lucky or the next day, or the next.

Marc Levy and Zofra had a private launch. He didn't want to create a scandal what with Daniels there who could write a nasty story.

"Get goin' on this yacht," he said to the crew.

"I think we should turn back, Sir,"

Marc didn't like people to tell him what to do, "With dis size boat nothin' can bother us..."

As he saw people exit the large ferry sick to their stomachs, his twitch began on his face and he thought twice. He thrust his oversized arm around a post, the boat left the dock, jolting all without being on the open sea. Now that the anchor was raised, Levy tried to settle himself, gripping the arm-rest of a nearby chair to stay seated and was thrown forward. Zofra had panic written all over her face. She lunged forward losing balance, Levy did likewise violently lurching in the opposite direction, unsteady, fear seized him, he began to sweat staggering to reach another seat. As seasickness took hold, a migraine of major proportions thumped. The agile crew tried to maneuver the short distance to the open channel believing it a mistake to continue. Twenty-minutes out going less than five knots was endless. Minutes seemed a nightmare. Levy staggered below and collapsed in the cabin. Zofra followed, unfastening his belt, opening his trousers, gasping deeply both sat heaving. Levy was petrified. The heat of his body soared to record high, perspiration ran down his face, and forced him to throw off his jacket, struggling for breath. Zofra was terrified. Levy was hurtled again, afraid to close his eyes fearing he'd lose equilibrium; his pupils budged toad fashion. He couldn't turn his head left or right, shortness of breath came next, a pain in his chest escalated, "Cardiac arrest, Shit! I'm havin' a heart attack....gonna die...Cardiac arrrr............!"

BOOM!..............**BOOM!** BOOM!..............**BOOM!**

Everywhere they looked, the sea commanded. Every menacing sound horrified the couple with the frightening, uncontrollable sea engulfing them with huge waves spraying the windows, as close as their fingertips.

BOOM!...............**BOOM!** thunderbolts crackled illuminating sparks igniting the bottomless sea. "Death, Zofra..." Levy sputtered..."We're goin' to die....we're goin' to drown....We're..." and he convulsed in vomit.

Zofra swallowed hard forcing down bile, sick as she was, holding Mark's hand, motioning to the crew, who had their own worries about safety following Levy's orders. Seeing the condition of Levy, the young mate held onto a post, steadying his footing, "You've been hit with severe seasickness, Mr. Levy. You won't…die..."

There was no need to speak further, the boat took the most violent jolt imaginable, gas emitted from Levy's stomach causing a putrid odor, he pulled his jacket to his face, once again unable to control nausea, vomiting uncontrollably, a feeling of claustrophobia overtook him, he turned white, from the torrent to his body, his heart beat wildly. "Get des god damned boat back..to Positano....Cardiac arrest...I'mm havin'.... Fuck Capri!" He bellowed, making the crew act with alacrity blessing his decision.

Zofra squeezed his hand, "Thank you Marc, thank you!" She put her hand on his heart. The storm overwhelmed them and bonded them as a couple. Levy never felt the nearness of death as he did aboard the yacht with a storm of this degree.

BOOM!...............**BOOM!** They disembarked trembling, soaked to the skin by the rain. "Thank God," Zofra uttered once on *terra firma.* Levy took her hand and put his other to his heart. Their limo had waited at the dock not believing Levy's decision to sail. That was fortunate, as streets were deserted. The lovers huddled closely in the Cadillac. "I'm neva gonna ever forget des. Zofra…I wanna tell ya…"

"Hush, Sweetheart…you're OK. We'll be safe…" She was wise to the power that arrived with the storm. Levy would idealize the situation telling everyone Zofra stood by him at the most frightening moment of his life. Once at the hotel after a grueling ride unable to see the terrifying drop from the Amalfi coast, the twosome blessed the fact they heard the Manager exclaim, "This always happens at this time of the year. Luckily we haven't rebooked your room…"

"I've gotta call Nigel in Capri." Levy said breathless.

"That will be impossible Sir. All phone lines are down in Capri."

"We'll catch him on the mobile…"

"Circuits are down too."

"Zofra, let's go to our…"

"Right this way, Mr. and Mrs. Levy." Zofra beamed at Marc. The couple had an affinity for each other and with all the grime from their seasickness, were blessed to be together and safe. Laughter ensued and panting Levy exclaimed, "Christ Almighty, I neva in my life saw a storm, like somethin' outta Titanic…thought I was havin' cardiac arrest..."

His loud words became contagious in the lobby as people witnessed the Hollywood couple who looked like vagabonds washed ashore rush to their suite at the San Pietro.

Levy looked at Zofra in the lift whose eyes swelled with tears of gratitude, "We're gonna' fuck like there's no tomorrow…" Levy beamed believing in God, love and destiny.

Sanjeev tried to call the main port from Nigel's mobile. "All boats have stopped running, it looks like a big one, a sirocco.…an all nighter til'tomorrow…" the port's Captain cautioned.

Hearing this, subtracting the guests that would not appear, he heard Daniels and Engleton, stomping wet feet, arriving at the front door, "I'm drenched to the skin."

"Shit! Mother fuckin' weather," Daniels said in a voice to match thunder.

"Never, never in my life have I seen a storm like this. Sorry Sanjeev for this mess…" fastidious Engleton added brushing the rain from his Panama hat and linen jacket that resembled wilted pajamas.

"No, no not at all Mr. Daniels, Mr. Engleton. Would you like tea sent to your room?"

"Yes, that would be lovely…" Jarvis said nasally turning to Monty, "You know Dante hated the sirocco, he wrote about it in the last book of his *Divina Commedia*, the *Inferno*....."

"Cut the shit, " Daniels shot back at his partner short tempered, turning to Sanjeev instead, "How's 'bout a bottle of Scotch?"

"Yes, Mr. Daniels. Certainly. Right away. Here…" the *Major d'uomo* passed two large towels to the men, now wrapped as mummies who retreated to their room, a maid following to wipe the floor behind them. Sanjeev picked up their sopping shoes, deposited them in the back atrium and quickly returned to the library hearing the buzz from the intercom.

Daniels and Engleton's amatory adventure had the gays spent. Attending a day's orgy of male hookers and transvestites on the island averted them from worries of the storm. They delighted with the assortment of hidden brothels and at last were at Villa Pina.

"Pardon me did you ring Mr. Arthur?"

"Perfectly all right. Yes, glad to be here where it's dry…yes… yes…" David Arthur spoke, "Although we Brits are used to showers, this is quite a storm!" He poked the fire.

"Matches the day," Elena D'Albora retorted.

"If you'll excuse me I must make some necessary changes for dinner as some guests have been unable to return by boat. Is there anything you require before the Pembrookes arrive?"

"Go right ahead, my good fellow…we're fine and when you have time **BOOM! ....BOOM..........!** send someone please with something to munch on…"

"Right away Sir."

Realizing the size of the party had decreased by twelve who were foolish to sail, Sanjeev quickly set the table, reworked details with the cook for dinner to be seated and busied himself with details should the storm worsen, which to his mind, it would. The hyperkinetic activity he required made him look like a comic pantomime moving from one part of the Villa to the next with a rapidity of organization worthy of a robot, his underlings duplicating his every move.

Windows were shut, *persiani* closed, candles put in position everywhere in case of a loss of power. Sanjeev directed the staff, and the cook and kept trying the phone and looking out to the vista of the island. The usual lights from houses interspersed on the mountain were in pitch darkness. It was just after six. Sanjeev penciled a seating list for tonight's dinner to show the Contessa or Mr. Pembrooke. There was an undercurrent of tension between them and the fact the house suddenly contained so many legal minds made him question everyone's motives and why things had changed to this degree.

He chose to wake Mr. Pembrooke first and convey the news about the regrets for dinner. That met without surprise. He'd been resting taking his blood pressure, listening to the rain pound the roof, hearing gusts of wind cause havoc to the garden, the island and himself. His frightened Labradors were hiding underneath his king-sized bed. Sanjeev lit the fire in his room. Nigel wondered if the old retainer had a clue as to developments.

"Observing the tempests of Capri is like observing people, Sanjeev. Each with our own tempest."

Nigel had been drinking all day to calm his nerves and fortify his resolve not knowing what to expect once he would be in the company of Esmeralda and her lawyers. His remark made no impact on the houseman. "Tell the gentlemen in the library I'll be down shortly."

"Yes Sir." Sanjeev went to leave. "I have a tentative seating list. We've changed from buffet to seated, care to see it?"

"No. It's a jigsaw puzzle. Handle it. Seat Mrs. Redat and Mrs. Jameson next to me. Distance me from those bloody lawyers please. Put Mrs. Pembrooke between them."

Nigel was in no rush to see the distinguished counsels whose sole concern regarding him would be to eliminate any hold he had on his wife's money. BOOM!...............**BOOM!** BOOM!...............**BOOM! ....**

"Fuckin' weather!.... Divorce is always War, God damn War!" I knew it would come to this! I can imagine how she wants to dismantle me! At least I've waited until there's some degree of time to make my exit serve monetary gains. He started to prepare himself and then slowed his pace, seeing a book of Auden's to distract him with something intellectual. He leafed through it and began to read aloud in his deep baritone voice,

"Of vineyards, baroque, la bella figura,
to these feminine townships where men
are males...
some believing amore
is better down south and much cheaper
(which is doubtful), some persuaded exposure
to strong sunlight is lethal to germs
(Which is patently false) and others, like me
In middle-age hoping to twig from
what we are not what we might be next, a question
the South seems never to raise..."

Food for thought. He closed the slim volume thinking damn shame Whitney and the others aren't around for some company. Told them it was a lousy day to sail. BOOM!...............**BOOM!** Damned Italian storm and Egyptian *sirocco*! Now I'll be stuck with that moaning Lynne, the gays, my bitch wife, the tart from L.A., and my only consolation will be Marco and Jacqueline. They're still around. How I envy those bastards in Ischia! They'll be shacking up at the swank hotel, privilege separates people, cozy and gossiping. God knows the reaction of my news Rupert will reveal.

Nigel believed his divorce announcement would be the height of importance, never guessing of the briefing friends would have into the wicked past of his wife, who slept peacefully in the adjoining room.

Serena's family in Ischia had a staff of equally competent people as were at Villa Pina. Once the storm threatened, rooms were prepared for guests to remain in comfort. The weight of revelations from the day's meeting was fresh in everyone's memory; all wished to digest facts and give opinions. Additionally, they questioned themselves, the prejudices they harbored, loyality and philosophy of life and felt duly uncomfortable to be at Villa Pina partaking in Nigel and Esmeralda's hospitality and blessed the fact the storm detained them in Ischia.

By seven the atmosphere was lightened by the burden being off Serena's shoulders. Spiga viewed the united front of the eleven friends presented to his client. The gale had its effect on this impromptu overnight turning into a dinner of good friends, sheltered from the storm and free to speak with candor.

The wrath of Lynne Jameson matched that of Cat Renoir's seeing their respective men desert them. Both understood they were two-timed and that betrayal did little to make either of them good company. Jacqueline viewed it all as Fate and tried to reach Samir on his mobile but she couldn't get through. Had she known that everyone on Capri was trying to get onto the circuits, she would have realized the impossibility of communication on a small island. BOOM!...............**BOOM!** BOOM!...............**BOOM!** BOOM!.........**BOOM!**

Lynne and Cat had no intention of calling Whitney or Levy. Both men behaved deplorably. Seeing Groucho yapping about the Villa, his surrogate Ms Zofra off with Mr. Levy, wherever they were, Cat prayed they would capsize and drown.

The wind kept howling furiously and the blackness of the night, unlit by any moon, made one shutter at the turn of the weather. The air was humid, fires had to be lit, all seemed chilled to the bone as the asphalt colored sky threatened lightening, again and again....

To experience a tempest at Capri made one shutter at the uncontrollable force of nature. Crackerjack thunder followed by bolts of lighting that threw brilliant streaks of electricity on the Mediterranean, BOOM!..............**BOOM!** sparking the garden, illuminating pristine rows of villas, the sky ablaze. To retreat to the warmth of Villa Pina, all counted their blessings. Shelter was everyone's concern and soon there would be a decent dinner at Villa Pina. It was better to be together.

Those that knew the circumstances viewed this differently, trying to reach offices in London and Rome without success, and those who didn't know the particulars of the day's happenings selfishly thought of their own set of circumstances viewing the miserable day as an omen to leave the island as soon as possible.

As the women dressed for dinner, Esmeralda was engulfed with thoughts of destiny and how most important things in life were out of one's control, rain pissed buckets and the tempest rose to fury.

No stranger to storms in Capri or Ischia, Spiga had the presence of mind to send a message to his contact at the Rome Bureau of CNN from his mobile phone just as the first crack of thunder hit BOOM!............... **BOOM!** and circuits went down. Serena had authorized the announcement underscoring her scheme. "It is not enough for me to even the score with Esmeralda financially. She's disgraced our name. I want her to disappear forever."

The text message was brief. It's power to shake financial markets staggering. Zianni Pharmaceuticals International stock would reverberate with investment portfolio managers panicky and clients dazed.

> **EXCLUSIVE FOR CNN. IMMEDIATE RELEASE. Fraud Revealed. Zianni family has announced Contessa Esmeralda Zianni (Pembrooke), who is the sole beneficiary from the legacy of Count Gianni Zianni, late husband, CEO of conglomerate, Zianni Pharmaceuticals International, is an imposter. Contessa Serena Zianni, sister to the deceased, is bringing the action to the EU Court before the statue of limitations expires. No comments are available. Fortune in excess of £3,000,000,000 GBP.**

He saved the message rereading it, pleased with its brevity, the impact it would have and the storm raged. Let's see what the effect the news brings. A sly smile grazed his lips. BOOM!...............**BOOM! .... BOOM!** Tamara Giordano will be thrilled to have the worldwide scoop and broadcast it from CNN in Rome immediately. He owed it to her; they were lovers ten years.BOOM!...............**BOOM!** All looked around as thunder lent its voice to the sinister events of the day. "Ever been to South Africa, Stefano,?" said Whitney, "heard Cape Town is glorious."

"The differences in South Africa - Cape Town and Johannesburg, a provincial city where exaggerated crime is matched by a dearth of culture, is a city that fascinates for its extremes. Mineral wealth for instance - diamonds, gold - have made South Africa a giant. Couple that with the wasteland of abandoned life, industry, mines, caves, walking distance from the city that can trace human life by millions of years.... add depravity, racial hatred, fear."

"Cape Town on the other hand," spoke Korthorpe, "is a mecca for elite Europeans fleeing winter, bringing culture and vibrant European life to a place far different from its northern capital."

"You all know I'm not one to interrogate people," Shabadiba changed the subject, in her deep throaty voice known not to dawdle with unnecessary remarks. She took a cigarette from the box on the table; de Gesu lit itBOOM!...............**BOOM!**

"Over the years what came to me was that although Esmeralda spoke with proficiency and accented her words with the highest degree of pronunciation, as I was taught, I sensed she was a foreigner who'd cultivated an English accent by elocution lessons like me. You see there's a fine line of difference if one listens to schooled English or English by birth."

"Eliza Doolittle!" Olympia interrupted.

"Yes," Shabadiba continued, "You and Nigel speak better than we do, just slightly," she smiled, "No one ever seemed to know exactly where she came from, schools she went to and I continually thought, which country did she came from? I mind my own business and never said this before, but now." The friends nodded agreement.

She took a long inhale, raised her chin high exhaling. "I agree with Serena, Esmeralda loved Gianni and I would venture to say Gianni was as ignorant to her background as we've been, and also the Baron. I met Martin Beck in Monte Carlo some years after they divorced. Sweet old devil," she smiled again, "He liked to play roulette. Mutual friends from Antibes introduced us. When I opened the subject that I knew Esmeralda, he stopped me abruptly saying, "I'm still in love with her. Anything you say will wound me." And walked away. I never forgot that."

The group exchanged opinions deciding once the storm passed they would return to Villa Pina, collect their things and leave. It had all become too complicated and delicate a situation to remain. Like friends everywhere, the least said would be best.

BOOM!...............**BOOM!**

Brian Korthorpe turned to Olympia "This is terribly upsetting. I read it in her eyes and never gave an opinion. Eyes give us a message. What's going on in the soul."

"Think so? As an artist, I've always concentrated on the mouth. Eyes can fool the viewer, Brian." Véronique sat close listening. "I always make a point," Olympia continued "to study a person's lips. They are the hardest part of a portrait to paint. Esmeralda's, though voluptuous, when studied, have developed a downcast expression either from guilt or shame."

"Maybe from depression." Véronique added.

"Yes." Olympia said with a twist of cynicism, her arched brows, gave way to a second message. "She hasn't had the best of life."

Nicky was off in a corner speaking to Rupert, "You know when I met her, touched her while dancing, I flirted, we're the same age, Gianni was ten years older and I'm a man who loves beautiful women. I studied her, Rupert, in doing so, I came to a conclusion. Gianni had stars in his eyes, I could have taken her to bed at anytime."

de Gesu joined the group, "I'm speaking about my impression of Esmeralda from early days, he expostulated, "As I said, I dined with her, took her on my plane, and frankly gentlemen, understood I could do something rotten to Gianni, take her to bed easily, but I didn't betray Gianni, hopeless fool was in love. Now in light of all this," Nicky grinned, "How marvelous to realize when all this is settled, and Nigel's no longer in the picture, I still could take her to bed and fuck her, but gentlemen, it's marvelous to understand, I don't want to." He downed his whiskey. "She's a million times worse than I thought."

Rupert in his toned down British style injected, "All that glitter, the glamour. The more I met her, the more it faded in my opinion. The first encounter, yes, I was bowled over. She was splendid. After, her superficiality outdistanced everything, I felt she wasn't genuine. I never felt I knew her."

"Like me…each succeeding meeting brought an emptiness…" Nicky toyed with the ice in his glass.

de Gesu studied the two men. He'd been Esmeralda's lover for several years until Gianni came into the picture. "Once she met Gianni, and this rests with us, I was her lover for a number of years prior, meeting her when she was wed to Beck, but once she met Gianni, she never allowed anyone near her. I do agree with Serena. Theirs was a love story." He gulped his scotch and the three went to the bar for another round.

Hours later after dinner, Nicky spoke to Jameson. "What do you make of the investment in ESCAPADES?"

"You mean now that Esmeralda might not have liquidity?"

"Right."

"I'm in for $10 million. Their stake, Pembrooke, that is, was double. What do you say? Split the ante?"

"Thought you'd say that." They shook hands. "When are you going back to America, Whitney...how do we move forward?" Nicky asked.

"I'll speak to Levy. He's a good bloke. We've got a winner in the film. Esmeralda will bow out, she has to."

"Exactly as I see it. You know Levy better than I do. Tell him I'll cover the investment with you and co-sign. Keep this between ourselves."

"You're on."

Nicky had received all the necessary information he required from the one brief phone call at Canzone del Mare. Spiga had acted for him. Frederico Spiga was aware some of Nicky's investments were tied to Zianni Pharmaceuticals. Italians, like Jews, protect each other. "Thanks for tipping me off, Spiga." Nicky turned as Jameson questioned, "What do you make of this?"

"Fraud, extortion, murder? Where does one start?"

"If that bitch is lucky, Serena will exile her." Whitney nodded to Olympia wanting his company from across the room.

"I'm of the same opinion." They joined the others for café finding Véronique holding court speaking of astrology.

"Don't you remember Brian I predicted as Whitney's boat came into port some days ago that we were all together for a specific reason?…Look at this…"

She unrolled a large paper that one would have thought was an architectural plan gone awry. "You see I've noted all of our zodiac signs and here in the centre, remarkably, they are juxtaposed, every one of them, with Esmeralda and Nigel's. Serena, I knew your details so I etched them into this astrological forecast, as you can see in blue when I learned we'd meet you." Véronique stretched the paper out on the coffee table and all stood watching in amazement.

"Remarkable Véronique!" Brian Korthorpe exclaimed, "And I thought astrology was a lot of bunk!" Samir defended her. "This ancient regard for the stars must be examined carefully. There are many proclaiming to predict the future but beware! Few have the gift of prophesy. Véronique… can you tell us more…" noted Samir, a true believer.

"Do you see how the 8th house of Nigel's is…" and the group surrounded Véronique as she delineated the mystique of prophesy.

Esmeralda knocked on Nigel's door. He'd been expecting this. "Come in Esmeralda." His mind returned to yesterday when she entered the same door and hell descended in his life. He was dabbing himself with Aqua di Silva. He didn't turn to look at her.

"Nigel, you know my lawyers are downstairs. Sanjeev tells me that several of our guests are unable to sail back for dinner this evening."

"Yes."

"Nigel do be kind please and keep up a façade! We have this journalist, Daniels here and…"

BOOM!....**BOOM! BOOM!.............BOOM!**

They looked to the window, then with a voice as smooth as silk, "My darling Esmeralda," he said looking over his shoulder, returning to his image in the mirror to comb the tuffs of his sideburns, "I should have taught you to play chess years ago. You adore manipulating people." He continued tying an ascot around his neck. "Sanjeev showed me the seating plan. I told him to seat the lawyers away from me, near you. Now tell me, Dear, what are your wishes?"

"Let's proceed as if nothing happened. It'll serve your purposes in the end. Today I've spoken to David and Luigi to prepare a settlement to dissolve our marriage without acrimony. I've too many other pressing matters." She tried to keep a cool head but her nerves gave her away.

"Esmeralda, your puppet husband that you wish to manipulate like a ventriloquist has a surprise, too. My lawyers are also preparing a document. Enmeshed as you are with other matters, may I be the first to tell you, we've frozen your assets."

Her jaw dropped, she was stunned.

"Besides a settlement, I want antiques and paintings. I'm particularly fond of the Guido Reni of "The Satyr" in your bedroom."

"Nigel! How could you?"

"Could I? …coming from you of all people?" He peered ruthlessly. She had emasculated him for years by her money, trickery and passive aggressive manner. The liquor consumed today eased his concerns for the future. There was no way he would exit this marriage without being financially solvent. That was a foregone conclusion. Esmeralda couldn't take him on contesting a divorce and come out in one piece from Serena. The timing for Nigel was perfect.

He intensified his viciousness, "Do calm yourself, my beautiful wife," and she was beautiful - standing before him with her hair tied in a long ponytail the way he liked it, in a pencil slim black Italian knit sweater he'd given her last summer when they were Venice. Her slim feet peeked from the hemline in red stilettos. "I suggest you take a good snort before I have the pleasure to escort you downstairs. Shall we go to your room?

"Not before you replace your wedding band."

"Oh yes," he reached for his ring on his bureau…"Now to proceed as you wisely suggested with *bella figura*."

His hand took her elbow and ushered her to her cabinet where she kept her liquor. He watched as she poured a shot of scotch quickly wishing the brew still her senses.

"Much better, Esmeralda. Now spray your mouth and shall we continue the masquerade of marriage?" His smile was cold-blooded, she returned it in like fashion and they walked to the living room resembling the stiff figurines of couple often seen duplicated atop wedding cakes.

Drinks were in progress as the host and hostess excused their lateness on the storm. BOOM!...............**BOOM! ....BOOM!!!**

XXV

The Tempest and The Dinner

"Jolly good to be together! I daresay, like Noah and his tribe years ago. Ha hahhaaa.." Nigel joked accepting a whiskey from a tray as he waltzed about the room dispersing kisses to the ladies. "Esmeralda and I are dying to hear about what you've been up to fighting the torrent of Capri so it 'twere."

"Nigel ya'll a hoot! En what's this I hear about Whitney? Neva able to get back from that stupid sailin' idea of his this mornin'. I told him it was wrong. If I didn't know him betta I'd question the whole thing."

"Ah Lynne, you should put your credentials through for the CIA." Nigel's light-hearted behavior was exaggerated and Marco Ricci, being the actor he was, saw through it immediately. Esmeralda thanked the day her husband was a jester. He'd learned to blab away when he was commentating killing time on air waves - the experienced, entertaining Nigel Pembrooke could out-talk everyone, small talk was his forte. At a time like this it was appreciated. BOOM!...............**BOOM!** BOOM!............... **BOOM!** BOOM!..........**BOOM!**

Daniels came to Esmeralda concerned, "I can't believe it, powers cut from the phone, I can't recharge my Blackberry, the broadband connection isn't working, Esmeralda I've got to phone in a story."

"Really Monty at a time like this it's impossible. The last meteorological reports advised that...."

"My mobile..."

"Ze mobile phones are not working, Sanjeev told me es ze circuits." said Jacqueline.

"Come, come, Monty, take a day off. Have a drink," Nigel advised patting the journalist on the shoulder. "Did anyone ever say before they die 'I should have phoned the office more often?'"

"Shit Nigel...you don't understand."

""What's happened to Zofra?" Nigel asked, "Didn't she and Mark make it back?"

Nigel realized as soon as he said the words he'd made a gaffe. Cat was listening and her blood froze. She fumed red from top to toe.

"Nigel," she asked preturbed, "Do you know where Mark is? Shabadiba left Groucho for Zofra to look after but he's in the kitchen. She's no where around."

"Now don't you think about anything, Cat," said Esmeralda moving towards her swiftly, taking the girl by the hand. "Come right here. I want you to meet someone who's your age and is very eligible." Esmeralda brought Cat (dressed to an outstanding advantage in a Dolce & Gabanna mini skirt and high Ferragamo boots) towards the only young man in the room.

"May I present you to Peter Evans. He's from my law firm in London and Peter do look after our guest from Los Angeles, please." Peter Evans, an inexperienced young man from Surbiton used to overstuffed Yob binge drinkers, never set his eyes on someone like Cat, "My pleasure. Please, you must tell me all about Los Angeles. I've never been there." He was plainly awestruck by the glamorous woman with a provocative name.

As Esmeralda introduced her lawyers to Jacqueline and Lynne, Jarvis Engleton joined the group and a discussion about global warning ensued. Daniels fidgeted with his mobile phone, moved to the landline on the desk trying to get a connection without any success. BOOM!...............**BOOM!** Nigel caught the eye of Marco and the two went to the backgammon table in the opposite corner shooting dice, standing together waiting for an announcement from the other.

"What's up?" said Marco…

"You might as well know. Before Rupert left for Ischia I asked him to tell the others…"BOOM!...............**BOOM!** BOOM!...............**BOOM!**

"What?"

"I'm divorcing Esmeralda." Nigel looked for some response.

"Nigel, obstacles are their own doing. Withdraw from the negatives. Live non-fragmented like me."

"I knew you'd have advice."

"We're on a soul's voyage, man. Do you want to be in a shipwreck? My new energy is my new career. Don't get lost in your senses."

"Are you competing for the Dalai Lama's job?" Nigel clinked his glass to Marco's.

"Divorce, remarriage, taxes, divorce, mistresses, winners, losers, remarriage, debts, credit ratings! We all die in the end. Make the most of it, Nigel." He exhaled Zen style and gave his friend a warm smile. Nigel appreciated the repartee.

"You know Marco, I remember I could've walked into a party like this but more fabulous, you know what I mean, and I could have scored with half the women in the room."

"Me too, so what's new?"

"Think I could do it again?"

"At our age it depends how much you have in the bank." He winked at Nigel. "Let's join the party." They walked towards the opposite end of the room and gave their opinion to the conversation still in effect on global warning. BOOM!...............**BOOM!** BOOM!...............**BOOM!**

Sanjeev announced, "Dinner is served."

Nigel extended his arm to escort Jacqueline, "Shall we?" He motioned to the others. Once seated, he began "I want to put all of you at ease. A storm like this always happens on the island, it'll clear by morning. Enjoy yourselves my dear old things. There's plenty to drink…"

"But the phone lines, Nigel…"

"My dear Monty Daniels, dedicated to journalism as you are, there's nothing one can do, my good fellow. The last wireless transmitter was found underwater in bits and pieces in '43 by Lt. Commander Ian Fleming when he was serving in WWII and it was retreived in Capri. Relax about communication...once the bloody circuits are reinstated, you'll be fine, that is unless power's cut. Then no one can recharge their mobiles. Imagine, if you will, what people did in the time of Tiberius with slaves and carrier pigeons to relate messages. Hahaha."

"Why Nigel whatteva will we do?"

"Let us imagine" he began, BOOM!...............**BOOM!** BOOM!...... .... **BOOM!** He raised his glass....lightheartedly speaking of history. "Tiberius himself is here tonight...in a vanquished world with a *strega*• that has ignited this evening!'

"Nigel," Lynne said again, "ya'll scarin' the dickens otta me..."

"Darling Lynne, have no fear that we'll have a key party. No! No! There's backgammon, dominos, chess, the piano. Put your fear aside, Capri has never felt a tremor since Tiberius' time from that beast volcano across the Bay, Mount Vesuvius."

"Nigel you're still scarin' me...en I bet others too..."

"Nonsense! Capri brings good luck. Don't give it a second thought that there's a four-hundred kilometer reservoir of magma lying eight kilometers below our Vescuivus...it stretches right out to the sea...the volcano will erupt again one day but not tonight."

"Hell in tarnation Nigel! I'm petrified..."

"You're safe here, Lynne, as the ancients were when Vesuvius erupted, as the populace were in WWII when no bombs fell."

BOOM!...............**BOOM!**

"We are free of terrorism, secure our seas are like our air rights, unpolluted ....corruption exists yes! but here we have Paradise: Greed is everywhere, less so on Capri." (The lawyers looked at each other and

---

• witch

then to Esmeralda. He was cheeky, terribly cheeky on a night like this to speak of greed.) "Even if scoundrels arrive from all over the world tainting some .. values ...the Capresi have their own society, like the Gaelic people of Ireland and speak in dialect as it chooses them to hide and keep their secrets! BOOM!...............**BOOM!** BOOM!...............**BOOM!** Secrets...as I was saying....secrets... we all have them....and this I am certain of now that I've presented a history lesson for our guests safe and secure at Villa Pina, this tempest will pass." He raised his glass to toast everyone..."Let imagination flow....our Capresi storm may suspend life without traffic on the sea, Internet, telephones, faxes...all will be restored - just a question of time...in the meantime let us reflect on the solitude of the past before the fast track society polluted us. Enjoy yourself! Esmeralda can play the piano after dinner."

"Zes is wonderful Esmeralda you can play ze piano?"

"But Nigel," Daniel pleaded trying to grapple with the situation, "I have to know what's happening in the world. BOOM!...............**BOOM! ...**BOOM **BOOM!** BOOM!...............**BOOM!**

"And this is our world...right now..."

"But Nigel! That's my business. I'm under contract to Morehouse papers and THE ENQUIRER, NEWS OF THE WORLD, THE MAIL ...PAGE SIX... if something's happening I've got to report it. News never stops."

"Monty, really I am sorry dear chap, but it's beyond my control." Monty Daniels instincts told him trouble was in the offing. The lawyers presence alone were a mystery, appearing with weather like this. Why were they here? Stress consumed him knowing there was nothing he could do. Certainly there's a story why Levy was with Zofra, that wasn't earth shattering news for his wide range of readers, he unrolled his thoughts like a skein of yarn, Hollywood gossip, that's all, another affair big deal....But these hot-shot lawyers on the scene - smells fishy. Everyone of them are concealing something I should know. A story's brewing under my god damned nose and I can't penetrate what the hell is happening. Jarvis is no use as a second set of ears. Why did those others go off to another island? Why did the Ambassador leave? ...and the young girl? Thoughts swirled in dervish circles. Daniels couldn't focus on conversation that took on a lightness avoiding important matters - N.C.S. - No Controversial Subjects were the rule at Villa Pina as the threatening indigo sky claimed the evening and any talk of law, divorce, politics, sex, scandal or religion were off limits.

Engleton exercised his knowledge of art and antiques, which bored the hell out of Monty and seemed to please Esmeralda. He never surmised Esmeralda was anxious far beyond anything he could have imagined as she blessed the fact the first two courses proceeded without incident. BOOM!...............**BOOM!** BOOM!...............**BOOM!** BOOM!.......... **BOOM!**

Hailstones pelted the stone terrace and torrents of rain continued throughout the evening with thunder in the distance and then edging closer. Sanjeev poured bottles of Chateau Rothschild's private vintage from '84, the cheese course commenced and considering the circumstances, the mood was agreeable. Daniels noted Esmeralda smile to Nigel never surmising he was witnessing two of the finest actors of his time.

Just as dessert was to be served, BOOM!...............**BOOM!** Rolling thunder dominated everything. BOOM!...............**BOOM!** a bolt of lightening followed, jolting the glass doors to the terrace. Everyone reacted as the house lost electrical power and room blackened......**BOOM!** The roar of thunder cursed the night again BOOM!.... ....**BOOM!** Dramatic lightening sparked to the right - to the left - **BOOM!..........** ..... **BOOM!** The morbid night caused all to think the end was near.

To be without electricity in Capri on a night like this was normal, yet guests were wildly apprehensive. Sanjeev ignited a multitude of candles burning on the table that reflected frightened faces, as if Caravaggio had arrived and painted their portraits.

BOOM!..............**BOOM! ...**BOOM!..............**BOOM!**

"Come, come now, don't be afraid," said Nigel to his guests. "A storm like this is a bitch, like some women..." His laugh was hearty but the remark was not overlooked by anyone..."One must know how to handle it."

"I beg your pardon Mme Pembrooke..."

"Yes Sanjeev,"

"Unfortunately, power seems to have been lost throughout the island. I have begun lighting candles everywhere, bedrooms are already lit. I came to inquire if anyone has special needs." A stilled silence met the room.

"Good erudite chappies like these fine legal minds might wish to remain this evening and not return to their hotel. Gentlemen, and Elena, I'm sure Esmeralda agrees. What do you wish?"

"How long do you believe the storm will continue, Nigel?"

BOOM!...............**BOOM!** BOOM!...............**BOOM!**

"David, that's hard to say. It's always like this on an island. Gorgeous one minute, tempest the next." He spooned a mouthful of black chocolate mousse into his mouth, pausing. "Since all the boats have ceased service, that's not a good sign, sorry to say chappies."

"Capresi take this in stride, could be a day or two before power's restored." Esmeralda added trying to show a united front with Nigel.

"A day or two?" Daniels echoed aghast. BOOM!...............**BOOM!**

"Yes, Monty." Esmeralda affirmed. "You'll be perfectly comfortable. We've been through this before, haven't we Nigel?"

"Yes, my Dear and I dare say it's best for our new guests for their own security to stay at the Villa. We've plenty of room. Trees have fallen earlier and with this present bolt of lightening, some may have blocked access to the road."

"That's fine by me, Nigel," said D'Albora looking to his daughter and then his host and hostess. David Arthur followed suit and his mignons nodded affirmation.

"Sanjeev will see to everything, he's a marvel." Esmeralda injected.

"Why I do declare, I'm always right. Whitney should'hav listened to me en nevva sailed off. En now...this es somethin' outta a novel or murder or.."

"Come Lynne, don't get overly dramatic," Marco said, "Leave the acting stuff to me. I've heard through the grapevine we have a talented pianist in our midst."

"Oh Marco, I'm really not that accomplished yet."

"Forgive me Esmeralda, I've created a *faux pas.* I was referring to Jarvis Engleton, who plays Gershwin like Bobby Short."

"Really?" Lynne turned to Jarvis. "New York music. I'm missin' New York." BOOM!...............**BOOM!** BOOM!...............**BOOM!**

"After dinner would you grace us with some music and be a jolly fellow, Jarvis?" Nigel asked.

"Certainly Nigel, my pleasure," said the emaciated guest delighted he'd become the hit of the party.

At this point in the evening, the Villa was lit as if it were the 17th century. Esmeralda felt a sense of relief. To a degree, the unexpected seriousness of the storm had distracted her from the pressure of legal issues. Dinner conversation continued and she looked about the table satisfied. She heard Nigel bellow advice, "The tempest will pass, it may suspend life..."

"...Reflect on solitude and higher things before the fast track of society pollutes us," added Marco.

The evening had two or three hours to go before she could retire, take a sleeping pill and prepare for tomorrow's difficult meeting, rain or shine with lawyers. Her mind swept with worry how to verbalize the story of her Mother, her baby.

Luigi D'Albora to her left was speaking with Jarvis Engleton and the junior solicitor from Arthur & Porter, discussed New York and music with Lynne. Nigel seemed relaxed surrounded by Marco and Jacqueline. Cat Renoir was being treated like a lady by Peter Evans who couldn't disguise his infatuation. To her right David Arthur, and Elena D'Albora were entertained by Monty Daniels discussing the time he'd sailed with Sofia Loren and Angelina Jolie. Esmeralda looked again. She counted. Her hand went to her heart that began to pound irregularly. "Oh my God, we're thirteen at table...a curse!."

Instantly with this revelation, the roar of thunder from Satan resounded, BOOM!...............**BOOM!** BOOM!...............**BOOM!** BOOM!.........**BOOM!** then a second rumble with twin bolts of lightening hit, then another. BOOM!...............**BOOM!** BOOM!...............**BOOM!** Everyone stopped speaking, petrified, looking towards the glass doors to the terrace. Esmeralda turned to David Arthur on her right, Luigi D'Albora on her left both of whom listened half attentive. "Please forgive me. I suddenly feel sick." Distracted by the storm, they sat awestruck not paying attention to her pronouncement, astonished by nature's spectacle intensifying BOOM!....... ....**BOOM!..BOOM!** With startling alacrity Esmeralda glided away in the dimness of the room with a only Nigel noticing she exited the supernatural scene, gazing at her exquisite *derriere.*

BOOM!...............**BOOM!** BOOM!...............**BOOM!**

She took a candelabra from the hallway and ascended the long staircase, reaching her room in time before she had a head rush, and Tachycardia began.

She had sensed it at dinner from the stress of the entire day, and then when she counted the omen of thirteen!....bad luck, someone would die, like Jesus when he was betrayed. She panicked. She threw her head over the side of her bed to avoid unconsciousness, her blood rushed, the pounding of her heart intensified, her breathing grew great with stress. A hot flash began sweat, then came a cold chill. Her heart raced in a panic attack, out of control with fright. She must have been in this state twenty minutes by the clock. Unable to stop her palpitating heart, alarmed beyond measure, her breath panted as if she'd been attacked. She remained struggling for normalcy the fever pitch of fear continued to grip her, afraid to move from her bed, panting, she finally crawled to her bath and prostrated herself on the cold marble floor to still her pounding heart to normalcy. She tore off her sweater and striped to the skin to have her smooth vanilla skin's temperature drop by contact with the ice-cold stone to shock her body back to its normal state. The rhythm of her heartbeat terrified her. All was pent up emotion. She couldn't control her trembling body, her throbbing heart, her fast-paced breath, her hands that gave way to carpo-pedal spasms, tears ran down her cheeks. Gianni once said her tears were the color of the sea at Capri when she shed them at his Father's funeral....

Her glockenspiel clock chimed eleven. She'd been in this furor an hour. Dimly she heard the melody of a Gershwin tune from the drawing room. No one would know she was in this state. She could die like this. No one would care. She lay still for what must have been a half hour more, her breath began to ease to normal rhythm, the cold marble floor shocked her heart to its usual pace. In the place where she lay so cold to the touch, the marble had warmed from the heat of her body.

The beat of her heart echoed in her throat, then it calmed. Her mouth ran dry and she moved like a zombie, slowly taking time to lift herself vertically to reach her sink and bathe her perspired face in cold water. Her reflection lit by the candle near the mirror startled her. She drew back, "I look like a witch." She whispered. "But I am a witch."

Her eyes viewed her reflection cruelly. Her mouth was etched with an expression she'd never witnessed before, her skin was pallid like a corpse. BOOM!...............**BOOM!** BOOM!...............**BOOM!** BOOM!......... **BOOM!**

Maybe this s what it feels like to die. She'd aged thirty years this night. She edged her way to her bed, staggering, holding the wall to steady herself, throwing herself her covers, starring to the blackness of her room....the terrifying thunder rumbled and returned.........BOOM!........ **BOOM!!**

BOOM!......**BOOM!**

The blackness of the sky bolted bright with lightening...her French doors shook from the gust of wind, she stared terror-stricken and winced.

She thought she saw a ghost....

XXVI

Demise

…was it a ghost? The ghost of death? Her husband Gianni? Surely she was dying. The storm's cyclic rage and sinister night noises fired hallucinations. The house, like all houses, had its peculiar sounds. Lying there, naked, she pulled the satin cover over her trembling legs. Terrified to look at the window she looked again unable to remove her eyes from it. **BOOM!** BOOM!……………**BOOM** A crack of thunder bolted anew. All was evil. Her mind raced to the sight of the apparition. The clock chimed one.

The last strains of the piano were heard. A mélange of voices followed reaching her ears as wind howled and rain cascaded on the balcony. The tone of guests words, their footsteps were dispersed bidding 'good night' throughout the villa. She couldn't make out the muffled speech. In the din of the storm, they drifted off as Nigel with his cackle bid, "One sleeps well on a stormy night." Then, an instant of silence. Attune to everything she waited. Nigel's door to his bedroom closed.

He'll never know what I've been through tonight, today, or tomorrow. If I die, he'll inherit a fortune. Maybe this is what he wants. Maybe all this is a conspiracy to drive me mad, commit suicide. Maybe he's plotting with Serena and others and tonight, crazed from panic, what if I swallow dozens of sleeping pills? He'll announce to the world he's bereft and rake in a fortune.

Nigel doesn't deserve my suicide. He doesn't love me. He never did. His affection is for himself. **BOOM!** BOOM!...............**BOOM..... BOOM!!!** Intermittent thunder exploded, lightening followed. A repeat combustion intensified minutes later. **BOOM!** BOOM!...............**BOOM**, She lay in bed with mental paralysis of black thoughts. How long would this last? The storm? The interrogation? How long would her lawyers and Serena's take before declaring the sentence to destroy her?

Her anguished mind met edgy nerves that gave way to frantic ideas. Across the room were 'dream bars.' The thought to move from her bed petrified her. The menacing idea to overdose lurked. She'd reached the pit of despair. In a downward spiral, her bed became a sarcophagus the rain continued...thunder roared **BOOM!** BOOM!..............**BOOM** far away. Another crack, **BOOM!** came closer....lightening sparked. For the instant, the room lit with an electric bolt coloring everything as a giant strobe from the devil.

Nigel's footsteps came to a standstill from next door. Soon he'd be asleep. Night sounds continued. The house clicked, cracked. Branches clawed the windows. Thunder was heard far in the distance, it boomed closer, lightening bolts were far, then near. Blustery wind rattled *persiani* shutters. A scratching noise was in her closet, no, it was outside her door, in her bath, on the terrace. The clock struck two. In the blackness of the night everything was exaggerated. A million thoughts consumed her. Her moral autopsy began.

Everything returned. All the denial, pain, delusion, the experience of her heart torn to shreds seeing the envelope from her Mother, knowing it was an omen of doom. Then - the deaths - Gianni's, the baby.

We were so in love with a million hopes for the future. She stifled the words in her pillow. Memories of her marriage enveloped Esmeralda. Forever she'd recall Gianni's classic Italian face - a face so handsome one would view it in Romanesque sculpture. The last look he gave her was vivid. It had never left her mind. He was so proud of her as his wife, to be a Father and take part in the sport he excelled for decades. As he strode to the field at Smith's Lawn on his Arabian stallion for that polo game at Windsor, he nodded to her seated in the Queen's box at the Guards Polo Club. This was their private salute of affection. Her eyes never left him, overjoyed to be his wife.

"The Sport of Kings. Polo,"....Gianni explained it to her.... "It's fast, rough, perhaps the most dangerous sport of the world, I love it! You go for goals and need to have a pedigree from champion stock perform with you." He showed her his assortment of horses. "A horse like Romany, with a sensitive mouth can compete at top speed, worth easily $300,000." Gianni had thirty of them and travelled with thirteen believing it his lucky number (seventeen is the bad luck numeral for Italians).

"Darling," he'd say, "I expect to get ten years of play out of a horse like Romany. A horse is the most important element in polo - speed, agility and (like the rider), the horse must be competitive. A horse - like a rider, senses everything - the control between the two is vital...."

"But how fast do you go, Gianni?"

"At top speed, we can do 35 mph or more but the animal can only play four minutes before being swapped."

"It's so dangerous....." she told him too many times....he would allay her fears, saying, "A polo horse is trained to stop on a dime, I control him through the reigns and how I sit on the saddle. " Gianni rode with a helmet in these competitions, four riders and four horses against four riders and four horses. A chukka generally lasted seven minutes, galloping full speed on the turf, the field is the largest in sport - the length of nine football fields.

Gianni's level of play brought intensity to the game. He'd broken his wrist several times within the course of ten years but that was all. Inside the field the only ones who could sense the speed and danger were those eight players. Like the Kings who had invented the sport in .....these men loved danger, adventure, seizing the moment to win, enthralled with competitive spirit and the camaraderie of the game.

To experience a polo match of this intensity was unforgettable.

The Hurlingham Association International Day staged the annual event that day, the greatest single polo jamboree in the world recognized with its dashing high goal matches, Royal involvement, its 20,000 spectators, illustrious military pageantry and lively area of hospitality tents. Major David Dollar was the present Chairman of the prestigious club overseeing the competition that began in 1886, now an institution in England and on the social agenda of aficionados who followed the sport. He had arranged a private tea for the players and their spouses with the Queen and Prince Charles in the royal confines of the white clapboard clubhouse after the exciting match.

The day was clear, brisk, a maze of flowers burst in bloom throughout the VIP section of the club flanking the two topiary statues of polo players on ponies at the entrance. She was wearing a banana suede coat from Gucci. Gianni had laughed because her tummy was too large to close it properly. The sprawling verdant lawn presented excellent conditions without a trace of dampness from early autumn rain. Peaceful hills of Buckinghamshire framed the picturesque setting.

It was two years since they'd met; two perfect years. Plans were to go to Annabel's and celebrate that night. Serena had come from Italy, Véronique was there with Shabadiba and Olympia. Samir had made a rare appearance. Nicky was eyeing the large sterling trophies on display from Cartier.

Gianni was extraordinarily handsome, toned, physically powerful, manly. His riding breeches clung to his long legs shoed in fine Italian leather boots. Strong, muscular hands gripped the reins, second nature to him to be in complete control of Romany, his favorite polo pony. The animal's splendor matched Gianni's.

Gianni excelled in the 'Sport of Kings,' taking the first three chukkas excellently. Whitney was on the field with him as goaler from America, the umpires were from Inter-Regimental forces. Rupert watched with other team members from the sidelines as the eight players galloped at top speed competing on the Queen's Ground. They were playing against Mexico and Argentina. Hugo Valesquez, his great friend, scored two points; Whitney and Gianni outperformed him.

Prince Charles was due to play the second match. The high pitch of action was exhilarating. BBC was broadcasting Nigel's voice. He was seated high in the stands under a huge umbrella, cameras filmed the match for international television audiences. VIPs huddled close to be near the royals; people attending were devotees of the sport, cultivated English gentry. Others had arrived from Argentina and France to support their players, some from Italy, Palm Beach and Mexico. This clique met frequently at worldwide matches, informally attired with elegance, speaking in hushed tones, sipping Veuve Clicquott.

The rumble of racing hooves from the strong thoroughbreds, the competitive sportsmanship in high gear heightened. All eyes were on the field, suddenly for no apparent reason, Romany refused to take the chukka and reared wildly, out of control. Gianni held on tightly. The immediate intensity of danger rippled through the crowd. Romany reared a second time without warning, the next second, threw Gianni to the ground. From the force, Gianni's helmet flew across the field.

Unmanageable action ensued. Gianni, lay on the field, curled in an embryo contortion to protect himself, crumpled at the exact point of contact where he was thrown, while his crazed horse galloped away. The other terrified beasts broke into a furious gallop, giving no heed to their riders' seizing their reigns to control them, the animals went wild with fear, violence ensued. The tragic catastrophe couldn't be diverted. All was split second timing, riders were unable to halt. Instantaneous action was instinctual. Stallions galloped with furious speed. Two reared in fright. To divert the tragedy was impossible. Players' anguish the BBC caught on camera. Gianni was trampled to death by three of the thoroughbreds. All witnessed the massacre. The uproar was colossal. Gianni was dead. Disaster claimed my husband's life.

Standing helpless, I screamed, a scream too hysterical to believe. It came from the soul of his baby. People grabbed me to remain in my place. I remember throwing off their hold with strength more vigorous than one could imagine racing to the field. I viewed the mutilated remains of my husband bathed in blood and then collapsed.

From what they told me, we were both carried from the grounds by stretchers. When I came to, I was in an ambulance, the baby kicked wildly in my stomach. My shock was indescribable.

That day I died with Gianni. I had no more desire to live.

This was one way Esmeralda remembered Gianni's death. The other was the reason for the tragedy. He was distracted. The contretemps they had minutes before he began the match overwhelmed emotional Gianni. His equestrian ability to control his horse failed.

It began with the letter.

Secure in her loving marriage, Esmeralda's anxiety about her past dimmed. Memories were blocked assimilating the life of Countess Zianni. This advantaged life was her right, genes shaped her from her Mother, her beauty, inherited. A refined patina she emulated from her two husbands. No one had cause to wonder about her lineage. Edited facts of her life were noted only if necessary for information and Esmeralda's past remained concealed. Gianni, similar to the Baron, was deeply in love without cause to interrogate his wife. The inclination of veneration stemmed, as is often the case, from the one in a partnership who loves to excess.

Weeks before his death, Gianni was called to New York for business. There he would meet his American CEO and have a visit with Samir and Jacqueline Redat. Esmeralda generally traveled with her husband. Now, however, she was six months pregnant and he wanted her to remain in Europe. It was decided she would take the short flight from Rome to London and they would rendezvous at Beaumont Manor in Wiltshire. There were interviews with nannies to tend, the nursery to design and medical checks in the UK should the baby be born in England.

Indian summer weather was exceptional that year. Esmeralda made it a practice to enjoy a late breakfast on the terrace of the Manor with its topiary garden. September was a choice month in the British isles. Morning dew had evaporated with the sparking English sun, the aroma of bittersweet boxwood intoxicated her senses coming from carved hedges in amusing animal designs. A mass of cabbage roses on the winding path vied for the eye's attention that stretched to a pristine lawn that loomed ahead. A meadow was beyond, touching the hillside with curves Gianni fantasized were the breasts and hips of a voluptuous woman. Emerald was her British Mother's name; the scenery reflected the same color. Only England with its frequent rainy weather produced a green of this quality. It was good to be back in the country she loved best of all. It had everything to do with her lineage and the good fortune Britain had brought her: first with Graham and Harrods, then Martin and Gianni.

Sherlock, a West Highland terrier shadowed her and presently rested near her chaise lounge. He was a sweet gift from Gianni to keep her company. Pampering herself, appealed to her, touching her firm tummy, feeling the movement of the baby. Only a woman can sense creation; the miracle of conception placed Esmeralda in another category of being. She was blessed beyond her dreams. She read *The Times*, *The Mail* and *The Telegraph*. She conversed with Sherlock as she had to Mercy, her dachshund in Germany, reading in English, reviewing critics' choices planning theatre events when Gianni returned or museums she wished to frequent. Appointments were in the afternoon. Cecil Jones, the man in charge of the London property, who rarely smiled, passed the day's mail to Esmeralda with her breakfast on the trolley, it made no impression on him.

"This courier letter arrived from Rome with additional mail, Contessa."

She waited until he was dismissed and opened mail. Gianni's secretaries handled most matters. Invitations were several and as she opened the courier piece from Rome she spied a familiar envelope; one she hadn't seen in years. "*Forward to Baroness Beck*" was scrawled upon the front of the large envelope, the signature and crest were unmistakable. Why would Martin write after all these years? How he loves to do things formally, she mused, still considers me Baroness Beck. Thoughts wondered to her ex-husband. Esmeralda retained an affection for Martin and appreciated his kindness never to intrude on her life with Gianni. Maybe he's going to remarry were her initial thoughts judging from the size of the envelope. She finished her breakfast saving his letter to read. Whatever he would write would be important. Instinct told her to distance herself from the stately mansion and take privacy to study his words in peace.

A loveseat hidden under a wicker arbor of jasmine was at the end of the long rose lined path. Her steps led her there, grasping the envelope, Sherlock was at her heels. She broke the claret seal embossed with the Beck coat of arms. One glace at the enclosure escalated to a diabolical sense of death. Attached to Martin's embossed card was a creased manila envelope.

> *My dear Esmeralda,*
> *This letter was received at our home in Bavaria.*
> *My thoughts are always of you. Martin*

The two envelopes were as different as black and white.

The brown envelope was sealed by glue and seemed to have made a long journey with its various stamps. She examined them closely, South African stamps. The return address was from the Convent. Her trembling hands tore open the envelope, like a Chinese puzzle, as one drama unfolded to another in her hands...yet another...a thin envelope of onion skin was enclosed. Her heart locked, the baby kicked. She swallowed a sudden lump that came to her throat. She tore the fragile envelope and froze reading the chicken scrawl text, dated 1987, thirteen years ago….

> *Daaugta Esse.*
> *Nuns helpin' me wriite yu*

A shrill of a scream resounded from her foreseeing a tragedy of wild proportions.

> *Dnot want to dye en my chile neva know*
> *Ize culdn't keep yu. ours blood es mixd*

yu fatha wan no abortin. me peeple don't want ya
Joburg that meen death to black ma.
ya gran'ma was white en same as yu en
eyes gren liken yu but polise kill her
Ize scared Ize don want 4 my Esse
whereva you are
if eva yu havin babee ya Ma es black
newspapa say ya fatha in jail yu run wey
Ize left yu wid him caz no otha wae en Ize
hope he neva hurt yu Essy yu hav
blod mixed en thers truble, killin'
Ize levin joburg. foregivme
Ma

Esmeralda's heart pounded and mind froze, dazed with the illiterate words. She re-read the letter, memorizing every misspelled word as creeping stiffness grew over her as it does to a corpse.

This secret of her parents arrived to rupture everything.

There was no doubt, the letter was from her Mother, a Negro, of an inferior race, a whore certainly.... "I'm a racist, raised a bigot, I detest the vermin! I am the vermin. I'm Negroid but never, never would I suspect miscegenation!"

Her hands shook, her mouth ran dry; a nervous quiver began on her lips, her forehead sprinkled with sweat that descend upon her body on the cool morning. Her heart palpitated.

The shock of her past returned with devestating proportions. Fragments of her life she could never fathom were now in place. Her bastard Father was an unmitigated liar, she, his victim. Everything was foul. She was the daughter of a whore, a swindler, a liar - a murder, a Negro, a half-breed, a mother fucking drunken bastard. Her parents had descended upon her doorstep from a distance of eleven thousand miles away to destroy her entire life.

The mystery of why she was at the Convent so long, why her Father viewed women so basely, why her skin was the color of vanilla like no one else's, beautiful, yes but too beautiful to be real was because she was mixed blood. My baby can be black!...were her initial thoughts. "I can give birth to a Negro," she said allowed, terrified of the consequences. A mix-breed child. "It can't happen. No one would understand. I'll be ruined. My marriage finished." She clasped the letter, holding her large tummy. "Gianni will think me unfaithful, a whore like my mother that I betrayed him with some black lover...."

Horrid as the revelation was, Esmeralda understood the contorted love from her mother whose warning came believing it right to protect her daughter. She's done me a horrible, vile favor. Esmeralda began to shake with terror. Tears burst from her heart.

"The shame, the shock! Gianni wants this baby with all his being! To see it born black will destroy him. I'll be destroyed. I can never explain this. It goes back too far. My history is tainted beyond anything I ever imagined. Our beautiful marriage, finished. A birth of a nigger! It can't happen." She re-read the letter. "It won't happen." Her voice was brittle and echoed in the hills.

The stillness of the garden was a blessing. The urgency to put in place a structure how to deal with this threat to her life, their life, the luxurious, aristocratic life of Count and Contessa Zianni seized her. Something must be accomplished before Gianni returns. Tainted birth can happen to others but it can't happen to me. I won't repeat the sin of my father's, my mother's and my grandmother's past.

South African bigotry was ingrained in Esmeralda, a victim of social rearing. She never spoke to a black, was a racist, like all whites living in Apartheid those horrid, insalubrious years. She came from a revered class. Inequality was never in question. She was white. She was better. The nuns told her so. Now this! What now? Negros were not equal. Her world was one that cursed minorities blaming them for the state of the world. Her privileged realm was one that no black could penetrate. Their race was different, a culture of savages. They spoke differently, uneducated like pigs. The pedestal Gianni erected to her, Martin gave her, Graham taught her was where she belonged. The truth was horrific. Her entire identity was wrong, she was someone else....

Bigotry was everywhere. Some people today sidestepped the issue, and feigned acceptance yet spoke differently in private. There was only one choice. All the bliss of feeling the baby's life inside her, everything pure and beautiful turned cold. Hate mixed with fear; joy was eliminated. She had to abort as soon as possible without Gianni's knowledge. Her marriage must be kept intact. He would never love her knowing her roots were guttural as this wretched South African truth revealed.

All her life believing her maternal blood noble, British, untainted, quality blood of heritage! Now this mark. No wonder she could never find records. The trauma descended. Yes, she was black, from perverted stock and sinful deeds. She detested her parents, both from the dregs of society, the slime of life. Everything she knew of their being was true. Too true. Her genes were theirs. Her blood, theirs. She was wicked, common, vulgar. She had disguised herself to be Graham's family, Martin's lineage, then Gianni's pedigree never knowing the truth. The entirety of her being was set before her as false. Revulsion filled every pore. She wished to take a dagger and kill the baby.

Who could she turn to? She thought for the instant and recalled her wedding day. She was utterly alone in the world. Her formed value system of propriety, her illustrious future set splendidly before her as this remarkable English garden that had been planned to perfection, her home in London, the palazzo in Rome, Villa Pina, Gianni's true love - all would vanish. He must never know the truth. It was entirely unacceptable for anyone, much less someone who adored her as a Goddess to condone. This dramatic twist of fate was too ugly, cruel, too unbearable. The enormity of the decision weighed on her mind, while at the same time she felt their six-month-old fetus squirming in amniotic fluid, safe for the moment. He, the heir to the entire Zianni fortune, was certainly black; this was the curse of her Mother's letter. The sin of her parents had come back to annihilate their grandson. An amniocentesis doesn't show color, it shows signs of normalcy, sex.

To plot an abortion was the only answer, Chinese did it all the time, infanticide....the word bristled. How can I manage in my sixth month?... without Gianni suspecting anything? Who do I know in England to help me with this execution and keep silent? Do it before Gianni returns from New York. Cockneys called children like this tarbush, who were proliferating London, the new trend and they didn't care but they never fit in. Common people took to multi-colored children sometimes yet there was always strife for mixed-breeds. Maybe in the future the world will take to colored kids …but never – never in our society. Esmeralda's blood ran cold. The answer to questions thumped resounding death. Sherlock barked at her heel breaking her sinister trance.

"We'll walk." She said "only you know my secret..."and she blessed the fact the garden was expansive and she could collect her thoughts. A dog cannot speak, what a blessing! Dogs are the only saints in this world....

To the right was an English maze of yew trees, the pride of Gianni's gardener. The nine-foot yew hedges shielded one from view, a perfect place for isolation. In and about, around and through the bushes she went with the terrier close beside. The staff would think she was taking her morning exercise. At the far end of the puzzle was the path circling around the house. Her watch noted the hour of noon. She came round the expanse with the lily pond and statues interspersed, and her mind was clear, her plan in place.

The blessed happiness she had felt with the thrill of being pregnant, carrying her beloved's child, loving the unseen creature was overshadowed by impending hell, a hell she would never risk. Her cold heart made a calculation too wicked to explain, "Women abort all the time," she said aloud alleviating the pressure of her sinister conscious. "Models regularly. Women in Italy use it as a means of birth control." Her heartless defense won against better judgment. I will not be controlled by a fetus or out dated Catholic conscious imbedded in dogma. Her jaw tightened. In the distance Clive, the gardener was burning leaves. She walked towards him.

"Good day, Contessa."

"Hello Clive. What are you burning?"

"Old shrubs, chippings we can't use for mulch." He rested for a moment on his rake.

The crumpled letter was in her tight fist.

"Just scraped up these things," the chipper gardener continued talking more to himself than to her. He turned his back to gather more debris.

"Beaumont's my pride and joy. Got to keep her pretty for you and Count Gianni." As he turned, Esmeralda moved closer to the flames, tossed the letter into the fire, watching the one and only piece of evidence about her black blood go up in roaring flames.

"Careful Countess. Don't get too close." He urged as he turned round smiling, his arms full of leaves.

"Just warming my hands. For some reason they felt a little chilly."

"You take care, carrying the young Zianni as you are."

"Yes. Clive. Thank you." She stepped back assuring herself every single word from the message burnt to extinction.

Having lived in London in the late '80s when she modeled for Graham, Esmeralda witnessed his low life in Soho. She was no stranger to the underworld that lurked on the streets selling tricks, drugs and any favor a person might require in a menacing situation. Money bought what one needed.

Her pregnancy was too advanced to have anything accomplished surgically. Drugs would induce the birth; she'd abort naturally. No one would suspect a thing. Seizing a rush of courage to create evil, she entered Beaumont's library, turned on the laptop, searched Google and found a group of names that would destroy the fetus. "Prosac, Zoloft, Paxil, antidepressants in a group of SSRI selective serotonin reuptake inhibitors" they were called, "used to treat depression, obsessive compulsive disorders, anxiety by increasing the amount of the neuro transmitter serotonin in the brain." Her eyes danced over the words and their precautions. She didn't fear for herself. She'd survive. "Taking SSRI can develop akathisia (inner restlessness that cannot be relieved) plus alcohol. All combined will certainly destroy the health of a fetus." She pushed another button, therewith appeared a list of amphetamines and sleeping pills. If the baby is born, he'll be born mongoloid. If I don't abort within the next few weeks, I'll seek a midwife. There are always ways, and in Italy everything can be done. Her thoughts were of the blackest motives.

Esmeralda read further "Misoprostol (Cytotec) induces labor. Cutotec, a cheap prescription drug for ulcers, a labor induction linked to uterine rupture and fetal tachycardia. Cervical ripening and labor induction Oxytocin is the drug of choice for labor induction when the cervical examination shows that the cervix is favorable. Amniotomy has been used as ether the only method of inducing labor if the membranes can be reached, or used with other drugs such as oxytocin or prostaglandin." All could be bought.

To the surprise of the staff, and those she was to meet for afternoon appointments, Esmeralda announced she'd received a telephone call that made it necessary to change plans. She would drive to London alone. Cecil Jones stirred with the revelation wanting to chauffer her to Kensington and received a polite refusal. Gianni had urged him to dote on his wife but her all-encompassing attitude was one of self-reliance; he had no intention to interfere. She seemed rushed, preoccupied, he conjectured.

The freedom of being alone in the car presented additional time to think. Quickly she maneuvered the vintage Alfa Romeo 'Berlinetta' from the circular drive, knowing once in London she'd park the unmistakable car underground at the Hyde Park garage and take a black cab. The car was too unique and would be seen where she intended to go. Her mind focused on her plan. She wound her way through the symmetric row of blue spruce and met the M4 to London. "So much of who I am is because of where I've been and where I am today. It's all too much of a difference -

this life and the other. I will never go back! My past is more horrible than I could have ever imagined."

If Graham's old pusher still worked the street, she'd find him. He'd helped when AIDS medicine wasn't authorized by the UK. Often she'd meet the crusty dealer to help alleviate Graham's pain from the deadly disease. No one spoke of matters like this. These people moved like rats in the night, an underground contingent in London, as in all cities, where money bought anything. She knew the location, the dim alley, with its urine stains, between the two theatres close to St. Martin's Lane, by the unmarked club Graham pointed out that gays frequented with rent boys, not far from the elegant one where she'd dine with him at the Garrick.

She crossed St. Martin's Lane for Drury Lane, Cranbourn Alley, Ruse Street. The puzzle of the West End was one she'd memorized long ago, she passed Floral Street, instincts led her to exactly where her rendezvous met with the drug kings of smut.

Who knew the real Esmeralda? From the moment she entered the world, hers was an education that no noble title or baccalaureate could never match. Swaddled in a rag of a blanket from her mother, dumped on her father's doorstep, schooled by nuns and now risen to being in a car custom made to her specifications, in a maternity dress designed by Missoni with Hermes purse stuffed with thousands of pounds and her precious title was her curriculum vitae. Experience plotted. Money achieved. Not a soul would squeal on her plan when she placed large bills in their avarice clutches.

Four years had passed from that nightmare in Soho and what followed after. The night's tempest and the pressure to divulge facts from her past were too vivid this night – a night that reawakened the witch that she was. Hers were roots of steel, her mind pragmatic. Survival! Survival! was the energy she had to possess. Everything would be for herself. Hours passed without sleep.

Faces loomed in her mind. Her Father's. Gianni's. The sleazy pimp who'd turned to trafficking in narcotics, meeting her surreptitiously trading drugs for cash three consecutive nights, her terror mounting should someone follow her, spot her, the police, the vapid street life, London at its sordid worst and she'd become a part of it.

BOOM!............BOOM!....BOOM...BOOM!

Capri's thunder terrified her, lightening cracked, blackness loomed. How well she remembered everything. Days followed in a sequel from the day before meeting the seedy man whose name she never knew nor wanted to know, paying him off, shielding her face, her hair, wearing dark glasses at night as if she were an addict. But she was an addict. An contemptible addict, addicted to *bella figura*, the sweet life of a bigot, to glamour, money, and 'respectable' society. Downing pills two at a time, in a race to make the deadline work before Gianni arrived from New York, feeling stabbing pain, faking her pangs on the pregnancy, lying to her Mother-in-law, Serena, friends who asked why she looked so sickly. Why was she remaining in bed? Was there anything wrong? Could they be of help? And her help, the paid performers to make her life one of ease never surmising anything all believing the third trimester was bringing on a physical change that was soon to pass tiptoeing by her bedroom, bringing her tea in bone china with the Zianni crest.

And doctors in London? To trick them was her greatest feat. Recalled to memory was waiting in the Harley Street reception room seeing other rich pregnant ladies, having been in their place days ago overjoyed with conception, reading a study on DNA published by NATIONAL GEOGRAPHIC that confirmed "all variously shaded people on earth trace ancestry to Africa some 150,000 years ago." Having her skin prickle reading "Genetic mutations act as markers Y chromosomes of native white man with mutations including M168," whatever that meant she wondered, "proving African ancestry…." The baby most certainly was black as tar. She remained speechless in fright, thinking of the butchery she'd inflict, as the feisty creature kicked in her womb. His strong genes and that of hers and Gianni's dominated. Doctors smiled telling her everything looked normal.

The concoction of pills didn't abort their son. Gianni returned and the morning he dressed to go to Windsor and take part in the match, while she dawdled preparing herself in the bathroom putting on makeup, her mobile phone rang. Gianni reached in her purse to pass it to her. It was then the eyes of the Chairman of the Board of Zianni Pharmaceuticals saw the pills. There were no words to describe his anguish. Lack of trust wafted through the room as the fire of lies she told him to cover her tracks stained the root of their union. The entire scene broke the bonds of matrimony as surely as if their wedding bands had snapped in two.

That is why Gianni was killed. He was heartbroken, distracted, knowing the power of every single pill and died. She killed him.

The grief she contained watching him die before her eyes was the worst experience in her life. The delicate state of pregnancy gave way to the shock of overwhelming depression and yet their strong son with all his Mother's overdosing of pills, moved, kicked and existed in her with the power of Zeus. The Italian family fawned over her, the last thing she needed. Gianni's funeral, the eulogy Rupert Davidson made which touched every soul in the Basilica where they wed, the aftermath with a thousand letters edged in black to read and answer, friends and doctors worried about her health, the pressure of the baby now certainly tainted with the variety of toxic pills she swallowed, would arrive disfigured and black. Nights were monsters, sleep impossible with the uppers and downers, the alcohol and the play acting day after day with the only subject on anyone's mind that sparked something positive was the birth of Gianni's baby.

When Gianni's Last Will and Testament was read, Esmeralda was dumbstruck. In all her wild imaginings she never considered Gianni would position her as head of the family. It was done because Gianni thought he'd live to old age and she carried his son. The money was entitled for the baby, not her, but life decreed something else, something terrible and she was caught in the avalanche of avarice vice. She was the Contessa Zianni, the widow to the scion whose legacy set her apart from practically all women in the world. She was one of the richest women in Europe. Everyone adored her because she was gorgeous, the tragic victim of circumstance, losing her young husband, carrying his heir all alone, without the love and support of her own family, young and exquisitely beautiful with a soul, all believed, angelic.

There were two months left of her pregnancy. The baby had to be terminated. The guilt of feeling his precious body day in day out, every hour with sleepless nights gave way to a form of madness bringing another emotion, hate. Desecrate this waste, free yourself of what was unknowingly a sin of your parents and caused Gianni's death. Without Gianni, life's worth nothing. Everything took on an ominous dimension.

After her seventh month of pregnancy ended, shrewd Esmeralda orchestrated the scenario confronting her. Contact was made with another set of powers. The Convento di Santo Spirito in Sicily was a respected clinic and sanatorium for the privileged to escape pressures of life. It was also a drug rehabilitation centre. They knew how to keep silent. She learned of their existence years ago when an industrialist, an acquaintance of Gianni's, committed suicide and his bereft wife, retired to the premises to avoid the media and gain control of her shattered life. Esmeralda seized her chance.

Using the excuse of her overwrought nerves from the death of her husband, the funeral, the pressure of responsibility from the extraordinary inheritance coming at a time when she was arriving at the term of her pregnancy, she set her scheme in motion, and announced plans to the family. She'd go into seclusion and rest for the next month. This was not unusual in the best of circumstances.

Gianni's Mother hemmed and hawed, not wishing to part from Esmerald wishing to accompany her. It was the last thing Esmeralda wanted. She needed complete privacy, told her doctor and he relayed it talking like a parrot to her Mother-in-law.

Once on the beautiful grounds in Taormina overlooking Mount Etna with the mild weather lingering in the southern part of Italy, the sea air gave Esmeralda strength of purpose. She assured everyone the baby's chance for a peaceful birth would be recognized some weeks later in Rome. For her security, a mid-wife was on staff and would meet with her daily. She'd continue exercising Lamaze breathing techniques.

Acclaimed doctors had ownership in the clinic and should the baby arrive premature, all respected the reputation of the renown clinic (even her mother-in-law). Esmeralda and the baby were not in danger. Although displeased to see the beautiful young widow depart Rome for a month, everyone empathized. Her exhaustion and grief was greater than the sum total of theirs, except, of course, Gianni's Mother who believed in Esmeralda's goodness as one believes in a child's innocence.

Once in Sicily, arrangements were made for labor inducing drugs to reach Esmeralda by the underground world of the Mafia that asked no questions and pocketed fees. Prussic acid was added to the list of toxicants. The rats at work, thought Esmeralda as she accepted the parcel from the dark face on the thoroughfare near the graduated steps to the sea. Gianni's seed would not be born and live. Premeditated murder was in place. It's cost £10,000 in cash. That did not include the cost of the clinic or the cost of silence from the mid-wife. There was no place for doubt in Esmeralda's plan. She viewed the baby as a demon to destroy. Remarkably she had the force of will to control her conscious.

One must design life the way one wishes to live it. Love and destiny can be controlled. "After Gianni there will be no more men to love. This baby like his family will be eradicated from my future if I am to survive."

Her reading matter avoided anything to do with religion choosing instead factual data contemplating over one million surgical abortions took place in the last twenty years in America alone, and how many in Italy? India? England? China? These thoughts eased any strain of doubt or pressure on her contorted conscious.

The 16th century convent was, as most important real estate in Italy, owned by the Roman Catholic Church from the time the Medici family controlled the Papal throne. In fortress style, it was set behind stone pillars and a wall of like dimension one viewed from the street. Once the weighty iron doors gave way to entry, an expansive pebbled courtyard bedecked with bougainvillea, oleander and geraniums of vibrant colors broke the austere setting of the white stucco edifice. Its Palladian windows were three meters high, leaded, opening onto terraces and gardens unable to be seen by anyone except those whose presence was accepted by the Mother Superior and the doctors of the clinic, whose consultation rooms were set aside as part of the magnificent interior. The specialty of the medical division was related to stress disorders, drug rehabilitation, births, deaths and patients in remission from cancer. The facilities were of the latest technology, perfect for a woman waiting the term of her pregnancy. Nuns, devoted to Christ, taking the vow of silence, had received vigorous training in nursing, serenity encompassed the ambiance, a sanctuary to peace.

Santo Spirito's grandeur was one of simple elegance with hushed voices, quiet footsteps, exceptional religious paintings on white stucco vaulted walls and dark heavy furniture that glowed with polish setting off Rococo curves. The rich arrived with their linens, maids, butlers, silver whatever they chose and claimed apartments that looked to the sea and the volcano, Mount Etna. Hallways were ten foot wide domed corridors with original pavement floors of terracotta stone. Priests cloaked in long black vestments were attached to a separate wing and visited daily saying mass, hearing confession and penance for sins, giving extreme unction to the dying and similar to physiatrists on staff, consoled those wishing guidance and counsel.

The Sisters of Convento di Santo Spirito, from the order of Santa Maria della Gracia, were Carmelites, attired in immaculate white linen covering them entirely except their face and hands. Long, black wooden rosaries hung at their waist reminding Esmeralda of the nuns in South Africa. All moved as phantoms, most having taken the vow of silence. Meals were private. When one entered the consecrated halls of the Convento di Santo Spirito a sense of being in another century, another world was its message, perfect for Esmeralda.

She had the foresight to bring many books and her laptop to stay in touch with the outside world should she care to. This lie she told everyone, but the truth was she needed technology to know more about how to terminate her pregnancy. Telephones were not encouraged nor was anything having to do with the word 'noise.' The Convent was one of sublime peace, pacific in its quest to avoid distractions from the outside world. Guests did not speak to one another and looked downwards respecting privacy if met in the garden, hallways or library. All were incognito.

"Oh! to be there now!" thought Esmeralda, as thoughts on this stormy night in Capri turned to serrated memories. Life never was the same after what she did at the Convent. She was scared. When I speak with my lawyers this day I will be vague in recollections. I'll say there are blank spots in my memory, delirium obscured my recollection at the time from numerous drugs given to save my life as I struggled to live knowing my baby was stillborn. He is sealed in his coffin, as I wanted him, buried in the family crypt. He rests with Gianni and with my sin. Lying had become a part of her daily life. To deceive her attorneys, those of Serena's, and should they discover the truth - to proclaim the prescribed pills she knew nothing about and possibly caused hallucinations. This would not phase her. No one would know the truth. She drained the infant of his vital breath, his juices.

After the first week at the convent, Esmeralda learned the routine using it to set her plan in motion. Doctors lived in villas throughout the enchanting village of Taormina and left the premises by seven at night. The nuns and one priest were housed on the grounds separately in a far off wing. A mid-wife, a woman of forty-five, Rosamaria Esposito, who brought over three hundred babies into the world, (or so she said – and God knows how many abortions thought Esmeralda) - lived below the hillside, outside the wall of the Convent in an unsavory part of the village of Taormina, the part tourists never see.

"Birth to me is a miracle and I shall be beside you always, Contessa. I'm here to protect you and shield you from anything you don't want anyone to know. You can tell me everything and I will understand."

"I was once so full of belief, so full of religion, and then my husband was taken from me in the most horrible tragedy. I tried to love God, but I am so sorry, so very very sorry, and I pray I'll be forgiven..." Esmeralda was speaking the truth yet with another truth unspoken never thinking that the wise woman from the hillside could grasp the greatness of her sorrow and wickedness of the act she wished to perform.

"I followed my Mother into this profession....seventy years we Espositos have been midwives...we have very few cases that ever happened where the little ones, the innocent babies were not protected...yours is thriving inside you. I can feel it, God and goodness will prevail...don't worry about anything....but if you care...and if you are...my silence is yours....."

One look at her prematurely aged face told Esmeralda she had an ally. It was only a question of money. The woman was in need. Shoes are the clue to a person's circumstances. The woman who visited her three-times day and in the evening before she left at six, later at eleven, had one pair of shoes that had seen the cobbler's hammer a dozen times. Their eyes met and in precise Italian Esmeralda began to discuss her sad circumstances about the death of Gianni, never giving a hint of what deeds she was constructing gaining the midwife's sympathy, hiding all evidence out of sight.

In a few days, she won Rosemarie's loyalty especially when she mentioned she would like to make a private contribution to her as Count Zianni would have done if he were alive. (One that the convent would never know about.)

"Surely," she stated flattering the peasant woman, "my mid-wife is more important to my well being than the nuns." This augured well with Signora Rosamaria Esposito, mother of eight children, believing all the stories she heard concocted over the twelve years she was in service to the privileged.

"Dearest Contessa, I am with you in all things, in everything you want. My experience, my wish is what I want for you. I am Sicilian. With me you have *omerta,* silence. Whatever passes between us, no one will ever know."

Esmeralda recounted stories, similar in deception to how Danny McSweeney fooled the nuns in Johannesburg. Esmeralda made a point to stress Gianni was of very dark complexion, with kinky hair so unlike hers and mentioned this while embroidering bibs for the baby to wear.

Rosamaria and the nuns viewed the care she took with her needlework for the infant, empathized with her sorrow, and believed in the young widow's wish to produce an heir she would love as no other.

"Experience has taught me, Contessa," said the wise Sicilian woman, "each of us has our own right to privacy. My vocation makes me a part of that privacy." She took Esmeralda's hand, looked into her eyes and kissed her cheek. "Still your mind, only God knows what I know." Her words never left Esmeralda and on this stormy night in Capri she called to memory the bond she had with a complete stranger who changed her life.

Yet the haunting memory remained and while the pressure to reveal facts within hours hung heavy in her heart, Esmeralda's conscious spoke. The strain of everything I'd experienced made me react as I did. Faced with the bizarre, I emptied my perfume bottles a week before and filled them with prussic acid and other toxic medicine. If the child survived the birth, before he took his first breath, one whiff of this toxic would asphyxiate him, the acid that leave a trace. That particular bottle I put close to my night table.

Her mind returned to the past.

Once she realized her plot was in place, it was a question of time. Which night she'd fuel herself with the mix of amphetamines and labor inducing drugs. They would have a dual effect breaking her amniotic fluid and begin the internal hemorrhaging to expel the baby. She wasn't afraid of the pain; she'd arranged everything for the lurid murder.

The umbilical cord is the clearest part of us from the placenta she recalled when she asked her Doctor how he would cut it. Inquiring further, Would it hurt? Deceiving everyone knowing her plan was to be alone. If illegal immigrants hid themselves in containers to expel a birth, she was no different. Survival made women betray their own. Her own Mother abandoned her to a savage. The drugs would begin to go into effect at eleven. Everyone would be asleep. She took a large white pillow and placed it beside her. There was an emergency button near her bed. She'd ring that in time. It was essential she was alone. It would take time for help to arrive.

The hour was near...Esmeralda's nadir had arrived. She took the drugs, swallowing them rapidly and waited. She kept a candle lit by her bed and extinguished her lights. The baby had been active all day exhausting her. It was as if he wanted to remind her he was alive. She refused to give way to his signs of life.

Twenty minutes. Thirty. Her body temperature began to change. She had consumed a larger dosage than necessary. There was no chance for a replay or failure. It had to work this one time. By forty minutes past the hour, one of the drugs began to take a stronger effect. It was a nightmare....she had to stay awake, not hallucinate...

How can I forget the shooting pains that raced throughout my stomach while the baby who was not ready to be born fought for survival? Contractions increased. It was past midnight and I was in full labor. I touched my vaginal wall believing I'd dilated to a large degree and the agony of pain continued. The hour was one, then two in the morning and I suffered like my baby through it all, not giving way to morphine smuggled into the room from my drug supply, tucked inside my pillow. The atmosphere was one of fear, terrible fear of the unknown. What I was doing to my baby and myself terrorized me. No one would understand how frightened I was. It mattered little if I would die. What I wanted more than anything - was for him to die - and for me - to survive the evil act of my wicked soul. I knew Lamaze breathing techniques and used them knowing I was going to deliver my baby myself.

There was no doubt to my intentions. I had made the decision and it was a question of when or if I would call for the mid-wife and later the sisters for help. I could silence the tongue of the mid-wife, the nuns took the vow of silence.

Pains increased, my water broke, blood gushed between my legs. Five in the morning, then five thirty, bells rang in the square, soon the nuns would be awake, called to prayer. My head was on fire. My body sweat with the fluids throughout my body as the baby pushed and kicked wildly out of control.

He was in a spasm fighting for life. I positioned my legs and back for the thrust I knew that was to come. It was close to six. My bed was the scene of a murder, blood gushed everywhere. The pain intensified. My breathing panted like a ravenous dog. PUSH...........PUSH.....push I told myself.....PUSH our eight-month old son from this body of mine with an indescribable force; the force of life - but this would be the finale, the force of death. With all my might, I struggled to expel him, my water burst, placenta spurted, a bloodbath ensued.

Suddenly he came drenched in amniotic fluid, placenta and blood, the sight of him I will live with the rest of my days. The umbilical cord wrapped round his neck, yet with us united hanging between my legs and his. In my exhaustion, before he could take his first breath of life, in the feverish pitch of hell, everything I'd planned happened quickly. I passed the bottle of acid under his nose, grabbed the pillow and held it down upon his face bathed in placenta and blood, black as I thought but for that instant seemed mulatto - or was he black?... with the slime of birth everywhere discoloring his wet hair. His face! A contorted face with a head smashed, too large! It was true. My roots claimed the race, from my white body, a black child that looked on this wicked night a mongoloid. His features were grotesque.

With the limited strength of my being, having endured the frightful night of a murder I'd created, I pressed harder on the pillow for him to lose life. His little hands and feet escaped in the last panic to catch breath slipping out from under the cushion as I continued to suffocate him by constricting his neck until he lost consciousness.

Then he lay concealed, lifeless. His struggle for life was over. It felt like a hundred hours for him to relinquish his control of life. I couldn't bear to see him, to touch him. I screamed for the midwife, she seemed to be there instantly - or was it my imagination? - removing the pillow soaked with blood and after-birth between my legs, his dead body lay lifeless between them. I collapsed, blew out the candle, pressed the emergency button, frantic and waited.

The wait was an eternity. I didn't want to look at the carnage. It was the second massacre in my life inside of a month. There were no witnesses this time, I was sure my baby was dead. I was never so pleased to rid myself of anything like this sin. The sin of mine, my mother's and father's. The sin that killed my husband. My act of violence was out of character. Thoroughly spent, I couldn't believe I'd done it. That night was my second murder, brutal like the first, my husband, Gianni's. I shook terrified at the ordeal of life and death. All seemed an eternity until the midwife arrived, but I was told later she was beside...she never left me...

Seeing my lifeless son, frightened me to death. I had killed. Murdered. I would go free. Play acting my part of the bereaved widow, the poor mother who lost her baby on a lonely night in Sicily alone, with no one beside her, whose husband's death created the dual shock, no one would know the difference. They would all view me as a saint. I had put a curse upon myself, creating the worst sin of mankind, infanticide. The guilt never left me. It took residence in the hardness of my heart and I wanted to die. I was wrong to kill the child. I should have killed myself.

My heavy door opened. I remember in my stupor I thought it was my midwife.

A nun rushed in. I became hysterical. The sweet sister on duty paid less interest to the infant seeing instantly it was dead. Her quest was to save my life. Within moments, in silence, two, three more nuns were tending me. All seemed an eternity...I was told later the midwife never left my side....

Everyone believed I'd given premature birth to a stillborn child and the midwife consoled me speaking a million beautiful words of kindness, the religious ones voicing silent prayers beside my bed, the priest - like a haunting dream - telling me, “He’s been baptized,” all sung to me like a hymn from another world with a dozen faceless voices, everything was gruesome. The midwife cut the umbilical cord and in my dazed state, lifted the child from the bed. I didn’t want to look at him. I shook with fear. As those good people tended to me, they never realized I was the Devil. The baby was dead and I was cold as marble. I fought the nuns and midwife who tried to sedate me.

No one understood the terror I’d inflicted on my baby, something impossible to forget. I begged them, “Keep the infant wrapped beside me,” they believed it was out of love. From a distance, I saw a contorted head as Rosemaria wrapped him in swaddling clothes and covered his dead face. I needed to speak to the mid-wife before delirium would take me with the sedation. They thought me brave. I was on fire with pain but it was of no consequence, hell was in my soul.

The nuns crossed themselves, breaking their silence, making the sign of the cross on me, “We will never forget you. We will never forget this baby. God will never forget the two of you.”

What I felt at that moment no words can describe. Drained of all emotion, exhausted from the poison that consumed my baby, my body and my mind, I met with God’s wrath. I will never utter this to any living soul.

“Don’t take the baby,” I pleaded, crazed.

“We will keep him here. The priest is coming,” said Rosemaria. Two nuns stood by, their garments full of blood from cleaning me and removing the baby whom Rosamaria placed in a small basket near my bed. She understood everything. Whether she thought I had viled myself having sex with a black man, I never knew. She would swear testimony and declare my baby was white and stillborn. Our eyes met. They said everything. I would speak to her when the shock and panic abated.

“We are giving you sedatives and pain killers. You must rest.” Rosamaria injected a drug into my arm. Her kind voice matched her gentle touch to my face. I urged her to come closer to hear my whisper.

"Please," I begged, "write on the birth certificate he was white and still born."

"But Contessa," she declared, "he is white...I've taken care of everything. Please Dear One, rest. I promise you, all has been taken care of."

Saying those words, I became hysterical, pulling her closer, whispering, "Our son was born white, I killed for no purpose...Our son was born white, our son was born white...." Those words were the last I remembered, the sedation took hold and I lost all senses.

Later, I came to semi-conscious. What I did that night was barbaric but no one except me and Rosamaria would ever know. The curse of this birth and death I would bear all my life.

"Where am I?" my voice echoed later, "What have I done?" thoughts raced in turmoil. I closed my eyes and renewed all the tragedy of my life. Before long I realized I was asleep. Waking again, my heart was seized with fear and emotion. I made my plan, resentment in my heart. My parents had destroyed me and my young family.

I slept, delirium took me, Rosamaria was always near. When I woke I heard her say, "I will send for the priest."

"No...no...not now." I refused to see him not understanding he'd been praying at my bedside, giving my son extreme unction. Out of my mind with panic, he thought, as the rest, I was hysterical because my beloved baby was dead. I was sedated again. Afterwards, lying in the unfamiliar room feeling weak, in a bed not my own, the moan of the baby's suffocation came to haunt me remembering how his little body shook struggling until death took him. I recalled his tiny feet, his hands clenched in a fist that opened without life at the end.

The midwife tended me, "Everything has been done as you wished. You must rest." Her comforting words closed the drama of my barren heart. The crime never left me and it never will.

Rosamaria and I never spoke about the birth, the death or my circumstances. She visited me everyday, sometimes sitting beside my bed holding my hand as tears flowed from my eyes.

"It is not for me to judge," she made the sign of the cross on my forehead, lips and breast and we sat in this way day after day. She was the only person I wanted beside me. Her wise eyes knew everything.

"I removed all the things you would not want here," she said a day after the baby was born, before Gianni's mother was to arrive. "Your baby is resting in the sleep of peace, ready to be buried when you return home."

"Has he been embalmed?'

"I have taken care of everything. Your secret rests with me. Rest, my dear Contessa. Rest."

"Grazie Rosamaria." All was unspoken, the Sicilian way.

The next day Gianni's Mother was beside me and never burdened me with conversation. Prior to her arrival, the baby's postmortem was handled by the midwife for no trace of the evil deed of drugs and his mixed race to be examined. His small coffin of bronze was sealed and kept at the mortuary in the clinic. When Sanjeev came to escort me and Mother back to Rome to bury the baby in the family crypt, I sat in a wheel chair weeping, wanting the coffin to contain me to lie beside my husband and our dead baby. I left Convento di Santo Spirito. Rosamaria was asked to come to see me in Rome giving her the money to do so. She dutifully came after the family's pilgrimage to the cemetery to bury the baby.

I wanted Rosamaria near. She had been witness to the second most tragic part of my life and never questioned me for the reasons why I had killed my baby. I surmised she thought I was a drug addict, had defiled myself with a Negro and saw the child was deformed. The birth certificate was signed by her, notarized and part of public records, as he stated, it said, *"White. Stillborn."*

After her visit in Rome, Rosamaria never had to work again. Through my bank in Switzerland, with my own funds, cash was placed in her hands that made her retirement at forty-five possible. Her allegiance to me was without a hint of blackmail. I came to understand as she tenderly held my hand during those meditative times when I only wanted her near, she was the victim of incest and had aborted a child her own father gave her. I never divulged the facts of my sin and never saw her again after she told me her story.

I return to my narrative…

My mourning brought everyone closer to me, something I didn't want. I distanced them and they attributed it to bereavement too overwhelming for anyone to assume. I was elevated to a status of martyr in the Zianni family and their idolization descended upon my vile character. Each embrace was a nail in my body knowing I was more evil than my parents.

With exceptional sympathy from everyone, Nigel Pembrooke entered my life as friend but he was in disguise. He was a suitor. It was no secret he'd been unhappily married for most of his years to Carolyn; cold, anorexic Carolyn who gave him little respect. Nigel made it a point to visit me frequently from London to Rome or when I was at Beaumont Manor or the house in Kensington. Life had become unbearable and he entered my scenario on time. I was despondent, depressed. The solitude of idle hours, calculating my miserable future, afraid I'd lost everything, including my mind, plagued me. With his attention, my vanity boosted and I saw my opportunity.

I recall it was winter and my need to be alone - confused as I was - made me return to Villa Pina. The house was deserted. Only Sanjeev was in attendance who left me alone. I couldn't gather my thoughts, my horrible experiences and vile soul made me turn to pills with frequency. To my great surprise Nigel followed me to Capri. His first words left no doubt to his intention. "I had only one desire," he said, "to see you again."

I was taken in by his charm. He seemed so sure, so much in love and made me smile about trivial things. After a time, he asked to marry yet, with respect, kept his distance. He knew how to maneuver me and I trusted him. I was alone, vulnerable and he appeared as a savior. Foolishly, I believed he could help resurrect a new life.

Considering these last years we've had, superficial as they were, Nigel filled the void. Nigel Pembrooke was someone my late husband trusted as a friend. Eight months after I'd lost Gianni, he made his intentions clear. Nigel cited he couldn't remain in his marriage any longer because of his feelings for me. I urged him not to change his life. I wasn't in love with him. My feelings were raw. He promised it didn't matter. His want was to protect me. He believed it his role to love me. "There's more to life than being dressed in black. I don't want to see you like this." He touched my heart, my cold brittle heart and his elegance promised another life. His wish to unburden me from death, help me assume the heavy duty of the Zianni mantle, being the widow whose sorrow was evident to all, was changed with his attention. Everything he said and did made me think of a new beauty to life.

He begged me to marry. I was so appreciative to have someone who knew so little about me be his next wife. Affection for him bloomed. His want was to look after my welfare, or so he said. He was consoling, gentle and amusing and he didn't push me to be sexually intimate. He would caress my cheek with his hand, but no more. Now I realize it was that his libido was not what I assumed, like most of Nigel, so much of what I assumed was not a part of his persona. In my delusion to remake my life, I attributed qualities to Nigel I never found once wed.

Time passed. I was almost thirty-four and needed someone to be beside me. I couldn't be alone. My sins were so great, I had to have distraction, I had to begin another play, another fantasy, another role and Nigel came to play my leading man.

At the time, I trusted Nigel, relied on him, a man seventeen years my senior. His guidance would help me, a father figure in a way. I never gave notice to his direction to assure me in my fragile state to be careful of all the financial decisions I had to make. He showed his intent and divorced Carolyn with alacrity. He became an important part of my life and privy to my portfolio. I took him into my confidence as a friend, I took him into my heart as an ally and I took him into my bed as a whore.

We married within eighteen months of widowhood and luck changed like the turbulent sea and this stormy tonight…and the extraordinary wealth of my late husband descended upon me, and with a calculating heart I managed funds, listened to Nigel and advisors, doing the minimal for Serena and Mother Zianni who eventually died of a broken heart. I distanced myself from all Ziannis. Nigel and his position in society, my wealth claimed our days. The mood swings of life with its color, scent, violence and peace, brought a new beginning with Nigel Pembrooke, yet ours was never a union of love. His superficiality became too evident, he bored me.

By our second year, I couldn't bear for him to touch me. His cocky aristocratic voice and personality became a monotonous broken record as he basked in the wealth my lifestyle that now, was shared as my spouse. I began to treat him as one does a dog you don't want to put down, whose sloth and parasitic character is tolerated and ignored. My life and his were viewed by everyone like a dream, as a Technicolor picture in a frame. That's all it was - an image of two individuals with *bella figura*. In truth, we had nothing more. Nigel served his purpose. I needed a husband and he filled his role. It could have lasted but I knew it would eventually end like this. Our union going to a divorce doesn't surprise me. I will give him as little as I can and let him resume his pontificating in treasured English halls and manor estates looking for his next wife.

Serena's allegations have come to call. That surprised me, my wicked Father wanting his financial due. Everyone wanting to claw me for money. I will endure and survive. I will see this through somehow… and somehow sleep came to Esmeralda as the storm raged in Capri and the clock chimed five.

XXVII

Legacy

By daybreak, the storm ensued without the violence of the night before. Esmeralda calmly coated pink varnish on her long nails. Her maid had served breakfast; Sanjeev occupied himself with details to settle unexpected guests.

"Indifference is power." She spoke aloud admiring her hands. "It all comes down to money." The monkeys had sufficient time from yesterday's meetings to devalue me, dissect me and today will be my greatest challenge. There were two attitudes one can take: That of the guilty or that of the innocent. She finished her nails, giving ample time for the polish to dry, thinking - always thinking.

What can I say to them?...that time has changed society to a degree. Yet, those years the trauma of Apartheid was a part of life that formed ideas, actions, values. There was a distinction to being white. The blacks were savages, rejected citizens without civility and any rights. Lawlessness swept the nation at the time I lived there, chaos reigned in black society, if you can call the uneducated society. It was more like harrowing hell in which they lived. I may ask these opponents:: Do you have any idea what my view of life in South Africa was when Botha• was Prime Minister

• Africaans nickname for Botha, The Big Crocodile

and President…at the time of my escape, President Botha, known to order over 40,000 people whipped as punishment, declared a State of Emergency, restrictions including house arrest were imposed. The military had sweeping powers. South African Broadcasting Corporation provided propaganda, everyone lived in fear. do you know of his paranoia that became ours? Have you lived through Apartheid? Do you know the fear? The prejudice? Botha controlled white thought, broadcasting, politics. Interracial marriage was prohibited, torture and death ensued if discovered, barbaric cruelty was the norm, etched on every black face for crimes and whites shuttered from fear as well, expecting at anytime to be victims of Negro angst. White power was instilled in me. It was the only way to live.

Today, strange as it may seem, though sophisticated society may embrace a mix of race, some cosmopolitans even lauding its virtues, little has changed in South Africa. Blacks are still isolated, impoverished, unschooled, living in squalor just as before without running water or sewage, there's vast unemployment and wildcat strikes that end in violence, always against the blacks. Children are too poor to receive a decent education and disease is everywhere in these communities, medicine out of date when it reaches the hospitals that treat them. The main beneficiaries continue to be white South Africans even with the end of the Apartheid regime.

They will question me……"What you did was violent."

I will answer: It was the price of extreme inequality. I was a victim, brought up in a country that officially ended Apartheid in 1994. But it was 1990 when I left, before the extraordinary change. My life was fraught with uncertainties and tension unable to be understood unless you lived through my passage.

Serena would scream. "Your husband loved you. He would have understood."

I don't know, I'd say, if he would have accepted what I had to confess. South Africa when I grew up was an sealed off country from the rest of the world. There was no Internet, CNN, mobile phones. The language itself, Africaans, was a way to keep South Africa isolated. There was an extraordinary inner struggle in opposition to Apartheid, a state-of-emergency law in 1985 had been passed. I can understand the horror that my Mother felt, her anguish. Police brutality was rising, arrests rampaged through the streets, all was berserk, mobs of anti-Negro protests produced violence unimaginable, I grew up in this environment, my white grandmother slaughtered because she had given birth to a mixed breed....had I been black, it was hell on earth."

I didn't want Gianni to be a victim of my history, or our child. I was without equality, and I am to this day too narrow, uneducated. In South Africa life was dangerous, a phenomenon that haunts me. Today, after streets have run in bloodshed and political compromises attained, the country, the world, is different.

Miscegenation will be considered fashionable by British society although people of all ages, races and creeds will continue to whisper about these things differently in private. In public, a face of tolerance will be shown to achieve the idea of liberal thinking in a liberal world yet even high blacks will want to breed with other high blacks and certainly associate with those of like mind. It will come down to education and how large a scope one's mind is. It will come down to money and *bella figura* and education.

She studied her reflection in the mirror, brushed her hair, fastened a gold necklace to her slender neck, full of self-possession. Her eyes evaluated her person in the Belle Epoque mirror as she slipped into a Chanel suit.

Her mind was contorted. Logic misconstrued. Misconstrued to survive. I committed a sin.... Who's to judge me? These lawyers? A priest hearing confession? Both have sinned themselves.

She painted her lips scarlet. Lawyers manipulate the law, priests do the same with religion. Self-righteous priests! Moral bullies! Who tell me if I confess I'm exonerated.

Last night brought a new prospective. With a different set of principles. Somehow I'll escape this witch hunt of Serena's.

She continued admiring herself, smoothing hand cream on her hands, to stall for time. One more coat of polish was added to her nails.

Serena, and these lawyers are the last people I want in my life. Not one of them lived as I. They'll judge me in ways they know nothing about. That's why the law is crooked, the Catholic Church a sham.

She recollected the last time she saw the priest in the Convent when everyone believed her a saint. The glint of judgment was in his eye.

"Do you wish to confess your sins?" He knew she was tainted. There I was lying half dead in a bed struggling to regain strength and he condemned me a sinner.

How can a priest speak of marriage, abortion, adultery and declare what's right without ever setting foot in that territory? The same is true of the lawyers, Serena and the others.. Did they walk in my steps? It's as preposterous as me trying to be a heart surgeon like Samir knowing I'm ill equipped to hold a human heart in my hand and try to save a stranger that means nothing to me.

With this resolve Esmeralda reached for her phone and dialed David Arthur's number in the guest suite. She paid no mind if circuits or if mobile phones functioned. They'd function for her.

"Are we to proceed today?"

As Serena Zianni's team met in Ischia, Esmeralda Pembrooke faced her attorneys to reveal further details of her past and accept counsel's advice how to construct her defense.

"A bad memory," Esmeralda said walking down her long circular staircase, "is a great convenience."

As she unraveled the second part of her history, her legal team sat absorbed with every word. In the confines of her library she spoke guardedly, "I'm human. Everyone has something to hide." The statement she'd considered. She watched individuals wince at her remark. They sit in my home, clocking fees and appraise me. In their own way, like my adversaries, they'll ultimately crucify me.

All are narrow minded racists, the type of people who disgust me, truly disgust me and will sprout forth with information how I will be dismantled. Their minds are shrunk in law books. Narrow minds lack elasticity. Their addiction is they cannot see. They cannot feel. I'm human. Life offered little choice. I am black. I am white.

Before elaborating on complex legal issues and financial ramifications confronting Esmeralda and Serena, it would not be out of place to speak of the others.

Once telephone lines functioned with a degree of success, the outside world made contact.

"What the devil are you doing, Monty?" Barked S. I. Morehouse, Chairman of Gazette News, the conglomerate of newspapers and magazines that was Monty Daniel's life bread.

"CNN announced one hell of a scoop last night. Get your ass in gear! You gave me some cocked up story about being *in* with the Zianni clan wangling big money out of me. We've been fucked big time out of one hell of a story!" Morehouse's angst came loud and clear. Monty was put on notice.

"Consider yourself in front of a firing squad! There's mud all over my face. Whose decision was it to run with this daft column of yours yesterday? What was it?...filler copy? Talking nonsense about Brad Pitt! Who the hell cares about Brad Pitt when every God damned newspaper has picked up on the Zianni fortune catapulting!"

Morehouse could have knocked Daniels over with a feather. The line went dead between Capri and New York as he gathered facts from his boss hearing the words thrashed through the static of the international connection. Panicky, he redialed taking copious notes.

"I urge you S.I., power was cut, it was the storm..."

"Bullshit about a storm! CNN got the story in Rome with the fuckin' storm!"

"I've got the inside story people will kill for, S.I. Don't panic. CNN will turn green. No one has what I'm privy to."

As Monty Daniels lied through his teeth, the line went dead the second time as rain pelted torrents. Daniels swore like a stevedore with his position at stake. "What the hell is the inside story?" he fumed to himself, mad as hell. Like a rabid dog fighting for a bone, he redialed New York.

As the scandalmonger tried to reconnect without success, Jarvis, usually high strung, lingered in bed undisturbed by the sudden stress of his partner.

"Holy Christ Jarvis. Morehouse tells me CNN announced Esmeralda's a fake!"

Engleton's face dropped non-pulsed.

"Hello…Hello S.I.…It's me again…"

Nigel avoided the company of everyone. His breakfast was served in his room with *The Times* as Labradors reclined on the marble floor by his side. The Englishman resembled a king in his counting house, counting all his money, listing assets of Esmeralda's, considering how much he could achieve financially. Access to some of their homes was necessary. After all, it was he who orchestrated buying Palace Gardens, the former home of Barbara Hutton? He wondered what more was possible. Entitlement to a few months at Villa Pina, Beaumont or Kensington's new manse was not out of line. He lifted his phone and dialed Baker, Baker & MacCloud.

"That you Reginald?" Hearing the affirmative Nigel continued, "My dear old thing, be a good chappie and go for Esmeralda's jugular. I'm making a list of antiques. Work a phrase in on the settlement I want use of the houses when the final split comes."

Nigel listened as his topaz eyes took on a mercenary intensity and a cunning smile formed on his razor thin lips. "Serena must have given that story to CNN. The whole world's going to feel for me, Reginald. I want to play this to the hilt. Pembrooke's Betrayed! I can see the headlines. An exclusive from the horse's mouth, by Jove! that's a good one! See which paper offers the best deal, *The Times* or *The Daily Mail*. Try *The New York Times,* too...maybe CNN. You get 5%. Squeeze them Reginald. I've got a great story. From here, I'll see what Daniels will pitch."

Nigel listened to the voice of his counsel. "Reginald, I have taken my weakness and I'm not afraid of anything. I've surpassed it by clear thinking now with this break.. Thank God I loathe Esmeralda." He signed off and thought of the Guido Reni painting.

Samir made contact with Jacqueline discreetly informing her to have their luggage ready to depart Villa Pina. "A drama's at hand." Nervously he urged "Don't break any links of friendship with Nigel or Esmeralda, make an excuse about the twins, say we must return to New York."

"En Samir, zee others?"

"Plans are to return to Capri as soon as the weather settles to sail, at best, tomorrow. Darling, just as we arrived on Whitney's boat with Shabadiba, Véronique, Stefano, we'll leave. Nigel's plan is to divorce Esmeralda."

"No Darling you are wrong. Hre zhey are very nice with each other."

"Don't believe it. Play along, Jacqueline. Everything's happened. Whitney's issued proceedings against Lynne. He's crazy in love with Olympia," he added, "things look very nice, my darling Jacqueline. Brian will join Naomi and drive to Tuscany."

"Oh la la, zis is very exciting. My Samir you be zee good boy?"

"Jacqueline. Jacqueline." And his phone went dead just as he began speaking erotic words sending her passionate kisses. She was a drug for him, his aphrodisiac. There was a gnawing urge to get back to her as soon as possible.

Whitney and Olympia had their own plans. Both had accessed how they viewed the future. Olympia agreed it best to leave for London directly from Ischia and shortly thereafter notify Tong their engagement was over - enough with her fetish for 'yellow fever.' Her belongings would be packed at Villa Pina and deposited on Whitney's yacht along with the others who sailed with Whitney from Portofino. An immediate exit from the Pembrooke's was everyone wish. Timing was perfect. This arrangement would produce no questions that Olympia was with Whitney. Lynne would welcome scandal wanting to name Olympia co-respondent. She wouldn't get her chance. Later, in London Olympia and Whitney would reunite.

Whitney's New York lawyers were contacted to commence divorce proceedings. "Contact Lynne at Villa Pina. Advise her a first class ticket from Naples to New York will arrive by courier. "Confrontation with my spouse is not something I relish. Handle the whole thing. Change the locks on the New York flat. Have her go to Greenwich."

As far as Whitney was concerned, he never would disembark the yacht, aptly christened by Lynne years ago, *"The Other Woman."* He'd enjoy the sail once the storm cleared from Capri to Portofino, from there fly to London and meet Olympia. Whitney's life was changing. He welcomed the artistic, younger ambiance that would bring him into another sphere of life. To offer Olympia the exhibit she wanted at the Tate was a delight. What delighted him further was her ability to arouse him and the promises she made that she would guarantee his books were published in London. He was making the right move. Soon he'd be an ex-pat, ex-spouse, ex-investment broker and rejoin the world as a new man.

Cat Renoir turned off her mobile phone. She never wanted to hear Mark Levy's voice again. She's asked Sanjeev to change her room. Her plan was to return to the centre of Capri while she still had Levy's credit card and purchase anything she could from whatever shops were open, including the array of jewelry shops along via Tragara. That would serve him right. Maybe life was to be in London with kind Peter Evans. He knows how to treat a lady properly.

Zofra and Mark Levy dawdled over breakfast in bed laughing at the weather praying for another intense storm. Levy had no inclination to call Cat, Nigel, Esmeralda, Stella or Marco. "Frig em in Capri, Zofra."

His hairy arm embraced her waist, "I knew the minute I saw you, you're the kinda woman I've been looking for all my life."

"I'm a cougar........I'll teach you some things, Mark Baby..."

He licked his lips, pushed the button that automatically lowered the *persiani* of their terrace, extinguished the lights in their darkened room and rummaged between the sheets to replay scenes from the night before.

Ring. Ring. Ring. Lynne took time to answer her mobile phone, resting in her suite. "I know its a guilty husban' ...Its ringin' like Chrismas en Whitney Jameson can wait." Abandoned as she was, furious pride niggled at her. She cleared her throat to sound unaffected by his betrayal. "Hellllooo"

"Mrs. Jameson?"

Startled, she replied, "Yes it es..."

"Bernard Epstein from New York."

"Whateva are you doin' callin? Ya'll lookin' for Whitney?"

"No Lynne," the attorney replied, thinking had Lynne been born a dog, she would have been a pit-bull. "Whitney's asked me to ring."

"Why in tarnation?" Her eyes went in circles, speculating.

"Sorry to break the news, Lynne. Alitalia will deliver a first class ticket for you Naples to New York non-stop. I've been advised by Whitney..."

"Why what eva es the matta?"

"Whitney's filing for divorce Lynne."

The South Carolina belle froze. "Why ya'll must be kiddin' me..."

"I'm sorry, Lynne, I'm not."

"Well now you listen here Bernard Epstein," her rant began in a shrill voice to make all birds in Capri fly off in terror. "You've been our lawya for goin'on twenty years en if Whitney's lost his mind, well ya'll tell him, I haven't lost mine!" Her lips shriveled as her high pitched voice gained volume, "En I'm refusin' yes Lynne Jameson is refusin.' I'm neva gonna consent to divorcin'. En that's final en whevea he is, tell him to drop dead."

"I'll pass along your message, but without alarming you, I do believe it best you seek counsel."

"Seek counsel? Why you brazen lawya! I'm not steppin' down from being Mrs. Whitney Jameson en that's final."

"Your tickets will arrive 10:30 tomorrow morning. A limousine will take you to the house in Greenwich."

"Tickets my hide. Bunch of traitors. It'll take more than tickets to have that coward of a two-faced Whitney push me otta his life! En Greenwich! Lynne Jameson is not goin' to any country house. I'm gonna live on Park Avenue."

Her goals for the future were all that interested her. Greed and envy had their place. "If there's eva is a third party, Mista Epstein, ya'll tell Whitney afta I'm finished with him, he won't live to kiss any hussy. I'm gonna take him to da cleanas." She slamed the phone shut.

Marco slept late. Whatever was going on, what did he care? He rang for his breakfast and listened to rain falling outside moving his naked body to the Persian rug beside his bed. Taking yogic position he began to chant, lost in meditation, serene, free of negative energy.

Shortly thereafter a pretty Italian maid with long brunette hair entered. Perhaps she was eighteen, dressed in a starched pink costume, she carried breakfast on a tray. Alighting from his favorite yoga position, lying in shavashana, Marco walked towards her. It was impossible for her to push him away, delicately he stroked her thighs then felt for her opening between her legs. Similar to yesterday, he was able to plant a succulent kiss on her moist mouth as she held the tray trembling. His hands began to wander. "No, no, Signor!" Her resistance was adorable.

"Ritornera?"• He asked as her sweet face blushed.

• You will return?

"Si." He put his index finger to her lips and lifted her chin for a kiss. He was Marco Ricci. She would keep her promise. That kiss had stirred his cock just as the phone rang and the Italian trinket departed. "It has to be Stella. She's got radar eyes."

"Darling I was just going to ring. Didn't know the circuits were…" He was speechless hearing her prattle about Serena's mission on Ischia, knowing Gianni's sister intended to drop an international bombshell.

His wiry body strode across the bedroom barefoot, evaluating her gossip, which brought one question, "Where does this put the film?" Once answered, he stroked his *coglioni* and replied, "I knew Nicky would bail us out. Stella, Stella Darling! I'm missing you like mad, when are you coming? I'm aroused by your voice like the Eiffel Tower at its pinnacle, fired by your absence, too alone, my treasure."

A gentle knock resounded on his door. Marco ended the call. He attributed his behavior to habits of a lifetime, his to keep and enjoy.

"Have you faxed everything to Capri?" Frederico Spiga asked his team. Hearing the affirmative he went to confer privately with Serena. The friends had studied documents, their disbelief proved as shocking as was Serena's initially. To everyone's credit there was no back-biting. Everyone supported Gianni's sister and had no wish to involve themselves further with Esmeralda.

Scandals were no stranger to Capri but no one wished to be embroiled in this one.

Nigel was another matter. In due time he'd divorce and re-enter the fold. Loyalty was a British trait. "Old school tie," some called it. Their bond united, all saw Nigel part of that bond.

Speaking of Nigel earlier, Rupert's shyness disappeared.

"Nigel's in love with people." He said to Serena. "I'm in love with you."

She didn't have to speak. Her eyes conveyed everything. To discuss matters of the heart at time like this Serena didn't want. He's poor now but his patina of pedigree makes him charming. A man can be poor if he keeps his dignity and remains a gentleman. The way he speaks never changes, or the way he holds his head, bows when he sees a lady and genuflects to a Queen.

"We've waited many years. Let's do everything properly." She rejoined the group to listen to opinions and answer questions. The onus was on her. Formulating the action she alone would take to protect her family name and see justice done weighed on her conscious. Serena stood to re-inherit a fortune.

Luigi D'Albora cleared his throat while David Arthur spoke in a toneless voice, "It will come as no surprise to you, Esmeralda, your investments are imperiled." The cerebral lawyer began. "Assets of private equity with stakes for start up investments have made your personal worth surge in these last years since Gianni's death. The momentary malaise of funds, therefore, with you pledging all assets constitutes your entitlement to 35% of the funds that were appropriated for taxes out of Panama since taking control of Zianni Pharmaceuticals International. However, these private securities have taxes that will be levied as a requirement to appease any lien the two governments, England and Italy will accept as collateral. This is just a quick overview until Ernst & Whinney's report."

"There is the issue as to selling stock to unidentified sources," noted D'Albora, "investment advisors have warned the UK regulatory agencies will fix their attention on this."

"What remains to be liquidated are entirely private securities from Baron Beck. These, we know, are strictly secret in Luxembourg. No one knows the account holder. Is that correct?"

"Nigel is aware of my securities in Liechtenstein and Switzerland." The attorneys blanched. "Serena has every right to have you indicted." Announced David Arthur. "There are a dozen ways to speak of fraud.

Unfortunately you fall into categories that cannot be circumvented in either country."

"Esmeralda" added Arthur "as the tax lien by the Inland Revenue will be assessed at £40 million pounds, this takes in property in the UK and holdings, of course. Our initial plea for bail we see would be conservatively set at about £8 million should you decide to fight this issue. The UK government will accept this collateral and Italy will coincide with England, under European Community laws or vice versa. Whichever country, you will be under intense scrutiny, house arrest and unable to travel."

"Naturally, we have the ability to go to postponement as much as possible," David Arthur remarked.

"As we did with Andreotti," added Luigi D'Albora.

A daze of lawyers drowned on with dour conformity about the complexity of the laws of fraud. Esmeralda did not return their stares. They carp preaching as if on a pulpit, driving me from possessions. Everything's about money. The sermon they presented increased her stance of cold reserve.

"Are you criticizing me?" she questioned. "Whatever you think of me is none of my business."

"Of course not." David Arthur said immediately, D'Albora nodded in agreement while he yanked his neck from what seemed to be a tight collar, as David Arthur fingered his cuff links. Esmeralda was an outsider. She looked around the table sizing up everyone. They're nervous. This kind of money, this kind of crime sets me apart from all their clients.

Her lawyers were not about to challenge her....lawyer/client privilege et al. Their fees justified they would protect their client, whether they viewed her guilty or innocent. In some respects, they could keep this case on the books years, brewing in the caldron of legal bureaucracy between international courts. That is, if she were liquid. Their legal coffers had to be paid to continue. The very idea of *pro bono* was not a part of their profile.

Spiga made it clear all Zianni assets were frozen once allegations went forward to Court, that included real estate. Pembrooke had already issued directives to freeze his wife's private holdings. She sat before them, one of the richest women in Europe thirty-six hours ago, soon to be destitute.

Luigi D'Albora paused for the moment, a brief stammer accompanied his next remark, "Lawyers w-wwill resign without fees paid. Your passport will be confiscated, and you can be imprisoned or deported."

"There's an escrow account waiting investment," Elena D'Albora interjected, "stock regulatory pricing is being evaluated in London by your financial advisors. You are aware they couldn't arrive due to the storm."

"We cannot liquidate on demand, funds on deposit or any escrow accounts." Arthur noted.

"Nigel's frozen those," Esmeralda answered stone still.

"Philanthropic promissory notes have been recalled," Arthur announced, "the investment in the film, ESCAPADES, from what we understand, will be assumed by Whitney Jameson and Nicky Viscounti." He looked to Esmeralda. Gianni's friends had done her a favor.

The news did not surprise Esmeralda void of expression. To her mind, the canaries chirping made her head dizzy with laws, accusations and the expanse of fraud her life created. D'Albora broke worst accusation. "Penal law dictates and sets this case aligned with civil issues. The other side wants to exhume the body of the heir Zianni for DNA purposes, born, as records state, stillborn."

A chill went through Esmeralda.

"We will counter this." D'Albora said quickly viewing the impact it had on his client. "In our opinion, as his Mother, unless we receive a subpoena from the Italian State, only you can approve this, and an examination of his DNA." D'Albora looked down averting his gaze sensing the birth contained lies too unpalatable to discover.

"Esmeralda," Arthur announced, "Luigi and I have spent half the night and all of this morning conferring. We have engaged in a lengthy discourse with Frederico Spiga in Ischia. He's meeting there, you might as well know, with Serena and the retinue of Gianni's friends, including Stefano de Gesu, who left Capri yesterday morning. They support Serena. You are on the brink of complete disaster, financially and personally."

"We are not here," Luigi spoke, "to judge you. Both advocates had an outward calm that stilled her despair. "Why you assumed this fraudulent life will be in question by Serena, the Judge and the jury. We will not discuss the press for one can only imagine how they will want to ruin you. We cannot see how you can win, Esmeralda. Our responsibility is to make the explosion of these documents and what repercussions they will have on the stock of Zianni Pharmaceuticals and your future...and protect you as best we can."

"Financially and otherwise," David Arthur interrupted narrowing his eyes towards Esmeralda, "If you choose to proceed, a verdict can be appealed to avoid prison."

The room was utterly silent.

Esmeralda's face reflected no shame or anger as her past was exposed and legal ramifications claimed her destruction.

In her hushed voice, knowing brevity is the by-product of vigor, she began. She had to retain a position of strength, weakness is contagious and weakness never succeeds in anything - especially when dealing with sharks. Everyone moved closer to her position at the table to hear what she uttered precisely.

"Ever since I have known both of you, I've marveled at your expertise to zigzag the law." Esmeralda locked her eyes on Arthur and then D'Albora. "Let Serena's legal team put forward their scheme. Let her believe she has the upper hand." Her cold control was remarkable. Not a trace of emotion changed the tone of her voice.

"We must meet together on neutral territory without outsiders - Serena, me, our lawyers, and no one else. Tell Spiga my intent is to protect the Zianni name. That will appeal to my sister-in-law." She rose from the table, standing like a marble statue.

"I pay you. It's up to you. Figure out the rest."

Without another word, she moved from the room, like a phantom. The last words she spoke produced an echo through the library.

XXVIII

Arrangement

To pause from this part of the story, it will come as no surprise the influence the CNN disclosure had upon stock markets throughout the world. Zianni stock, which traded at £233.072 at the time of the announcement, plummeted to £125.864 within hours then teetered at £99 to £89.3. Brokers handling multi-national corporations and clients with formidable portfolios conferred in Tokyo, New York, London, Frankfurt. A money chase was on…gaining and losing echoing throughout the world as the economic crisis of Zianni Pharmaceuticals International shattered markets. Chaos was staggering.

Zianni's New York CEO conferred with his counterpart in London frantic for details. The Italian Chief of the conglomerate, Pietro Anselmi was livid. In a conference call to his Board colleagues, he took a brave initiative, speaking his mind, designing the only plan he could fathom. Over the last sixty hours, he had gorged himself on 'comfort food,' swallowing stress with every bite, increasing his girth considerably.

"We'll counteract this. I'm going to announce our new drug on Alzheimer's."

"What?" came astonished voices across the wires.

"Fuck The World Health Organization if they keep stalling on tests and didn't give the go ahead on this product. Screw the USA politicians!

God damned swine with their two-bit lives wanting to show constitutes they can hold up the Food & Drug Administration meddling with medicine. They don't know a god damned thing about science! A bunch of Motherfucking pansies afraid of taking the leap to the future to help afflicted whose brains will rot without ZHIMERS." He barked his plans, certain of his decision without giving one moment for anyone to contradict him. "This company will not be toppled by them or some tart Gianni was stupid enough to marry!"

He rang his legal team on the other phone, 'Put all on conference mode." Crisis management began with the alacrity known to those whose financial survival is at stake.

"Make a blanket statement. Quote me. ZHIMERS, our latest miracle drug that the World Health Organization has been testing for eighteen months and we in Europe, Asia and Latin America, New Zealand, Australia and China see as a cure to detain this dread decease by a decade (or more) will be released today to physicians worldwide. Any patient with the early effects of the disease will benefit from ZHIMERS. In fact, make that ZHIMMERS is the CURE to increase memory and regenerate the mind of the elderly and let's give it a percentage - 97%."

He paused collecting his words, "Let this be like the AIDS medicine that damn FDA and kiss-ass politicans held up for years. If they ask about the FDA our stance is they've been tardy to eradicate the disease in America and detain its advancement exactly as they did with AIDS. That'll get those cocked up Senators fuming."

He was on a roll, imagining how Bloomberg and NASDAQ would spotlight Zianni Pharmaceuticals International, confident in every respect, gaining control of his monumental decision...fantasizing how huge blocks of stock would trade within minutes. "I want it to read like this, "Since Sir Brian Korthorpe - whose work with the National Institute of Health, the Ecole Polytechnique Federale in Lusanne, the center of the EU's research project, isolated his findings of tobacco as a significant part in the remission of Alzheimer's ten years ago at the Zianni Centre at Cambridge University, with the most outstanding bio-tech scientists in the world - along with the knowledge of the World Health Organization - we at Zianni Pharmaceuticals International have furthered his findings with a remarkable pill to exit world markets today...that will revolutionize how this dreaded disease will be thwarted." A smile came to his lips. "ZHIMERS has a positive benefit-risk profile. Clinical trials have been extraordinary. Understanding the brain will take decades but with our work stem cells will be transformed into neurons and cultured thus providing substitutes for brain tissue. We stand behind our newest drug that has been studied by the Institute of Safe Medication Practices, the nonprofit, watchdog group in America that studies medication usage."

"ZHIMERS tested in senior care homes in ten diverse countries – you can detail those - add this – to over ten thousand people - without any side effects- make Zianni Pharmaceuticals International abide by their medical findings – stress this: patients who were doomed to this dread decease have shown a remarkable stability of mind once consistent treatment has been initiated using ZHIMERS, the Zianni miracle drug."

"Anything more?" came his Director of PR, somewhat nervously.

"Yes, this will scare the hell out of everyone...give the world the truth: By 2150 one-third of the world's population is expected to succumb to Alzheimer's."

"Are you sure?"

"Positive." Anselmi was pleased, his esteem surged considering what this meant for him and the company. "God damned stock will rollercoaster, soar, split and I'll be richer. I'm not about to have the company I devoted my life to go belly up."

"Do me a favor," he added to his legal team, "Check the Rockefeller Foundation. Ask if they want their name linked to this press announcement. They invested £20 million believing in Korthorpe years ago. The guy's a genius. That'll give added credence in the marketplace. I want this released within the hour......it has to go viral but first have the PR people smaltz it up with details."

He closed the phone, went to his bar and poured a triple scotch. "Get Brian Korthorpe on the phone," he said to his secretary.

"Surein' me honey I'm gonna get meself a first class ticket to Europe en be a rich man." Danny McSweeney guzzled his Guinness and looked to the redhead seated at the pub in Johannesburg. "Es just a matter of time til me eyes see the beautiful daughter of mine whose money is gonna take care of her Daddy in style. You ever hear of the luck of the Irish?" McSweeney pulled at his ginger hair and shoved his gut closer to the railing of the bar,

"Give me another, me luck's comin' I can feel it en I'll be takin' a little kiss from this here pretty lady." He plonked three rand on the sticky wooden counter roaring with laughter. The redhead moved closer. "Ya women are all alike. Like men when they struck gold."

She lit a cigarette with her wrinkled lips splashed with greasy paint and smiled showing agate teeth matching those of Danny's. He took the cigarette out of her mouth and shoved it in his own while his dirty hand caressed her ass. "A miracle's a happenin' me fair lass en a leprechaun's arrangin' a nice surprise. He's a'comin' with a pot a gold fur Danny McSweeney."

In Munich, Zumwelden & Zumwelden were briefed of the investigation by the Studio of Frederico Spiga from the beginning. When Serena Zianni received Danny McSweeney's letter, her hope was that the Baron would shed light on Esmeralda's past before she undertook a detective to validity McSweeney's allegations.

On a chilly day in Germany, while the sun shown in South Africa, the skies were clear in London and Rome and a rainbow began to form over the Bay of Naples, Zumwelden & Zumwelden sat waiting for their client, Baron Martin Heindrick von Beck to arrive. Had the choir master of the Basilica in Rome been in attendance, he would have recognized the skeletal figure of Rolf Zumwelden, the man who sat alone like a leper six years ago when Esmeralda Beck married Gianni Zianni.

The current of time was in the Baron's favor with all his advanced years of three-score-and-twenty. The Zumwelden brothers lauded their favorite client recalling the painful day years ago and how they orchestrated the Baroness' life.

"Gentlemen," the portly figure of Baron Beck addressed his lawyers arriving without anguish of the situation or the pain from his gouty toes. "Brief me on the state of affairs with the CNN's announcement yesterday." He was a man of keen intellect, in good humor. All would be arranged as he wished.

"An honor to meet you, Your Majesty." Elizabeth MacKenzie curtsied to Prince Charles and then Camilla, the Duchess of Cornwall.

"Prince William tells us you are a sculptress." Said the Prince whose manner made Elizabeth feel like she was Rodin. Her Mother mentioned he had the exceptional quality to concentrate on whomever he'd engage in conversation and to Elizabeth's delight everything she imagined was true. He addressed her as if she were an authority. Her ego was fired with enthusiasm. The Prince's Trust for Art was a legend throughout the world. Prince William had invited her to Highgrove. They shared mutual friends from St. Andrew's University in Scotland.

"We'd like you to see our garden, my pride and joy," began the royal. "Perhaps you'll consider designing a statue for our Young British Artist's competition next year." His words overwhelmed Elizabeth.

"What an honor that would be for me!"

"Sources tell us, Elizabeth," said the Duchess of Cornwall smiling warmly, "your initial moquettes received rave notices at the Chelsea Arts Club. They're in a partnership with us to encourage young talent such as yours."

"So very kind of you. I've been studying in Rome. Bernini's statues inspired me. That's how I began my first moquettes."

Elizabeth wanted her Mother beside her to share the thrill she was experiencing at a moment like this. She had wondered if life was ever fair. Do those who want everything and give nothing always win? Do those who break hearts ever have theirs break in return? Do the ones who use people get used? Do those who take advantage of vulnerable people for money and affection always score? And what about the cruel ones, who cheat and complain, ruin families and leave a string of broken dreams in their wake. Those miserable people who move forward in society with pockets full of money and glib remarks shattering the lives of good people...Do they ever look back? Maybe life would turn right for me and Mother. Maybe there's fairness, a happy ending, after all in this world.

"Two great talents in one family!" Said the Prince smilingly, "A poet and a sculptress. My! The Dartworth genes are impressive."

"Thank you, your Majesty, your Highness."

"Come now, shall we walk the grounds together and speak of how Camilla and I can have you design something for Highgrove?"

While on the Amalfi coast in Positano…

"Mark, I think it's only right to call Monty," said Zofra.

"Yeah. A good idea. Maybe he can tell us what's goin' on with this CNN announcin' the Zianni fortune's at stake."

"You think it's a joke, Mark?"

"Whataya crazy? CNN would be smacked with a libel suit to knock ya socks off. Don't make me *mashuga shikas* like you neva know about business."

Zofra began dialing the columnist from their suite in Positano. She blessed the day Daniels had the foresight to bring her to Capri, a trip that changed her life.

"Wait a minute, sweetheart." Levy called from across the suite. She closed the phone. "Let me get Nigel, or Whitney, ya know the money men for ESCAPADES." Levy began dialing his mobile sweating. "Even Nicky Viscounti." He spoke to himself, looked around cobra style and smiled at Zofra, his equivalent of a Hungarian Goddess.

"Nigel's phone's switched off. Thank God da circuits are workin'. I'll try Whitney. Ok's ringin.' "

"Whitney, what's happenin'? We're here in Positano, you still in Ischia with this god damned storm? Almost lost my life, what's the score?"

Mark signaled his bombshell, Zofra, to come closer. His face was aghast, then it settled, the twitch returned throughout the call. All Zofra could hear were Levy's replies. "Yeah," "A ha," "Right," "Smart," "God," "Shit, no foolin'. Finally Levy let out a big sigh petting his large stomach. "Thanks, Whitney. Dat's class, real class. Tell that to Nicky. Yeah."

Again he became intent seizing every word from the Boston society boy. "No kiddin' God she must be fumin' yeah, ya got lucky."

He looked to Zofra and winked. "Whattif I told ya I'm sittin' in Positano, the best hotel in the world, with that sweet cookie from Hungary? Mme Zofra makin' me forget all my troubles." A roar of laughter followed. His eyes twinkled eyeing Zofra who unwrapped herself with her large pink breasts exposed. He gave her his Hollywood smile showing all 32 sparkling white teeth from his beefy mouth.

"Now that I've spoken to ya, Whitney, yeah I think it's best just get a copter from here to Naples and fly to L.A. Hell with the stuff at the Villa. Cat can find her way back, nothin' serious there. I don't wantta get into a tangle with Daniels, ya know huntin' for a story en be a louse to Nigel or Esmeralda. They were good to me, ya know what I mean? I don forget that."

He listened to the investor. "Yeah meet me in L.A. Zofra en I well we'll give ya a dinna. Tell Stella." He winked at Zofra who looked him and knew her ship had arrived.

Meanwhile, Daniels in Capri was about to burst a gasket. The vein in his forehead pulsated and he felt a migraine form stinging his eyes. He searched all over the Villa. No one was around. The topography of Capri exists of precipices, cliffs and abysses, all impregnable and now even the library's locked! "Shit!" he bellowed.

Sanjeev saw him jiggling the door, "I'm sorry Mr. Daniels but a conference is in session. May I help you?"

"Sanjeev, what do you want? I'll pay anything. What's going on?"

"Sir, I don't know what you mean. The weather is clearing. Did you see the rainbow…"

"Screw the rainbow! What's with Esmeralda? Nigel? The lawyers?"

"Sir, I truly do not know and furthermore I am obliged to be loyal to the Contessa and Mr. Pembrooke."

"Where's Marco?"

"Mr. Ricci is resting in his room as is Mrs. Jameson. Miss Renoir has left to shop in Capri now that the weather is less threatening."

Daniels couldn't believe he was sitting on top of the most important story of his career and he couldn't wangle one iota of a fact out of anyone. All were in hiding.

"What happened to Levy? Zofra?"

"At this point, Mr. Daniels, I have not heard about Mr. Levy or Miss Zofra. He was detained in Positano."

A stream of new curse words resounded from Daniels.

"Will that be all Sir?"

Daniels howled, "YES!" He hated patient people when he was at his wit's end. He tore back to his room. Jarvis was exiting the shower. He ordered, "Call Lynne Jameson. Better coming from you than me. See if she can shed light on what's happening."

"Monty, she's such a barnacle. Really do I have to?"

"Do it!" He ran his fingers through his tousled hair.

"Jarvis, I've got to get a story."

"The cloud over there..."Jarvis dialed Lynne, spoke about the weather droning on, as Monty paced the room sweating from nerves. Jarvis was getting no where except to hear Lynn's voice resound through the receiver say "I'm always right,"

Monty's mobile rang.

"Monty, it's Nigel. Care to come to my room for a chat?"

His heart leapt with excitement. Now he was getting someplace. Nigel would squeal. He owed Daniels big time. With this, Morehouse would be apologizing. He took the stairs two at a time, knocked on Nigel's door breathless, and waited.

"Jolly good, my dear old thing. Do come in. Have you had café?"

"Nigel. What the hell's going on? I got a phone call from New York, Morehouse himself, threatening to break my contract telling me the Zianni news: fortune is toppling, everything's at stake, Esmeralda is a fake. What the hell's happening?"

"Now calm yourself Monty."

"Calm? You expect me to stay calm? I'm here but CNN scoops the whole damn world! I'm on the carpet and this damn storm and you say stay calm?"

"Yes." Nigel took a *stogie* slowly from his case, inserted it into a tortoise holder and lit his *cigarillo*. Daniels fumed. "Best thing, dear chappie is to begin by telling you *The Times* and *The Daily Mail* have offered a hefty sum for an exclusive from me. This is not to mention the Italian papers, and of course, others....HELLO MAGAZINE, TATLER.... I called you because as you are a good friend, here at my home, I do believe I should give you first dibs. Name the price Morehouse is willing to pay for the whole works. I'm speaking six figures to seven, high range."

"Holy Shit, Nigel, that's a lot of money."

"Start dialing New York, while I put on CNN." Nigel's ploy worked wonders. Puppet style Daniels began speaking to Morehouse beginning by telling him "I'm standing in the bedroom of Esmeralda Zianni Pembrooke's husband's, Nigel, yes, that's right. S.I., that's clout. No one gets a step in the door like that," he added. "CNN, The*Times* and *Daily Mail* are negotiating with Nigel for the exclusive. He wants six figures. What are you willing to put on the table?" The Machiavellian Nigel stood guard.

"Sure," he heard Daniels say, "I'll pass you to Nigel."

"Dear S.I., how are you good fellow?" Nigel listened to the media giant's spiel jewing him down, which he expected.

"Don't trouble yourself with this, my dear old thing. My intention was, of course, to give Monty the cream of the entire grisly tail, but if what I want is out of your range, we'll do another story at another time. Forgive me but I must alert other journalists and take their…" He halted.

"What did you say?" Nigel listened owl like. "Oh yes. Wise of you. Doing this direct, shall we say, without my lawyers cut does save you some S.I." Again he waited hearing the mogul's complaints about the punt. A sudden smile came to Nigel's face while Daniels waited having taken in every word he spoke. "So it is £1,850,000 with serial rights for the exclusive. You have my word. Stephen's right here near my Labradors listening to every word. Shall I pass you to him, good fellow?"

As Monty took commands, Nigel inhaled a long leisurely drag on his *cigarillo*. He'd check with Reginald MacCloud before he did his complete kiss and tell for Monty Daniels.

It isn't everyday I make £1,850,000 yet my eyes are fixed on the plum of a settlement I'll wangle for the divorce. Nigel admired himself in the mirror. The arrangements to rid myself of Esmeralda are looking better and better. Thank Goodness I had the patience to wait until hell broke lose and she was worth divorcing.' He removed his heavy bifocals, ran his long fingers over the dome of his head, People take to the underdog he mused.

"I daresay, Monty, shall we view CNN for the latest news flash and then begin...? Keep in mind....I want to OK final copy....."

XXIX

Denouement

In the halls of neutral territory, the elegant Caccia Club in Rome, away from snooping press, guests and servants, advocates met, speaking civilly. At first all went smoothly, the atmosphere of the opposing legal giants lent quiet tension to the room, discussing matters in hushed voices waiting for their respective clients. It was five days since the diabolical news announced by CNN made world headlines, flushed the financial market place only to have the boomerang of Zianni stock soar, exactly as Anselmi orchestrated announcing the wonder drug, ZHIMMERS. Zianni Pharmaceuticals and Countess Esmeralda Zianni remained front page news in every city of importance in the world.

Paparazzi were posted for prized photographs alerted that the Zianni Contesses were meeting at the Hassler Hotel atop the Spanish steps. It would take them twenty minutes to descend the 278 steps, rush down via Condotti dodging traffic to the private club's position close to the Tiber as the street's name changed to Fontanella Borghese, meeting closed iron gates twenty feet high once they learned where the real rendezvous was arranged. By that time, the two women would be ensconced inside without meddling photographers snapping their entrance to the imposing establishment. Ubiquitous gossip erupted by satellite, newspapers, magazine, television, radio, journals, SOS, text messages, faxes and Internet; word of mouth moved fast speaking of Esmeralda Zianni Pembrooke, a wicked Goddess without specific facts.

She had lied, was a spy, was a Negro,, a call girl, a two-timer wrote the columnists stripped of assets noting legal bills would reach the five million mark to her lawyers, her husband was betraying her, divorcing her and her possessions would be auctioned at Sotheby's within a fortnight. (Privately Nigel's lawyers advised delay on the core of the story until after this Caccia event.) An exclusive serial began about Esmeralda's life, dominating front pages about the startling story with photographs of Esmeralda's past, spotlighting Apartheid, published in all of Daniels' twenty-seven syndicated newspapers while Daniels shadowed Nigel everywhere. The NAACP held a protest march in New York claiming prejudice against Esmeralda because she was black. Ophrah Winfrey wanted exclusive rights to her story citing mixed-racial marriages were the new trend and the Italian Countess was a victim of bigots. Barbara Walters had leading anthropologists on her TV show speaking of mutations of races, believing it close to impossible the rich heiress with her porcelain skin could be black.

Rumor ran wild with figures tripling in size from the scandal worshipping public. Everything was out of proportion as the press clamored for the most startling story. She made great press, everyone had an opinion and the journalists fanned the fire.

Esmeralda arrived in Rome accompanied by her lawyers in a private plane. Nigel flew to London to sign papers with Baker, Baker & MacCloud. Guests left the villa. While the fiasco of the Zianni event reverberated throughout the world, Italy, England, New York and Hollywood was where press gurus tracked down those who had recently been with the Countess paying for recollections about her. Lynne Jameson, was anxious to squeal, wanting to see her name in print, noting what she had to say was "Gospel Truth!" The scandal made the film ESCAPADES receive triple the amount of publicity as the cinema event of the century, since Esmeralda Pembrooke had originally been a backer.

The world waited for every parcel of news about the exciting tale. Smeared across television screens and on Google searches were photograph of Esmeralda, Gianni, Nigel, the wretched Father Danny, Harrods magnificent advertisements and a scant few of Baron Beck. All chewed on any juicy tidbit of rumor flabbergasted, at the same time the miracle drug surged Zianni stock, fueling financial analysts to add their comments the story.

Brian Korthorpe was flown to Cambridge, England, in a Zianni jet for hasty news conferences. It all happened in a flash. The authority on Alzheimer's was sought for interviews globally regarding his research developing the miracle medication, ZHIMMERS, and the alternative of patch therapy and revolutionary chip inserted in the brain, while columnists slipped in questions, "What happened at Villa Pina? What connection to the Countess do you have? How well do you know her? Her husband Nigel?"

"I speak only about science. Sorry." He said kindly keeping his private thoughts about the finagling of biotech giants ability to change the world.

Korthorpe's name was spotlighted alongside the story of the heiress as the savior of the insidious disease, Alzheimer's. TIME MAGAZINE photographed him for their cover. Flanking him throughout all interviews was Naomi. The couple, free at last to be able to come forward publically, marveled how Fate changed their life, announcing plans to marry. The event at Villa Pina though catastrophic for some, was their miracle, now united.

Hospitals and doctors were besieged with calls worldwide. Visits from their patients and the family of their patients to get the drug went viral. Care homes throughout the world were creating a bidding war to have ZHIMMERS exclusively in their city. The demand for the drug was record-breaking news.

While on everyone's lips was talk of the ravishing jewel of a woman who shined through all misfortunes, lost her husband, then her baby, venerated by all who followed her life's story as it unfolded. Was it all a plot to destroy a beauty?

A new chapter came into view, her dismantling. Esmeralda's name circled in every drawing room, beauty parlor, secretarial pool, nursing station, resort hotel, news dealer, library, restaurant, airplane, subway and night-club in the world. The toast of international society, the exquisite icon of Harrods, the elegant, soft spoken turquoise eyed woman of mixed blood had won the attention of men and women from Kings to taxi drivers and was now a public figure. The void of Princess Diana with people living vicariously through media was fired with news of Esmeralda, Contessa, Baroness, wife of the Englishman Pembrooke and con artist. Delicious blurry facts seized the public while extraordinary acclaim was given to Zianni Pharmaceuticals and the great scientist, Sir Brian Korthorpe. All the news was devoured by men who revered science, women whose compassion sensed there was more to the story of the Countess, (certainly she had been beneficial promoting the acclaimed Korthorpe's work)... then there were the activists speaking of equal rights, the Human Rights Commissions worldwide gave vent to their programs of tolerance being considered in this case, there were the bored whose emotions either loved her or loathed her, respected her or reviled her, everyone had an opinion. Everyone judged everything.

One great scientist was a story overtaken by two women - two Contesses - Money, youth, a dead husband, mixed blood, a dead baby, spiked international drama. It made extraordinary news, Serena, the good sister and Esmeralda, the bad wife.

The first to enter the Caccia was Serena, dressed in a black gabardine suit and low-heeled shoes. From her appearance, she looked dressed for a wake. More than her zodiac sign, the character of Serena, a scorpion, was obvious. She had plotted and her web was intact.

The club's guard unhinged wrought iron gates that led to the massive arched courtyard. Serena walked through eyeing towering statues that seemed to touch the endless blue Roman sky.

A small crowd lingered near the entrance of the club, mostly tourists remarking on the beauty of the edifice, once the home of the Borghese family, later the Spanish embassy when Italy was ruled by Spain for two hundred years, not recognizing they were witnessing another type of history.

Serena would sting, like the Scorpion sign of her birth. She could be deadly. Her wish was for Esmeralda to disappear, be assured no one would hear her name again. and dismantle her wealth. Serena wanted Esmeralda to never to utter the word Zianni again after justice was enforced. Serena wished Esmeralda dead.

A tell tale frown mark had begun to form on Serena's face from all the stress or was it jealousy and greed haunting her? Her decision to press forward legally, and hers alone would decide Esmeralda's fate. What a wretched position. Was there goodness of her soul? The tension of the last six months' investigation had reached its climax. "A certain vindictiveness is in me. I will remain blameless for this change in character. But is it a change?," she thought to herself alone.

Rupert's security gave Serena the strength she needed to face this horrific problem. Tonight they would be together, as they were in Ischia, lovers at last with a future they never dreamed possible.

How Esmeralda intended to live out her deceit Serena couldn't fathom. If it hadn't been for Danny McSweeney's letter, this deception would have remained a complete enigma devouring the wealth of Ziannis. Serena judged her former sister-in-law vilely, her rancid character, evil deeds, her complex nature...under the surface there's nothing but horrid sins churned in Serena's fixed mind. She, like everyone, had bias and greed percolating inside her. Anyone who's lost a fortune to a relative, spouse, ally, partner or lover harbors hate. Nonetheless, Serena, a lover of the truth, was tormented with a case of this severity. To know Gianni was duped to this degree, to have his baby in question! Thank God he isn't alive to see this, and Mother and Father – all saw Esmeralda at her best, believing her a Goddess.... all too impossible to believe. And, Nigel, although mercenary, he didn't deserve this. It doesn't impress me he's intent on publishing his version of the facts of this story. It will be slanted to make him look like the wounded spouse and bring dishonor to the Zianni name. What else can I expect? The last thing Nigel is, is innocent. Facts ran through her mind in overload. What are the true ingredients of Esmeralda's character? Will I ever know?

Serena walked down the Caccia's main corridor slowly, passing the member's photos of Prince Philip, King Umberto, Prince Charles, the Raniers, viewing the oversized portraits of the greats of history painted by masters whose work hung at this club and museums. The quiet ambiance was perfect for a meeting such as this. Privacy is the benchmark of the Caccia, the only place we could select as 'neutral territory,' where no one from outside can penetrate. To think years ago it rang with laughter and dancing until wee hours when Esmeralda became Contessa Zianni. Life was giving lessons to everyone, nothing lasts forever, everything changes. *bella figura, bruta fugura….*

The lawyers rose when Serena entered. Everyone knew Esmeralda would be late. It was a part of her control. Tension mounted as the clock ticked ten. It was a reenactment of the scene at Caesar Augustus some days ago except this time was Esmeralda's denouement.

The sleek Mercedes drove to the entrance of the Caccia moments after Serena alighted. The driver had been waiting on a side street with Esmeralda who wished to give her opponent, Serena, ample time to strut to the library of the Caccia unhurried feeling superior while Esmeralda searched for the tone of voice that would inspire compassion in her former sister-in-law..

Her lawyers had clearly unveiled the depths of her chicaneries and the repercussions of how a jury would judge her guilty. Esmeralda detested surprises and feared the worst was to come.

My beauty formed me to attract the opposite sex without the knowledge of the wiles of men. The pious South African nuns singing their "Gloria Halleluiah hymns" made me prejudiced against anyone of color, against people who weren't Catholic or of another class and I was ill equipped to prepare me for life, this raw life - I just knew the Convent, the lies of my Father I believed…the admission of my Mother, the cruel twists of destiny make me ignoble. I'm not a person who's evil. And then she stopped herself, dead to shame.

No one kills their own flesh and but an evil witch, a killer, a person deranged. I'm set apart from everyone I know, worse than my Father who killed in a jealous rage instantly, not premeditatively. Her being was stone. Everything was too deep to feel any longer. Nigel was creating tales that reviled her. Thank God I had the presence of mind never to divulge what happened at Convento di Santo Spirito.

A costume of beige wool trimmed in black twill by Valentino was her choice to appear without any degree of mourning. The lines of the suit skimmed her body to perfection. She looked as one to be presented to a head of State; instead she was attending her mortician's plans for her burial.

Who will speak first? What will I say? Will Serena be civil? Hard? Cold? How will she crucify me? Thoughts collided.

This is what I owe my Father. His sin and what my Mother forced upon me.

Esmeralda tried to shed the mantle of her own responsibility by living in denial, passing the sins to her forbearers but she was no fool. She was a racist and a bigot. Her soul was encased in evil; she was doomed for hell, a killer.

It was all too evident to everyone involved the Zianni family was on the brink of events that would be catastrophic. Within days every detail of this case and will be blasted around the globe by the media. "We can't keep a lid on these matters, but" thought Esmeralda, "maybe I can try."

She entered the room and Serena's greeting was too courteous to be polite. Esmeralda smelled a trap.

Her first words came quickly. "You're too much of a lady to do me a bad turn," she said greeting her sister-in-law whom she hadn't seen in three years.

Lawyers began with reciting legal stipulations, showing Esmeralda for the first time original documents in their possession, proclaiming their point of view as to the severity of her crimes. It was akin to a tommy-gun, and they, a firing squad but she held herself magnificently, listening.

To read Esmeralda's face was not easy. She was exquisitely beautiful and had taken time to have her makeup highlight that beauty, her abundance of strawberry-blonde hair was combed to perfection, the jewelry she wore understated. Her skin was alabaster cream and her voluptuous lips displayed the only hint of emotion as she curled them from time to time reading documents.

She was seized by her Father's crude letter.

After she read it, she shot a glance to Serena. Envy and resentment was written in mean eyes that grew cold with Serena's stare, threatening Esmeralda. She had betrayed Gianni not caring for the needs of his sister and Mother in the exorbitant fashion they had become accustomed. Esmeralda's greed had created this event. Yet, Esmeralda's greed was reflected in Serena.

Frederico Spiga was speaking about an indictment that would come once Serena gave him the authority to proceed. He detailed what this would mean to Esmeralda. Spiga's words echoed those of her advocates days before. Esmeralda's blasé attitude unnerved the aggressive Italian. He kept the tone of his voice at his maximum pitch and clenched his jaw annunciating the words "prison" and "restitution," like a melodramatic actor to break Esmeralda's resolve.

Serena's face was one of emotion. She struggled with her position as adversary.

Esmeralda saw this and viewed her chance. Retribution and the honor of the Zianni name was more important to Serena than justice. She had not assimilated into the clan without being trained. They revered their high standard of privacy. The Ziannis weren't café society. They were society.

Their kind didn't print photos in tabloids or give interviews to magazines speaking of stately homes. The last five days of the journalists spewing forth bile must enrage Serena. The Ziannis don't take well to seeing their name in the press. The press was there to note their births, marriages and deaths in the past four hundred years and that was enough! Everything else was private. Now because of this scandal, everything was open for public display and it disgusted Serena beyond anything she could have imagined. *Paparazzi* by dozens gathered at her doorstep each mourning hounding her every move throughout the day.

Esmeralda never intended for it to happen. She had lived a lie, but she had lived her lie elegantly, which brought no disgrace. Inner shame was her sin, her evil sin that would torment her forever.

Who are these people? She kept asking herself the same question. What do they really want of me? What they say is true but where do they come from to pry into my life as they have? What is left to live for? I have no wish for another man, another marriage, another child. I've lived in the finest cities of the world as a Baroness, a Contessa, a woman idolized. Where can I go? I will live forever in loneliness and despair. Better to take my life. Let the whole wretched ugliness be lost in suicide. I can leave this meeting today, go to my splendid palazzo, take my pills and never face tomorrow but not until the divorce to Nigel is final.

The drone of legal voices hummed as wasps in a chamber of providence.

My past has been obliterated. My present destroyed, my future annihilated. Self-imposed resignation springs from my soul. This is my wake. I hold one trump card.

Esmeralda stood at the long mahogany table eyeing everyone, composing what she would say.

"Equals speak stating what is the truth easily." She looked with a penetrating glance at Serena. "You now know, Serena, we are not equals. Who gave you the right to dishonor your brother's wife as you have is something I detest. I have revered the Zianni name. I have never brought shame to the family. A deranged Father who wished to make me, an innocent minor, threatened as his victim for incest to blacken my life with vile blackmail is whom you have listened to, an ex-convict, without giving me the dignity to speak before this horrific case was exposed internationally."

The room was dead quiet.

Esmeralda's stance never wavered shoving the documents in front of her to one side. "You see my wit, charm and gaiety have evaporated because of your malicious wish to eradicate me as a human being. Call me a deceiver, call me a cheat, defile my character. May God forgive you. Never did you, privileged as you are, walk in my shoes."

Her soft spoken voice was even with extraordinary impact. Those who viewed her in the austere ambiance on this dreadful occasion would remember the quality of her profound dialogue forever. To achieve understanding from those who judged her - knowing she had no other defence was her purpose.

"I escaped a lurid father and tried for a better life, changing my name so he would never find me, never being a disgrace to anyone, working without a blemish on my career, my first marriage to a noble person without a hint of scandal, never having promiscuity darken my door. Your brother with his loving and loyal heart full of goodness wanted me as his wife. I never betrayed his love. Had he lived, Gianni wouldn't have cared if I were the daughter of an aristocrat, a car mechanic whose larcenous character taints me or a black mother.

She changed the course of her defense.

"What will dragging my story through the court do to enhance the Zianni name? The Pharmaceutical giant's position?" She never took her eyes from Serena.

"Will it make you happier? Richer? Will you find stars beaming brighter in your sky because your lofty virtue has failed to see another whose path crossed yours and was not pristine?"

Tension built within her, the shape of her mouth tightened. "Maybe you prefer war. Peace is too unsettling. I have tried to keep a replica of peace since the tragic death of my husband."

In a drama of emotions, Esmeralda questioned: "Is your want to destroy me completely? Call in a mortician. You've presented an avalanche of reproaches against me. How should I behave? How would you behave with the same set of circumstances?"

She paused dramatically. "Strip me of resources, deny me my home, cut out my tongue, exhume the body of my innocent baby, call me a fraud, a con-artist. I embellished my past because of its tainted nature. I had nothing to do with how I was born. Whether I am white or Negroid, Chinese or Indian does it matter? My first impulse was to run away when I was a young girl in South Africa. I had no recourse and took life as it came. Don't most of us do that?" The group sat transfixed.

"Isn't Fate a dictator to our circumstances? I have made my sins. I am no angel but until one walks in my shoes, do not crucify me. I've been appraised of the law, of what the penalty is for living in fraud. It was not me who named Esmeralda Zianni the sole heir to the Zianni Pharmaceuticals International empire. Gianni did that believing he would live to an old age, and his son would follow him. He trusted me."

She stopped. Took a sip of water from a goblet in front of her. "Strip me of everything and jail me if you like. Let me be the constant reminder of the Zianni scandal for decades. If that is your wish, I know I cannot contest this in Court."

Her voice never lost control.

"I ask that no money be given to my Father. His vile voice is a lying voice. Do not fuel it with money. I never knew of my Mother or that she was alive until years ago when Baron Beck sent me a letter he received via the nuns in South Africa. I was pregnant with Gianni's child. Gianni was in New York on business." She continued her entreaty.

"Nigel and I have filed for divorce. This fact you know. He wants to exit financially solvent. Everyone's wish is to be financially solvent." A slim smile graced her lips. "Nigel's claws are on possessions I had before I came into my marriage to Zianni. I do not wish him to have any possessions that belong to the Zianni family."

Esmeralda's strength of purpose dispelled the hate in the room.

"Now if you will excuse me. I have said all I have to say. I will return to the house Gianni saw fit to give me. You can speak amongst yourselves how you will make arrangements for my future."

She looked at Serena once more and left the library walking slowly from the Caccia towards her waiting limousine.

It was mid-September, the best time of the year in Rome, the sky was splendid illuminating the warm terracotta colors of *centro storico.* Esmeralda had exhibited an extraordinary part of her persona, one that rarely was illuminated. She had more than pride of an elegant woman. The words she expressed were simple. They were words from her intellect and her brittle, broken heart. Moreover, with the set of circumstances that confronted her, viewing her life in the last five days she had achieved what she thought was impossible. Whatever they would do to her, Esmeralda's courage conquered her fear.

PART FOUR

THE EPILOGUE

A passerby making a detour in Germany saw a plaque

The citizens of Munich
Express Gratitude to
Baroness Esmeralda Beck
Establishing the Bavarian Centre for
Abused Children
December 1991

People on vacation saw another

Sisters of Mercy
Carmelite Order of Santa Maria della Gracia
Taormina, Sicily
Bestow Blessings
to
Contessa Esmeralda Zianni
Benevolent Benefactor of
The Neonatal Intensive Care Hospital for Angels
Dedicated to the memory of her Son
Giovanni Zianni II
5 November 2000

2004...Prince Charles scanned the front page of *The Times.* He recalled when he was with Esmeralda and Nigel unveiling a plaque...

HRH Prince Charles
and
The Royal Boroughs of Westminster, Kensington and Chelsea
London
Express Appreciation to
Esmeralda Pembrooke
For
The Homeless Women's Hospice
Christmas 2003

XXX

The Funeral

Spring, 2006…

Eighteen months passed….

Bells from Old Chelsea Church in London, marked the hour of five. Thomas More called this *his* Church on the Embankment of the Thames. Henry VIII worshiped here and married Jane Seymour, his third wife, in this historic landmark, no stranger to the rich and distinguished who gathered this day five hundred years later evading issues politely speaking of trivialities, sorrow and happier days.

In Capri, a diverse contingent gathered in the piazza. The sixth century *Torre dell'Orologio* struck a similar hour as in London.

Appearing like a setting in a play, the bustle and confusion of the square mixed nobility with fishermen, *nouveau riche* tourists with housewives and screaming babies and then there was the small contingent of 'regulars' who gathered opposite the sea waiting. Who would be the first to speak of that September two years ago?

In London, the Vicar called to mind confessions about one individual while preparing his vestments in the sacristy for the service. Everyone had an opinion. Speech carried people away from themselves preferring to dissect the hidden life of another.

Whispers could be heard in the Church while whispers were heard of the same person in Capri. Few sealed their lips. Those that did understood the reasons why this woman's life had impact on their own.

Everything that had transpired was exaggerated beyond proportions, there were different versions by the hundreds percolating from different tongues in different languages fanning the flames of reckless gossip.

Some called her Machiavellian. Some crucified her. Some crowned her. Passion for curiosity made all listen, judge and form opinions.

By not being in attendance, Esmeralda Pembrooke drew more attention than if she were among the decorated people holding court in the piazza night after night and in London at the solemn Church service.

Dusk came, the hour ticked away. The religious ritual began in London.

"Véronique knew from the beginning the stars would chart everyone's destiny," whispered Brian Korthorpe respecting his friend's profession.

As she foresaw, Véronique succumbed to cancer within eighteen months, clinging to life after leaving Villa Pina. Samir alone knew she carried this tragic secret and respected her confidence. Now he and Jacqueline along with Sir Brian and Lady Naomi Korthorpe, stood alongside Stefano de Gesu wrought with sorrow, bereft, shedding tears believing their own end was suddenly closer.

At the moment of death, Stefano came to realize the depth of his love for Véronique Joulin. The dignified Ambassador had been inconsolable for the last several days. To the final moment, he lingered by Véronique's bedside until she departed for another world.

Shabadiba was with Olympia and Whitney, who'd announced plans to marry giving the exclusive to Monty Daniels who stood nearby in attendance not wishing to publicize this tragic event. He'd done enough stories that stemmed from Villa Pina. This memorial for Véronique needn't be one of them. Jarvis was out of his life. Mark and Zofra Levy sent a huge basket of lilies expressing condolences.

Off in the distance was Cat Renoir dressed demurely in a black suit with Peter Evans. Nigel Pembrooke sat alone, across the aisle from Lord and Lady Rupert Davidson. Bells tolled, the organ began its haunting sound and an array of people Véronique had advised throughout her years, took their places.

While in Capri, waiters at the cafes served Campari, listening, watching. Men smoked *cigarillos.* Silence dissolved in air. All spoke of one woman, the Contessa… mystified about events.

"Who are these people?" Waiters questioned among themselves. "Cafe philosophers? Do they speak the truth about that beautiful creature or jealous gossip?" They, too, were wise to understand speech carried people away from themselves, preferring to dissect the hidden life of another.

While in London, all talk was about Véronique's life, another life that had impact on their own. Strangers wondered who was the handsome Italian man, the one seated in the front pew whose eyes were wet with tears.

Questions would receive surprising answers and whispers could be heard in the Church while whispers were heard speaking of similar people in Capri. People would listen satiated with the passion for curiosity. Few sealed their lips. "Nature has her own way of controlling individuals, much like the stars," Véronique would say. "There's a mood to life," she'd advise "and one to the seasons."

Dusk came as the Vicar continued his opening words and people regarded the printed Church program with an astrological map of the stars….In Véronique's cursive script was written:

> *"Once, we had celestial symmetry, twelve zodiac signs, seven lights in the sky continuously moving. The Sun ruled Leo. The Moon ruled Cancer. Each planet ruled two signs apiece. Mars*

governed Aries & Scorpio. Venus; Taurus & Libra. Mercury; Gemini & Virgo, Jupiter; Sagittarius & Pisces, Saturn; Capricorn & Aquarius. After 1781 when Uranus was discovered things changed, astrologers attributed it to Aquarius. The 1846 discovery of Neptune was given to Pisces. By the 1950's Pluto belonged to Scorpio. So... what will Ceres, Xena and Charon end up ruling?"

The eulogy, Véronique requested, was given by Marco Ricci who'd arrived in London from Los Angeles with Stella, taking a break from the film in production with Mark Levy as the Producer. Marco, dressed in a dark suit with black tie, climbed the steps to the pulpit thinking the gadfly, the gossip, the artist whose career ignited, egoists who stalk every party, the hack, the old, the young, the seekers, the followers, the prude, the bore, the intellectual, the gifted, the meek and the blowhards, everyone in decline and the wannabees are all here....and he began....

"This is one role I didn't wish to have. Véronique and I spoke about what she wanted to convey. I don't have to elaborate on our tragic loss and speak of laurels about the great friend she was to us all. Death has brought somber thoughts to us. I want to recite her words, which she gave me a few days ago when she knew she had brief time to live.

Slow down sooner, live longer later. Dare to be crazy.
Remember you have the right to draw your own confusions.
Be a part of your stars. Keep the faith, and if you can't keep it or don't want to keep it, FIND IT.
If all fails. . . Remember...No one gets out alive.

Marco smiled and the church had a ripple of laughter at the light heartedness of the eulogy.

"Paint lovely colors of the mind, look inside yourself.
That's where you'll find light unending. Wherever you go,
go wildly with love and understanding. You're the Master's

Child. Paint your canvas. Sing your song - even though the road is long and difficult – follow me to Magic Land – but not too soon.
I love you! Véronique."

As music commenced and attendees dispersed, close friends kissed with sincere embraces, brushing away tears exiting the Church in unity marveling that every prediction Véronique had made came true.

......while in Capri, fog descended over the Amalfi coast creating a hazy silhouette of the great Vesuvius. Clouds moved with a menacing urgency foretelling a storm brewing, stars disappeared that had begun to emerge in the twilight. Afraid of a tempest, the Italians dispersed from cafes, gesticulating, kissing each other with promises and exaggerated embraces.

"*Domani,*" they declared, "*Si, Si... domani...*" emptying the piazza like a ghost town, scurrying to their respective villas, assuring the others to meet, as they met every night at this time was the scenario...and what had been - became legend.

XXXI

Nigel Pembrooke

From the precipice of Villa Pina, he spied the ship from the Bay of Naples coming across the *Coast' Amalfitana*. The promise of another season was beginning, April in Capri. Soon birds would feather their nests while lizards and butterflies remained asleep until June. Here and there a patch of bright color from old blooms of bougainvillea and geraniums that had miraculously survived frost spotted the landscape.

The reaction of the dogs was restlessness. No servants were about, only Sanjeev. Grapes from last season that hadn't been picked were raisins, dry and tasteless, hundreds on the ground that were of no consequence. Peach and lemon trees in profusion had buds beginning to form. They colored the terraced garden below in patches of green, without bloom, while a patch of brilliant blue broke through the clouds illuminating the rocky crest of the mountain painting the towering cypress chartreuse.

Nigel Pembrooke's be-speckled topaz eyes remained fixed on the slow pace of the three-mast schooner and its contours coming towards Capri. A chill met his cheek, remembering and he buttoned his cashmere sweater and fell under the hypnotic spell of nature, lost in thought. Villa Pina was his past.

The tourists, far below in Capri were not a part of this life, his life, languishing on the terrace away from the masses. It had suited him, this life, well, to a point. Obsequiously tending his every need, devoted Sanjeev, the Sri Lankan manservant doted on him. Oranges were peeled from the market, espresso *corretto* poured with the exact measure of anisette placed in his cup.

"Our marriage meant nothing to Esmeralda. It was always in a perpetual crisis, perhaps that was its pleasure..." He adjusted his ascot thinking. "It meant nothing to Esmeralda. But it did to me. She aroused me with her indifference." He studied the scene.

The few villas in the distance closer to the sea were closed tightly with shutters. This view from the peak was majestic seeing the white caps form as far as the eye could see, this villa, finest in all Capri, with its Doric columns, ancient ruins, unparalleled panorama at the promontory, where the two parts of the island converged at the summit had been home, Capri and Anacapri.

This isle - full of history, mysticism and me - an English aristocrat who learned from bourgeois people, clowns, lovers, fraudsters, artists and millionaires. All were a part of my life here in Italy and arrived that September to experience a moment of time on a rock in the Mediterranean, invest in a film and change life entirely. The Chinese say '*tis better to travel with hope than to arrive.*' They, rightly, referred to life. These have been difficult years. How much more difficult for Esmeralda. There are moments when I've longed to see her. But moments, that's all.

Timetables and connections are my future. The privileged make their own arrangements. The masses who shove and sweat next to each other to arrive and depart from Naples to be in this paradise, the weather beaten and tired, those crude Italians, except a rare few, will have me as one of those rare few. Packing up as I have this week, seeing she left her wedding ring, ends this chapter in my life.

She acted civilly as had Serena. After the shock of the decision and the divorce, once well from the sudden attack of uremia, (taken for observation overnight as tension mounted, knowing it was the panic of stress), seeing my avarice scheme succeed - I recall lying in the London Clinic. When the nurse thrust a hypodermic into my rump, being sedated after the drama of emotions, side stepping the avalanche of Esmeralda's wretched past, *cornutti* one journalist for another, securing the settlement I wanted, it was all tremendous, too great to take in one lifetime.

To let me have some time at Beaumont for a month and then Palace Gardens before Serena reclaimed the property and that lucky Rupert began to live there was good. Yes, he maneuvered his chances. Lord Rupert Davidson and Lady Serena inherited everything that Gianni wanted for Esmeralda. Nigel contemplated their virtues not deceiving himself that they were free of vices. No one was.

He thought again...

I wasn't about to complain to anyone. Now to be given this month at Villa Pina, all was with courtesy. Courtesy can be so cold. My intention always has been to resume being in the grace of those who make up circles where I originated. I may have betrayed myself and to a degree old friends, but that's rectified.

Our kind sticks together. No one will mention things. Or if they do when we've had too much to drink, I'll feel the guilt I should. I can gaze at my Guido Reni painting and no one will dare say a word. I will be tolerated. Eventually accepted again.

I worked my marriage to Esmeralda to my advantage. She would have destroyed me had I stayed her pawn. To reclaim my aristocratic privilege and speak of the suffering I have known - trying to be a good husband to the imposter she was, learning how wicked was her past... and he paused taking a *cigarello* from its case.

He inserted it into his tortoise filter, ignited the tip with his gold lighter, pressed the *cigarello* to his aristocratic lips, lighting it slowly gazing to the view. Many will laud me.

Villa Pina will not crumble, or will Beaumont or the manse at Palace Gardens. It all seems a dream, a terrible nightmare. No one could have imagined this life, a life too true, too real, too candid, too grand a plot to have been real.

The sea was calm, a soft blue met the horizon without a definitive mark. The only break in the scene was the wake of the ship as it moved parallel to the shore then took a leisurely turn towards Marina Grande. Island mentality, he mused. This island has taught me, England has rescued me. Capri changed me. Me of all people learning from a piece of granite in the middle of the world, but it's true. My life had everything here except integrity, truth, dignity and happiness. I must guard against it ever happening again. I need to go into the world as before this all happened. I have to strive and return giving the best of my ability. I don't have to pretend to be one of society. I am society. The crowd is another matter.

In this paradise boredom sat at my table, this change was inevitable. Change is what I've learned watching the tempests of Capri turn into glorious days, like people. I must be prepared for them to arrive again... the tempests but this time, I'm wiser.

Within a half hour Whitney's yacht would be at Marina Grande, his crew would descend on Villa Pina to collect Nigel Pembrooke's belongings. He would be the only one aboard. He relished his solitude spying the flag flying from the mast with binoculars.

He reached for *The Times*, scanned the headlines. The Prime Minister was making a speech about the United Kingdom, speaking of his country in Western Europe, which comprised England, Scotland, Wales, and Northern Ireland. Tony Blair spoke about its beginning with the kingdom of England; created by three acts of union: with Wales (1536), Scotland (1707), and Ireland (1800). At the height of its power in the 19th century it ruled an empire that spanned the globe. London is the capital and the largest city. Population: 60,000,000 of the United Kingdom and soon it would be 60,000,001.

"I've changed." he said looking at Sanjeev.

"I beg your pardon, Signor?"

"I was remarking about a phenomena, Sanjeev, private thoughts after all of this. I've changed, everything changed."

"One can never escape one's karma." The tobacco skinned *major d'uomo* stopped what he was doing and moved towards Nigel. "Is there anything else you require, Lord Pembrooke?"

"No. Go along, I am quite content."

Content! Phenomena! I'm content, at last. No more a rat in a cage and phenomena? Ours was a strange love. I never possessed Esmeralda. No one ever did, not even Gianni. I often wonder if I wanted to possess her. We had a common purpose. Yes, it was an ambitious marriage. Friendship? Never. No one could be friends with Esmeralda. There was an affection in the beginning but to discuss coitus with her would be impossible. She was the one woman I had where the element of truth was missing. I felt trust was missing, something was hidden or what she offered superficial me. I see now it was her extraordinary fear of being exposed.

Nigel took a deep sigh. We were never truly lovers. We were in partnership and that partnership, unlike the rapture of a romance, came with a fairly equal equation. We both brought the same degree to the table. It could have worked. It wasn't real - that's why it could have worked.

Financially solvent today, money has reached my clutches from sources I never expected. He inhaled his *cigarello* deeply and sighed a sigh that would have brought him an Oscar if this were a film…but was it a film? We had made our movie, took in our own drama and lived in legal offices negotiating settlements and houses, plans to make life work, the legal cutting room added and deleted people and scenes from life to survive this charade with a better spectacle.

Wasn't it Marco when he received the Oscar for ESCAPADES who said the same thing and soon he'll arrive in Hollywood, with his *amante*, that ball buster, Stella to collect another trophy for the second film they've done with Levy. Sweet Levy who thinks he found true love in Mrs. Zofra Levy. Amazing.

Nigel's mind wandered back to the peace of solitude. Suddenly, it was shattered by the sound of the piano. "God Damn it! Who in hell is playing the fucking piano?"

He took wide strides to the *salotto,* his hand reached for the buff colored Labrador at his feet that followed him, kicking it aside. His curious, angry eyes peered into the gilded room.

"Forgive me if I've disturbed you. I didn't intend to make a sound," Sanjeev addressed Nigel covering the black baby Grande with a large white sheet. The entire room was covered with sheets. The once gorgeous villa was a room of phantoms.

Everything for Nigel was finished here.

"It's time to begin the intercourse of people, view the clowns and be one myself."

He smiled at Sanjeev put his hand on his shoulder. In the tomb of a room, he took a long drag on his smoke, stretched his frame broadly, and paused returning to the terrace to see if the boat docked and took one more look at the sea, thinking of his souvenirs.

"Let there be this silence. I'm no longer a part of her life. This is no longer a part of my life. Her needs do not concern me, nor mine hers. It was a vacant marriage devoid of desire. I interpret it all to be the greed and weakness of us both."

Nigel Pembrooke, whose tempest was over had seen a unexpected finale with an unforgettable climax. His superficial life was a thing of the past. Esmeralda's settlement would keep him in lifetime luxury, his twin brother died without issue, he inherited the title he longed for. His last taste of Esmeralda that remarkable morning when the same three-mast schooner was preparing to enter the waters of Capri were the last time they made love.

We were lovers that morning, enflamed by desire, I fertilized her. It was a once in a lifetime orgasm for me, and she...she was sweet, loving ..but...that word *but*...that changes everything...we didn't know until months after I filed for divorce Esmeralda was pregnant."

He stroked his high-domed head and slowly took another *cigarello* from his silver case, stomping out the first, inserting the next one methodically into a tortoise holder, igniting the tip, inhaling deeply.

He had remorse, how was it possible not to have felt her suffering? At times he longed to see her and knew that was out of the question. The revelation she carried our child - my only child - had made me quake in her presence. Her expression, I shall never forget, it was as if she foresaw everything that was to happen...Through the legal proceedings she endured the ordeal of the pregnancy.....Nigel's eyes brimmed for the first time allowing emotion to swell...."and.... a baby daughter...." he said aloud, swallowing the lump in his throat remembering ....in the beginning he'd been unable to feel any love for the infant, but she was his, indisputably his, DNA documents linked Esmeralda and he forever with this, their only issue, this mulatto enchantress with kinky strawberry-blonde hair who won his heart. She was christened Nigella, by Vicar Grylls in Norfolk and outside of her birth certificate noting her race - mulatto, nothing more was said.

His years with Esmeralda were never to be forgotten. Cruel Fate had condemned her and there was and would always be the extraordinary life that was theirs alone and their child. She had done the worst things in the world to him and with this baby, his baby, the best. There were few things in life that one can appreciate as the birth of a baby, completely innocent, non-judgmental, offering love to all....this is life's greatest pleasure and the few other things that make this journey tolerable, a sunny day, this view from Villa Pina, a good breakfast, music.

Strange how years pass too quickly and March becomes November and aches are the first thing you feel in the morning instead of caresses, your teeth show your years like the lines in your face and you try to exude some sort of *bella figura*....that's the least one can do in this frenetic world, be elegant. Women should be beautiful, not look like some unmade beds...but this is superficial. I have been taken out of the ordinary to the extraordinary by the full custody of my only child. Now perhaps I'm learning how to live....

Colored people didn't mean what they had once meant to Nigel or to anyone. Racial barriers were diminishing with the passing of every day. Nigella's birth kept the Pembrooke legacy intact.

In time, reckoned Nigel, the world will change. Change - the only thing one can be certain of in this world. Prejudice will remain, people will judge because we are human, but education and money will open doors once closed to miscegenation. The world will come to think it chic, special and then not even give racial difference second notice.

Lord Nigel Pembrooke, seventh Earl of Pembrooke Manor, Norfolk, stretched his height to maximum, breathing in the untainted sea air of Capri. He remained in ecstasy of this wondrous scene as the wind swept up from the sea, the sky became a clearer blue than he could ever recall, the sun glistened, the sea glittered with what seemed hundreds of sapphires, hues of emerald and twinkle of turquoise diamonds, like Esmeralda's eyes.

Indelible in his memory was when they were first wed and came one Christmas and there was a froth of snow on Vesuvius. Yesterdays.... that was yesterday, thoughts turned to the future, his health, whispering gratitude to the Divine that saved him from drowning in disgrace, sending a prayer into the Universe for Nigella and her Mother. Off in the distance, the campanile from the *piazza* marked the hour.

Tiberius was 69, a good number, when he left Rome for Capri. He never wanted to see that city again, believing it had become too corrupt, nauseating his taste. He was oppressed with the games of the Senate, the populace, the marriage that left him wanting, the phonies who latched onto him, suffocating his freedom and every thought. Empty, continual talk by average seekers wanting to leap from their mediocrity and gain power. To escape power and find peace was his intention, experiencing a new existence. Though younger by years, I am an old fox, escaping Capri for reasons quite similar. This life has cost me. Everything costs. It might not come in the cost of silver, gold and money, it can come in the cost of happiness, self respect. Time....that cost is far greater.

Turgenev said "the impression of Capri will remain with me until I die."

He bent down to pet his Labradors, "*Andiamo*," he commanded.

Sanjeev, stood transfixed. Nigel Pembrooke shook his hand. The devoted houseman and he locked eyes in a long take. Words were impossible.

Nigel exited the terrace, seeing the three- mast schooner docked at port and with his pets following along, Lord Nigel Pembrooke left Capri never to return again.

As narrator of this story, I have tried to convey a faithful portrait and not be judgmental.....

A legend in her time, this sensitive beauty, Esmeralda, came to mature as a Baroness, Contessa and paradox, looking for answers from her experience of life, a brutal and beautiful life. In many ways, she followed the motto of the famous Swedish Doctor, Capri neighbor, Axel Munthe, "*Oser, vouloir, savoir, se taire...*" to dare, to want, to know, to remain silent.

When she first accepted life in an orphanage and later confronted wretched conditions as a sixteen year old girl, in the land of her birth with toxic history, she refused to be vexed by circumstances that precipitated a dramatic life change. This was to be her pattern as she moved into the third decade, one of diminished progression.

Her original intention was to enter old age with style and retain *bella figura* where once she had simmering sexuality. Those were the days when she walked with an air of energy, darting from cloud to cloud, without effort, engaging every facet of life positively, grasping the limit of people's understanding, tailoring her remarks accordingly with a passion for respectability.

She suffered emotional loss early as an infant and later an adolescent compelling her to leave the complex country of her birth and begin her journey meeting exceptional difficulties. Gradually she achieved an understanding of society, and the set of values it imposed for acceptance, she made giant steps designing her future, varnishing mistakes through secrecy. Huge mistakes if one is to judge. But I am not here to judge but to write that through all of this, she survived showing character.

Class always knows class was a fact she gleaned from life; and once she received her Mother's letter, she understood she would be forever an outsider. The climax of this traumatic tale illustrates another side to her guarded life and to life itself.

Miscengenation was hers at a point in life when her identitiy had been set by bias, in her third decade she learned the truth of who she was.

One never knows the trajectory of tomorrow. When it arrives, life brings maturity studying the puzzle that constitute what decisions are made at the time. In Esmeralda's case, the hidden reality of her past, was a mark of racial prejudice taught by Caucasian bigoted nuns living in the Apartheid regime. Once she learned her true roots from her Mother, a woman she never knew, Esmeralda never expected to have her life broadcast throughout the world. Her want was concealment.

As I complete my narrative, who am I to speak of bigotry, racial or religious hatred? I am a born German and the stigma of my people's stains of sin from WWII remains upon me and on any decent person of my nation. There is a racist and bigot in all of us. To be motivated by prejudice is when we are not our higher selves.We all judge and we must eradicate or at best temper judgements with tolerance and forgiveness.

I understood Esmeralda and with my head bowed, let me return to the end of this story....

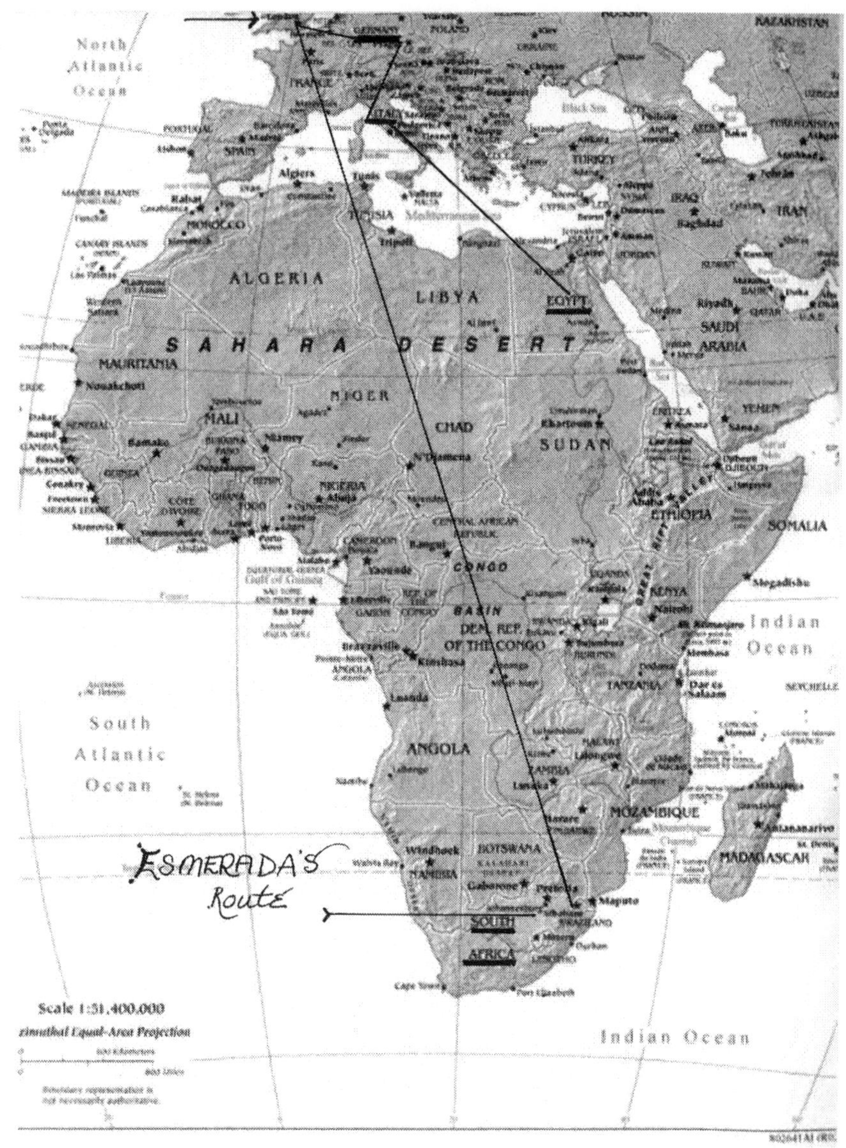
North Atlantic Ocean
KAZAKHSTAN
GERMANY
FRANCE
ITALY
SPAIN
Black Sea
TURKEY
IRAQ
IRAN
Algiers
Tunis
TUNISIA
MOROCCO
ALGERIA
LIBYA
EGYPT
SAUDI ARABIA
SAHARA DESERT
MAURITANIA
NIGER
MALI
CHAD
SUDAN
YEMEN
NIGERIA
ETHIOPIA
SOMALIA
CAMEROON
Gulf of Guinea
CONGO BASIN
KENYA
DEM. REP. OF THE CONGO
Indian Ocean
TANZANIA
South Atlantic Ocean
ANGOLA
MOZAMBIQUE
MADAGASCAR
BOTSWANA
NAMIBIA
ESMERADA'S Route
SOUTH AFRICA
Scale 1:51,400,000
Indian Ocean

XXXI

Esmeralda

Exiled to a country she never wished to know, days were spent as a recluse, in a remote compound, far from peering eyes, adjacent to the tomb of the Aga Kahn on the Nile near Luxor. She had servants, food, peace and her conscious.

The world shuns her without hope she will be vilified by anyone who will restore her broken life into any other ending.

It has been nine months. The time it takes to have a baby, she thought, staring out to the Nile. Here in this ancient country, with the world's longest river, and a vast swamp of papyrus and aquatic plants, the authorities in Europe couldn't touch her, protected from indictment, taking asylum and the misery of growing older everyday alone, her skin scorched crisp from the sun, worn and haggard...living as a misanthrope that passed from the human scene.

Days were spent hiding her once gorgeous body in a caftan. She had forgotten what the touch of a man meant, the promises, the sweetness of romance, the spice of life. Like the waves that lapped the shores of the Nile, with its high tide and low tide, her mind had a rhythm of continual thoughts, drifting to the same conclusion, she betrayed herself.

She walked barefoot, uncombed, avoiding mirrors, which she once sought to assure herself of her beauty. Her bedroom was painted black, everything was black, the covers, the chairs, the walls without adornment.

When she exited her balcony, or sat in the shade of the terrace sipping *chi* she would hear bird cries of the Nile in concert twittering with amorous messages darting across the sky on their way to adventure or the sounds of the feluccas sailing leisurely to Aswan. Her thoughts were of her children, the one she killed and the one she relinquished. She could never forgive herself. Forgiveness was the greatest gift to have and receive.

To forgive herself for her little son's death was impossible. To torment herself, she fantasized how life would have been if....but 'what ifs' don't matter. The pain of her sin marred her for eternity. Although she realized she was a woman gone mad the moment she knew of her Mother's existence, insane with a bigotry of magnified proportions – although she recognized she lived in a world of Apartheid that made her a racist and bigot, forgiveness was not a part of her equation. She was taught the fear of contigation was what these people contributed to the world, lowlife undesirables - parasites on society, beneath her. The nuns, politics and the segregated live she knew formed her. Once the truth was known, her crazed mind produced a distortion that could never be forgiven. No priest, no physiatrist could convince her she was anything but evil....this penetrating evil chewed on her fiber day after day; brittle, bitter anguish engulfed her.

The Fate of life was to be pregnant with Nigel's child, conceived that one time just before guests came to Villa Pina. In my excitement, I'd forgotten my diaphragm. Ours was a marriage of espionage, two spies, never trusting each other, cursed and then blessed. Life is a continual dance of confusion.

It was better they took Nigella from me immediately after I gave birth. The thought of seeing another infant come from my body was overwhelming. My womb was tainted. I didn't want to connect in any way with her. I wasn't worthy of her. There was no other solution but to give full custody to Nigel, use our daughter as barter – Nigel would give her a better life than she would ever know with a Mother like me. Nigel wouldn't lie, not like her horrible Father, but when the time was right, he would tell Nigella the truth of my past when she's old enough to understand.

Nigel now has a daughter, born of his blood and mine, a mulatto daughter – with strawberry-blonde hair, half Negroid. Maybe my little girl will bear a child who'll be black, or white or mulatto. Maybe one day she will forgive me as my Mother wished me to understand and forgive her.

Anthropology struck her. "We don't venture too far afield from our place in society" said the learned professor Gianni brought to Villa Pina one night. She shuttered at this revelation then. Now she believed his words true.

In today's world, she contemplated, will race matter? Some believe it fashionable. Some are convinced that's how we all began and how the world will develop, all will be of color. Nigel will swallow his conservative way of thinking mocking bigots now with a tarbush, heir to his title. He is, like every single one of us, bigoted but no one admits to this. People are hypocritical and muddle through society, as superficial human beings to make life work. The Catholic Church is exactly the same.

A rare few have courage to live in the truth, speak their minds and not judge, this includes how black people view whites or - Jews Christians, heterosexuals - gays, Muslims - atheists, Japanese - Chinese, and so forth... the few truly tolerant people are not the majority who lie to themselves and others. People are snobs. Class differences, gender and age bias, financial circumstances....People don't want less when they can have more or better. Time changes everything. Yet some things remain the same. What lasts forever? … my guilt will ebb…yes, maybe even my guilt ….will ebb...

Her position was on the narrow strip of land on the Nile, protected from Egyptian locks that made the large tourist vessels impossible to reach this point, resplendent with tall reeds, the dead remains of the Muslim world, herself and crocodiles.

At the hour of ten, before the scorching sun dominated life, tour guides on the feluccas, resembling Egyptian virile primates, would halt their sail speaking loud enough for her to catch a faint echo with set phrases they memorized. Their want was to give drama to their tourist's holiday in Egypt.

"Here's where the Aga Kahn is buried, see the simple tomb, one of the richest men in the world lies there. Beside it is the home of his wife, the Begum, who lived there until her death. Now she is entombed with him."

"What's the other villa?" someone would inquire spotting the hidden house nestled in reeds and bamboo.

"Ah yes! That's the villa of the famous Contessa Zianni. Today she lives in seclusion from her sins. Our country forgave her but she never leaves her villa. Her servants are sworn to secrecy. Some say she considers suicide late in the night. Once it was rumored she tried to leap from her balcony, with her jewels on to weigh her down hoping the midnight current of the Nile would carry her away."

Tourists would be awed, remembering the dramatic story. "Tell us more!" they'd exclaim curious to invade Esmeralda's life from a guide who earned his tips spreading hearsay.

"How she spends her days no one knows. She lives with many cats and lets them dine at table nibbling from her plate so she doesn't eat alone."

"Is she still very beautiful?"

"Oh yes!....very beautiful but never speaks to anyone. A tragic story with an ending waiting for death." The tourists would sail on and speak in hushed voices about their opinions of the famous Contessa. For that moment in time, Esmeralda's memory would be revitalized on the Nile, south of Luxor where the sun beat ceaselessly. Cicadas, lizards, egrets, crocodiles, camels and donkeys were the only sign of life the exquisite Esmeralda saw. Days followed in sequence without change. Thoughts dominated her troubled mind.

How can one escape one's destiny? Had I known my parents life, mine may have been different. What if I never went to that Convent and worked the streets like my Mother? I've worked other streets - the streets of society. Only my love for Gianni was authentic.

Time illuminated her rememberances....

How strange Graham Anderson came into my life. He could have been a suitor, a killer, a pimp, instead he was a believer, a dream builder, a homosexual and I needed a man and a dream to believe in. I didn't believe in myself. All that excitement of going to London believing myself half English! The aura of glamour from my life as a model, the passion for respectability.

Martin, wonderful, controlling Martin who wanted me to be his last love and loved me without conditions. de Gesu meant nothing to me. He was one of the characters in the novels I dreamed about come to life, but Gianni, that was different.

The pain of his death, the remembrances of the fleeting joy and horrific death of her husband and son came back to haunt her. The solitude of Luxor tortured her mind but thoughts were not as deranged as in Sicily. Here she was her own jury and made her summation to the only judge she knew, herself.

Nigel didn't have the depth to understand me, she thought, superficial Nigel was a man I thought I could control by the pretext of a marriage of means. He's has received is rewards. Yet those rewards come with the fear of an imminent heart attack, vengeance has struck him, too, from a Higher source. I never respected him. Not as I respected Gianni and Martin.

Trust is another matter. Whom did I trust?

No one after Graham – not even Gianni - for once I knew my past I realized he would never have continued to love me as he did. He saw me as a Goddess, like Martin, but Martin's eyes were seasoned. Martin was something else. Deception made both men view me differently.

One needs more than love. One needs trust and respect. In all ways I gave Gianni the depths of my love, respect and trust, but my wretched character of a bigot, wanting my… *Bella figura*!

Dignity is something no one can take from you. I lost my dignity and any shreds of integrity the day I killed my baby with the first pill. May God forgive me!

Is there a God?... or is this hell - penetrating loneliness, an empty void, alone in the desert, that's all? Once the sun has set, once one has lived life and made mistakes...all is barren sand.... is that all there is to existence?

Hidden from view, Esmeralda watched from her terrace the passing of the tide, the white and blue feluccas, the animals. The eternity of silence penetrated life. Like a caged animal, ashamed, she lived without hope, without friends ...but what are friends? she'd question....there for you only if it suits their interests. We have so few friends in life. Acquaintances by the hundreds but friends? A different entity in one's life - like music when it is perfect...music can linger but friends, true friends...do they linger? Perhaps life is a huge orchestra and then one exceptional instrument lingers....a cello, or a violin....a haunting flute, or a harp....like friends by the hundreds and then just one...I wonder if anyone is thinking about me?

The roar of the fast track pace of life has died away. This is perfect, the hum of bees, the twittering of birds, the lull of the Nile. Its peace interrupted when a tour guide for bored people who seek the fantasy of my life sail by, scared of their death thinking it should come to me and not them.

Soon it will be Christmas. I will not deceive myself. Christmas will be another day. the twenty-fifth day of the twelfth month of this year and it will pass into oblivion as I will soon. The tender pain of looking at faded photographs of Christmas past will be endures again this year, as last year and the year before that.

This is my Fate, my *Maşallah*. I was led here by the kindness of Samir who remains a silent voice in my life. Ponderous hours move day after day, week after week, month after month, without change, without word from the outside world, cut off from life, expectant of death that has already seized me.... how much longer before the end?

Then as Christmas passed and New Year approached, as she sat under the shade of the large umbrella, lying on the chaise, her caftan pulled to her thighs, she imagined footsteps....I'm dreaming....it's an apparition....

The slow footsteps came closer. They were not those recognizable from the Egyptian servants scuffing their sandals on the floorboards, driving her half mad …these footsteps she recognized – she'd heard before, long ago - and she remained still wondering is this another dream like the ones that seize my unconscious night after night? The footsteps... came from behind...then they stopped.....

"……….All alone and so beautiful?"

The voice was unmistakable.

The voice, the tone, sweeter than she remembered it - was this some crazed dream?..or was it true? Real? The accent was exclusive to him ...

"I am here because I love you and my desire is to replace all your sorrow and eradicate your horrid memories, enemies and the torment you've been through. I bring my heart that beats for you alone with hope that you will accept me again."

"Martin...."

There was nothing more she could utter, not believing the shock of his presence…He took her hand in his, no words could express how he had touched her deepest emotions, his elderly face was that of an angel.

"Now you're mine, as you were intended. I am here to change your world."

Everything was stilled. Martin Beck kissed the palm of her hand.

"You will always be, as you always were - mine - the Baroness Beck."

Overwhelmed to be with her at last, overjoyed to see the one man who had loved her to excess, understood and forgave her, hours passed as Martin spoke of extraordinary things, and as a galaxy of stars appeared over the Nile, life returned to Esmeralda.

***

Narrator's Note

As promised when I began this story, I would reveal myself....

The Legend of Capri, my Esmeralda, never knew until that night, we were never divorced. My lawyers went along with my egocentric idea to keep her legally bound to me, crazed as I was to possess her forever.

When she wed Gianni believing it a marriage sanctified by the Roman Catholic Church, she was still married to me. Unknowingly, Esmeralda became a bigamist, unaware of this twist of Fate I orchestrated, the same result with her marriage to Nigel Pembrooke. It was all a sham because no could read - or took the time to translate - the plethora of German documents produced by Zumwelden & Zumwelden, gold sampled, "DEGREE NISI," written in calligraphy with seals and ribbons all over them. Everyone thought they were authentic. I had the last laugh on both of these contenders and their advisors for my Esmeralda.

Lying, lying, everyone lies. Everyone has secrets.

Because she understood me, Esmeralda forgave me...just as she forgave the fact that throughout all the years away from me in this masquerade of Contessa Zianni and then Madame Pembrooke, I had my team of people who told me her every move. I achieved a double bluff. It was just a matter of time.

Some may call me paranoid, they would be right but they too would come not to judge me - a man whose age made him seize the last remants of life - (as my beloved Esmeralda understood). Time is our greatest enemy. It goes too quickly when we are happy. Tonight, with her permission, I finalized this story, the night before death is to take me.

I brought young Gianni into Esmeralda's life, the innocent issue she believed she killed at the Convento Santo Spirito Clinic in Taormina. As she suspected, I read her Mother's letter. I knew Esmeralda would take a decision that was fired from bigoted thoughts imbued in her South African life, a life I knew all about before I married her.

I made a pack with the sainted midwife who realized Esmeralda's horrific plan when she viewed the poisons in her belongings. She drugged Esmeralda that set her in a frenzy of hallucinations the night she went into labor. At the last minute seeing how the birth of Gianni Zianni's child would be, plans were put in motion to protect Esmeralda from any suggestion that she had strayted from her marriage and taken a black lover. Once the midwife saw the infant Zianni was born black as ebony to ths porcelain Goddess, compounded by Esmeralda (in delirium) speaking to Rosamaria of her fears of a mixed breed, the problem was easily solved should the baby be born Negro. It was a simple situation of switching babies with one born hours earlier, stillborn, from an unwed mother in the village. Substituting this white baby, Rosamaria saw to it that the white infant was immediately embalmed. The infant was buried in the Zianni tomb and then later was exhumed at the time of Serena's witch-hunt.

The beautiful Gianni I cared for within a week of his birth, away from prying eyes, behind the gates of my castle in Bavaria waiting for the right time when his legal position was strong and I could bring him together with his Mother, my Esmeralda. His birth was documented in France where I know the authorities, (the French are color-blind and tolerate racial matters).

I paid the midwife, Rosamaria Esposito, to remain these years with Gianni keeping her close by with her family on the grounds of my estate. No one questioned anything. Money talks in these matters. All who knew, thought I had done something wonderful to care for a baby born mute. That is what Esmeralda's drugs inflicted on Gianni, only that, otherwise he's perfect.

In time, after I brought Esmeralda out of Luxor, Gianni was reunited with his mother. Their love is unparalleled. Seeing her son bigotry vanished. Her vision of life has become beautiful and she will forever remain ashamed of her limited prejudiced pass. She was in someone else's skin.

Legally, Gianni, with his cat-green eyes, now five years old, has had his DNA authenticated to be that of his late Father's Giovanni Zianni and Essy McSweeney (Esmeralda's). Zumwelden & Zumwelden, my attorneys worked ceaselessly to assure our beautiful son his rightful, uncontested inheritance through the European Union's Supreme Court, thus becoming the sole heir of Zianni Pharmaceuticals International.

Today little Giovanni Zianni II is a billionaire. Serena and Rupert were denied access to his fortune by the Judiciary and have had to return everything. Truth prevailed although the racial hatred and jealousy of his Aunt Serena will be hers to live with forever.

Nigel was flabbergasted at what I had done. Being of an aristocratic mind and now mellowed by the birth of his daughter - and Esmeralda's generosity to let him retain the financial settlement from their faux divorce, we understand each other. When I met him one last time in London, some weeks ago, he gave me his word to have the siblings of Esmeralda come to know each. Money will pave their way in a new tolerant world where their Mother will be exonerated and open-mindedness prevail.

She will live as she was intended to live, freely, like the Goddess Botticelli painted, and the world will view miscegenation one day as nothing out of the ordinary.

I close my eyes as a new moon rises and a new world begins.

Baron Martin Heindrick von Beck
Bavaria,
3 January 2008

With appreciation to
Annalisa Mignona Merlino
my Italian 'sister'
for her sensitivity to life and our many happy years
in
Capri

Made in the USA
Charleston, SC
08 June 2013